THE DEATH AND LIFE OF

AUGUST SWEENEY

A NOVEL

SAMUEL ASHWORTH

sfwp.com

Library of Congress Cataloging-in-Publication Data
Names: Ashworth, Samuel, 1985- author.
Title: The death and life of August Sweeney : a novel / Samuel Ashworth.
Description: Santa Fe : Santa Fe Writers Project, 2025. | Summary:
  "Legendary chef August Sweeney has served his final meal, dying in the
  middle of service in the very restaurant he built to secure his legacy.
  When Dr. Maya Zhu, a guarded, intense autopsist, is summoned to
  investigate, she discovers she must operate under strict conditions
  Sweeney himself dictated before he died. As she digs deeper into his
  immense body, everything that can go wrong, does, because August Sweeney
  isn't about to let a little thing like death stop him from raising hell.
  The Death and Life of August Sweeney finds two people drawn together
  across the barrier of death. In her ruthless drive to excel as a doctor,
  Zhu has walled herself off from almost everything. As she dissects
  Sweeney, teasing out the mysteries hidden in his body, she begins to
  understand that she is doing an autopsy on her counterpoint: an equally
  ruthless artist who made excess his muse. As she obsesses over what
  happened to Sweeney under the strangest conditions of her career, her
  life- and August' s death- will never be the same"—Provided by publisher.
Identifiers: LCCN 2024030691 (print) | LCCN 2024030692 (ebook) |
  ISBN 9781951631413 (trade paperback) | ISBN 9781951631420 (ebook)
Subjects: LCGFT: Novels. | Medical fiction.
Classification: LCC PS3601.S585 D43 2025 (print) | LCC PS3601.S585 (ebook) |
  DDC 813/.6—dc23/eng/20240709
LC record available at https://lccn.loc.gov/2024030691
LC ebook record available at https://lccn.loc.gov/2024030692

COVER DESIGN: Benjamin Shaykin

Published by SFWP
369 Montezuma Ave. #350
Santa Fe, NM 87501
www.sfwp.com

Praise for *The Death and Life of August Sweeney*

"*The Death and Life of August Sweeney* is one of the most sumptuous and inventive novels I've read in years. In language that sings with seductive detail, Ashworth twines the stories of a magnetic celebrity chef with the obsessive doctor assigned to his autopsy. Not since Jim Crace's *Being Dead* has death contained all the drama and intrigue of life. I flew through this novel but the aftertaste—of pleasure and passion and longing—lingers still."

—Tania James, National Book Award-longlisted author of *Loot*

"An enchanting, captivating narrative, with extraordinary characters at its core. In unerring detail and confident prose, Ashworth immerses readers in a rich tapestry of events. A masterful debut."

—Weike Wang, PEN/Hemingway-award winning author of *Chemistry* and *Rental House*

"Visceral in every sense of the word. In Ashworth's assured and exacting prose, what could so easily be disturbing becomes decadent. Divine, even. A triumph."

—Roshani Chokshi, NYT-bestselling author of *The Last Tale of the Flower Bride*

"*The Death and Life of August Sweeney* is a (literally) visceral tale of loves familial and romantic, sins of the spirit and flesh, redemptions little and big. In carving out a fictional space within the celebrity chef world for August Sweeney, Ashworth charts decades of our culture's shifting relationship to food with deft humor and memorable characters. This is the most fun I've had reading about an autopsy since Mary Roach's *Stiff*."

—Isaac Butler, National Book Critics Circle Award-winning author of *The Method: How the 20th Century Learned to Act*

"Samuel Ashworth has turned the concept of character development inside out with *The Death and Life of August Sweeney*. Working backwards from death, we trace a man's life through his clotted arteries, pockmarked lungs, and a brain spotted with lesions, and learn far more about him post mortem than he ever would have revealed in life. Funny, disgusting, incisive, and anatomically correct—it's a brilliant debut."

—Elizabeth Gonzalez James, author of *The Bullet Swallower* and *Mona at Sea*

"This is a generous book. A sumptuous and delightful feast of observation into the literal, physical human heart, as well as the metaphorical one. Ashworth has a talent for creating characters so detailed and alive that they are practically three-dimensional. Flawless."

—Rion Amilcar Scott, PEN/Bingham award-winning author of *The World Doesn't Require You*

"With prose as sharp as a scalpel and rich as haute cuisine, Ashworth brings his characters to life (and death), along with their passions, idiosyncrasies, and grudges. This impressive debut is a New York story at its best, brimming with visceral detail, smarts and humor."

—Sarah Seltzer, author of *The Singer Sisters*

"A novel told through the process of an autopsy might sound morbid, but *The Death and Life of August Sweeney* is about passion and verve and, yes, sometimes viscera. The two protagonists, a chef and his autopsist, are erudite and poetic within their areas of expertise, and author Samuel Ashworth weaves together the language of both, crafting an intricate hymn of praise to life and the bodies that contain it. A triumph of form and humanity."

—Zach Powers, author of *First Cosmic Velocity*

"Hilarious, accurate, and all too familiar. I loved it!"

—Bradley Whitford, star of *The West Wing*

For Shannon,
Who knew.

Never know who will touch you dead.

—James Joyce

FINAL AUTOPSY REPORT

Patient: August Robert Sweeney
Demographics: Caucasian Male, 52
Date/Time of Death: 1/8/2022 9:56 PM
Date/Time of Autopsy: 1/9/2022 8:30 AM
Pathologist: Zhu, Maya X, MD
Service: NYU-Langone Medical Center
Restrictions: None
Case ID: AU-8818

Final Anatomic Diagnosis

I. Cardiovascular system: History of arrhythmia secondary to atherosclerotic cardiovascular disease **C2**

    A. Heart: Acute hypertrophy (weight: 1530 g) **A2**; myocardial infarct due to thrombus in lower coronary artery **A1**

    B. Lungs, bilateral: mild centriacinar emphysema (weight: right 600 g; left: 550g) **5**

    C. Aorta: acute atherosclerotic plaque **A2**

    D. Liver: mild cirrhosis (weight: 840 g) **A3**

    E. Esophagus, lower third: Esophageal varices **A3**

    F. Gallbladder: Black calculi **A4**

    G. Bladder: pouchlike eversions **A5**

II. Head and Nervous system: Brain, temporal cortex: encephalitis due to herpes simplex virus-2 **A2**

III. Other findings
    A. Colon, sigmoid; Diverticulosis; ulcerative colitis **A5**

TYPE: Anatomic (A) or clinical (C) diagnosis

IMPORTANCE: 1-immediate cause of death (COD); 2-underlying COD; 3-contributory COD; 4-concomitant, significant; 5-incidental

1.

All night the stench had gestated. Indifferent to the chill in the room, it gorged on warm flesh and grew. As the hours passed with nowhere to go the stench became dense, folding in upon itself until it was thick and volatile. It pressed at the walls, aching for freedom, and when at last August Sweeney cracked the seal of the walk-in refrigerator, the stench saw its opening, curled into a fist, and struck.

August staggered. Ghk, he said.

Something big was rotten.

Covering his nose and breathing through his mouth, he began tugging plastic tubs from the shelves. He probed marble-white slabs of tripe; plump yellow poussins brining in salt and sage; slabs of congealed duck's blood ready to be cubed and eased into vats of bubbling chili oil. When he found the source, sorrow clubbed him in the chest.

It was the pig's head. Just yesterday it had belonged to an exquisite Mangalitsa he'd hand-butchered. Even tightly wrapped in Saran the jowl had sloughed off the cheekbones, and the once-proud nose had wilted. The lower jaw which in life had pulverized black walnuts, chestnuts, and acorns, looked melted; all up the back of the back of its head, pustules wept. The lovely pink of its skin had gone the gray of mortar.

Guilt sank its fangs into August's heart. It was such a waste. He inhaled, inviting the stench into his lungs, and retched. This was justice. It was right, he felt, that even slaughtered, flayed, butchered, decapitated, bled white, and smoked, still the pig had found a way to sock him in the mouth.

The mouth that truly wanted socking, however, did not belong to August Sweeney.

Chucho, you hairless fuck! August barreled out of the walk-in, bearing the pan with the pig's head like a father carrying a murdered child.

Hola Chef, said Chucho Rivera, switching on the hot lamps and the Lungs. Chucho was indeed as hairless as a dolphin from his head to his pubes. August had seen it with his own eyes.

I should put those smooth balls of yours in the fryer and make you eat them. He rarely spoke to his cooks like this these days—it didn't fly anymore—but it was good to know that the old muscles had some life left.

His back still turned to August, Chucho fired up the giant stainless-steel stockpot on the range.

Your sister said to tell you hello, Chef.

Chucho, tell me what happens if you wrap up hot meat and put it somewhere cold.

That's between me and your sister.

A slimy piece of the pig's ear hit Chucho in the back of the head with a satisfying whack.

Hijo de—

Motherfucker, mira. Look at this! I told you yesterday to smoke this and then you wrapped it up hot and left it in the walk-in. Now what happens when you do that?

Chucho swallowed hard. Pinche, he spat. That stupid pinche cabron. The new guy, Chef—the trainee. I had to jump onto the line because Claire cut herself real bad so I told his skinny ass to take it out the smoker at seven. I wasn't watching him. Maybe he don't know...

Hal would have known, thought August. Hal knew that if you wrap food when it's hot you get bacteria out the yin-yang. Decay at warp factor 5. Obviously the new kid didn't. August hadn't bothered to learn his name, and now he wouldn't have to.

Yo, I could fire him for you, Chef? Chucho asked gently. August nodded, a sigh emanating from somewhere deep inside his enormous body. August was tired of having to fire these kids himself—he didn't enjoy watching their dreams collapse. Whenever he'd take them on they'd be so thrilled they'd practically levitate; they knew he could change their lives. One after another they came crashing to earth.

It was his fault for trying to find a second Hal. Once—once—he'd struck gold with an untrained, uneducated kid he'd hired on the grounds of he showed up gnawing on raw garlic, and then the kid broke his heart. Now the universe kept sending him fanboy clowns who wouldn't know the Maillard reaction if it seared their skin off. He considered that maybe he should just give in and hire the culinary school kids.

August didn't even have a damn sister. He had a daughter but Chucho knew better than to bring her up.

Holding their breath Chucho and August lugged the rotten one-eared head out to the dumpster, and before they heaved it in they both looked at it for a moment. Its eyes were black, like slimy dull olives, and the way its jaw sagged, exposing its teeth, made the pig seem to grin. A big hideous yellow molar-showing grin like the Cheshire cat with leprosy. Chucho was making the same face, with his eyes crossed and his tongue hanging out. August glared, Chucho stopped. After five years together, he knew where the line was. It made them both angry to lose the head. How many pig heads does a man get to cook in his lifetime? August had been planning to turn it into sisig, a spicy hash of cheek, tongue, chili and liver that Santos, his sauté guy, had been pushing him to put on the menu. Now he'd have to start from scratch because of some kid who was lucky all they were going to do was fire him. Back in the day the punishment would have been medieval.

It was 10am. Seven hours to service and they were about to be down a cook. As a young man he'd relished last-minute improvisation—it was one of the things that had made him so compulsively watchable on television, until, of course, he wasn't—but now the mere thought of crouching down to forage in the lowboy made his knees ache. He was only fifty-one; he was unprepared for his body to be this old.

They grunted and swung the head up and over the side of the dumpster where it landed with a whump. There it would sit and rot until the trash guys came Thursday, by which time the head would be so acrawl with flies that the minute the dumpster tipped into the truck, it'd detonate in a maggot-bomb, and August felt suddenly he was next.

He'd been having these morbid visions more and more lately. He knew the score. Dr. Kaufman had been adamant that Lipitor could only do so much, and when the patient was of August's size and cholesterol level, that was very little indeed.

He would have to make a change, but he couldn't do it. August Sweeney would be God damned if he was going to live out his days without butter. Or any of the other things Kaufman had prohibited. It's the choice between life and death, Kaufman'd said, handing him a pamphlet with kale on the cover.

If I choose your way, August had replied, I won't be able to tell the difference.

The pig head slid greasily into a pile of trash bags. There wasn't so much difference between this and getting laid in a glitzy coffin, in a suit with a corsage in the lapel—which was ridiculous—and they stitched your jaw shut like trussing a chicken and clipped your fingernails because they kept growing and they tossed a wreath in after you and then you went into the ground and the exact same thing happened to you that happened to this pig. You rotted and spoiled and stunk and liquefied like everybody else.

He'd been thrown on the trash heap before. Deserved it, even—he understood this now. But he was climbing out, finally. He'd done his penance, his years in the wilderness, and, when it was over, he'd come home and launched Sanglier in the middle of the restaurant apocalypse and turned it into a fucking beacon in the darkness. As of tonight they were booked three months out. He couldn't be done. He was only getting started.

But as he washed his hands off, August couldn't stop himself. Me prometes algo, papa, he said. I ever die on the line, you cure me like we do the prosciutto, with pink salt and the juniper berries. You wrap me in cheesecloth and hang me in the liquor closet with the rest.

Chucho looked at him funny, but said, Okay, chef, but if you die, I could get your knives, right?

2.

Most of us will die with our eyes open, but 289's were practically bulging out of his head when I freed it from the white body bag. He had died painfully but his eyes were gemlike now. Or at least they would be until I pulled them out. I was pleased: the ICU gotten him to me fast. There was none of the milky exudate of eyes that had been staring for days, indifferent to dust or sunlight. Consistent with cause of death, the pupils were very dilated, black as the obols the ancient Greeks placed on the eyes. His irises were brown gold. The pupils would have widened as he died, sucking in the last glimmers of light as blood stopped flowing to his brain and his vision blurred and funneled to a pinhole. Of all the lies the movies tell, the most sinister is that when we die the eyelids lower themselves peacefully, of their own accord. Death is not an accord.

"I love the way the new ones smell," India said.

"I'm sorry?" I said.

"The body bags. You know what they smell like?"

I did not.

"Kiddie pools. Like the vinyl ones you fill with a garden hose? It's so clean."

I took in the rest of his face. Matted dark hair, wrathful thick eyebrows, a sharp goatee. Mouth agape and teeth yellow. Smoker. I thought about telling her garden hoses and kiddie pools were not features of my childhood, but I kept silent. Nothing to be gained by letting her think about me as a child.

I liked India, but if I responded to this line of conversation I would be required to respond to everything that fell out of her mouth for the rest of the day, as if I were trapped in the window seat of an airplane next to a married man in a suit who went to China for business one time and came back with opinions. Meanwhile in 25 minutes the students would arrive. My plan was to make them start with the eyes, make them look closely. Tell them they're looking for *tache-noir*. Give the discomfort time to bloom in them the way tea reddens water. If I had to let them invade my lab, the least I could do was make sure the ones who had no business in this life didn't make it through the first hour.

I said, "You can unzip the rest of him now."

India had to do a full lap around the gurney, unzipping the bag carefully, stretched as it was around the massive shape of the man inside. She freed his feet and checked the toe tag. His toenails were yellowed and chunky and jagged.

"Been a minute since you were able to get down there with the clippers, huh, big guy?" Then she flung open the body bag, and there on the table was the largest man I had ever seen.

I was silent a long time. My silence was uncontagious.

"God *damn*, Dr. Zhu."

"He's a big one."

"I'm glad they're coming today. No way we get this guy on the table ourselves."

I was not glad they were coming, but I saw her point. On my own, I would have had to do the autopsy right there on the gurney. Maybe one or two of the students would hit the floor when they had to lift him. He was less a man than a hemisphere, naked and domed and white as an exsanguinated chicken.

"Weight?" I said.

"You don't want to guess?" With a blue-gloved finger India pushed her frameless glasses back up her broad round nose and grinned. "I'm going 385."

This was what was expected of me. Levity. Banter. I went with it because India was a good tech, and I needed her. I stepped back and appraised.

Patient number 289, age 52. Stated cause of death: myocardial infarction caused by chronic ischemic cardiomyopathy. A bad heart stopped. Truth be told, I was annoyed: I now had to spend the next ten hours handholding kids through every last valve and sphincter of a body whose COD was so straightforward even the fidgety little resident who pronounced him last night could not have fucked it up.

Yet, as I took him in, I was struck. I'd had fatter men on the table, but no one as *big*, not even the NFL players whose brains needed to come out. A man of this size should have showed the signs. Dead people tend to look as if they *should* be dead. Purple edema surrounding the lower legs. Clubbed fingers. But not 289. Instead, in his thighs I saw a kind of vulpine power. His neck was a craze of blue vasculature: there was still blood in there, deoxygenated and inert. His forearms were frescoed with tattoos, his radial muscles coiled like boat-ropes. His hands could have crushed rocks. On the ring finger of his left hand was a faint stripe of whitened skin: the last trace of a wedding band.

As fat as he was, I could see muscle there. And muscle was denser. I was still annoyed, but now, quietly, I was getting interested.

"405," I said to India. She checked the chart.

"Damn, Dr. Zhu." I'd impressed her. "403. Good guess!"

"I wasn't guessing."

India took the tape measure off the wall and handed me the clip end. From scalp to toe tag, he was six feet nine inches. Two inches longer than the autopsy table.

"You look like someone," India said to him.

"Everyone's someone," I said, inanely.

She clicked her tongue. "I *know* you look like somebody. I'm gonna figure it out. But for now," she said, patting his head, "I'm gonna call you Hagrid." She was right—he did look familiar. But this is a common trick the mind plays on pathologists: one of our recurring nightmares is having to dissect someone we know. I usually wake up concerned at how easily it comes to me.

In any case I found her glee excessive. But I let it pass. India was quick, strong, efficient—more so than the other techs in this building—and I needed her to like me. I'd only been director of autopsy pathology for four months and I still felt like I was on probation. I could be curt, but I could not be humorless or bossy. At least, not with India. Students were another matter.

Students. Just the word made my lip curl. Students weren't supposed to be part of the deal—the living weren't supposed to be part of the deal. I had no idea what to do with them, how to speak to them. It's not that I disliked people, as some of us do. People were benign, mostly. I just didn't care. I didn't care about their trouble sleeping or what they'd been watching lately or their nieces or vacations. I was aware that I was supposed to, so I faked it, capably. But what I cared about were their bodies. Their ligaments, their white blood cell counts. Their sciatic nerves. Their ovaries. Their bile and tear ducts. The unimaginably precise vibrations of their tympanic membranes. The cells billioning away inside them, the fireworks of their synapses, the three pounds of feces on its slow commute through their intestines. That was interesting. Humans are at all times a few millimeters away from death. Our bodies are barely-contained whirlwinds of blood and shit held in place by membranes so thin you can see through them and if one of those containment systems fails, the whole house caves in. It is important not to think about this too often. But the autopsist's job is to think about it daily, to study why those systems fail. That was why I did this: because it offered a life of bodies, without interference from the people inside.

Med students, meanwhile, were only people by the most liberal definition of the word.

Residents were one thing, as fumbling and nervous as they are—but med students were like the schools of carp Nainai used to take me to feed, in the fish pond in Fuxing Park. The way they'd swarm for the grains of rice she'd toss, thrashing in the water, fighting for each crumb, their mouths gawping mutely and horribly. She'd stand there at the water's edge, a cold faint smile on her old lips as she'd toss one fistful here, one there, each time forcing the carp to chase it in a crazed wriggling mass. I didn't know then why she did it, but as the years passed, I understood. She'd been in the war with the Japanese. I'd never thought to ask her what she'd seen and she would never have told me. Anyone who lived through as much history as she did had earned the right to forget it. Whatever it was, she poured it all, all her disappointments, all her sadism and pain, into the revolting carp, so that for me there was nothing left but love.

"They'll be here at 8:30, right?" India asked, pulling a stack of stainless-steel pans off the shelf.

"Yes, but these are med students. They'll be early." All craning their necks and standing on tiptoe to see over each other, gawping their carp-mouths. Hungry for every rice grain of approval. *They* were my job today. They wanted to know what an autopsy was. I was going to give it to them good and hard.

"How many?"

"Four. Dr. Mandragola said his lawyer set the whole thing up months ago."

"So this guy knew he was gonna die." India asked, scratching her head, her elaborate braids bunched snugly under her blue surgical cap. "And he wasn't terminal or nothing?"

I shook my head, examining the scars and burn marks embossed along his arms. They were everywhere. The arms reminded me of my father's, but hypertrophic. I was not about to admit it to India, but he did seem familiar. Not his face so much as a tattoo on the anterior side of his left arm, an anthropomorphic pig licking his lips and holding an outsized chef's knife. I'd probably seen something like it on a t-shirt at a mediocre barbecue place. But clearly he was a cook. A lifer, from the look of him. He would have spent his days in a restaurant kitchen like my father's, but how? He was huge—the counters would have been thigh-high for him, his spine kyphotic and knees arthritic from the constant bending. Looking at the stippled burn marks I could see him moving quickly, too quickly, dropping a slab of meat into a pot of boiling oil to fry it, and, on contact, the oil surging up the wet surface of the meat to envelop his forearm, blistering the skin down to the dermis. Over time, it would have cooled, turning from pinkish-red to mauve. These burns were recent. He had still been working almost right up to when he died—a death he knew was coming.

He had my attention.

Strictly speaking pathologists are not supposed to do this. Speculating about the patients' lives is considered gauche. We use numbers, not names, nor do we guess at what kind of lives they lived. Certainly we are not supposed to linger over any sense of familiarity. The psychological toll is too great, they say. "Professional distance" is paramount. Over and over as a resident I was told distance was the only way to do this job day after day, corpse after corpse, without fracturing. And there was truth in this. Distance didn't come naturally to anyone, and I was no different— we had to practice it, hone it until it felt light and fluid in our hands. But even then all the autopsists I ever met cultivated some form of emotional release. Some went to all-night raves. Some obsessively maximized airline points. One man I knew was also a Presbyterian minister. I took strangers to bed to find out how their bodies worked when they were naked and trembling. I consumed women and men alike. I did not ask for names or numbers. I did not stay the night. I wasn't there to sleep. I let them go from my memory like blood down a drain.

Yet I always considered it craven that the way I was supposed to practice distance was to just…ignore that the person inside had ever been alive. That did not seem sustainable to me. The only practical approach was to confront the patient's humanity head-on—to stare into it as I was planning to make my students stare into this man's eyes—and require myself to feel nothing.

Not that I ever said any of this aloud.

I did not know what India did for a release. It was the one thing she did not talk about, and I had never asked.

I handed her the camera. "They told me about it when it was decided. We were just waiting for the body. Get some pictures of these burn marks, and the hematoma here on his shoulder. Looks like he fell hard." When Dr. Mandragola first told me, I'd experienced a quiet thrill. This wasn't just an autopsy. *Every possible utility from the cadaver,* that was the instruction. *Cost is immaterial.* Anatomical gifts are always exciting, but someone who actually understood the research value of his own body? Whoever this man was I'd have liked him even while he was still alive. Then Mandragola told me teaching was part of the deal and "invited" me to "take point on that," like it was an honor, and the gilt crumbled off the lily. Last night the email went out two hours after time of death, "first come first served," and by 3am all four spots were filled. So the children about to come clomping into my lab weren't just med students, they were the most sleep-is-for-the-weak med students.

I had a terrible thought: what if the students *liked* it? What if next week Mandragola came up to me smiling his smile where his lips don't actually part and said, *They just loved it so much, how would you feel about making this a regular thing?*

No. I could not allow them to enjoy this.

"I heard he made some kind of donation when he died," India said, the shutter clicking.

"Apparently. Whatever it was, it was generous enough to get Dr. Mandragola to set all this up."

"But not enough to get him to teach it himself."

Careful here. I caught the edge of my lips twitching into a smirk and tightened my jaw to keep it from spreading. India was expecting me to laugh, to give a friendly the-sisters-are-doing-it-for-themselves chuckle to let her know I wished it could just be the two of us down here, working on him together, sharpening the routine she and I had been building since I'd started just three months ago. But we were not friends. I knew what letting little remarks like that slide could lead to. Today it would be Mario—who deserved it—but tomorrow it could be me. Authority is a condition, not a pedestal.

"I'm the autopsy pathologist at this hospital, it's my job," I finally said, lightly. Then I changed the subject. "We have to take him down to the skeleton."

"The beetles!" said India brightly.

"Yes. Contact the dermestid lab and arrange for pickup. But make sure you read the form carefully. No calling the family, only the lawyer. Eckstein."

"Okay, that's strange, right?"

"It's uncommon. But the family gets the final report."

"No funeral home, I'm guessing." *That* I laughed at, to make up for ignoring her last joke. India needed to think she was funny. That was part of how she kept her distance.

On the table, 289's eyes were fixed on the drop ceiling, as if the panels were a puzzle he had to solve. His shoulders and chest were constellated with tiny black and red moles.

"When was the last time you removed a spinal cord?" I was watching India closely for hesitation here. Spinals were less common, usually for cases of degenerative neural disease. If she wasn't surehanded sawing through vertebrae it would take forever.

India made blue-gloved finger guns at me. "Like taking string cheese out of the packet."

"Good. I'm going to review the medical history. If they get here, help them suit up." I peeled off my gloves and headed for the door. "Oh, one more thing. We're doing the eyes today, too."

India stopped. Eye removals were the rarest of all. Here, she hesitated. So much for that.

"I'll be doing them," I said.

India relaxed. "*Man*, Dr. Zhu. It's like you're *trying* to freak them out or something."

For the first time all day I smiled.

Patient is a 52-year-old man who collapsed
at work in his restaurant at 8:49pm on
the night of January 8. EMTs were called
to the scene and CPR and defibrillation
were attempted, but patient was already
in asystolic heart failure by the time
they arrived. He was brought to ER and
pronounced dead at 9:56pm. Patient was DNI
and DNR.

Patient is a 51-year-old man who was admitted
to the ER at 7:55pm on the night of February
20 with acute pain in his chest, dizziness,
and shortness of breath. On arrival patient
was perspiring, hypertensive, with BP
181/110, with labored, raspy breathing.
EMTs diagnosed tachycardia (211bpm) and
1500cc electrolyte solution was administered
intravenously. Once in the ER EKG revealed
atrial fibrillation and patient was given
10mg warfarin. Patient was hypoxic with
O2 levels between 80-85mmHg and was given
supplemental O2. Patient appeared to have
been brought in under duress by a co-worker,
and was impatient to leave, saying he had to
get back to work. Patient was uncooperative
and unwilling to provide medical history

because it would "take too long." He refused
strenuous recommendations to stay overnight
for observation, and once heartbeat had
stabilized, he demanded to be discharged. He
said that the New York Times food critic was
in his restaurant. Mr. Sweeney was given a
prescription for Coumadin.

Patient is morbidly obese with LDL
cholesterol levels of 178mg/dL and resting
heart rate of 91bpm…Patient was advised
to make serious dietary and lifestyle
changes. Patient laughed. Ensuing cough was
hacking and wet; subsequent X-rays confirmed
emphysema.

August Sweeney, 49, was referred to me by Dr.
BEN KAUFMAN for suspected liver fibrosis. Mr.
Sweeney was highly dismissive of questions
pertaining to family history but declared
he had recently "dialed back" his daily wine
intake to "just a bottle a day. Only the good
shit." Patient was emphatic that this made it
acceptable to consume in such volume. He also
asserted that given his (considerable) size,
a bottle of wine was equivalent to a glass or
two for "a normal person." Patient refused
transient elastography on the grounds that he
didn't "have time." AST and ALT blood tests
were ordered.

This is the third visit from Mr. Sweeney, a

```
45 year-old chef of some renown, for reddish
urine and pain while urinating...
```

```
...Patient has been treated for a number of
sexually-transmitted bacterial infections,
including gonorrhea, chlamydia, and Zika...
```

I shoved my chair back from my desk. My office door was closed; I was, for a few more precious minutes, alone.

The medical history read like Murder on the Orient Express—the heart was the one that got him, but every other organ had been lining up behind, knife drawn. I wanted—no, needed—to get inside him. I tell people, you never know a man until you've held his heart in your hands. This is my joke. It makes people laugh, uncomfortably, and then they stop asking. Which is for the best. People are children about death. (Children, however, are not.) The worst are the ones who don't stop asking, who get suddenly excited and start in with the *what's the grossest thing you've ever seen* and the *is it true you shit yourself when you die.* These are the idiots who go to torture porn movies and read morbid little cartoons online and went to the Bodies exhibit one time and haven't shut up about it since. They're spectators of death, fanboys. They remind me of the wealthy white people who'd ride out to Civil War battlefields in their carriages, hoping to get a good seat to watch the battle. Because my joke is not a joke. The living lie. The dead can't.

But that doesn't mean they give up the truth easily. I took a sip of tea from my thermos. This medical history was mystifying. Why would a man so patently uninterested in doctors in his lifetime spend all this money to get a doctor to tear him apart in search of answers that would never do him any good? I felt a tug of curiosity somewhere between my ribs. If this were a normal day, it would have just been me and India, alone in the lab, teasing out the mystery. But what Mario wanted, Mario got. I had a job to do. 289 was just another body, and there were more where he came from. There were always more.

From out in the hallway, a heavy metal door clanged open, and sneakers squeaked on the buffed linoleum. I inhaled, relaxed my facial muscles. My face went smooth, masklike. I was Dr. Maya Zhu, 32-year-old chief of autopsy pathology at New York University-Langone Medical Center, and my students had arrived.

3.

On January 20, 1970, on a snowy winter's night, all eleven pounds and three ounces of August Robert Sweeney were pried bloodsoaked and cyanotic from his howling mother's uterus, slathered with vernix caseosa like a turkey rubbed with thick pats of butter, and destined for excess.

For hours in the waiting room Thomas Sweeney, Jr. had paced and smoked, smoked and paced. His tie was loosened but not untied. As he paced he tried to distract himself by cataloging all the apparati in the hospital which bore the Grayson brand: EKGs, X-rays, microscopes, spectrometers, hyperbaric chambers, dialysis machines. His brother Jack had come and was making conversation with Thomas' brother-in-law.

Two days! Two days she had been in that room. It was a hard birth, the doctor had told him, and the child was rather larger than they had expected. Isabelle had no one to blame but herself, either. She was the one committed to this "natural-birthing" business. And even though Thomas had attended the classes when he could, Isabelle had been firm that he would be waiting outside when the baby came: he was not to watch the bloody spectacle. She did not think it was right for a wife to let her husband see her screaming and flung open like the hood of a Buick, and that was fine with him. But two days! If something were wrong, wouldn't they tell him? Of course they would. Isabelle was no fragile-boned sparrow, either. She was a redoubtable woman and she was bound and determined to deliver this baby in full command of her senses. She had heard what twilight sleep did—the mother woke up a day later with no memory of the birth, only a horrible emptiness, and they would hand you a child and tell you it was yours and you just had to take their word for it.

And so, Thomas paced. She would probably come through it all right, he told himself. This was 1970. At least the money wasn't a worry anymore. They had waited, the Enovid flooding Isabelle's womb with deceptive, uncatholic hormones and giving her nausea and fits of what they agreed to call "the blues," until his position at Grayson was secure. He was making twenty-nine thousand, seven hundred and fifty-three dollars per year now, before the bayonet of taxes pierced his heart. His son would not have to grow up in a home where meat was only for special occasions.

Thomas's parents, Thomas, Sr., and Margaret, had come over as newlyweds from Leitrim in 1933, over the shouting objections of Margaret's people, because Thomas's brother Alfy was in with the dockworkers and assured him he could find a job, even with the country in the midst of what Alfy, in his usual decorous way, called "the rain of swan-diving stockbrokers." To the surprise of Margaret's people there was indeed work to be had on the docks, and Thomas, with his brawn and fondness for spirits, his good cheer and his imposing size on the picket lines, found himself right at home, and the Sweeneys set down to the business of making a life in Hell's Kitchen. They also set down to the business of making babies in the ferocious Irish idiom. By the time Thomas, Jr., came around in 1936 to receive his joyous father's name Catherine and Deirdre were already on scene, and there would follow Darragh, Louis, Lizzie, Maeve, Fiona, and Jack before Margaret's hardy womb boarded up shop and closed for business.

Yet none of his siblings had taken this long, Thomas thought, chewing on his cigar. In fact one day when he was six he was helping his swollen mother fold laundry when she suddenly gasped, straightened up, and said, "Tommy, love, will you run out and hail your Mam a taxi." By the time his father had arrived at the hospital from the docks, stuffing his cap into his jacket pocket, Fiona had been born, swaddled, and his mother was putting her things back into her purse, insisting that she had to get home and make dinner.

Which was no trifling concern in the Sweeney home. His father's income was steady, but meager. They did not starve, but nor did Thomas ever remember being full. His mother's talent was not for cooking so much as it was for stretching: stews would be a salty, watery broth redolent of cabbage, with some over-the-hill vegetables, and on rare occasions a tough, savored chunk of boiled mutton. Pasta was served with what his father jovially called a "soup's on" of oil and oleomargarine. Thomas learned to live with a quiet, almost tender gnaw in his stomach.

That was all behind him now. He had studied his way out of Hell's Kitchen, graduated high school and then City College. Most of his siblings had done well, too, except for Louis, who fell in with the Westies and was doing fifteen to twenty at Attica for a rosary of offenses. Still, it was a good showing for the Sweeney clan. Isabelle would not have to work. Maybe later when there was time she could go back to Harcourt Brace, but there was no need for that now. Twenty-nine thousand seven hundred fifty-three. He turned the number over in his head as he drew deeply on the ritual Cohiba, and an orange ring glowed around the perfect cylinder of ash.

Food for Thomas Sweeney was something you either had enough of, or you didn't. It was much like health: if it was there, it was good; if it wasn't, it was bad. To be sure he had likes and dislikes like any man: runny cheese, charred steak, lima beans, and hardboiled eggs sprinkled with salt in column one; blackberries, pickles ("embalmed vegetables," his father called them), oysters, and cold soup in column two. But these were not *passions*. Passions required that one be picky, and pickiness was unimaginable to him. Except for the days he was compelled to lunch with other Grayson executives at their clubs and favored haunts, each day at lunchtime Thomas would park himself on a stool at Maud's Diner on 48th and 3rd and they would bring him the fried chicken and a bowl of the soup of the day. Once it was gazpacho, and with the utmost composure he asked if they wouldn't heat it up, which they did without judgment; this wasn't Café des Artistes. Not that Thomas would have much enjoyed Café des Artistes. He returned to Maud's day after day, year after year, not merely because he knew Maud and the girls as well as he knew his own family, but because he liked knowing what he was getting every day. His fried chicken and soup made him happy because it made him secure and to Thomas, they were the same thing.

A middle-aged nurse came down the hall toward them, the ticktock of her footsteps glancing off the green tiled walls of the corridor.

"Mr. Sweeney? She's asking for you. Please come with me."

Thomas coughed violently on the smoke and stabbed out his cigar. He could feel his hands go cold as the blood rushed inward, his heart rate accelerating. As he neared, he heard a scream come through the door, rising and falling and rising again. In her life such a sound could never have come from his wife. Something was wrong.

The delivery room when he entered reminded Thomas, for some reason, of the floor of the New York Stock Exchange, with machines pinging and lights glaring and bodies swarming, except that the bodies were all swathed in blue and the floor was wet with blood and the thing they were swarming around was Isabelle, whose face he just could make out through the crush. Her hair was plastered to her forehead, her face crimson from tears and screaming. Her lower half was tented by a blue sheet, into which a doctor was burrowed.

When she saw him she called out his name. He rushed to her side, his leather shoes skidding on the blood, and seized her hand.

Are you okay? he asked, and she stared at him like he was insane. He'd never seen such terror in his wife's eyes. She had always been so solid to him, like a great oak planted in his life, but now she seemed so fragile and trembling that he wanted to throw himself over her and shield her with his body from the doctors. Then a scream came from her at a pitch that about sheared his eardrum, and she clenched his hand with bone-snapping strength.

"FUCK," Isabelle bellowed, and the doctor emerged from the tent holding a bloody scalpel. He flicked it into a pan.

"That should do it," he said. "Now I need you to push, Isabelle, just keep a steady pressure." He dove back in.

Thomas imagined his fingers splintering like dry twigs, but he gritted his teeth and held on. So this was what it felt like to be useless. This was his only job, to let her pass some of this pain on to him, and not say any more stupid things. He tried to remember what they'd learned in Lamaze but his head was swimming from the sight of blood and the smell of shit. Isabelle screamed again, and held the scream as the nurses around her slowly counted down from ten.

"Almost there," came the doctor's voice from under the tent.

"Breathe?" he said, hopefully, and the glare she shot him was withering.

"I *am* breathing," she snarled, and to prove it unleashed a roar so loud it seemed choral, as if the entire room were screaming in unison. Pain shot up Thomas's arm, but he held tight.

A prolonged squelching sound like a boot in mud, and the doctor emerged holding a massed creature soaked in blood and gray exudate. A *whoosh* of warm clear fluid flooded from Isabelle and splashed the delivery room floor. They wound the placenta from her gently, tugging it out in a gush of blood, and scissored the umbilical cord. Nurses set upon the infant with suction nozzles to vacuum the mucus from mouth and nostrils, drops of stinging erythromycin to splash in its eyes, and a wet cloth to wipe clean its ears and body. Then the doctor took it by the ankles and slapped it once across the buttocks. Thomas watched, agog, as the infant August filled his lungs with air, puffed out his chest, and let fly a cry that rattled the obstetric instruments in their steel pans.

"Mr. and Mrs. Sweeney," said the doctor, panting slightly, "you've got one big healthy boy."

Thomas watched, catatonic, as they laid his son on Isabelle's heaving chest. Trembling, she took his tiny, curled hand in her fingers.

"August," she whispered. "Hi."

Isabelle looked at Thomas, all the fury and pain gone. His whole body flooded with gratitude. She had done this for him. For them. And he would take it from here. He felt fear creep into the joints between his bones. Thomas knelt down beside his wife and took her hand and pressed it to his cheek. Everything, he vowed. He would give them everything they needed.

Thomas would be true to his word. He would provide August with everything: school, braces, good shoes, summer camp. But of all the things August Sweeney's father gave him, from a mistrust of Protestants to blepharic eyebrows, from a dependable penis to a love of the blues, I imagine August could have done without the death sentence woven into the short arm of his nineteenth chromosome.

4.

Once my friend—I do have friends—brought her dog to my apartment. She'd said, I got a dog, you have to meet him. I said okay, because she is a good friend, who invites me to the ballet with her sometimes and isn't vegetarian. She came over and I opened my apartment door and the dog, a tubby, slouch-bellied dachsund, took off as if spring-loaded. It charged around the room on its absurd legs, braking and skidding and changing directions. My studio apartment is sparsely furnished, with a few bookshelves, a desk, a table by the galley kitchen, a few orchids in pots I tend carefully, like fragile genitals. Still, there was nowhere for her to go. She caromed off cabinets, accordioned up the carpet. I'd thought what I had was sufficient. I'd thought of my little room like a Tang poem: spare and small, every syllable of it spacious with meaning. Yet now the spaces between everything contracted. I saw how close my bed was to my desk, how precariously perched my orchids were on the windowsill, how my table blocked half the entrance to the kitchen. Finally, she wore herself out and fell asleep on the carpet, but by then it was too late: the moment the dog had entered it was as if the walls of my studio had begun to close in.

Now the same thing was happening in my beloved lab. They were all packed in, four of them, mummified from head to toe in smurf-blue polyester. Suddenly my quiet little lab felt like my father's kitchen whenever the health inspectors would roll through with their ancient laptops. I'd just gotten it set up how I wanted it, too, with my supply cabinets lining one wall, and on the other, an array of glass cabinets housing dozens of plastic jars with tissue samples floating in formalin. And there, still on the gurney, was the vastness of 289 covered by the flap of the body bag (I'd asked India to cover him back up, for theater's sake), around which we gathered, a shuffling, anxious ring of blue. Beside us waited the great rooted stainless-steel bed of the autopsy table, its holes and faucets ready to drain pint after pint of his blood, and perpendicular to that, the dissection table with its water jets and sink. The metal shone, sterile, in the fluorescence of the room. Shadows were abolished.

I couldn't tell them apart, and I hadn't bothered to ask their names. From their build and hair bundled under their surgical caps I could make out three women, one Asian, two white. Potential problems. The women, especially the Asians, were prone to thinking of me in a sisterly way. They wouldn't see the youngest director of autopsy pathology in a US hospital, they'd see their *jiejie*. They'd expect me to be warmer, friendlier. And when, inevitably, I was not, they would feel betrayed.

The male, tall and angular, pulled out a phone and pointed it at himself.

"No selfies!" I snapped. The phone vanished instantly, and a suitable voltage of shame went through the student. I considered going full Milgram-experiment on him, to fry him thoroughly in front of everyone. But I held back. Men are easy to humiliate but then they devote their lives to getting even. I wanted them to be afraid of me, but there was no benefit in having them loathe me. Better to let 289 do the talking. So I threw open the flap of the body bag and there he was.

You talk about voltage.

Even swaddled in layers of protective fabrics I could see the air go from their lungs, like bystanders to a silent detonation. Behind their blue sheathing there were tremors, flinching, but since the only exposed part of them was the eyes, the uncertainty of where to look was the most pronounced.

He was hugely, opulently naked. He was the size of a sarcophagus but soft, terribly and visibly soft and vulnerable, with nothing but his tattoos for covering, and a girthy, uncircumcised penis laid primly over his smooth globe of a scrotum. It was this, most of all, that they were persevering in not looking at. I gave them a moment to take furtive glances. Let them see what dead really means.

"Meet 289," I said. We refer to bodies as numbers in our files for privacy, and in our lab for distance; they didn't need to know the name of the man on the table. He was the 289th autopsy that year.

"They look a little different in here than they do in anatomy class, don't they?" said India. Some emphatic nods, some mumbled "uh-huhs." "No formalin in this guy." She patted him on the shoulder. "We get 'em fresh here."

I thought she was laying it on a little thick, but it was working. They had thought 289 would resemble the cadavers they'd studied in Gross Anatomy: his blood replaced with embalming fluid, giving the skin clay-like firmness and the hue of an oyster, that leaden gray that reassured them that this person on the table was very irreversibly dead. They'd assumed the body would be respectfully draped. But here was just a naked stranger—so much so that they seemed embarrassed to be seeing him like this.

"We need to transfer him to the table," I said. Again, the silent alarm rippled through them. No one had hit the floor yet. Steeling themselves they gripped the white body bag, as they had been trained to do with ER patients on blankets. India stifled a snort next to me.

"No, no," I said, calmly. "What do we need the bag for? We're not dissecting the bag. We need to move *him*." India shook up a bottle of foaming Lysol and liberally sprayed the awaiting autopsy table with it, not to disinfect it but to grease the way. There was a pleasurable scent of lemon. "Come on, grab the nearest load-bearing part of him. Not the hands. Get under the shoulders, the head, the thighs, and on the count of three—"

He was still warm.

The tall boy, the selfie enthusiast, seemed to go soft. There it was. Vasovagal syncope. Somewhere in his autonomic nervous system, he'd glitched. He had maybe one second. Norepinephrine had been pinballing around the efferent pathways of his brain, bouncing from one neuron to the next, when panic rocked the machine, the silver ball jammed, and the whole system went on tilt. The heart muscle slowed: his blood pressure plunged: warmth grew in his legs as the blood vessels there dilated, pooling the blood that the brain craved. His urethra was relaxing itself and I worried he might urinate on my floor. He swayed once—he was trying to fight this, his brain using up its last molecules of oxygen to broadcast the message *don't embarrass yourself.* Finally, deprived of blood, the brain banged the emergency shutdown button. For an instant, he was death's perfect image: his body intact, with nobody home. No stiffening, no histrionic seizing-up like 289 experienced when his heart froze. This boy only wilted. Fainters become dead weight instantly; they fall fast and hard and in any direction. I didn't want to be explaining to Mario how a student wound up with a head injury on day one.

I said, "Would someone please catch him?" His knees failed and the rest of him followed, as if shoved, all six feet and change of him lurching violently sideways. There were gasps and reflexive lunges and a girl wrapped her arms around him. They both hit the floor together, almost like lovers falling into bed, but then he tumbled off her and rolled to a halt on the linoleum tiles.

When he came to we were ringed around him and all the students were telling one another to give him some air. One had her fingers on the radial artery of his wrist. They knew enough not to be frightened. They had a vulturish look, the hunger all med students had to capitalize on every opportunity to actually use the information they'd gone through such pains to memorize. Their fingers ached to stitch wounds, set bones, compress chests. They went through their day hoping catastrophe struck. I admit I liked that about them.

The tall boy's glasses were fogged up from the surgical mask, and one of his colleagues knelt to remove both. His eyes opened. He sat right up, mortified.

"Take it easy," the girl with his glasses said as she handed them back.

"I'm sorry," he said. "I didn't see that coming."

The girl said, "Hold your arms over your head." He did so, breathing slowly.

"I'm really sorry," he said, pleading without conviction.

"There's a couch in my office," I said. "Go lie down there for fifteen minutes. Then you can head home." I spoke gently, unjudgmentally, but he was done here.

"That's never happened to me before. I've watched surgeries. I don't get it." How astonished he was at his betrayal by his own body, at the power of the fear he thought he was equal to. Doctors are stupider about death than almost anyone else, but medical students, who spend their days and nights dreaming of defeating death, even undoing it, are even more hopeless. Wobbling, the tall boy went out of the lab.

I always thought that if I were an HR manager, and this is one of many reasons I am not an HR manager, I would want to see MRI and brain scans of anyone I was going to hire. I told my friend with the dog this once. She called me a fascist. I think she is right. I am a little bit fascist. For a long time I hoped I was a sociopath. It would simplify so many things.

"If anyone else is uncomfortable," I said after the heavy door shut, "There is no shame in leaving. I've seen a lot of people who thought they had strong stomachs go down like that." I gave them a minute, but no one moved. It would take more than this to thin the herd. Well, more was coming. "All right, let's get him on the table."

With a great collective intake of breath they all slid their hands under his lukewarm bulk. They'd expected him to be cold, almost reptilian. But even after a night in a refrigerated room, a man of his size takes a long time to lose his internal heat. Fat insulates. I could see them wince, shiver, look away, but they held firm. On three, we lifted and groaned and pulled and—dear God—he was heavy. Even with ten hands on him we had to move him a few inches at a time, thumping him crudely from gurney to table. First, we got his head and shoulders on, his skull hitting the panel with a clang. Next, we gripped under his buttocks and heaved him over, but his left arm wound up pinned under his torso and we had to tilt him to pull the arm free. 289 went right on staring out, eyeballs frozen in place. Pulling by the arms we worked his trunk over the Lysol-slick table, until only his log-like legs remained on the gurney. Two students took his heels and swung the legs over; they projected a few inches beyond the edge of a table meant to accommodate any human shape. A little more shoving and grunting, and he was in place. His mouth gaped as if in pain. Everyone was panting from the exertion. India balled up the body bag and stuffed it in the red hazmat bin. I took a blue block from the counter and parked it under his skull, like a Ming dynasty headrest.

We were ready to begin. And then the phone rang. A glare sent India to the far wall to answer it.

"Autopsy pathology...Yes...Well, she's a little busy...What's his name...Hold up—what?" Her voice dropped to a whisper: "For real?" She listened for a long time, and her brow creased and she glanced at me, then at the students. Finally, she said, in a professional alto, "I think you should ask Dr. Zhu directly. Please hold."

Annoyed, I removed my splash shield, stripped off my top gloves, and came around the body on the table. As I took the phone from her, India made a facial expression at me I could not quite read.

"This is Dr. Zhu."

A young woman's voice. "Dr. Zhu, this is front desk security. I'm sorry, but, uh, we've got a gentleman here who says he's your father?"

5.

In the summer of 1983, when he was 13, August attended—or rather was driven to and tenderly dumped at—Chum-Chump-Wa sleepaway camp. Sprawling over fifty acres of Maine, Camp Chum-Chump-Wa was co-ed, very swank, and full of tanned, towheaded boys from Connecticut and Westchester who all played golf and knew how to reef the halyard and tie a bowline and called one another "Chief" and lightly-freckled girls with perms and braces who reapplied their lip gloss after making out and turned out often to be demonic serve-and-volleyers whose mothers were on multiple boards and councils and whose fathers had actually wept over Nixon's resignation.

And the moment August Sweeney arrived at Camp Chum-Chump-Wa, the thirteen year-old Irish colossus of Manhattan towering over all of the blond, avian-boned children of Greenwich and Darien and Scarsdale, those children swiveled their guns on him. It wasn't just that they assumed he was dumb. They were weak before him, and their weakness made them mean. They sought safety in numbers. They spoke faster, used preppy slang he didn't understand. The jokes that worked at Catholic school didn't work here. They had different jokes, camp jokes, that August didn't think were funny but made the other kids wet their khaki shorts.

Then one day at lunch the camp cook, a sensitive, harried lesbian who kept trying to feed the campers eggplant, was gone. Standing at the pass-through in her place was a savage-looking man, lean and grim, with hair right out of *The Warriors*. The camp director, a pink-cheeked man who told the kids to call him Big Rick, which did not go how he had planned, rang the announcement bell and the clamor of Bakelite plates and cutlery quieted.

Campers, I have some sad news and some great news. The sad news is, after five summers with us, Marianne has had to leave us unexpectedly. (Snickering from some of the girls' tables.)

But fortunately, Victor here...what's your last name?

Victor's plenty, the man said. He didn't smile.

The camp director looked unnerved but rallied. Victor it is! Campers, let's give Victor a warm Chum-Chump-Wa welcome holler, why don't we?

OLOLOLOLOLOLOLOLOOOO! The rafters of the dining lodge echoed with the ululating Indian battle-cry of three hundred voices tapping their right hands over their mouths and tomahawk-chopping with their left.

Huh, said Victor.

When the din resumed one of the other new kids in August's cabin, Iggy (whom August had already learned not to associate with; Iggy had brought actual *tap shoes* with him to camp, and that was the end of him, socially), pushed his horn-rimmed glasses up his nose.

He looks like a sphinx, Iggy said, looking at his fellow Loons for a response. When he got none, he pressed on undeterred: Most people think that 'sphinx' just means someone who doesn't talk a lot. But in Greek myths the sphinx would come up to random people on the road and ask them questions, and if you didn't get them right, it would tear your throat out!

August decided he liked Iggy—and Victor. There was an imperiousness to Victor, a leathery quality that became apparent that night, when he was forking out thin pink slices of roast beef and a corpulent little Muskrat in front of August in line asked, quiveringly, if he might have some chicken nuggets instead?

Victor sank the fork into the wood counter of the pass-through and let it stand there, wobbling. He folded his arms and a blue tattoo of Latin words the St. Ignatius Loyola Jesuits would have been depressed to know August couldn't translate twitched over the radial muscles of his forearm. Victor narrowed his eyes to cold slits that peered out through the curtain of scraggly grey hair. His voice was a panther's growl: No…*nuggets*.

Wobbling with fear the little Muskrat accepted the roast beef, and August fell in love. Here was a man—shamanic, stubble-jawed, with crow's feet branching like cracked earth from the corners of his eyes—who terrified the polo shirts. August had never wanted anyone's approval more.

Approval was not something August was used to craving, but then, neither was he used to feeling left out. Since the day he began kindergarten, August's December birthday and eager-to-please pituitary gland had made him the largest and oldest kid in his class. He was Pantagruel in overalls, and the natural order of schoolchildren conferred imperial status upon him at once. August wore his mantle comfortably. He was an intuitive leader, and power suited him. As he grew older and vaster he experimented with bullying, especially when he discovered that by administering—then merely threatening—noogies he could get Sidney Feinbaum to do his homework for him. August's heart was never entirely in the noogies, though. He gave them because they were expected of boys his size. August didn't have the helpless rage that gives a true bully inspiration. His parents were too competent. Bullying was a means to an end, one he deployed rarely, but which grew more essential when in sixth grade he moved to St. Ignatius Loyola, where the rising tide of homework began to drag him out to sea.

In the twelve years August attended school the only academic exercise that would ever truly excite him was the 6th-grade dissection of a fetal pig. From the first soft slip of scalpel through slick skin, he felt an authority and a calm come over him. He was mesmerized by the complexity of the pig's insides, their precise arrangement, his big fingers finding an unfamiliar dexterity as they carefully freed the heart from its tethers and palpated the tiny, bruise-colored organ. For the first time he found himself so engrossed in something he forgot to make fun of Sidney Feinbaum for fainting. He heard a rumor that in senior year they got to dissect a whole cat, and was crushed when this turned out not to be true.

On the first day of school in 7th grade the St. Ignatius Loyola football coach all but threw himself at August's feet. At twelve he was already six-one, one-ninety, and only getting started. August played fullback and linebacker, and as much as he loved scoring touchdowns, he *lived* for the hitting. The larger he grew, the more fragile the world around him became—things that came into his orbit just seemed to break more often. He had to be careful when hugging his mother now, or when loading the dishwasher at home. But on the football field he didn't have to worry. He found an odd peace, an unambiguous purpose, in lowering his helmet like a battering ram and hurling his full mass into someone with no motive beyond bringing that person down. It was as if August had been purpose-built for football. He didn't even mind the brutal practices, with its musclenumbing crabwalks and wind sprints; his body craved heat and sweat and motion. He loved the tribalism, too, the sense of being in a wolfpack with its own internal code of behavior. As a 7th grader, of course, he was mercilessly hazed, but he took it with martial stoicism and soon won the respect of his teammates—especially when he started flattening opposing quarterbacks with routine efficiency. And with Coach Salerno now acting as his intercessor with the academic authorities, he was able to turn from bully to protector of his former victims (for whom he had always had an oddly paternal feeling) from other upstart bullies, with Sidney Feinbaum as his consigliere. By the end of his first season he was a star.

It was a shock for August, then, when he was packed off to Chum-Chump-Wa that summer and found that his size and athleticism meant squat. These were the *really* rich kids. St. Ignatius Loyola's, being tuitionless and Catholic and therefore full of Blacks and Hispanics and Irish and Italians, was avoided by the eliter WASP and Jewish families, who sent their litter to Dalton, Riverdale, Browning, Spence. He had met these kids before, usually when his father was invited up to a colleague's Greenwich country club and dragged the whole clan onto the Metro-North for a day of "August, why don't you and Sebastian play a little tennis?" then being spanked around the court by a whippet-thin, side-parted boy, and being stuck in a rowboat with Jack, the brothers paddling futilely and yelling at each other while their parents sipped old fashioneds by the pool. He hadn't liked those kids then. Or at the stifling joyless Park Avenue apartment parties hosted by the other executives, when his father forced him to cram his bulk into a wool jacket and tie (he hated that tie, just *hated* it) and his father would make crude jokes about his mother that he would never have made at home, and the other men would laugh. The other boys at those parties would fit so splendidly into their blazers it looked like their jackets had gestated around them in the womb and could no more be removed from their shoulders than could the white from their skin. The only redeeming thing about the parties was that August learned early how easy it was to sneak whiskey, and how easy it was to sneak girls whiskey, and what happened when he did.

But at Chum-Chump-Wa (fight song: *Hail Chum-Chump-Wa/We'll thum-thump ya!*) there was no whiskey to sneak, and the girls seemed afraid of him. He didn't speak their language, didn't wear their clothes, didn't know their music (Neil Diamond, all night long), couldn't get to first base. Thus the fear Victor inspired in these kids was like a salve for August's vengeful soul. The other campers made up stories about him: he'd been in Vietnam, he'd been in jail, he was a rapist. But Victor was tolerant of August, because August had once come up to the service window and told him his meatloaf was bitchin'.

Then one day, as August walked alone through the woods, late for one activity or another, he saw Victor fucking a counselor. He stood there on the path, eyes wide, dick swelling. They were doing it standing up, against a tree. Victor saw him (the counselor, her eyes closed in obvious rapture, didn't) and winked.

The next day August saw Victor out back behind the dining lodge, sitting on a propane tank with a massive FLAMMABLE sign, smoking a cigarette. As if he'd said it a thousand times August asked if he could bum one. Victor shrugged and lit it for him. Pinching the cigarette between his thumb and index and middle fingers, as he'd seen Clint Eastwood do it, he took a deep, seasoned drag and it punched him in the throat. He tried so hard to keep from coughing that his eyes began to water. Victor laughed, a short phlegmy bark, and spit out something unliquid and greenish.

It's not a dick, kid, you don't have to take it all at once, said Victor. August steadied himself and put it to his lips again, feeling his upper lip gently grip the fibers of the tipping paper. He drew more humbly than before and, this time, felt a warm efflorescence of smoke fill his mouth. He liked this. No wonder his parents did it so much. They smoked quietly together, and August began to grow lightheaded and confident. He decided to ask about the kitchen, so Victor came down off the propane tank and showed him around, pointing things out with the ember of his cigarette. He let him try out the big swing-armed dishwasher that shook and whooshed when he lowered the hood, pointed out the prepped meals prepped waiting in the walk-in, and showed him the huge tubs of butter and thirty-pound bags of pre-cut French fries. And the young August, who had always been the child who wanted to help his mom cut potatoes and play in mud and who liked the sticky feeling of glue in his hands and the way the racks on the dishwasher slid smoothly back into place, was enchanted. Then and there he told Victor he wanted to be a chef someday, and Victor laughed so hard that he started to cough up little mucosal chunks of lung.

August spent much of that summer in the kitchen, trailing Victor like an adoring baby elephant. Victor accepted his presence, as long as he did not talk too much, but the Bulgarian teenagers who made up the rest of the staff were thrilled. Not only could he lift the heaviest boxes and reach the items on the highest shelves, but they discovered he would do anything if the request came from Irina, a pretty sixteen-year-old who wore her chestnut hair in a tight ponytail. He would help her wash dishes, shell peas, peel potatoes, and in August's overenthusiastic hands helping usually meant doing all of it. At night his dreams were consumed with her, but he dared not touch himself. One boy in his cabin had already been betrayed by the vinyl of the mattresses.

Irina seemed not to mind August's awkward efforts to brush up against her (sometimes she even would ruffle his hair like a dog's). He was too chicken to do more. But one morning, when Irina was refilling the cereal tubs, August saw Victor steal up behind her and lay his hand on the exposed skin of her neck. She didn't move a muscle as Victor's craggy hand roved downward, to her lower back. August could not see Irina's face, but Victor spotted him there, watching. Grinning, Victor snaked his fingers into the back pocket of Irina's blue jeans, looked straight at August, and winked.

In the final days of camp, August grew bolder. He would try to play with Irina's hair, or touch her exposed midriff, but each time she would go stiff, then catch his hands and place them back down by his side. She seemed colder to him after that, and he couldn't understand why. Maybe he was just too young, or not smooth enough. He had to learn to be more aggressive, he thought, so that he wouldn't be so awkward next summer. For months after camp, he thought constantly of Irina. He dreamt of how it would feel to touch the soap-white skin of her belly, to probe his fingers below the waist of her jeans.

When Thomas and Isabelle dropped him off the following June August leapt from the car without so much as a goodbye and headed straight for the dining lodge. He burst into the kitchen and there was a stout old lady with bushy hair and a pukka-shell necklace, directing the Bulgarians. There were lots of new faces. Irina was nowhere to be seen.

Hello, said the woman. Who might you be?

Where's Victor, August asked.

Who? said the woman.

He is cook last summer, said a crew-cut Bulgarian August recognized, pointing a finger at his ear and making a corkscrew gesture.

Oh! her eyes widened. Him. Oh God. Yes. Don't worry, he's long gone. There's nothing to worry about now, dear. Would you like a brownie?

By the time registration for the summer of 1985 rolled around August informed his parents that he had had it with campfires and lanyards and color wars. Fortunately, it so happened that Grayson had gone public in the fall of 1984, and in an unprecedented fit of fiscal euphoria Thomas and Isabelle had bought themselves a summer house on the South Shore of Long Island. It was more of a cottage (fiscal euphoria had limits), but it had a fine view of Shinnecock Bay. Thomas bought a little Sunfish sailboat he capsized the first time he took it out; Isabelle and the boys nearly died laughing and cheering as he clambered, soaked, onto the upturned hull, and hauled irately on the daggerboard to try to right the boat. Jack, who was thirteen, observed that at least his father seemed to know how to *swear* like a sailor. Thomas never stepped in "that damn canoe" again, but Isabelle turned out to be a preternaturally-able mariner, and most mornings was to be found skimming her way across the bay, enjoying the perfect quiet before returning to a house where she was outnumbered three to one.

August was far too large for the Sunfish and had a higher calling that summer: Thomas, who felt that the routine, responsibility, and respectability of a proper job would iron out some of the more brazen impulses he'd lately detected in his now fifteen-year-old son, arranged for August to work as a dishwasher at a Italian restaurant in Hampton Bays, called Sprezzatura. The moment August heard the word "restaurant," he agreed.

Sprezzatura was the dominion of their neighbor in East Quogue, Jimmy Luisi, a gleamingly-pompadoured Italian who pronounced "beautiful" with four distinct syllables and wore silk shirts unbuttoned to the sixth rib. August's parents and Jack would come up on the weekends. The other five days a week, August was unsupervised, with money in his pocket, a snarling 1974 Mercury Cougar, and everything to prove.

The very first morning he arrived in the kitchen, all six feet five inches and 270 pounds of him, the skinny, manic cooks marked him as a perfect vector for chaos. Wedged into the small alcove of the dishwashing station, August could neither dodge nor duck whenever moldy fruit, wooden spoons, or rags soaked in Russian dressing were flung his way. He soon learned to catch and wing them back, and before long he and the cooks were trading artillery fire across the kitchen. August took his hazing nobly because he loved it. He loved it all—the car, the women, the fluid, noisy, adrenal blast furnace of the kitchen, the smoking over the garde-manger, the women, the depraved conversation of the men (and women), the war stories. The women. Within a week he'd spiked his virginity like a finished dupe receipt on the line. She was a gelatinous, sleepy-eyed bartender named Natalee whose flaplike breasts, when she was underneath him, moved like water in a bathtub. They were all sitting on the beach, around a fire. He was three cans past the point of no return, and she was forty-two; he'd told her he was nineteen, and she didn't argue. They did it on a towel, right there by the fire, in full view of the others.

Even vasodilated by Ballantine's, and with his neuronal pumps lazily burping out ions, these things were bolted to August Sweeney's memory like a plaque to a plinth: her muscular tongue pugnacious in his mouth, the uneven ridges of her teeth, the plasmoid feel of her tits, her big belly yielding like rising dough, the uric tang of her labia, her yelp-laugh as his penis stabbed bunglingly at her pelvis, and then the unearthly sensation of finding the entrance and sinking into her. After that he remembered very little, and certainly not the part afterward where he ran giddy and naked, softening penis flopping like an eel, headlong into the cold Atlantic Ocean.

The next summer, 1986, Jimmy Luisi let him peel potatoes, chop onions, rinse salad, and then began to put him on the cold station on slower days. He changed kegs and scraped out grease traps. He liked the movement, the noise, the heat. Maybe it was that superhuman anaerobic respiration, but for a big man, August loved heat. He had loved it in late-summer football training camps, and he loved it now. A kitchen, he philosophized, was more or less a house on fire, and so he accepted the heat the same way he would walk, not run, through heavy rain because he was going to get wet anyway, so why not have some dignity about it? To deal with the heat all he had to do was accept the reality of constant perspiration. His underwear would get sticky and wet. His socks would be soaked in his sneakers. He learned to enjoy the salt taste of a single bead of sweat trickling into the corner of his mouth, the same way he was always compelled by the taste of his own blood when he accidentally cut himself. To August, the kitchen of Sprezzatura felt—though he wouldn't even have been able to spell the word—amniotic.

In his junior year, August—now at Xavier High School—brought sacramental terror to the Greater New York Catholic School Football Association. He was so certain that the college football recruiters would be beating down his door that despite his parents' exhortations he had let his already-dismal grades go completely to hell. But his door remained on its hinges; Manhattan was not exactly East Texas in terms of raw football talent-incubation. By the spring of 1988 it was clear that August was not going to college—or graduating high school. Thomas was enraged and insisted that August make up the work and reapply the following year. In the meantime, he declared, August was going to work full-time. None of this farting around the Hamptons. He would work at Grayson, Thomas decided. He would begin as a copyboy, go back to school, graduate, then come back in through accounts, then sales, then corner office, then gold watch and the long goodbye. August told his father he felt roughly the same way about this as he did about becoming "a professional enema-tester," which caused days of heavy silence at the Sweeney dinner table until destiny came calling in the form of ruddy Mediterranean ethnic omnibus Timo Pruno, who ran a restaurant in Queens, and who happened to be the father of his fellow lineman at Xavier, the regrettably-named Bruno Pruno.

The job was only supposed to be for a year.

6.

From the moment I hung up the phone, it took just over four minutes to reach the hospital lobby. It was a walk I'd timed three months ago, on my first day. That included fifteen seconds to pull off and throw out apron armguards gloves smock and booties, and, in this case, another fifteen to lie to the students: "Sorry, everyone. Histology needs an emergency consult; I'll be back as soon as I can. In the meantime, India, can you please take them through first cuts? If you finish that, show them some samples from the cabinet. There are some good ischemic hearts in there." I held eye contact with her, silently conveying my gratitude for her quick thinking and discretion. Inwardly, I was grimacing: now she had something on me. Then it was three and a half long minutes through the subterranean cinder-block tunnels, walking briskly but never running, never let them see you run, past laundry bins, stacks of shipping pallets, folding tables, unmarked doors, slow-rolling robot carts that froze like startled deer when a human crossed their path, past workmen in heavy boots and sneakered orderlies, up two flights of concrete stairs, through a fire door and into the airport brilliance of the main lobby. All told, four minutes for my head to turn itself inside out trying to understand why my dad, who was supposed to be at home in Forest Hills, recovering from a stroke, could possibly be at the front desk of my hospital. Four minutes is an eternity in brain-time. Hypnosis patients who have been under for all of thirty seconds report having seen entire days go by. As I walked, whole scenarios illustrated and erased themselves in my mind, like time-lapse shots of the jungle floor in the Planet Earth movies, green shoots squiggling upwards to burst into flower, then withering and palsying and turning brown before shrinking back down into the earth: he was miraculously better. I was secretly adopted. This was an elaborate prank. It was not my dad at all, it was a scammer; my mother saw scammers everywhere, like my great-aunt Yurong saw ghosts. There was an entirely different Maya Zhu in this hospital and she and her father had breakfast together once a week and she confided in him about her lousy dating life and he told dad jokes. Not one of these scenarios involved walking into the warm sunshine of the lobby to discover my father standing there in a burgundy tracksuit, filthy with dust and grime and grinning triumphantly at me.

He looked like a cartoon science experiment had exploded in his face. The black hair he had kept neatly parted and combed since the day he picked me up at the airport when I was six was wild, electrified; his glasses were bleared and his whole face was florid; however long he had been out in the January cold, it was long enough for the capillaries in his cheeks to crack.

"Tongtong. I missed you so much," he said in Chinese, his voice hoarse and weak, and before I could stop him he wrapped me in a hug and I gagged; he reeked of rotten meat. He clearly hadn't showered in days, and he'd soiled himself. Alarmed, the security guard started toward us, but I shook my head at her. The entire lobby was staring at me in the way that New Yorkers stare, where they avert their eyes but train every other sensory faculty they have on you. There was no time for questions now—not here. I needed to get us out of this place where patients and colleagues could see us.

"He's with me," I told the guard, who was only too happy to get him out of there.

I led my dad back through the basement hallways. The workmen and nurses blanched and pressed themselves up against the wall as we approached, a doctor in scrubs leading a feral old Asian man in a tracksuit. "I wanted to see you," he kept saying. Every so often he saw something down the wrong hallway and veered off in that direction and I had to corral him like an orderly in a mental institution.

Finally, I got him into the basement sanctum of the autopsy wing and down the corridor to my office. As I put my hand on the door handle, I realized the student who fainted might still be in there.

"Wait here," I hissed at my father, who was admiring a laminated poster detailing the gross pathology of Dilated Cardiomyopathy. I eased open the door and peered in. No sign of the student. I exhaled. I pulled dad inside and closed the door quietly behind us.

"This is your office?" he said, disappointed.

"Drink," I said, handing him a cup of water.

"Not even a window. Tongtong, you need a window. It's very gloomy down here. You'll get depressed."

"Ba, how did you get here? Did you walk?"

"You should ask them for an office with a window."

This was not my field. None of this was my field. Literally any other doctor in this hospital, even the most venal radiologist, was more qualified to deal with a man in this condition than I was. And there was no way I could call any one of them. "Look at me. Ba." I snapped my fingers. "Did you walk here from Queens?"

"Yes, I walked. I lost my Metrocard." He finished the water, and I got him another. His hands were shaking. I had to get him cleaned up. Then maybe I could get him to sleep on the couch until someone could come get him. Mom. Ming-Yan. Anyone.

I took a spare set of scrubs out of my drawer. They weren't big, but they would do. He was never a large man, but the stroke seemed to have shrunk him. I had not seen him for weeks. I led him quietly across the hall to the locker room and switched on the shower. There was a spare towel. When the water was warm I told him to get undressed and get in the water. He seemed dazed, but compliant. I left before he could remove his pants; I'd never seen him naked and I was not about to start now. I stood outside the door listening until I heard the sound of the water change, and I knew he'd gotten in.

Back in my office I shut the door and called home. No one answered. Of course. The man was recovering from a stroke, why would anyone be taking care of him? I called my mom's cell phone.

"Wei?" I heard street sounds; she was outside.

"Mama, Ba is here. At the hospital."

She shrieked. Literally shrieked. "*Aiii!* Such good news!"

"How is that good news? Mama, he's filthy and completely out of it. He says he walked here. From Queens! It's freezing outside!"

"Well, he's been gone for two days."

I stopped pacing.

"Two *days*? Gone where? Gone like missing? Mom! Why didn't you call me?" I was trying to keep my voice down, paranoid that even through two steel doors they'd hear me across the hallway in the autopsy lab.

"Well, we didn't want to worry you!" she said, as if it were the most obvious thing in the world. As if I should be grateful. "We thought he would come back, or that someone in the neighborhood would pick him up and bring him home. That's what usually happens."

"*Usually?* What do you mean—he's done this before?"

She was quiet for a beat. "Once or twice."

"Once or twice."

"Who can count."

"Mom! And you didn't tell me? This is serious!"

"Ai ya, Tongtong, don't scold me!" she said in her most wounded voice. "You told us not to bother you when you were working!"

I dropped to the couch. "I don't *believe* you," I said in English. But of course, I did. Because I had told them that. Not that I'd needed to. They knew.

They hadn't pushed me into medicine. They hadn't pushed me into anything. (They did push me away from certain things, such as the time in high school I joked that I'd make a great CIA agent, because it was true, and for the next month it was wall-to-wall Wen Ho Lee horror stories at dinnertime. "And he was Taiwanese," they said. "Imagine what they do to mainlanders!" Even fifteen years later, my mother still forwarded me every article she saw about Chinese grad students getting busted for espionage.) Instead all they demanded was that I crush my competition and make good money. So when I told them which branch of medicine I wanted to go into, I was entirely unprepared for a volcano to erupt.

"Dead people?" my mother asked, the color draining from her rigorously-moisturized face.

"It's called an autopsy, mama. I exam—"

"We sent you to medical school," my father hissed. "We paid. For *this?*"

"It's medicine, Ba. It's important. And I'm good at it."

We were sitting at the table, eating. I don't remember what. I just remember I'd brought melon cakes. I had gone to a Chinese bakery to pick them up.

"You know in China this is shameful," he said, his face reddening. "It was forbidden before the communists came. It is not a job for a doctor."

My mother clicked her tongue and looked to the sky imploringly. "Does it pay well?" she asked, twisting her napkin into knots. Somehow this gesture—the trite, pathetic artifice of it, like a paid mourner at a funeral flinging themselves onto the coffin and wailing—set my teeth on edge. My whole life I had done everything they had asked of me, without a flicker of complaint. Most people would have snapped in half if they'd had my childhood.

I laughed harshly. "Nope."

"Who cares how it pays," said my dad, his voice low with danger. "You are *mutilating* people."

I slammed the door on my way out and took the melon cakes with me. We didn't speak for weeks.

"How fast can you get here?" I asked my mom. "I've got him in the shower, and he can rest in my office for a while. But I have students, I have to get back to work."

"I can't come this morning. I'm going to the restaurant right now. There's a banquet for thirty people, corporate, and ever since Baba stopped being able to work the kitchen is completely wu li hu tu. I don't trust the new second chef. You know he's from Fujian?"

"That doesn't mean he stea—you know what, forget it. Can Ming-Yan come?"

"Eh? Ming-Yan is in China. Didn't I tell you? She's trying to sell Gong-gong's house. Apparently she knows someone who can help her get money out—"

"*Mother. The dead man in my lab is literally decomposing as we speak. I do not have time to take care of Baba.*" Every minute I was dealing with this was another minute for his adrenal glands to autolyze and melt into the surrounding fatty tissue.

There was a knock on the door, and Dad entered, wearing scrubs that were too small for him, and toweling off his hair. With the grime washed off he was pale and gaunt. When had he gotten so old?

"Better?" I asked him. He nodded and sat on the couch. "Lie down," I said. "Rest now."

"Is that him?" Mom asked. "Just let him sleep. I can come after lunch, at four."

"That's in seven hours!"

"Eh? You're in a hospital. What could happen?"

I hung up. I couldn't deal with her. I sat in my desk chair and put my head in my hands. I needed to think but felt lightheaded and out of breath. Between the students and India and the virtual certainty that Mario would come down to check out 289, whose bequest was morbid enough to capture even *his* depraved attention. If anyone knew my father was sleeping in my office, they'd never take me seriously again— or worse, pity me. No sooner did I think this than I was awash in guilt.

Part of my father's brain had died and he wanted to see me so much he walked from Queens to Midtown Manhattan in late December. Maybe my mother was right—the hospital was the safest place he could possibly be.

"Tongtong?" His voice seemed to be coming from somewhere far away.

I kept my head in my hands. "Yes, Ba?"

"You need a window."

"Yes, Ba."

When I reentered the lab, 289 was flung open like a giant soft-cover book, his eyes still staring upward. Even after a few hundred bodies I still enjoy the soft little burst of amygdalar static I get whenever I walk into a lab mid-autopsy. Their faces are always untroubled, oblivious to the carnage happening just below.

India hadn't gotten very far. Ordinarily, in the twenty minutes I'd been gone, she would have the sternum and anterior ribcage clipped out and would be scalpeling the organs free of abdominal fascia. Vigilantly I checked the students for any signs that India had been talking about what she'd heard over the phone. No awkward averting of eyes, no great shows of concentrating on minute things. And up close, now I could see there was nothing ordinary about 289. His entire torso was encased in the thickest layer of gelatinous yellow adipose I had ever seen. It was like aspic. Clearly it had taken her the whole time just to reach the ribcage, much less cut it.

"This is crazy, Dr. Zhu," said one girl, in a dazed voice not entirely unlike my father's a minute before.

"No kidding," India grimaced. I could see her splash shield beaded with moisture. She was sweating as she cut. I put fresh protective garments on and came around to take the scalpel off her hands for a while; she shook her wrist out as if dispelling a cramp.

The white girl said, "My anatomy cadaver was a tiny old lady. She barely had any muscle. I've never seen fat like this."

"You want to be a doctor in America, you better get used to it," said a short one with a tenor voice. At first I thought it was a woman with a ponytail tenting her cap; now it seemed to be a man with a Bushwick bun.

"She was like a walnut," said the girl. On the final word, I heard her arytenoid cartilage squeeze together in her throat, and her vocal cords slacken: vocal fry.

I didn't comment. My scalpel wrote its way across his ribs, tracing deeper into his life, into his death.

Scalpels are silent. Tracing the blade lightly from clavicle to sternum, like a pencil, causes the skin to unzip itself, like an exotic flower opening. It is not the cutting I grew up with. The cleavers of my father's restaurant were percussive, whacking arrhythmically onto the plastic cutting boards. Ribs, backbones, cloves of garlic, blanched tripe, whatever the question, the answer was: cleaver. It was the soundtrack of the kitchen, the whack and sizzle and scorch and Z100. But this was not the cutting my father wanted for me, as much as he loved it.

I could feel my heart rate coming down. It was me and the dead man, and a dead man will never wander off on you. I had no idea what to do with the man across the hall, the man whose cerebral artery had been momentarily blocked by a one-millimeter speck of coagulated blood and fibrin that smote his parieto-occipital junction like a thunderbolt, and now couldn't be trusted to control a cleaver because he couldn't make his hands do what he told them. But this man in front of me? He was mine.

Soon the ribs were a beautiful orderly gridiron of white bone, red intercostal muscle, and orange tissue. The loose rubbery skin of his chest went into the red bucket beside the table with a sound like a fresh fish being slapped onto newspaper.

My phone buzzed in my pocket. I ignored it. I stepped back from the table and wiped the blood from my hands on a blue cotton towel.

"India, if you would?"

She picked up the long-handled pruning shears from the counter and clacked them together. "Just a little off the top?" She was enjoying this entirely too much, showing off for the students. But if she got any more of them to drop, I'd buy her a gift card. They were used to medical technologies being sleek, expensive, sterile, humming with electronic intelligence. They were not used to a pair of clippers that cost $39.95 at Home Depot.

Once I saw a battlefield autopsy kit that was used in the Civil War. It was a little rusty but everything looked more or less the same—saws, shears, clamps, mallets. I thought, I could get the job done with that. The body didn't change. We had so many new ways to heal it and kill it, but the ways to take it apart were the same as they had ever been.

India stuck the points of the shears into his intercostal muscles and squeezed the handles: *crack.*

Vocal Fry went veering away from the table with a cry. She hopped in a circle and flapped her hands as if trying to get something sticky off. No syncope here: the fight-or-flight reflex had chosen Option B. She danced from foot to foot, trying to collect herself. I wondered what would have happened if it chose Option A. Would she have just punched the person next to her? Under the surgical mask I found myself smiling.

"Keep it together, Katz," hissed the Asian girl.

"It's just so *loud*," she said, sucking breath in through her teeth. "My old lady had osteoporosis, we could practically snap her bones with our hands."

Crick. "Look at this one," said India. "Shears went right through it."

"Probably a broken rib," Bushwick asseverated, and I was annoyed: he was probably right.

They didn't know how lucky they were that 289 had died the way he did. He probably didn't think about how lucky he was either. Most of the bodies that wound up on this table, especially the ones whose eyes were closed—having died "peacefully"—spent weeks in a hospital bed. Doctors kept them alive, barely: a heart rate above zero. That wasn't life. That was arithmetic. They ceased to be people, and became battlefields on which the doctors went vainly to war with death. If they were in a good hospital that had avoided a staff shortage, a few times a day a nurse would come by to turn them. Catheters were tunneled into their urethras, colostomy bags stuck with tape to their stomachs. Their skin would grow papery, so much so that when we lifted them onto the table it came right off like the peel of a boiled tomato. In the worst cases, sacral ulcers developed: a hole the size of a baby's fist would open in the lower back. But for me, the worst was always the PICC line we had to pull, inch by slick plastic inch, out of their veins: it's how we feed people who can't eat. But at that point, why bother? Life ends when the body stops being able to eat. After that it's just death by degrees. Painful, boring, humiliating degrees. This is how most Americans are made to die.

I tried to suppress the thought that this was especially how many stroke victims died. But my dad wasn't dying. This much I knew. The blood clot had been a warning shot from his cardiovascular system that years of stress and heat and standing for twelve hours a day in non-orthotic shoes had done a number on his arteries. He could have died, to be sure, but my mother got him to the hospital in time. As long as he took his statins and warfarin, he'd be okay. The hand tremors would probably fade. They couldn't be sure about the brain damage, though. The brain was tricky that way. The personality changes might go away, or they might be permanent. There was no way to know.

But 289 had shot past all of this. He had died so suddenly, so cleanly, we would be able to tell what his last meal was.

Meals. I hadn't even thought—God knew when was the last time my dad ate was. That was why he was delirious. The man's stomach was probably devouring its own fat right now. If I could get some food in him, he might be ready for me get him out of my office and into a cab home. But I couldn't leave the lab again, and I certainly couldn't send him out on his own.

Grunting, India snapped through the last rib and dropped the bloody shears with a clank in the dissection table sink. Then she picked up the bone key and wedged the blade into a seam in the manubriosternal joint. She twisted and with a slick sucking sound the entire breastplate popped free. "Like a Tupperware lid," she said, and passed around the slab of meat and bone for the students to hold.

India already knew he was here. She knew whatever the security guard at the desk had told her over the phone. And despite the fact that she was typically as discreet as a train derailment, she'd kept her mouth shut.

I pulled my predecessor's (Mario's) broken-spined copy of *Netter's Anatomy* off the shelf and handed it to the Asian girl. "Before we go any further, I want you to inspect the organs *in situ*. Use the book if you need, though you shouldn't. Without embalming fluid, everything will look and feel different than it did in anatomy. Work together and identify everything you can. Note anything that looks irregular. We'll be back shortly." A nod to India, and she followed.

"Remember no selfies," she called over her shoulder. The students cracked up. She was good with them. Better than me.

I led her down the hallway, past my office—the door still closed— to the cold room. I punched the code and the steel door unsealed. The room was tight, and made even tighter by the cadaver sheathed in a white bag on a gurney. A woman. Cancer. Yesterday's work. The funeral home hadn't come by yet to collect her. In the chill we could see our breath, but this wouldn't take long, and I wanted to make sure we weren't overheard.

"I'm sorry about that," I started, pulling down my surgical mask.

"So was it really your dad?" she asked.

"It was."

She let out a low whistle. "Man. Is he all right? Is something wrong with him?" she said, then caught herself. "Oh sh—sorry, Dr. Zhu. You ain't gotta tell me, it's none of my business."

I assessed this woman who worked for me. She was a few inches shorter than me, with a stocky pugnacious build, like a field hockey goalie. Her skin was deep brown—she was half-Cuban, half Creole. Not that I had asked. She just told me. This was our relationship. She talked about herself, and I didn't talk much at all. On weekends she went home to Pelham to visit her parents and came in on Mondays with these phenomenal leftovers. If I had to trust anyone in this hospital, it might as well be her.

"One month ago my father had a stroke. Since then, on a few occasions he has wandered off."

India nodded. "My great-grandma used to do that. They kept finding her in the aisles at the CVS. She thought she was going to the movies."

"This time he came here. I have gotten him showered and into some scrubs. He's sleeping in the office right now, but he has not eaten in a long time and appears—" I forced the word to come out cleanly "—delirious."

"Then we gotta get him some food. Fill up the tank. You want me to run to the canteen?"

I was relieved she did not make me ask. "That would be very kind. A sandwich or something bland, I don't want to irritate his stomach."

"Oh, they got plenty of bland up there, don't worry. You get back in there." She smiled. "See if you can get any more to go down."

I let my eyebrows flicker upwards as if to say *We understand each other*. She punched the red button that released the door from the inside and shouldered it open. Before we exited I found myself compelled to say it: "I hope you will keep this matter between—"

"Please. Won't breathe a word. You hear that, lady?" she warned the body bag. She mimed locking her mouth closed, then pulling out her bra and dropping the key into her cleavage. So ludicrous, so nakedly ingenuous was this gesture that I was filled with the urge to clench her to me. But that would have been impossible.

7.

August was moving smoothly between four different burners and the flattop, where two beautiful T-bones, from an innocent steer who had never harmed anyone in its whole life, were blackening and shrinking, the flesh clenching into brittle pucks.

Where are my steaks! Maria Enescu came banging through the double doors. I fired them ten minutes ago!

August grimaced. Tell those suits to keep their toupees on, it takes time, it takes time to ruin a steak.

Chef Ivor Stojko came over and put a hairy arm around his shoulder. Is a tragedy every time, no?

They want it well done, I'll fucking give them well done, August said. Maybe rub it between my sweaty ass cheeks, make it salty.

Is my boy, beamed Ivor. This is for seven?

August checked the dupe. Uh huh.

Govnari, Ivor snorted, prepping a bowl of goulash for table twenty-three.

August knew this word. He had picked up a lot of Serbian words in the two years he had worked under Ivor at Timo's. Of course the only thing the words were useful for was starting a fight. But that was all right with August.

I need more salad plates, said Luna from the cold station.

Coming! said Toussaint, the Haitian dishwasher.

August checked the underside of the T-bones. Still grey. He knew this type of client—bottom-feeding brokers, penny-stock guys, who swaggered around Queens in Beemers they could barely make the payments on and came to places like Timo's to act like big shots because they couldn't afford to do it in Manhattan. And nothing made them feel more big-shotty than sending food back. August figured if they were going to do it anyhow, he might as well give them a good reason.

Behind him a yelp and a pulpy crash, followed by

I VILL CHOP YOU IN PIECES AND FEED YOU TO MY CATS.

Toussaint scrambling for a mop to soak up 23's blood-red goulash, now splattered all over the kitchen floor.

LEETLE TINY PIECES

Staggering under the weight of a tubful of salad plates, Toussaint had accidentally bumped into Ivor, and 23's goulash had ejected from the chef's hand halfway to the passthrough and gone spinning through the air, red sauce pinwheeling in its wake, before bursting in a meaty splash on the tiles.

LIKE KEEBLE

Sorry chef! said Toussaint, swabbing hard at the still-steaming stew and the shards of white enamelware. Sorry sorry chef!

Calmly August reached up for a clean bowl and ladled out a new portion of goulash from the huge stockpot simmering on the 6-burner range. He spiked it with a prim dash of red wine vinegar—*food with no acid is boring as life with no danger*, Ivor had taught him—stirred it, then he sprinkled a pinch of parsley over the stew, ran his kitchen towel around the edge of the plate, and placed it on the passthrough.

All up on twenty-three, he called.

Still waiting on T-bones! Maria rapped her wedding ring on the stainless steel passthrough. If you're done shouting at poor Toussaint.

Oh my god it's a wedding ring, said Ivor. Guys, do you know Maria is married? Do you know she had wedding ring? I don't think she has ever mentioned before. Is first I'm hearing! Congratulations Maria!

Fuck you Ivor.

Right now? In kitchen? At least buy me drink first.

I'd rather fuck that TV alien, said Maria. What's his name, Alf.

Not even real diamond anyway.

Meanwhile table seven still has no T-bones.

T-bones for seven, said August, handing them up to the pass. If those fucking suits don't like it tell them they can come back and tell me themselves.

Out went the forlorn steaks, burned black as klinker brick, along with Maria's upraised middle finger. Ivor watched her go, the hint of a smile flickering under his bushy mustache. His hair was black and thinning, with a feeble comb-over covering his accelerating baldness. His nose was knuckled at the bridge from having been broken with some regularity. He stank constantly of garlic.

Checking the next dupe—stuffed peppers, dolmades, chicken marsala—August fantasized about the suits actually coming into the kitchen, rabid with coke and machismo, demanding to speak to the chef, only to find him, August, looming like the Marshmallow Man from *Ghostbusters*. He imagined calmly taking hold of their power ties, feeling the silk fibers, admiring the pattern, then yanking downward, keeping their faces inches from the searing surface of the flattop.

I'm so sorry you didn't enjoy your steaks, he would say in a soothing professional voice. Would it help to understand how we cook them?

Lately these violent thoughts had been growing in him. He did not quite know why.

He liked the customers at Timo's. He liked everything about Timo's. He especially liked Timo himself, a paternal, thick-accented, club-fingered buffalo who wore a suit every day and loved offering guests free shots of his uncle's homemade brandy from whatever country that table's people happened to come from—and in Forest Hills, Queens in 1986, people came from everywhere. The point of Timo's was that no matter where a guest came from, be it Greece or Poland or Hungary or

Portugal, he would find at least one dish that reminded him of home: moussaka, pierogis, chicken paprika, pastels de nata. It would not be a particularly good rendition of that dish, but the genius of Timo Pruno was to realize that his clients did not particularly care how well-made a dish was, so long as it looked enough like what their mothers had made at home.

No one seemed to be able to figure out exactly which country Timo Pruno was from; *I was born on a boat in the middle of the Mediterranean,* he would say, *the sea is my mother, so beautiful all of Europe embraced her.* He seemed to speak the language of every customer who came through his door, even the Chinese.

With the marsala bubbling redly on the range and stuffed peppers blistering in the oven, August wiped his hands and station down and went over to the kitchen door to look through the porthole window. From there, he had a clear view of Maria depositing the steaks at 7. The men were leaning back in their chairs, the front legs off the floor, and leering up at her. One checked her backside as she bent to put the plates on the table.

Ivor, c'mere, said August. Ten bucks says the suit on the left goes for it.

The chef peered through the porthole. He snorted. No chance, he said. No chin. Total pussy.

Remember last time? I thought she'd chop his fucking arm off, said August.

Is not the only thing she chops off, said Ivor.

The one with the chin raised his martini glass to her and said something. Maria stiffened, straightened and looked straight at him. She laughed coldly and said something in reply. The front legs of his chair hit the floor. The chinless one smirked at the other, who was rapidly reddening. Maria stepped back from the table. She folded her arms across her chest, spoke again, and the one with the chin tossed his martini in her face.

August had always been fast off the line, but Ivor was faster. Or rather August let him be faster: for just a moment, August hesitated. He did not know why. It was as if some chill hand suddenly gripped his shoulder and said *stay*. It was only for a second, but a second was enough. The swinging kitchen door hit the wall with a bang that silenced the whole packed dining room. Every head swiveled as a furious Serb in a white jacket barreled out of the kitchen aiming a long boning knife like a bayonet.

In an instant, Ivor was on the suit with the chin, grabbing him by his collar. He hauled the man to his feet and pressed the blade of the knife to his quivering pink throat.

Apologize, Ivor growled.

Holy shit, the man squeaked.

Ivor released his collar and slapped him across the face, hard. Instantly the man's cheek flushed red, blood rushing to ruptured capillaries. Ivor seized him by the tie and pulled him close, the knife hovering millimeters from the man's jugular.

I asked you, Ivor said.

I'm sorry, he gasped.

I can't hear you, Ivor said, and if I can't hear you, *she can't hear you.*

Are you insane? he said.

August had followed behind to cover Chinless. He folded his arms and glowered down at the pale little man, silently warning him not to interfere. He could feel something shimmering in his chest like sunlight on the water, a fluency in his muscles. Everything seemed to have slowed down—he felt exquisitely aware of everything that was happening in the room: the panicked recoil of the diners around them. The color draining from Timo's face where he stood by the bar. Maria reaching with trembling fingers for a napkin to wipe her face. His limbs felt tuned, strong. Like he could have hoisted Chinless over his head and pitched him clear through the window if he wanted.

Yet at the same time August knew that he must not—that Ivor had crossed a line that he could not afford to cross himself. Timo's was his whole world.

Ivor choked up on the man's tie. I said she can't hear you.

Okay! Okay! I'm sorry! Jesus! I'm sorry!

Not loosening his grip, Ivor looked at Maria. Was that loud enough?

Are you crazy, Ivor? she said softly. Did you lose your mind? Let him go.

Ivor stared at her for a second, confused. Then he pulled back the knife and let the tie slip from his fist, and the man's legs buckled. He crashed to the floor and began scrabbling backwards on his butt toward the door, his pinstripe pants scrunching up to reveal ridiculous lime-green socks.

You crazy fuck! He screamed as his chinless friend tried to help him up, but he batted his hands away. I'll sue! Do you know who I am? I'll sue every last motherfucker in this room! This isn't Moscow, you pinko fuck! We have laws in this country! I'll ruin your whole *life*! I'll have you and your skank deported!

He finally got to his feet, turned, and ran directly into Timo, whose face was a stormcloud.

Please, you will leave now, he said, circling around him, bulling him toward the exit. Thank you for coming.

You the owner? said the man, knocking over a chair as he backpedaled. Oh, I'm gonna get *rich* off you.

You're all witnesses! the chinless one cried.

Shut the fuck up, Lenny, said the man, fixing his eyes on Timo. You'll be hearing from my lawyer. I *promise*. And as he backed out the door, with every eye in the restaurant on him, he looked at Ivor and gave him the middle finger. August felt acid flush his veins. He saw himself seizing the man's upraised finger and ripping it right out of his hand, like a cork from a wine bottle. But he didn't move, the door slammed, and they were gone. There was a hush in the room, as if a clanging bell had been suddenly stifled. Nobody moved.

Finally, with a soft grunt, Timo bent down to pick up the chair and set it upright, banging the legs into the floorboards to puncture the silence. He gazed around the room, meeting each eye. At the Hungarians at table 3, at the elderly Chinese couple at 11, at the trembling children of the Cypriot family at 17. Then he grinned.

I love it! he said, gesturing broadly to the whole room. Is just like being back in the old country!

And just like that, laughter rang out once more in Timo's Ristorante, and there was homemade brandy for all.

A few weeks later, August was awakened from a marvelously erotic dream by the telephone. At first he tried to ignore it, hoping to linger with the naked giantess a little bit longer, but he didn't have an answering machine, and the damn thing wouldn't stop ringing so with a groan he rolled out of bed and lumbered over to the far wall of his studio apartment, where the phone was.

It was still dark in the apartment, thanks to the blackout curtains left behind by the previous tenant. Disoriented and detumescing sullenly, August had no idea what time it was and he decided to see how long he could go without finding out. It was his day off; time was no object to him.

What, he said. He slid down the wall to sit on the floor of the kitchenette. He was completely naked. The seafoam-green linoleum felt cool on his bare ass. A little gritty.

August, it's Timo.

Shit, Timo, said August.

Shit Timo is right, said Timo. Ivor is gone. I need you to come in.

In the bed, a woman (Kera? August tried to remember) murmured, Tell them to go away, it's your day off.

It's my day off, said August, closing his eyes as he rested his head against the kitchen wall.

You tell 'em, said probably-Kera, sleepily.

Not anymore, said Timo. Now is your day on. Ivor is gone. I have no chef.

He's not *gone*, said August. He's just drunk in a gutter somewhere, he'll show up. Yesterday was probably Serbian independence day or something.

Serbia is part of Yugoslavia, it's not independent, came Kera's voice from the bed.

Whatever, said August.

August, he's gone, said Timo. He called this morning. From Michigan.

Michigan? August said. Kera slipped out of bed, padded over, and insinuated herself, warm and naked, into his lap. She ran her tongue up the curve of his jaw and reached down to take him in her velvet hand; August retumesced.

He tells me the fucks who throw the drink on Maria, they are pressing charges. He has priors.

What? You're fucking joking. That piece of shit? August bit his bottom lip, half from rage at the suit, half from pleasure at what Kera's fingers were doing.

I know, I like to kill him, but what I can do? Ivor is gone. Didn't even say where in Michigan. Timo sounded wounded.

It's cold there, maybe he'll be happy, said August, not knowing what to say. In his chest he felt a dim flare of guilt. Ivor was his coach, his mentor, and he had just stood there. Useless.

How soon you can be here, Timo asked.

You don't really *want* to go, Kera whispered in his ear, humid and low. Pressed against his chest, her skin felt on his skin the way egg drop soup felt on his tongue, silken and concupiscent.

Timo, man, I had a whole day planned, August said, trying to come up with some plans beyond the one sitting in his lap, but none seemed vital enough to get him off the hook. Can't Luna cover?

Augusto, you don't hear clearly—I have no chef. I need a chef. You are the chef now. Is no more Ivor. You are my chef.

Kera went down on him but she was too late. August had already begun devising specials.

8.

Before reentering the lab I checked my phone. It was a text from Mandragola. The human scalpel heard from at last. For a moment I had forgotten about him.

You're welcome.

Only pedants and anatomists put periods at the end of their texts, I replied.

He's fascinating, isn't he?

He would be if three students weren't draped over him all the time

I thought there were four students.

There were. I put the phone back in my pocket. It buzzed one more time, but I didn't bother to check. He wasn't wrong. I *was* fascinated. But he wanted me to feel indebted to him, and that—no.

In the lab two of them were standing over the body. The Asian girl was consulting the book, and Bushwick was slumped on a stool with his splash shield off and surgeon's mask slung under his chin. The instant he heard the door he leapt up as if the seat were electrified.

"So?" I asked the women. "What do you see?"

The Asian girl spoke. "Enlarged heart muscle suggests chronic hypertension. Staining and color of the lungs implies he was a smoker, and—"

No, no, no.

"Stop," I said. "I didn't ask what do you *think*. I asked what do you *see*. You've had him open for five minutes, and already you're making diagnoses. That's not how we do this. In this lab, we don't make guesses. We don't imply, or suggest. That's for their doctors to do, and then they get it wrong. That's why we're here. Put the book down. Tell me something: in a hospital, what happens when a person dies?"

Blank looks. Well, if they were here to learn, I might as well teach them something.

"We haven't covered—" started the girl.

"Let's go through it. Your patient's heart stops. Blood oxygen goes to zero. Neural function ceases. Paddles don't work, intubation doesn't work, you shine your little penlight in their eyes, you call time of death. Okay? Your patient is no longer your patient, they're your decedent. Now what."

"You have to do the death certificate," said Bushwick, his confidence restored now that he was no longer woozy from 289's innards.

"Wrong. First you have to tell the family. They'll teach you how to do this at length. They'll hire actors who can cry on cue. You'll be professional and compassionate but above all you will be clear, you will not use any soft language like 'he's in a better place' or 'we did all we could.' That language is intended to make *you* feel better, but it does nothing for the family. You will say 'died' and you will say it quickly because you will want to get out of there as fast as you can. The family will be allowed to view the body before it is sent to the morgue. Then comes the death certificate, and this is where you will screw up."

I led them over to the computer and pulled up a blank death certificate on screen. "The US Standard Certificate of Death form looks like a W-2. The main parts you need to concern yourselves with are Part 37, Manner of Death, and Part 32, Cause of Death. Manner is easy: was it a homicide, a suicide, an accident, natural, or a mystery. Either you know or you don't. Cause, however—cause is hard. The form asks for immediate cause of death, and then the underlying causes, going back as far as the medical history will allow. But for all the time your professors will spend coaching you on how to tell families their grandfather died, they won't spend ten minutes explaining how to determine exactly what killed their grandfather. What percentage of US death certificates, do you think, have an error in the cause of death section?"

"Ten?" hazarded Vocal Fry.

I made eye contact with all three. "Fifty."

That startled them.

"How is that possible?" the Asian girl said. If I was going to be teaching them, I really needed to learn their names.

"Hypothetical example." Too late, I realized I was not accustomed to impromptu lectures. It came out before I could stop myself. "A healthy, active 65-year-old man is rushed to the hospital after having a sudden ischemic stroke."

I left out that it was a Sunday, and the man was cooking pork, wearing his boxers and house slippers, and that his wife, who was the only one at home with him when he hit the floor, insisted on forcing pants onto him before the EMTs arrived.

"According to his wife, he has never had heart issues, or diabetes. He is neither obese nor a smoker. No previous complaints of chest pain. Prefers Chinese medicine to Western whenever possible."

"What's the family medical history?" asked Vocal Fry.

"The man is an immigrant whose parents died under Communism. He does not know." Neither did his daughter, the one who would have known the symptoms of a stroke if she had been there, which she was supposed to be because it was Sunday and her father was cooking, but instead she was in her lab listening to Chopin and looking at slivers of renal infarcts under a microscope. "He is put on life support when he arrives at the hospital, but he dies."

"So he dies of a stroke. That's the cause of death," Vocal Fry said.

"The stroke caused the death. But an undergraduate volunteer EMT could have told you that." An undergraduate volunteer EMT would have probably been at her parents' house when she was supposed to be, too. "The reason you get to put Doctor in front of your name and get a fancy parking permit from the NYPD is, you have to explain what *caused* the stroke."

"How are we supposed to do that?"

"Well, if you're like most doctors, you guess. So go on. Guess. You're a first year resident, you've just had your first patient die in front of you. You're not doing so great. But there are other, live patients, and if you move fast enough you might avoid a second. So you want to make this quick. I mean, it's a stroke, it's probably cardiovascular *somehow*. So do it. Guess."

They were looking at each other, bewildered, and I, suddenly, was hot in the face. I found myself goading them with my voice.

"Come on, what's the worst that can happen? He can't die twice. Guess."

"Mitral stenosis?" said the Asian girl, timorously.

"Great. Done. Put it on the form. Ischemic stroke caused by cerebral artery blockage, originating in chronic mitral stenosis. Put it on the form, move along. You might be wrong, but you're *probably* right."

"But was I?" she asked.

"Oh, God no." I laughed. "The man has—*had*—hypertrophic cardiomyopathy. Usually asymptomatic, very hard to diagnose unless you're looking for it. But also completely hereditary. Passes like a ghost through walls from parent to child." A child who was going to be getting EKGs once a year for the rest of her life. A child who knew how close her father came. "This is why what we do in here matters. We don't just tell you if you made a mistake in the cause of death, either—we tell you if you made a mistake in treatment. And in about one in ten cases, you did. As doctors, you will get things wrong. That can't be helped. But you need to know when you do, so you don't get them wrong twice. That's our job. So before we think, we *look*."

It was so quiet I could hear the whir of the computer. They seemed less struck by what I'd said than how I'd said it. As if they hadn't expected this volume of moral authority to come from the lowly autopsy pathologist (who hadn't expected it to come from herself, either). I wondered what they had heard about me upstairs.

It occurred to me that this was a perfect time to show them the eyes, now that they were properly unnerved.

"Come around here." I cupped my hands under his head to turn it from side to side, so all of them could see clearly. His black hair bristled my gloves. I couldn't help checking his scalp. It was whitish and flaky; dandruff sprinkled my gloves. I wondered, if I knew I were dying, would I still spend as much time taking care of my hair as I do?

"Look carefully at his eyes" I said. "In the cadavers you saw in anatomy, the eyes were milky. It looked like everyone had glaucoma, because—"

The door opened and standing there in blue scrubs was my father.

"Tongtong!" he cried in Chinese. "I heard your voice!"

In movies, they always show the disasters in slow-motion. The camera arcs lovingly around the bullet swirling the air, or the suddenly airborne car. Faces contort into expressions of astonishment or horror. I like these moments when the sound gets sucked out of the scene, because the director is letting you linger over the full anatomy of the image. It is also accurate. There is a word for this effect: tachypsychia. In instants of grave alarm—like, say, when one's father bursts into one's lab and sees one holding a dead man's head in one's hands—epinephrine zooms out of the adrenal medulla and into the bloodstream, throttling up the heart rate and dilating bronchial passages. Time very literally seems to slow down, and people commonly report sounds becoming muffled. It can also lower sensitivity to pain, drain the color from one's vision, or—as seemed to be happening to me—short-circuit motor function. I should have been launching myself at him to bundle him back out of the lab before he could say anything else, because if you had given me the choice between a slow death and letting these medical students leave here and tell everyone that Maya Zhu's daddy came to her lab to check up on her, I would have asked, "How slow?" Instead I found myself frozen as Dad barreled up to me and blew what was left of my mind by wrapping me in a bear hug.

"Wah! So this is what you do?" he said in Chinese, looking at the blubbery scarlet crevasse of 289's torso. I covered the face with my hands—I didn't want Dad seeing. I didn't know how he would react. Had he ever seen a cadaver? And since when did he hug? But instead he looked up at the equally-gobsmacked young people around me. "You have students now? You're a professor! You should have told us!"

Where was the man who just half an hour ago was half-dead from exhaustion? And moreover, where was my father, who hadn't bear-hugged me in decades, and had now done it twice in less than an hour? I didn't have time for these questions. I'd done my ER rotations, I remembered my training: contain the bleeding, stabilize vitals, then figure out what's going on. I needed to get him away from here before anyone figured out who he was. But my father wasn't on a gurney, and he was—probably—not psychotic, and anyhow there was nothing here to sedate him with and meanwhile, 289's head was still in my hands and his brown-gold eyes were staring up at me and my father was shaking hands with the students.

"Hi! I'm James T. I'm her dad!"

Bushwick almost choked on his own name. "Scott?"

"Hi, James T. I'm Maya's dad."

"I'm Eva," said Vocal Fry. "James T. like Tiberius? Like Star Trek?"

"Exactly!" He saw the Asian girl and fixed her with a look. "Chinese or Korean?"

I had never prayed before. I had never seen the point. But somehow I found myself gripping 289's seborrheic scalp because he was the only one in the room on my side and silently imploring him, as if he had some sort of intercessory power in this situation: *please, please, please, not Chinese.*

"Wo jiao Wei Wei."

This day just kept getting better.

"Ba," I smiled, firmly taking his arm before he could start asking Wei Wei where her parents were from. Steering him toward the wall of tissue samples, I spoke Chinese under my breath. "You should be resting."

"Wo mei shi le," he protested.

"You can't be here." I could sense my authority leaching out of the room.

"Are these organs?" he asked, staring amazedly at the clear plastic jars, each with tranches of liver or heart floating in tea-brown fluid. "It looks like pickled vegetables."

From Wei Wei I heard a snort of mirth, and I made a mental note to ensure she was heavily involved in running his bowel. If we ever got that far. Just then the door banged open and India entered holding a styrofoam carton, looking panicked. She saw him and exhaled, but then gathered in the climate of the room. For a long, confused moment, she looked back and forth between my dad and the students like a woman who realized she had definitely not brought enough for the whole class.

"I got you a BLT?" she said, holding out the carton to him.

"You are too nice," he said. "I'm James T., Maya's dad. Are you a student too?"

"No, I'm her tech. Her assistant," she clarified. As she passed him the carton she took his elbow lightly and said, "We can't eat in here. Too many chemicals. Come on back to the office with me." To my relief, he nodded. I saw his shoulders slacken, and he shuffled forward after her. Suddenly he appeared so fragile, so withered, that I couldn't look at him. It felt like seeing him naked. I turned back to the students, trying to remember where I'd left off and how I could get this autopsy back on track.

"Aiiiii!"

I whirled. My father—out of whom I had never heard such a sound emerge, not even when he cut himself with a cleaver—was staggering backward from the autopsy table, the styrofoam crunching as he clutched it to his chest in panic.

At first I was terrified he was having another stroke, or worse. It was as if he'd seen the giant dead body for the first time, but that wasn't it. He'd seen it before. He looked right at it. I rushed to him as his knees went. A choked sob came out of him, and in his eyes I saw the welling of tears.

My father didn't cry. I knew he was exhausted and strokes could cause behavioral change. But *my father did not cry.* And even if he did now, he was goddamn well not allowed to do it in my lab. There were always plenty of people to cry and grieve, but there was only one of me, one person whose job it was to see this body without sorrow or pity. And now the man who taught me how to be that person was slumped on my floor, tears coming down his cheeks.

Trembling, he pointed at 289's open mouth and sightless eyes. "My friend," he croaked. "August."

9.

Timo swacked a rubber-banded bundle of receipts down on August's desk. They were in the cramped, unheated chef's office, the walls of which were so covered in post-its and pushpinned menu ideas it looked as if August were tracking an international crime syndicate.

Foie gras. You ordered *thirty pounds* of foie gras.

Blood was surging into Timo's face, spreading the flush evenly from his scalp to the sides of his neck, which like all middle-aged men of his Mediterranean gene pool was as wide as his head.

What in fuck we are going to do with thirty pounds of foie gras? Maybe we paint the bathroom. Maybe make a sculpture. But you know what we don't do with it? Sell it. Is no one buying foie gras. Is no one buying—Timo picked up the stack of receipts and started rifling through them—Chilean sea bass…King Crab…oh my God, *caviar*?

We actually sold some of that to these Russ—August began to say, and Timo silenced him with a furious glare. He'd known this was coming for weeks. Money was a new concept to August. As far as he understood, Timo's was a success, so it had money. If he made it better, with better food, it would have even more money. It was just math. And yet the walk-in was bursting with gorgeous, expensive meats that night after night, went unsold and were now steadily and inexorably rotting. But he couldn't help it; every time he looked at the purveyor lists, something came over him. It was as if a valve was opened in his chest, and his imagination burst forth. Without even closing his eyes he could taste, literally taste the foie gras melting sweet and salty on the back of his tongue. He felt his teeth snap the crispy skin of the sea bass, drizzled with lemon, and his tongue collect the fragrant white flesh below, and he had to have it.

And then what they do buy, half of it you fuck up! cried Timo.

Not *half*, he groused.

So he'd been a little overambitious. Who could blame him? Sometimes he would look out over the kitchen, see the familiar faces shuttling back and forth at their stations, and feel an obscure dread drape itself over his shoulders. Was this all there was? He loved Timo and the other employees, but more and more he feared that no one would ever notice him out here—and certainly not if he was slinging wrinkled little dolmades. So quietly he had begun looking for new recipes in old cookbooks, and they were full of these French names. Bocuse, Point, Brazier. He did not know who they were but the names shimmered in his mind—even if he pronounced the last one like the feminine undergarment. Cooks could be famous. Why not him? He felt his power acutely, like a gun nestled in its holster, waiting to be drawn.

The problem was that *making* those recipes had turned out to be like playing the piano blindfolded with his toes. A significant amount of the foie gras, for instance, had gone into a squab pie. The recipe seemed straightforward: line a hotel pan with a hot-water crust, bone and dice the squabs, put them inside the crust with hard-boiled eggs and thyme and potatoes, lay sliced lobes of foie gras down the midline, bury it with filling, cover, bake, and blow people's minds. Turned out the thing it blew wasn't their minds, it was their colons: The foie melted to a pink congealed paste, but since August had never worked with squab before, he didn't realize that the pale pink color meant it was undercooked until it carved its way out of him like Tim Robbins tunnelling out of Shawshank. He was determined not to make the same mistake with his attempt at beef Wellington, and overcooked it so much that a hundred dollars' worth of prime tenderloin wound up javelined into the trash.

After that August gave up on wrapping meat in crusts, but even so, he still wasn't able to pull off the truly refined shit—he no more understood the art of saucing than he understood how his television worked—and even on the rare occasions he *did* get something right, no one bought any. After five beautifully-baked lobsters thermidor went completely unsold, he turned almost vengefully to the recipes he found for stuff like kidney in mustard and parsley, or lamb's brains braised in red wine. He intended it as a little bit of a fuck-you to the people who weren't buying the luxury ingredients on his menu, but to his surprise, they sold like crazy. This was further confirmation that he was cooking for philistines. But he'd win them over. He just needed more time.

August raised his head, defiant. I'm gonna get it, Timo. And when I do it'll be fuckin' great. Isn't that my job? Make the best fuckin' food I can?

Timo looked perplexed, as if he had never heard such a crazy thing in his·life. Where you think you are? You think this is Paris? You are Escoffier? People come here for a taste of home, that's what we give. We make it cheap, we sell it cheap, everyone is happy. So you make a delicious duck a l'orange? No one will know because no one buying it! So why you do this to me? What, is Gael Greene is coming? You think New York Times is going to review us? We are in *Queens*. Gael Greene doesn't even know Queens exists.

Timo was shouting by now, his red cheeks aquiver. There was a sourness of bile in August's mouth, and a catch in his throat. He wanted suddenly to reach under the desk and flip it over, then seize Timo by his ridiculous red blazer and heave him through the front window of the restaurant, sending him tumbling in a rain of shattered glass across the sidewalk. The thought of having to go back to slinging shitty goulash and paprika chicken was like having his balls kicked in. He had *just* gotten started, and now he had to stop, go back? How could he? For the first time since he was bearing down on panicking high school quarterbacks he knew who he was every day. He was working sixteen-hour days, cramming his bulk into the walk-in to inventory, checking every dish that left his kitchen, poring over cookbooks in his freezing office, barely sleeping at night. The pay was still lousy, and worse, for two weeks a mysterious pain had burned in his stomach, as if he had swallowed poison ivy and it was burning him up from the inside. He was giving his very body for this shitbox of a restaurant because he was a man completely in love and now Timo was tearing it all away from him because of money?

Timo could see the hurt in August's face, and he softened.

Augusto, you are a good cook, Timo sighed. Better even than Ivor.

August snorted. He knew he was better than Ivor.

But is more to being a chef than just cooking. You cook with this—Timo thumped his heart—but you *chef* with this: he tapped a clubby finger to his temple.

No shit, Timo, August scowled. I've never done so much fuckin' math in my life. This above all was what he resented. As a line cook, it had all been muscle memory. The goal was simple efficiency: do the most stuff with the fewest possible movements. Suddenly, he had to issue orders, expedite the dupes, check the plates, keep an eye on every cook, waiter, and runner, and that was to say nothing of the sheer amount of calculation he had to do—how many quarter-chickens they had left divided by how many covers he expected on a Tuesday night, or how much to charge for a plate of four seared scallops if the wholesale cost per pound from the Phylaktou Fish Brothers was $12… his head hurt so much he had taken to pulverizing aspirin on his desk and snorting it like cocaine. He had also taken to cocaine.

So what you want? An Olympic gold medal? This isn't little league, this is your job. Get up from this desk. I want you to look at something.

August rose and squeezed himself around the edge of the desk, sucking in his gut. Timo stood in the doorway, which gave on the whole kitchen. It was 11am, an hour to lunch service, and the white-tiled chamber was a hive of activity. Look, Timo said, gesturing.

Oh my God, is that a...*kitchen?* August clapped his hands to his cheeks in astonishment. I've heard of those. Do they...do they make food in there?

Not what, you idiot. Look with your eyes. You see Luna?

Luna, his sous since Ivor left, was shivering her knife through an enormous bunch of parsley, her knuckles crooked to guard against the knife's rapid action. She was a squat cheerful woman. August knew she had a daughter, but he didn't know anything more about her.

She came from Mexico. Walking. In sandals. With her daughter on her back. Five years she works for me. Now she owns apartment, her daughter gets straight As. You see Toussaint?

The Haitian was tightening the swinging arm of the dishwasher hood with a screwdriver. Most of the time August had no idea what he was saying and he routinely showed up hungover, but when service rolled around he was a machine.

From Haiti, in a boat. With what's the word, paddles. Whole family dead from Duvalier. So he drinks.

Waiters whisked in and out of the kitchen, refilling ketchup and olive oil bottles from giant cans; collecting wine glasses from the dish station and bearing them out, eight glasses hanging from each hand; using ice-cream scoops to portion little spheres of the Irish butter August had insisted on into stainless-steel ramekins. Prep cooks were parboiling pasta and patting grape leaves dry with paper towels. Luis, the grill guy, was dusting flatiron steaks with salt and chopped garlic and pepper and parking them in a tub to marinate.

Look at Maria. Her parents come from Romania, fleeing—he pronounced a name that sounded to August like Timo had a mouthful of peanut butter. She comes as a child and her father drives a cab and her mother cleans houses. Then her dad gets sick and she has to work, so she comes here. She could run this restaurant if I died. Doesn't want to. Wants to go back to school.

Okay, I get the point, August muttered, chastened.

No you don't, said Timo softly, putting his hand on August's shoulders. You are their boss.

Right, so they work for me.

No, my friend. You work for them.

10.

When I was six, at the Number Four Elementary School in Luwan, we went on a field trip to a cemetery. It was a cold spring day, I remember. They herded us onto a public bus, and I had to hold hands with a known biter named Feifei, who used the sleeve of her jacket to wipe her nose. They didn't tell us where we were going, but then the bus let us out at Jiading Cemetery, in the north-west of Shanghai. Hundreds of people were there already, thronging the graves. The long rows of headstones were draped with colorful wreaths and garlands of flowers, and everywhere people were sweeping the graves with whisk brooms. Some people had little jars of red paint and were painting in the faded characters on the headstones. The air thrived with incense, the sweet smoke of joss and burning paper money.

It was Qingming Day. Jiading was the martyrs' cemetery, the final resting place of what my teacher called the heroes of the revolution. Feifei announced that her grandmother was buried here. My grandmother was still alive, I told her, spitefully. She bit me and I socked her.

That afternoon, back at school they taught us a poem. It was about Qingming Day in a village, *where it is raining softly*

Qingming shijie yu fenfen
People in the streets are full of sorrow
Lu shang xingren yu duanhun
A stranger asks where he can find a place to drink
Jiewen jiujia hechu you

A peasant boy points into the distance, toward Xinghua village.

Mutong yaozhi Xinghuacun

My teacher told us the poem was written by a man named Du Mu, who lived 1200 years ago. She said it was about how on Qingming Day we all have to do our duty to the dead, take care of their graves, give them respect. But I kept hearing the last words, xing hua cun. My teacher said it meant "the village of flowering apricot trees." It sounded like a painting. I had never seen an apricot tree (or for that matter a village), but I knew that apricots were special treats. My grandfather sometimes brought them home to us in a black plastic bag, and he would nuzzle the softness of the fruit against my nose before all three of us would eat them in one go. He told me that if I planted the pit in the ground, a new tree would grow. It was the craziest thing I'd ever heard.

Over and over, the words repeated in my head. Xinghua cun. Xinghua cun. The poem was about death, but it hadn't made me sad. Instead I was thinking of a village full of flowers and apricots on trees.

When I got home I told my grandparents I had learned a poem and they asked me to recite it, but I'd forgotten how it went, I just remembered the final words. "Oh, everyone knows that one," said my grandmother. "All cultured people know it!" My grandfather wrote it out for me.

清明时节雨纷纷
路上行人欲断魂
借问酒家何处有
牧童遥指杏花村

He taught me to read it, and explained how Chinese poetry could compress lots of big words into one single character. "Like how there's a whole tree inside an apricot pit," I said.

He nodded, then he said, "when you go to live with your parents in America someday, you should recite this to them. They'll be so impressed!" That's how we always talked about the day I'd leave: "someday." My grandparents were not in a hurry to get rid of me, and my parents were not in a hurry to receive me. They missed me, they said in letters and calls. They were excited for me to see their restaurant when it was ready. This was what they talked about, the restaurant. The restaurant was why I couldn't be with them yet. When it was done, they said, that's when I would be able to come. They'd gone to America when I was two, and I had barely ever met them since.

A month later my grandmother got sick. Multiple sclerosis. My grandfather couldn't take care of both of us anymore. Suddenly "someday" was here. They decided to move me to America before the end of the summer so that I could start school.

As the date of my flight approached I would wake up in the middle of the night, sweating through my pajamas. I wanted to go into my grandparents' room but now I knew I had to let my grandmother sleep. So I'd put my pillow on the carpeted cement floor and lay down on it to try to cool off. To sleep, I found myself thinking of that village, its trees heavy with flowers and apricots. Old people walking through it in the rain, drinking wine. It all ran together, like clothing dye in warm water. I'd repeat the name, Xinghua cun, Xinghua cun, over and over until I fell asleep.

I decided to memorize the poem. I made my grandfather teach me to write it. He would help me roll up my sleeves so I wouldn't stain them with calligraphic ink. I practiced and practiced reciting, declaiming the poem as I stamped martially up and down the hallway of our little apartment:

QINGming shijie yu FENFEN
(stomp stomp stomp)
LU shang XINGren

On and on for days. I saw myself delivering it to my mom and dad when I met them. I would get up on a table and recite it to them beautifully. I would tell them all about the village of flowering apricot trees and they would know that I, too, was a cultured girl, and they wouldn't care that I had come to them so much earlier than they wanted. They wouldn't mind that I had come before the restaurant was finished.

It is strange how well I remember it all—I can see the memories as if projected on a screen: I arrive at JFK with a suitcase, clutching the hand of my aunt Ming-Yan who has accompanied me on the flight from China. I try to walk bravely—under my breath I repeat my poem to myself—but I am afraid that my parents won't recognize me. But they do, they are there with a stuffed tiger and hugs and my mother smells like jasmine and they pick me up and put me on my dad's shoulders, and from up here things look different. Dad holds my ankles, and the whole airport strobes with newness.

I'd seen pictures of New York, full of tall buildings and yellow cabs, but the apartment was far from both the buildings and the cabs.

"Welcome to Queens," said my dad. "Can you say 'Queens?'" It was the first English word I'd ever heard him speak. All I knew how to say was "yes," "no," and "restaurant," which it had taken me days to learn. Resaraun.

The apartment was small. They were just a month away from opening their new restaurant then, and the apartment was crammed with boxes; they took up fully half of my new room, which faced a shaftway.

At dinner that night my mother cooked a huge meal of her native Shaanxi food, and they kept asking me questions about home, about my grandparents, about school, all things I did not want to think or talk about because I did not know if I would ever see them again so abruptly I stood up and announced, "I have a poem for you!"

"A poem?" My parents both put their chopsticks down.

"*QINGMING SHIJIE YU FENFEN*," I began, my voice sounding much louder in the small apartment than at home. I saw the surprise on my parents' face. They looked at each other, then at me, perching forward in their chairs.

"*LU SHANG XINGREN YU DUANHUN.*"

They were smiling, but their brows were furrowed. I felt my food in my stomach, in my throat—it was heavy, the oil and spicy meat mixing together. Her food tasted different from my grandmother's. I wanted to go back home, I missed my grandparents. I had to recite this poem so that my parents would let me stay but I wasn't sure that I even wanted them to.

"*JIEWEN JIUJIA*—" and then I blanked on the next word. I tried to think back, bring up the poem in my mind, but instead of the characters I had written on the paper over and over there were just swirling black shapes. All I wanted was to get to the village of flowering apricots but there was a whole ocean between it and me.

I looked at my father and mother, imploring them to tell me the next word, the way my grandfather would. My mother opened her mouth but my father put his hand on hers and stopped her.

"Let her," he murmured. I was on my own.

I did not love these people. I barely knew them. How, then, could they love me? I didn't know where I was but I knew it wasn't home.

And then the word reared up in my head, huge and black. 何. Where?

I finished the poem in a blaze of martial glory and my father sprang up from his chair and took me in his arms and his eyes were glimmering.

"Xiaotong," he said, "I'm so happy to meet you."

That night they decided to name the restaurant Xinghuacun. The English sign read *Shanghai Palace*, but that's not what the Chinese characters said. To us it was only ever Xinghuacun.

It was the restaurant my parents had dreamed of. After years of grinding and saving and slinging pork fried rice on Mott Street, my parents had gotten together with a group of Chinese investors—one guy ran a taxi cab company, another was a dermatologist—and leased a narrow space on 48th, between Madison and Park, in the shadow of Rockefeller Center. The goal was simple: instead of serving orange chicken and sesame chicken and General Tso's chicken, Xinghuacun would offer steamed whole red snapper with leeks, Dongpo pork, hairy crab, light, flaky scallion pancakes, and most of all, proper soup dumplings. It wouldn't be fancy, but it would be real Shanghainese food, or at least as close as my dad could get. And he wanted to do it without the gaudy chintzy paper-dragon Shun Lee bullshit. It was 1992, and my parents and their partners were betting that New Yorkers were willing to pay a little bit more money for authenticity and good service.

We opened just after my 7th birthday. The night before we opened, rather than go all the way back to Forest Hills, we slept in the restaurant, just the three of us. My dad cooked us dinner in the kitchen, making huge flames jump from the wok for my amusement, and we ate in the long empty dining room, the lights turned low. I was so excited I could barely eat. I remember asking question after question: "Will people come? How will they know we're here? Do foreigners eat like us?" Then we pushed back the tables and laid down thin pallet mattresses on the red carpet, and I thought back to the weeks of sleeping on the floor in my grandparents' apartment. I missed them, but even then I was starting to forget their faces. The memory of a seven year old is a soft, easily-eroded thing, it shifts like sand dunes in desert winds; since the prefrontal and parietal cortices are still forming, children must dive into the hippocampus as an all-purpose bucket for memory, which is like neural bobbing for apples. Because the connection to the prefrontal cortex is weak, visual images fade especially quickly.

So I lay there, awake, listening to the rain. Inside the restaurant, it was dark, but the streetlights cast an orange glow through the front windows. From time to time a taxi would slish by and its headlamps would make the shadows wheel around the walls. I tried to think of my grandfather and grandmother, remember the cool of their floor, the way they smelled, the way my grandfather always ate his noodles boiling hot. But I kept opening my eyes to look at my parents sleeping side by side. I'd never watched them sleeping before. My mother's hair was carefully tied up in a silk handkerchief; my father's bare feet poked out from under his blanket. Each had folded their glasses and laid them by their pillows. They were mine now, somehow. They had been entrusted to me. I had to take care of them.

A few months later, Mimi Sheraton wrote a piece about "Shanghai Palace" in the *Times*. The headline was "Where the Secret Menu Is the Menu." By that time I had started reading English so well that before service my mother had me translate it for the staff. Big Pao, the second cook, lifted me up and stood me on the bar, and I read the whole thing in the same loud, brassy voice I used to recite my poem. I could feel the language of the article coming into my head in English and leaving my mouth in Chinese. I didn't know all the words—even now whenever I see the words "pungent" or "gossamer," I remember that article—but I knew enough that by the end, my mom pulled the fanciest bottle of Wuliangye we had off the shelf and poured everyone in the room a shot, which was, for her, an act of insanity, and all the grown-ups roared a toast to Mimi.

In those early years my parents were always at the restaurant, so after school I would go over to a neighbor's house and do my homework until they came home. But on weekends or days off or holidays I got to come in and help out. Some days I'd read, other days I'd find things to do, like make change, fill water pitchers, fetch ashtrays. One day, on a dare from Big Pao, I consumed twenty soup dumplings and after that the employees called me Baobao. I called them *ge* and *jie*, elder brother and sister, and they let me boss them imperiously around.

Most days, though, I would sit and watch all the foreigners. What amazed me most, at first, was how white people ate. They scrutinized the food, lifted it up to look underneath it as though it was hiding something. They tasted it timidly sometimes, taking little nibbles, the way our class hamster, Gooey, would eat carrots. I got in trouble once for laughing at a woman who boldly speared a soup dumpling with one chopstick, lifted it to her mouth, and sprang back as hot soup hit her right in the chest.

Xinghuacun became my personal zoo, where I could observe docile white people in captivity. Their bodies looked so odd, so different from people in China. Older ladies with their fingers knobbled with rings and the skin drawn papery over their angular facial bones. Pink-faced fat men with little neck but abundant chin, and strands of hair on the backs of their hands. Teenagers with acne and protrusive Adam's apples. They all looked…richer.

I began to watch the foreign customers with almost predatory fixation, trying to imagine what they were like under that rosy skin, inside those bones. It was not hard to think of them as foreigners then. Not only was that the word we all still used, laowai, but I really didn't know many—most of the kids I went to school with in Forest Hills were immigrants, too, and my teacher was Mrs. Huerta. Americans just *seemed* foreign, so out of place, especially at Xinghuacun. I'd watch the way their faces would redden with spicy food, the flush starting from the forehead, sweat accumulating there like water condensating on the outside of a glass. When they ate the steamed whole snapper I could see them roll around the white flesh in their mouths, not swallowing, probing it vigilantly for lurking bones.

I started to wonder what they all looked like under their clothes. Were they pink like that all over? Did foreigners have lots of hair everywhere, like the kids at Number Four Elementary school claimed? What did the backs of their knees look like? Did they pee and poop like I did?

Poop was a particular concern. I didn't know what happened to the food my dad made when it went inside them. I knew that there was meat in there, and organs and blood, and I had a vague sense of its order because whenever I watched Big Pao prepare meat he would show me where on himself that meat came from. When he was hacking pork ribs into chunks he would slap his chest; when it came to tripe soup he would trace his finger in a coil all over his stomach. Soon he began to quiz me: he'd hold up a slab of raw, dripping flank steak, and I'd point to my thigh. But I still couldn't understand what happened in between their mouths and their butts that took in steamed pork belly with pickled mustard greens at one end and turned it into poop at the other. I asked my mother this and she looked horrified. "Xiaotong, we are *eating*," she hissed. I didn't see what was wrong with asking, since they were constantly warning me not to eat this or that American food that my friends brought to school for lunch, like salami sandwiches or Dunkaroos, because I'd definitely get diarrhea. Apparently it was okay to talk about my poop, but not other people's.

But I couldn't stop thinking about it. Why did people get diarrhea? And for that matter, why did old people's hands crook like that? When people got fat, did everything else inside them get fat too, like beachballs? I started taking books about the human body out of the library. I'd hide them from my parents behind a copy of *Highlights*, obscurely shamed. I'm not sure why, since these were books the Forest Hills Public Library had no trouble loaning to eight year-olds. Somehow I knew that this was not something people liked to talk about, that it was my job to hide these truths from my parents. But I couldn't help it. More and more I needed to know.

As I drifted deeper and deeper into the hidden worlds inside humans, Xinghuacun kept churning along. More articles appeared, to be laminated by my mother and taped to the front window. I got into Hunter when I was 11 and began going to school in the red-brick fortress on 96th street and Park. After that I knew that as long as I maintained high grades I could get away with anything shy of murder, or veganism. Mama and Papa Zhu did not come to my field hockey games, and I did not expect them to. I was independent, which was good for them, since Xinghuacun was as much their child as I was, and a much higher-maintenance child at that. I did not resent this, much. The restaurant was less a rival than a sibling. Its needs superseded our own, because the restaurant was the earth our lives were rooted in. My parents didn't take a single vacation until I was fourteen, when we went to Puerto Rico, and even then my mother ran up a giant phone bill in the hotel room calling every night to check on receipts. There was no space between who they were, and what they did. Because, in truth, they loved it. And we had what my parents had never had growing up in China in the '60s: stability.

We renovated and expanded in 2001, and then two months later the planes hit.

We'd never been so busy as that night, and I had never been so grateful that Xinghuacun was there. I threw on an apron and waited on tables. The whole city had spent the afternoon hypnotized in front of the television, and as night fell, the whole idea of cooking seemed somehow unconfrontable, so everyone left their apartments, floating into the streets like driftwood on the tide, to discover that everyone else had had the same idea, too. That night every bar and diner and restaurant in New York was full, people spilling out into sidewalk cafes in the warm September dusk. My father was a demon in the kitchen, my mother frantic behind the bar; I and the rest of the staff raced from table to table, taking orders and running food, and the customers seemed to be looking around them, astonished that it was all open for business, that we were open for business, that they could still order off a menu and dumplings—the defiant power of a single dumpling!— would still arrive and still be hot and they could hand over money and that money still worked and somehow they knew, we all knew, the city was *here for us*.

And now I was my father's city. With the streets of his neighborhood melted together in his mind, he had crossed canals and bridges and freeways, starved and deranged, to find me. He was a stranger, looking for a place to rest. Xinghua Cun, for now, would have to be here.

11.

Silverware pinged on porcelain, crystal glasses chimed. Wreaths of conversation and soft laughter were absorbed by the red carpet and velvet banquettes. Golden sconces on the walls tinted the water in the glasses bronze. Fragrant steam whispered from the glossy surface of soups. At a central table there was a whoosh as flames burst blue and high from a copper skillet handled by a white-aproned waiter. Applause. A woman at table 34 placed a toast point beaded with black caviar on her tongue. She collected it into her mouth, and six salivary glands gushed in greeting, the flavor of sea-spray and wood-smoke and butter inhering into the saliva, which poured lavishly over the papillae stippling her tongue, which passed the toast backward to the molars to crunch it to brittle crumbs, and the pearls of caviar forward to compress them against the back of the incisors until they burst, cold and saline and viscous and expensive, while the amylase in the saliva (a fraction of the liter and a half her glands would produce over the course of the day) worked itself into the toast, the starch crackling, forcing scented air into her nasal passage, and thence to her brain, while breaking the starch into malty sugar and the caviar to a liquid, fusing them together into a concentrated mush, which she let linger, warm and glittering on her tongue, the flavor coursing like electricity through a cable up her glossopharyngeal nerve, until at last her tongue arched its back like a woman in ecstasy, her epiglottis retracted, and as the work of a hundred hands that lifted the sturgeon from the sea, ultrasounded its belly, sliced it open, scooped the delicate, bloody black eggs from its ovaries, sieved and cleaned them, chilled and salted them, tinned and shipped and hauled and plated them, slipped down her throat, her brain went soft with memory, and she sighed, and had another.

At table 35, August tried to take it all in, twisting in his dinner jacket, a grey blazer that cinched his armpits. He'd bought it at Woolworth's, the biggest size they had, because Timo had told him he'd need a jacket for tonight and the last time he'd worn one, it was his high school graduation, when he weighed an ascetic two-seventy. That was, coincidentally, the last time he'd been to a fancy restaurant, where, as ever when the Sweeney clan marked a special occasion with a perfunctorily expensive meal, he'd watched his father order chicken and his mother order chicken and his brother order chicken, so he ordered duck.

But this time, as a thank you for a year of devotedly running his kitchen, Timo was paying—and ordering, which was just as well, because the menu at La Grenouille was entirely, stubbornly, in French.

Don't be nervous! Timo had said when he'd handed back the leatherbound menu and wine list to their waiter. Finest French restaurant in New York. Is going to be an adventure.

August *had* been nervous at first, when he walked in the door and instead of the wall of sound that would hit him at Timo's, there was hush. But as he watched the waiters swishing past each other with plates poised on their fingertips, their posture perfect, one hand behind their backs, the nervousness melted into something else. How did they move like that? How did they seem to know exactly where to be at exactly the right time? He began to feel the way he did his first day at Jimmy Luisi's when he was 17 and Jimmy handed him an apron and led him to the dish station—like he had been brought into the inner sanctum of a temple.

In a voice low with marvel August said: It's so *quiet*.

Maybe, said Timo slathered butter glinting with sea salt on a warm, crusty roll, But inside kitchen? He jabbed the knife at the velvet-upholstered double doors at the far end of the *salle*. It is war. With a general, and officers, and the ones they send into battlefield to be exploded.

I like war, said August.

Heh, grunted Timo. I liked it too when I was your age.

A dollop of butter flew off Timo's knife and landed on the tablecloth; without breaking stride a passing waiter wiped it away with a cloth. The seamlessness of the action took August's breath away.

Suddenly he wanted—needed—to get into that kitchen more than anything in the world. All those big projects he'd tried and failed? He just knew that back there, they had the key. They could teach him.

You gotta have a buddy here, right? said August

Timo snorted. Here? Here they don't talk to a guy from Queens. You want in? You work your way in.

As August gazed toward the kitchen door in longing, the wine arrived, their waiter's lower half hidden by his pristine white apron, so that he appeared to sail toward them like a schooner. Deftly he corkscrewed it open, gave a brief sniff to the reddened tip of the cork (neatly pocketed), and holding the bottle primly by the punt poured a mouthful out for Timo. Timo sipped as the waiter held the bottle silently for review.

Is poetry! he laughed, and gave the waiter a jovial thumbs-up and said loudly, Good job! The waiter's eyebrow flickered upward.

Holding the big Burgundy glass as Timo and the other diners around him had, with three thick fingers lightly pinching where the stem met the base, August lifted it to his nose and inhaled the way he knew he was supposed to, even though it always just smelled like wine to him, and he couldn't understand why the whole point of wine seemed to be to make it taste and smell like something *other* than wine, like chocolate or fuckin blackberry, and if that's what you wanted why not just fuckin drink *that* in the first place, which is when the first long-bottled scent molecules met the lining of his nasal cavity, and the neural artillery of a million epithelial cells fired a single volley straight into the center of his brain. August's vision was suffused with color. He could *see* the smells—the brown wood of a barrel, ringed with sunburnt orange, then giving way to a maroon, a deep red-ringed maroon that seemed to pulse in a living halo around his skull.

August stared at Timo, his expression one of astonishment, even accusation.

Timo grinned. Now see what happens when you drink it.

They'd drink three bottles between them that lunch, but compared to the food, the wine was only the cloud of dust that rising, catches the brilliance of a sunbeam.

As the dishes arrived at the table, August tried to fix each one in his memory—he wished he'd brought a camera. Over and over, he asked Timo what these things were called, but the French names all slid off his memory like butter off a hot knife. But the music of it, the song each bite sang along his lips and tongue—he knew these would remain with him all his life.

The appetizers came, a kind of cold salad involving lobster with slivers of grapefruit and avocado, and a spiral of pine-green oil. Skeptical, August arranged it on his fork and raised it carefully, uncertainly, to his mouth. The first bite went through him like the opening electric guitar-chord at a heavy metal concert. The flavor, the coldness, the citric zing strobed in his skull like stagelights madly pinwheeling around the darkness of the stadium. Another bite, and now August heard rhythm, a thump at the base of his spine. He tried to make the feeling last, chewing slowly and thoughtfully—Timo could have been saying something, he didn't know—trying to hear every note the food was playing. By the time the salad was gone and its dressing mopped with a piece of bread it was as if he himself were in the crowd, chanting and stomping his feet as the bass pulsed through the floor.

When the waiter lifted a silver cloche to reveal a sumptuous whole turbot, steaming on a platter, it was as if the band had suddenly quieted, the only sound a trancelike shimmer of keyboard. He watched in reverence, trembling, as the waiter ran the blade of a knife along the length of the fish. Holding two silvers spoons like chopsticks he then laid the fillets on two waiting plates, beside two rosettes of perfectly conical carrots, before finishing by spooning a creamy sauce over the fish. And then, as August's teeth closed over it, the skin delicately crackling, the flesh like a soft kiss, the whole band joined in, a wave of rock crashing down on him.

From that moment onward everything felt turned up to eleven. The wine swirled around all of it, lights beaming mad colors to every corner of his brain. Even the bread between courses thundered from the amplifiers, the crust and dough hymning with unctuous salt-flecked butter like two guitars wailing in harmony.

And when the steak came, fat and crowned with a thick pat of herbed butter, and with white gloves the waiter drizzled a green liquid over it from a silver sauce boat, it was as electric as a smashed guitar. With every bite, the music crescendoed, the sound gathering wave upon wave until it was nearly solid, driving him backwards, lifting him out of his very shoes.

By the time of the desserts and coffee August had stage-dived and was being borne by hundreds of fluttering hands over the surface of the crowd, light as a beachball. And with the final bite of profiterole, the ice cream cold and choux pastry warm, the last golden chords died away, echoing softly in the stillness.

August's whole body had gone slack with pleasure, his head lolling around on his shoulders like a newborn baby's. He felt as if he were encased in a delicate soap bubble, floating around the room, brushing lightly against the heat of the wall sconces. And yet, even in his drifting orbit, August knew: he could do this. He could learn.

Timo, how much they pay here? he asked.

What do I pay you now?

You know exactly how much you pay me.

Twenty-four thousand. Here maybe you get fifteen.

Bullshit, said August, snapping back to reality, and causing the caviar-eating woman at the adjacent table to click her tongue disapprovingly. Look at this place.

No bullshit. If you are head chef here, sure, maybe you get the money. But here you would be commis. Potato guy. You start at the bottom. For six months, you peel potatoes, boil potatoes, and you hope maybe the salad guy break his leg so you can take his job. This, for years. And why, when you are happy now? I pay you good. Look how I take care of you, Augusto—Timo gestured to the crystal and silver wreckage of their meal—You know I love you like my son.

August slumped in the velvet seat, discouraged, his jacket pinching him cruelly. Timo paid him well, he knew. And he had been happy working for him these past years. But it was as he'd suspected: his happiness had been a fiction. He'd only been happy because he didn't know what he was missing.

I love you too, Timo, but you gotta teach me this.

Timo almost spit out his wine. I can't teach you this, are you crazy? This kind of thing, they only teach in France.

Where? August asked.

What you mean, where? Is the whole country! They worship the god of Michelin.

What, like the tires?

Exactly like. But also they make a restaurant guide. They review restaurants, give them stars. If you are three-star restaurant, you are the very best in the world.

Are there any in New York? August asked, his mind forming the dim contours of an idea.

Timo snorted. Europe only. They don't think about USA. Because

Americans, they don't care. They eat like raccoons. But in France, everywhere is like this, with the craziness about food.

Seeing the look on August's face—he was staring into the distance like a movie was being projected on the far wall—Timo laughed, not unkindly, but not warmly, either. What, you want to go to France now? You want to be big French chef? You?

Yeah, said August, slowly. Yeah. That's exactly what I'm gonna fuckin' do.

12.

Shredded lettuce and tomato slices had spilled out of the busted styrofoam and onto the floor. This was exactly why there was no food allowed in here. Two rules! No food, and no crying! In five minutes my father had violated both. I needed to get him away from there, give his overheated brain time to cool.

My father's brain was damaged—that was all. It had suffered the neurological equivalent of a Florida sinkhole, the kind that yawns open suddenly in suburban backyards and swallows swing sets and trampolines and Hyundais whole. Now, jarred by the ordeal of the last forty-eight hours, some frayed wires in his fusiform gyrus had brushed against each other, sparked, and tricked the temporal lobe into thinking it recognized the man on the table. Intracranial fake news, like déjà vu. The name he could have gotten from the toe tag, or the autopsy form in my office, anywhere.

I tried lifting him by the shoulders, but he sagged like dead weight. I flashed back to my first ER rotation, trying to muscle a heroin overdose off the floor and into a wheelchair. India moved to help, but he wrestled free.

"This is my friend!" he shouted at me in Chinese. "What happened?"

"He's not your friend, Dad," I said as quietly as I can, my face burning with shame at the thought of Wei Wei understanding everything he was saying. "He's just a cook who died last night."

"He's not just a cook!" he shoved me away, indignant. "This is August Sweeney!"

A gasp from the students. India released my dad's arm.

"What?" I asked them.

"Oh my God, it's him," said Wei Wei, staring down at 289's face.

"Holy shit," squeaked Bushwick.

"August Sweeney's dead?" said Eva, lurching away from the body. "And that's him?" She whipped out her phone. It was the first time a phone had come out of a pocket since the attempted selfie. She covered her mouth in shock.

"Wait," I said, but they weren't listening. Even India looked stunned.

"I *knew* I recognized him," she breathed, looking back at me accusingly. As if I had kept this information from her. Why did they all seem to know this random man's name? How did my dad?

"I don't get it," I said. "Is he famous?"

Eva showed the screen to me; there was a New York Times alert.

Celebrity chef August Sweeney, known as the Orpheus of Offal, has died at 52.

They were gazing at me with a collective look I'd seen before, whenever I was called on to engage with pop culture I was supposed to know. It was a look that said *how do you even get through the day?*

"He used to have a Food Network show," said Wei Wei, her gaze going from me to him to my father, who had risen to his feet and retreated to the far wall, where he was staring mournfully at the body. "Like a bunch of them. There was a food competition. *No Guts No Glory.*"

They all started talking at once. Apparently his show was all about organ meat and making contestants use every part of the animal. His whole career had been about this. He did game, too, from rabbit to ostrich to elk. It seemed there was a whole elk special, where he went hunting, shot it on camera, and then field-dressed it, butchered it, and cooked it for two hundred people. I was astonished at how much they seemed to know about this man I had never heard of. I'd dissected celebrities before—mostly former football players, and some famous overdoses—but never someone who rated a New York Times push alert.

"I mean this guy is the reason I learned to like liver," said Bushwick. "And not like foie gras, either."

As they talked, my father shuffled over to listen to them. I still didn't understand how he knew this man—both of us hated cooking shows. He wouldn't watch the Food Network for the same reason I never watched the shows where every episode has an autopsy. Not because they were inaccurate—it was television, not a textbook—but because they made the business of taking a body apart look clean and surgical, like a drone strike viewed from 30,000 feet. It was the same with cooking shows. Gauzy-voiced white women in colors that popped on TV were forever standing over counters so clean you could do organ transplants on them, dicing chicken breast and effortlessly chiffonading parsley with pristinely-manicured fingers light on the knife, like concert pianists. They wouldn't have lasted ten minutes in my dad's kitchen, amid the fire and grease. I knew it wasn't the food they made that attracted viewers, it was the serenity with which they were making it. It caressed you, drew you in, said, *you too can have this kitchen, you too can have this calm.* Give me a break.

I read an article once about how when they advertise food on TV, they always have to show the food in motion somehow—steam rises from pasta, a steak backflips over a flaming grill, ice cubes tumble into a moisture-beaded glass of Coke, lettuce and tomato fall into place on a revolving hamburger. Because still food on TV unnerves us, like one person facing the wrong way in a crowded elevator. It looks, for lack of a better word, dead. Which is why food styling is effectively mortuary science. Watching food ads makes me feel somehow turfy. That perfect beaded moisture is just WD-40 sprayed on the glass. Those beautifully plump burritos? Stuffed with mashed potatoes. The steam curling from the pasta is a tampon soaked in water and microwaved, and the healthy glow of a man in a casket is rouge and foundation. The youthful fullness of his cheeks is Formalin pumped up through the carotid arteries I carefully leave intact. Even the curve of the eyelids is faked; the vitreous gel of the eyes collapses postmortem, so morticians cover it with a cap to keep the eyes from looking sunken and wasted. And they do beautiful work, but unlike the food stylists, you never really believe it.

I looked back at 289's craggy nose and yellowed teeth. It occurred to me that my father had been at home in bed all month, convalescing—maybe he'd been glued to Ina Garten and whoever this man was? His brain was just so haywire it had convinced him they were friends. At least now it made sense why I'd been so sure I knew this man, too—I must have seen him on TV at some point, or on the side of a bus, and his visage filed away in my perirhinal cortex, just posterior to my nose, where subconscious memory is stored in dark, dusty archives.

And then as soon as I had this thought I realized it was not true, for at that moment the perirhinal cortex unearthed a single memory file and shot it up the pneumatic tube to the information desk of my frontal lobe, where it arrived with a bright *thoonk* to be unfolded and smoothed and read.

"Son of a bitch," I breathed into my mask. I knew *exactly* who this man was.

In my defense, so much of what makes us recognizable relies on movement, on quickness. The way a person's eyes crinkle when they smile, the way they bite their lower lip when thinking hard. These are the things that make a person a person, not just a statue of flesh.

Also, the beard was new.

For autopsists, when you see 300 bodies a year, all in the same frozen, rictal attitude, you learn to dismiss any sense of recognition as a trick of the mind, and an unhealthy one. A similar thing happens when you have sex with a large number of people: their faces are the first to vanish from memory, because faces are not that interesting. Faces can lie; flesh can't. I only care about holding onto the parts of their bodies that spark joy—a pectus excavatum scooped out of the bony sternum, the pleasurable give of cellulite, hyperextensible elbows, dainty toes. These I file carefully and tenderly in my memory. If I had ever seen August Sweeney naked there would have been a dozen different things I would have recognized the second India unzipped the bag—the tattoos alone; I never forget a tattoo. But put that thought right out of your mind. That wasn't what happened.

Years ago when I was a resident, I don't remember what year or what rotation or anything else, I left the hospital one night, my whole body tingling with that exhausted energy you feel as a resident when you've been up for days and are tired in the marrow of your bones and yet your brain is so on fire that if you go home you just know that instead of going to bed you're going to do all of your laundry *and* fold it, so instead I drifted over to Xinghuacun for a late dinner.

It was almost 11pm, when the streets of Midtown were empty and the skyscrapers on 6th avenue all blaze with wasteful light. There were still a few tables finishing up when I walked in. In the corner a gigantic man was eating by himself. There were multiple plates and empty Tsingtao bottles around him. I hugged my mother and slumped into a booth. The kitchen was about to close so I asked her if I could have some noodles and a beer and she clucked her tongue and I rolled my eyes.

I was scrolling my phone mindlessly when I heard a man's voice.

"Hey, are you James T's daughter?" The gigantic man was looming over me, ruddy and sweating. Clearly he was drunk and had eaten something too spicy for him.

I am usually less than friendly when strange perspiring middle-aged men approach me when I am not in the mood. But this was our restaurant and he was a guest.

"Yes," I said. "I hope you enjoyed your dinner."

"Your dad is a genius. I mean it." He paused, his eyebrows raised. He seemed to be waiting for a certain kind of response—now I realize he expected me to recognize him, and to have the reaction people are supposed to have when a very famous person bellies up to their table. I just stared up at him dumbly. A grin crept over his lips.

Big Pao arrived with the noodles and beer and I got up to greet him, but before I could the man wrapped his arms around him woozily.

"Powpow!" he cried. "The crab this evening. Food of the gods."

Big Pao blushed and waved away the compliment. I was boggled. My mom and dad were the face of the business, but even our white regulars didn't know Big Pao—his English was weak and he rarely left the kitchen.

"You must come here a lot," I said as Big Pao retreated to the kitchen.

"Whenever I can. But I never saw you here before."

"I work late," I said defensively. "I'm a doctor." It was true, though. Ever since the night I'd told them I was going to specialize in autopsy, I had been coming more and more rarely, and only at times when I knew my dad would have already gone home. I still went to their house for Sunday dinners, but at least their house was still my house, with my room. At Xinghuacun we were squarely on his turf.

"Oh yeah, I heard that. What kind of doctor? Mind if I sit down?" he asked, sitting down.

I snorted. "Oh, didn't they tell you. I do pathology. Mostly autopsies."

"Like with dead bodies?"

"Preferably."

"Damn." He glanced at me, almost shyly. "Could I ask you

something?" Not waiting for me to reply, he asked, "What could you guys see in a dead body? Could you see, like, emotional problems?"

If medical students are like scavengers, hungry to practice medicine on any injured body, residents are like fresh converts to a religion, their minds shimmering with faith and hearts ablaze with evangelical passion. But even by that standard, I was a zealot.

"There's nothing I can't see," I told him, my voice almost dangerous with self-assurance. And then I started to talk. I told him how I could scalpel open a human body, pull out its organs and see the very molecules of the person's disease. I told him what it is like to liberate an entire human reproductive system from a person and what I look for in a healthy testicle. I gave him the full force of what I was capable of, and as I spoke—as I said out loud what I could never have told my parents—I found myself astonished, even grateful: this was the power I'd dreamed of as I sat in this restaurant and watched our customers masticating, and now it was mine. It was all real.

"No shit," he breathed. "No shit. So take a look at me. What do you think you'd see if you cut me op—"

"Psh. You're easy. I wouldn't even need to." I'd seen it the moment I really looked at him. It wasn't in his eyes, which I assume were the kind of eyes that people describe as "sad"; I am not a good judge of resting facial expressions—but just above them. "I can tell you right now. Your heart is in trouble. You have xanthelasma."

"Never met her."

"Those beads on your eyelids. You've seen them in the mirror, like little pebbles. You think they're moles, but they're not. They're cholesterol deposits. I bet your hands are cold a lot."

"How do you know that?" He jammed his beefy hands under his armpits as if embarrassed.

"There's so much excess cholesterol in your system that it's seeping into your skin. I can see it there on your elbows, too—see where they bulge a little?"

"So?"

I took a long sip of beer. If I had been his doctor I would have said xanthelasma is usually harmless, but it can be a sign of possible heart disease, so let's do tests. I wasn't his doctor, and I could see every imaginable sign of excess cholesterol written in giant glowing letters on his skin and he had been kind to Big Pao and I felt that entitled him to the truth, because maybe no one else would tell him. And furthermore, given how many empty beers were on his table, he was not going to remember this conversation in the morning. But I would. And I'd always wanted to do this.

"So you're going to die."

He snorted and started coughing.

"Yeah," he said. "How old are you?"

I didn't give that information away. No one wants to think about their doctor's age. "How old do you think I am?"

"I think my daughter's around your age. She hates my guts."

"I'm sure she doesn't—"

"Oh, no, she does. I don't even blame her. But let me ask you—when you cut a person open, can you tell what was wrong with them. I don't mean like disease. I mean, like, in their brains? Could you tell a person's kid how come they were such a fuck-up?"

"That's not what we do," I said, realizing it was time to go. It was always time to go when middle-aged men started talking about their daughters who were my age. "Why don't you just tell her yourself?"

He laughed and shook his head. He took a packet of cigarettes out of his pocket and offered me one. It looked tiny, almost feminine in his huge fingers.

"Hey, come outside with me," he smiled. "I gotta know more about this, and I could use a smoke." So he was that kind of man. The kind who go weak at the knees around cold women. It was too bad. I liked him. He had the kind of vulnerability that you find in men who don't have a thing in the world they're compensating for. When he trained his attention on me it was like a floodlight, banishing all shadows and places to hide. Poor guy—if we'd met at a bar I'd have asked *him*. But not in a million years was I going to pick up a person who knew my parents.

"Sorry, buddy," I touched his hand apologetically. "It's not happening tonight."

He gave me a sad, understanding smile. "Worth a shot." He stood and took a fat roll of bills out of his pocket. "Well, I guess I'll be seeing you. Tell your dad I said hi." He peeled off a healthy number of twenties—way more than the value of whatever he'd eaten and drunk—and threw them on his table. He gave my mom a hug, and then he was gone. I never mentioned him to my dad. I didn't even know his name.

The students were trading notes on their favorite episodes. I was glad I was behind multiple layers of PPE, so they couldn't see how my armpits had begun sweating, or my cheeks were going red. They might have noticed pupil dilation and my mask inflating and deflating rapidly as I began breathing hard, but they weren't paying any attention to me.

"He butchered a whole pig live on Good Morning America," said Bushwick. "I saw the video."

"PETA went bugfuck," said Eva, who saw me and looked contrite. I waved it away; I barely noticed her swearing. Their enthusiasm unsettled me. It felt indecent—to say nothing of unprofessional—to be star-struck by a cadaver.

I started sizing up the students for real, as if they were predators. Wei Wei chewed her words. She spoke English like someone who learned it patiently and carefully, whose voice remembered the hurt of not being able to make herself understood.

Eva was the opposite. Central-casting JAP. She was young, probably right out of college. I could see her doing summer public health projects someplace like Guatemala, where she wore cutoff jean shorts and showed old women selling beads how to play with TikTok filters and worked so hard they brought her back year after year.

Bushwick stood with his arms crossed, his legs spread apart. This stance, and the way he kept looking around the room, surveying it as if he were thinking about buying it, persuaded me that he had spent excessive amounts of time on the bow of a sailboat, wearing designer sunglasses.

I'd been silent for too long. They were going to notice something was wrong.

"I didn't know they let people cook brains on the Food Network," I said.

"Well, he's been off the air for a while. I think he got cancelled," said Eva.

Bushwick snorted.

"Wait, how did you know him?" said Wei Wei, and it took me a moment to realize that she'd said it in Chinese. To my father. And silently, irrevocably, a line was crossed.

He, too, was startled to be addressed, and when he spoke his voice was quiet. He was always quieter in English.

"I have a restaurant. In Midtown. Shanghai Village. For many years, every month he comes to eat in my restaurant. He use to come with his friends, all chefs. They eat so much! Then he came alone. He always ask me to have a beer with him, or show him how to make food. Many times I show him in my kitchen." He swallowed and his eyes welled again. "Tongtong, he said Shanghai Village was the best Chinese food in New York."

The words stung. I was proud for him and furious that these other people, strangers to him, were seeing him so diminished, so maudlin. The man I knew would never let others see him like this, not even my mother. Nor would I.

"He is famous?" Dad asked the students. They nodded. He turned to me. "Then why did he die?"

I looked down at the vast bloody tangle of August Sweeney's organs. He had asked the right question. Not how he died, but why.

How was the question the zombified kid on call last night could have answered. *Why* was what took me eight years of medical training and two licensing exams to answer. *Why* was the reason I hadn't been home all month.

"I don't know yet," I said.

"It's your job to find out," he said. It was not a question.

He was right. However bizarre a coincidence this was, I didn't have time to think about it. I am phenomenal at not thinking about things; my shit can always wait. I have always assumed that someday there will be a great time of shit-reckoning for me, when maybe I go to a silent yoga retreat halfway up a New Hampshire mountain with goat milk and I sit crosslegged and topless with cool wind in my hair and crawl into my own cerebellum for three weeks and when I come out all of my shit has slid from me like snakeskin and lies in crinkled translucent piles.

I folded the memory of this man, of his hands offering me a cigarette, into its plastic cylinder and sent it back down the pneumatic tube.

"I will. We will." I gestured to the students.

"Can I…" he hesitated, and when he spoke his voice was soft with humility. "Can I watch you?"

He had never asked me for anything in this tone. All my life he had instructed. He had required. When I shrank from a challenge, he had coaxed. But he had never implored. The doctor in me knew he needed rest. But the daughter in me wanted to show him what I do. So did the anatomist. This body was my religion; this table my altar; this lab my temple. And now my father was asking for my blessing. He wanted to watch me work. I thought of all the times he patiently showed me the way to kill a fish (cleaver shunted into the spinal cord) or gut a rabbit or squeeze and store the blood from a duck. He never hid the reality of his job from me. Had our places been reversed, he would have let me watch. He would have trusted me. I realized I wanted him to watch me answer it. If he could see what I did, then maybe he'd understand why I'd given them so few of the things they'd asked.

And what the hell, this day was already a shitshow.

"Okay, that's enough chitchat," I said, and led us back to Mr. Sweeney. "We have 405 pounds of him to get through. India, can you get my dad suited up?"

Even as they pulled their masks back over their mouths and lowered the splash shields, I could see the excitement glitter in their eyes, marveling at these famous organs.

"He gave his body to science," I cracked my knuckles. "So let's do science."

13.

Nothing came more easily to August Sweeney than falling in love. It would hit him silently, like a falling air conditioner. He fell in love indiscriminately, without regard to availability, size, race, age (within reason) or even level of sentience: there were knives and dive bars that August loved with as much warmth and protectiveness as he had ever felt for a woman. He loved men, too, less sensually but with equal heat. The problem wasn't getting people to love him back, for people fell easily in love with August; they would do so all his life. With his size, his dynamism, his appetites, he exerted gravity like a planet. No, August's problem was staying in love. His ardor was volcanic: love would gush from him like magma, consuming anything in its path, then sooner or later it would go cold and rigid and sullen and dark.

But while he loved, all was right with the world, and at this particular moment, he was utterly under the spell of a large tub of squid.

They had been delivered that morning in a little blue Renault *camionette*, driven by a stocky middle-aged woman with magenta hair. Chef Baratin had greeted her warmly, kissing her on both cheeks, addressing her as what August heard as Madame Fanooy. He commissioned August and Julien, the sous-chef, to unload six large coolers from the truck. Eager to impress Chef Baratin, August waved off Julien, bent down to grip the handles of the biggest one, and hoisted. Through sheer clean-and-jerk force he lifted the cooler off the bed of the truck, but before he could take a step backward, something sank its talons into his spinal column and said *drop it*. August complied and the truck jounced with the impact.

Behind him, Chef Baratin gave a little aristocratic clap. He said something in French to Madame Fanooy, and she flexed her biceps with a masculine growl, then all three laughed. Chef Baratin clapped August on the shoulder, and motioned Julien to come over and grab a handle.

A kitchen, it's not one person, *hein?* he said.

When Madame Fanooy's truck had rattled off down the dirt driveway in a cloud of orange dust, the coolers turned out to contain vast amounts of fresh fish, shrimp, langoustines, and squid all packed in ice and water. The one August had undertaken to lift held four full-grown octopi in water, though August did not actually know whether they were full-grown, since he had never seen a whole octopus in person. Even at his most profligate, these were not the sort of deliveries that the Phylaktou brothers made to Timo's. It wasn't just the octopi, either—they almost never got whole fresh fish like this. They'd get trout or mackerel, frozen solid, which they'd roast whole with lemon and parsley. Everything else arrived cleaned, boned, filleted, portioned, and vacuum-sealed. By comparison, the fish of Madame Fanooy were from another planet: huge, glossy, blue-grey, slick, their fins barbed. August had no idea what they were called in English, but simply looking at them made his palms itch. He wanted to get right to learning what to do with them, but then Julien handed him a big stainless-steel tub.

These are *encornets. A nettoyer.* You clean, he said.

August gazed into the tub. It was a mass of pearlescent whole squid, their tails lightly freckled with pink dots and their heads a wreath of tentacles. Their eyes were tiny black beads. Julien, a tall, clean-shaven, knobby-elbowed young man who looked like a broomstick standing next to August, led him to a large sink in the little alcove where August had spent most of the last week. He set a big colander in the sink, and on the counter beside it parked the tub of squid and two empty hotel pans.

Watch. You pull 'ere. Julien flicked on the faucet and, as the water rumbled the steel sink, ran his forefinger inside the tubule of the tail, then pulled the head free, drawing with it a glop of innards. The head he threw into the far pan, and held up the tail, now an empty casing with an arrow-like fin at one end.

This, clean. Like this, he said. He ran the tail under the flow of water, scooping out any remaining guts with his stirring finger. Then, with a motion so deft August couldn't follow, he inverted the tail neatly over his thumb so it encased the digit in translucent blue-gray.

Looks like a condom, August muttered.

Justement, said Julien, brightly. He ran the tail under the water to rub off the remaining guts, uninverted it, and tossed it into the near pan. Like this, okay? *Bon, au boulot!* Whereupon he left, sauntering off to do whatever flambéing or sautéing he did in the main kitchen while August was stuck here, in the glorified cubbyhole where his head almost scraped the ceiling, with a bucket of squid.

Grumbling, August picked up his first one. It was floppy and cold and smooth. Sighting down the length of the squid, he thrust his meaty finger into the space between head and tail and something salty and viscous shot right into his mouth. August spat it out and dropped the squid. He could see black liquid oozing from the tail. So that was really a thing, he thought. Squids have ink. Despite himself, he was impressed. Dead or not, this thing could still hit back.

He picked up the violated squid and tried again. He stirred his finger around the inside of the tail, feeling the organs detach easily, then pulled the whole works out. He inspected it carefully. Beside the deflated dark mush which must have been the ink sac, there was a soft golden lozenge. Curious, he pressed it with his thumb, and it oozed molten copper.

Huh, murmured August.

Turning to the business of cleaning, the first thing that August found was that the fin on a squid's tail was wider than the hole he was supposed to push it through. So were his thumbs, which dwarfed Julien's bony pianist fingers, the correct tool for this job. He tried to squinch up the fin to push it through the little hole, but the fin was slick and wouldn't stay squinched. He would get one side through, but the other side would pop free. He tried to pinch it between thumb and index finger and use his old friend brute force, which caused the entire tail to rupture. Embarrassed, August tossed it into the trash can and hid it under some paper towels.

He took up a new squid. This time he liberated the head and guts with no discharge, and patiently worked the fin until he began impatiently working the fin, at which point the tail burst again and the squid joined its predecessor.

On the next one, August calmly, slowly creased and pressed the tail, sweat beading on his eyebrows until he got it, fold by fold, through the hole and flipped over his index finger. Exultant, August raised both hands and did a little dance. It had taken four full minutes. He washed the innards off and peeled away a thin spear of transparent bone he hadn't noticed before. It ran the length of the tail, like a kind of spine. He tossed the clean intact tail into the pan with a triumphant splat. On the following squid, he hooked the little spine with a fingernail, detached it gently from the inner wall, and drew it out in the same stroke as the rest of the head. This time the tail was much more responsive to manipulation, and he got it done in two minutes. Inspired, August set to work.

Outside, Provence was in the full shimmer of summer. The sun was like a warm compress. The lavender fields and vineyards thrived with bees delirious with industry, and all day long the trees sang with the chirr of cicadas. A steady breeze tempered the heat and made the landscape feel restless, the fields rippling softly, the wind susurrating in the trees. The dining room of Le Roi Ubu was full nightly with vacationing Parisians, Lyonnais, Brits, Germans, Dutch. The roads abounded with rental cars and the markets resounded with confidently-bad French. It was 1992.

Inside, for a week now August had, with increasing impatience, been stuck in his alcove plucking cilantro leaves from their stems and deseeding tomatoes and peeling potatoes and shelling beans and scrubbing the tiled kitchen floors. Timo had warned him this would happen, but August hadn't believed him. Timo was the reason he was here at all, though. Realizing that August was serious about this France business, he'd let him leave for the month of August, when anyway the streets of Queens were so empty and astonished by heat that tumbleweeds practically rolled down Roosevelt Avenue. He didn't know any of the big Michelin chefs, or even the small ones, but he agreed that as long as August promised to come back by September, he was willing to call an old friend from his youth, Chef Baratin. August promised—he loved Timo very much—and they shook hands. Maybe you even learn some French while you chop onions, Timo'd laughed.

August had imagined working in a glittering temple to foie gras like La Grenouille, with straight-backed chefs in spotless white toques. Le Roi Ubu turned out to be a small, humble restaurant of 40 seats with only three weathered copper pots, reserved for making sauces. It sat on a hillside overlooking the village of Buoux and the imperial purple carrelage of lavender fields that surrounded it. August spoke no French, and had no car. Le Roi Ubu had a dormitory out back, in a squat stone building that seemed to have been built a few hundred years ago. Three others lived there, too: an apprentice patissiere named Anouk and two young waiters named Magnus and Albert. It had no air conditioning. No one seemed to have air conditioning in this country, but that was all right with August. The air was dry, so that the sun seemed to cause not sweat but glow, and shade was a fine refuge from the heat. Magnus and Albert were fascinated by August, both by his size and by his Americanness, frequently asking him to say their favorite catchphrases from American movies. He would say, *Yippee-ki-yay, motherfuckers,* and the two of them would shriek with joy.

Everything was different at Le Roi Ubu. It wasn't just that he had gone from the head chef to a lowly stagiaire. Timo'd been explicit about this. But once August made a decision he was not to be turned from it. Still, he hadn't quite expected this kitchen to be a completely different world. For one thing, there was no music. Where August had always kept the radio at Timo's tuned to Hot 97, Chef Baratin's kitchen had no music at all. The only sounds were those of cooking, or of Baratin barking out an order, and Julien and the commis, Petra, automatically calling back *Oui chef!* And because he had to clean the kitchen twice a day, all the surfaces were shinier than at Timo's, where grease and grime were a fact of life; August had never imagined a kitchen could be so clean. Going to work felt like going to church. There was no shouting, no allegations about cooks' mothers pingponging back and forth. No one threw dirty kitchen towels at anyone. But he could have borne it all were it not for the fact that even after a week, he still wasn't allowed to cook anything.

On his first day, August had been handed a bag of onions and told to chop "very small pieces" so he did it as fast and tiny as he could, his knife skills fluent and bold and his eyes liquefying with tears. When he was done, Chef Baratin took one look at the bowl of soggy, pulverized onion, sighed, and dumped it all into the trash. August was shocked. He had done this to his own cooks over badly cooked plates, but never for prep work.

Cut very small pieces, it means cut very small pieces, not abuse! Baratin said. I thought Timo said you were his chef. Come, watch.

Baratin took an onion from the bag and halved it from root to tip. Cutting off the tip, he made a series of thin slices through the domed onion, just shy of the root. He rotated the onion and did the same, but parallel to the cutting board. Then he pressed firmly down with three fingers and carefully, slowly, drove the blade downward, and the onion seemed to molt into a pile of perfect miniscule cubes.

This is broon-waz, said Baratin. For the soup. Do ten like this.

August, for the first time in a long time, was faced with the strong possibility that he did not know a single fucking thing about cooking. He'd always prided himself on his knife-speed, but the whole business of broon-waz and jew-lian and shifonad bewildered him. Even the way that Baratin and Julien could take a spoonful of caponata and then do this rapid swiping-together of spoons and deposit a perfect football-shaped dollop (a kenell, they called it) on the plate looked like some kind of street magic.

But now, the squid had begun to feel congenial in his hands. He had learned not to look at the squid as he folded it, for his eyes were stupid and would only distract him, and rather to trust his fingers. From time to time his excavations of the tail would dig up a tiny white crab fastened grimly to the inside, or a brittle starfish, or a whole sardine—proof, to August, that these squid had come straight from the sea, unmolested by commercial seafood processors or whoever had peeled and deveined and blast-frozen the shrimp he got at Timo's. He timed himself with each one, checking his watch before picking up a squid and looking up at the ceiling as his fingers solved the riddle of each tail, for each was different. Small ones needed delicacy lest he tear them; large ones required firmer discipline. His time dropped from two minutes to forty-five seconds, and there it stayed for a good eighty or ninety squid. But August knew he could go faster. He had to concentrate, cut out unnecessary movements. Planting his feet farther apart in a rock guitarist's power stance, he closed his eyes and poured himself into the squid. Rinse, scoop guts, detach spine, pull, fold, flip, rinse, flip back, next. The noise of the kitchen beyond quieted to a hum. He lived in the space between seconds. Every ion of his volition was funneled into his fingertips. It was him and the water and the squid and the stopwatch and he was happy.

On squid number 158 it happened: the rectilinear black numbers on his Casio read 29.88. A sensation went through August that he could only compare to the moment he first sank into Natalee the bartender on the beach in Hampton Bays.

He finished the tub in a trance and when he was done he gazed upon his work like God the father surveying his creation and deemed it good. Pristine tails piled in one bus tub, a mass of severed tentacle-heads in the other. Four hours of work. He loved these squids as surely, as protectively, as he had ever loved anything.

He brought them to Baratin like a son bringing home a girl to his parents saying "Mom, Dad, this is the one." August was already thinking of how he would cook them. It had been a week of prep work, he figured they would agree that he had earned the right. But he had never eaten fresh squid before—how would he go about cooking them? Did you sauce them? Or maybe something so fresh, you just grilled it with oil and lemon? Did you have to boil them first, get the rubberiness out? Chef would explain.

Baratin was tying pieces of rabbit into tight cylinders. He put down his string and picked a few tails up, admiring them. Then he took the tub from August.

Bon. Now you do the heads. Julien, *montre-lui comment faire.* He stuck the tails into a lowboy fridge and went back to his rabbit.

Viens, said Julien, walking him back to the alcove. He pulled out a cutting board and showed August how to slice the heads just in front of the eyes, preserving the tentacles, then press down on the mouth so that a hard little beak popped out, and to pare that away. "Much more easy," he said, but August was barely paying attention. Chef had just taken the squid away from him. Just like that. He held out hope that they would call him back, put him on a station—even the cold station—so that he could at least watch them work tonight. But as the minutes ticked by, and beak after beak was sliced away, the call did not come. His hand ached from gripping the little paring knife. His back and feet ached from standing in one place for hours; at home he was able to roam the kitchen, be constantly in motion. August began to despair. They didn't need his help; they wanted him to stay back here, out of their way. No one was going to teach him how to cook these squid. He would never see them plated. All he was to them was a pair of hands. Baratin had let him come as a favor to Timo, but that didn't mean he was going to teach him.

He finished the squid heads sullenly, slowly, so that it took him almost all of service. He felt like a child. After service ended and the heads went into the fridge next to the tails, he mopped the kitchen floor again and polished all the stainless-steel countertops with vinegar, again. Then he walked the dirt path back to his room, the moon high and crickets whirring, and folded his bulk into the little European cot in his little European room, his face burning with humiliation. He could hear Magnus and Albert and Anouk outside smoking and laughing. He had never felt so far from home.

The following morning August entered the kitchen to find Baratin standing at the sink in his little alcove, holding a large fish, his right arm smeared with blood. A heap of whole fish, each the size of a woman's thigh, was piled like wet shiny firewood on the counter beside him.

Ah bon! Baratin greeted him, cheerfully. Today, it's for surgery!

Whereupon he thrust his hand into the fish's yawning mouth, sinking down to the elbow. August could see Baratin's fingers troubling the fish's silver belly, then he pulled out a fistful of ragged purple guts and tossed them *flatch* into a waiting bowl.

August picked one up and almost dropped it: it was lubricated. He gazed at it, ran his hand against the bristle of its scales. He had never had to clean a fish before. Well, he was here to learn, so holding it as firmly as he could he followed Chef's lead and reached inside. Everything felt like cold wet testicles, but he duly grasped whatever his fingers could reach, and he pulled. There was a satisfying ripping of tissue and he produced for Baratin a great bloody fistful of fish innards. Baratin nodded his approval.

Is a strange life, *hein?* he said.

August laughed, and together they made short work of the pile on the counter. As they worked, Baratin told him the fish was called *dorade* in French, or sea bream in English. It had to be eaten fresh, and the way to know if it was fresh was to check the eye. If it was clear, gemlike, then it was good, and you did not need to do much to it, just salt and pepper and lemon. If the eye was fogged, though, it was good only for soup. Freshness, said Baratin, was everything. In America, he knew—for he had visited—it was hard to get food fresh. "Your tomatoes, it's not tomatoes. It is maybe a kind of baseball you hit with the bat, but it's not a tomato." August could only nod, and listen. It was the most Baratin had talked to him all week.

When they were finished, Baratin said, You know how to fillet, yes?

August wasn't sure what to say. Or rather he knew he was supposed to say *Oui, Chef.* But he absolutely did not know how to fillet a whole fish, especially one of this size. Baratin was looking at him closely. He wanted August to prove himself. Really, how hard could it be? He glanced at the pile of them in the sink. There weren't that many—just twelve. It wasn't like the squid, where if he fucked one up it wouldn't matter. You couldn't cover a trashed sea bream with paper towels. And these were indisputably beautiful fish, their eyes like jewels and their scales iridescent. It would be a crime to waste one. He thought about the onions, about the coolers, and about all the things he'd insisted on doing by himself to show Chef he was the real thing. But he was not the real thing. The real thing would know how to fillet a fish.

I'm a little rusty, he finally said.

Rusty? said Baratin.

It's been a while. Like you said, not a lot of fresh stuff in New York.

Of course, said Chef dubiously, sharpening his knife. Watch carefully.

What happened next was so swift and effortless August could barely follow it. Baratin's long thin knife glided through the fish like an oar through water. He cleaved it at the head and then drew the blade calmly down the length of the spine once, twice, three times, and the whole foot-long filet came free in a gorgeous pink slab. Then he flipped it around and did the same on the other side. The only sound was the faint snicker of the blade through the pinbones. It wasn't the complexity of the technique that entranced him, but the speed of it. Never had he seen a chef move so assuredly and deftly, not even Ivor, whose movements now seemed to August as balletic as a drugged bear. The whole dazzling dance took thirty seconds but to August it was as if he'd watched a whole movie, and he wanted to see it all over again. He picked a fish out of the sink and held it humbly out to Chef Baratin.

Show me, August said. Please.

14.

Mr. Sweeney's entire bowel sat there, piled and slimy and shining. It almost overflowed the steel pan on his thighs. The clamps at either end stuck out of the jellied mass like chopsticks in a bowl of glutinous rice noodles. The smell in the room was softly fecal. I scooped a section of Mr. Sweeney's large intestine out of the bowl and ran its length through my hands, more slowly this time, feeling for abnormalities. The intestinal walls felt like rubbery calamari tails, pockmarked and thick. Too thick, and still squidgy with mucosa. The obvious causes came to mind swiftly: elevated cholesterol, diverticulitis, ulcerative colitis or Crohn's, or just plain gas; and then the sexier ones like lupus, cirrhosis, or rare signet-ring cancers, which don't form masses and therefore lurk undetected by better-paid radiologists until it's too late. I knew I was getting ahead of myself, but I always got excited around bowels.

"The ancient Romans," I said, picking up a pair of round-ended scissors, "used to employ a person called a haruspex to perform divination. They'd slit open a living sheep's belly and collect its entrails, then spread them still steaming on a table. There would be a question they'd be looking for an answer to, a yes-or-no question. Like, 'Should I marry my daughter to this man?' 'Should we march into battle tomorrow?' And the haruspex would carefully pick over the intestines and liver, probing them for answers. We don't know exactly how the haruspex read them, but we know the organs' judgment was final. A single anal polyp could send a hundred men to die. India could you unclamp the colon, please?"

Blanching slightly, India removed the clamp at the bottom of Mr. Sweeney's intestinal coil and took a step back. Then she took another, and another, until she was somewhere in the neighborhood of 2nd Avenue. The rest of them, my father included, were still gathered in close around me. I felt a glitter of malice at the thought that they did not realize what I was about to do.

"If there's one thing you learn about medicine today, it's this. Listen to the patient's bowels. They will never lie."

I flicked on the faucet and slit open the rectum and began sliding the scissors up the colon. Bits of feces crumbled into the sink. For a second all was still. And then the students and my father were flung backwards.

When I was eight, most days after school I went to our neighbor Leonora's house. My parents were at Xinghuacun constantly, and I was still too young to go alone on the 7 train. So I would walk the three blocks from P.S. 196 back to our apartment building, and Leonora would buzz me in and I would do my homework while we watched cop shows together. Leonora was a security guard at the Queens Museum, which made her the closest thing to a cop I knew, and she did nothing to disabuse me of that notion; she kept a running commentary through every episode ("See that? How they hold the perp's head as they put him in the squad car? You gotta do that otherwise they whack their heads on purpose so could they sue you."). My reward for finishing my homework was getting to see her gun, a thick-handled black weapon I couldn't have imagined a woman holding. She was childless and twice-divorced, once from a cop.

The English that I learned from these shows was hard-boiled and lushly idiomatic, and I began to use crude Chinese versions of it when I spoke to my parents. But the English phrase that stuck with me the most was one they all seemed to use in every episode, even though it seemed to make no sense at all: "trust your gut."

It was a ridiculous idea. The gut was where food turned into poop. Why would you trust it more than your commanding officer? And yet the TV cops would say it all the time, invoking their guts with religious reverence—their guts were constantly telling them things or disliking things. My first thought was that these men seemed often to have a lot of gut, and that being fat meant they were successful. Leonora thought this was hilarious, and eventually she explained.

"You know when you get nervous, you get like this feeling in your belly like butterflies?" I nodded. "But then you know how it's a different feeling when you get excited? Well, that's your gut talking. Right here." She slapped the swell of flesh that rose from the waistband of her grey sweatpants. I knew exactly what she meant. I always imagined the odd feelings in my stomach like a pit of tiny snakes like I'd seen in *Indiana Jones*. Most often they slept, but, when kids made fun of my hair or clothes or the things I said, the snakes would wake up and start writhing and hissing, their scales cold and slick.

When I said it in Chinese—"have confidence in your stomach"— my parents were baffled. It made me feel sorry for them. How were they supposed to learn this country's language if they didn't have time to watch TV?

It wasn't until decades later, when the mysteries of the enteric nervous system were revealed to me, that I understood that "trust your gut" wasn't just a figure of speech. The snakes in my belly weren't an illusion. Those entrail-fondlers had it right: the human bowel is oracular.

The gag reflex is elegantly simple. It's one of the very few reflexes that can be tamed—or at least, it's one of the few anyone tries to tame. It can be set off by touching—or merely menacing—the soft palate at the back of the mouth. Like most reflexes, it's a simple and instant loop: the glossopharyngeal nerve senses a foreign object and alerts the vagus nerve, which barks ABORT at the soft palate and pharyngeal muscles, and the offending object is rudely expelled.

Like most reflex actions, gagging does not need the brain's input; the two cranial nerves connect to each other directly and cause a very simple, contained motor function. For revulsion to graduate from gagging to retching, however, is much more complicated.

Retching is an odd creature, as reflexes go—it achieves very little. It sort of simulates the experience of vomiting, with none of the benefits. It also comes from the same place: the brain stem's chemoreceptor trigger zone, or vomiting center. This is a tiny little node in the medulla that's exquisitely sensitive to toxins in the blood (like chemo drugs); it can be activated by panic signals from the inner ear (motion sickness); it can also be caused by exterior stimuli, such as one's attending physician pulling a giant compacted brick of human feces from a decomposing intestine. In this case, the vomiting center responds to afferent impulses from the piriform cortex, right between one's ears. But retching can also be caused by the mere sight or sound of retching, because in a group of people, those vomiting centers in the brain are wired together like smoke detectors spread across a large house; if one goes off, they all go off. Hence the scene unfolding before me.

The smell could have caused turbulence in a small-engine aircraft. All medical professionalism was abandoned; they were reeling around the lab, gasping and heaving like soldiers under attack from mustard gas. I wasn't immune, either; I could feel my abdominal muscles spasming and my throat closing. I had run countless hundreds of bowels, many of them constipated, but this one put them all to shame. But I wasn't about to let them—let my dad—see me crack. I don't know if whoever came up with the line "no way out but through" was talking about feces, but it certainly applied.

I steeled myself and pressed onward with the scissors, holding the small intestine under the faucet as I sheared through its rubbery walls, and then through all thirty-nine ribbonlike feet of it, the chyme and feces flowing off it in yellow-brown curtains. I knew I should have been talking them through this, narrating it like David Attenborough describing the mating dance of an exotic bird, but the first thing that happens during retching is that the glottis slams shut, which protects the windpipe from anything that might be making its way back up toward the mouth, but also makes it impossible to speak. Instead, the only sounds in the room were the hum of the fan, the sibilance of the scissors, the drum of the water on the sink bottom, and my father's wracked coughs.

Normally this was India's job, or whichever resident I was training, but I wanted my father to know I could do this. As I drove the scissors through the jellied coil and the rotten fragrance filled my nose, I retreated into the memory of my first day of medical school. I remembered the way that as soon as I walked into the gross anatomy lab, the stink of forty bodies saturated in embalming fluids shoved a fat fist down my throat and squeezed, and in that instant I remembered how my father had taught me to eat lobes of abalone, pulpy jellyfish, gelatinous cubes of duck's blood.

I was still a child, eight or nine. One day he'd sat me down in the kitchen at Xinghuacun, a range of bowls spread before us, shiny with sinister substances.

"This," he had said, his expression deadly serious, "is real food. This is what real Chinese people eat. In American it is all salt and sugar and—" he waved the word away like an irritating fly "—ketchup. But flavor is not the only thing. Texture—kou gan—is just as important. Taste this."

He plucked out a trembling piece of jellyfish and held it delicately in his chopsticks. Dutifully, I ate. I chewed, but my teeth barely dented it. It was rubbery and spicy. When I tried to swallow it my soft palate recoiled in horror, and I gagged. I wanted to spit it out but I saw my father's eyes, hard and imperious. I squeezed my eyes shut and swallowed.

"Hao. Zai lai yi ge." He fished out another piece. "Do not fight the texture. Yield to it. Be *patient*."

I tried again. And again. Over and over, one sloppy wet morsel after another until I learned that the trick was not to force myself to swallow, but to allow the food to express itself fully, to absorb it, savor it, and then, when it was ready, swallow. To yield was not weakness, it was strength.

This was what I remembered that day in the anatomy lab, how to yield, and just like that the stink of death released its grip on my throat, and I was clear. That was the day I understood the control I would need to exert over myself if I wanted to be great: the discipline not to fight, but to endure.

I had kept to that, all these years. But he hadn't. That man was not in this lab today. Whoever was inhabiting his exhausted, fragile body, it was not the man who trained his daughter never to choke.

Finally, my larynx unsealed. There was still some of the compacted feces in the colander in the sink. I picked a little vial off the counter, a tiny spoon attached to the cap, and showed it to the students.

"Who would like to do the honors."

"Don't look at me," India said, "I quit."

"I'll do it," said Eva.

The others swiveled their heads at her, like startled meerkats. She popped off the cap and examined the little scalloped end of the spoon. Then she took a deep breath in through her mouth and went for it.

One night my parents didn't come home until late and I stayed at Leonora's, and we watched a new show called *NYPD Blue*. Halfway through, David Caruso and Amy Brennaman started kissing. Boring, I thought, kissing made people look like birds eating off each others' faces. But then he pulled off her shirt. And pants. In his white undershirt David Caruso lifted her off the ground, his hands gripping her thighs as she wrapped her legs around his waist, then he dipped her, slowly, his mouth never leaving hers, to the bedsheets. The window behind them was open to the blue New York summer night, the gossamer curtains swaying in the breeze. And then they were naked, completely naked, amber-skinned and glowing, the slope of their butts bared to the sky right there on Leonora's boxy, wood-paneled television. The camera lingered on Amy Brennaman's back as a lone long muscle tensed, once, like the hammer of a piano key striking a single wire. Slowly I reached back to feel the same place in my back, but I did not feel that muscle; I couldn't make it go. In my guts—the very place Leonora had told me I should trust—I felt something go cold and shivery and wonderful. I glanced, panicked, at Leonora, sure somehow that I was not supposed to be seeing this, but she just sat there, as mesmerized as me.

Amy Brennaman's and David Caruso's were the first grown-up naked bodies I'd ever seen, and they would be the only ones I saw for years. The cops on the show always looked harried and exhausted, in lumpy wrinkled clothes, but once they took those clothes off, which they did with satisfying regularity and tormenting brevity, they became transfigured, fleetingly, into these beings of gold and shadow, clenched together on rumpled sheets or rising bare-assed from beds or standing naked and brave in locker rooms. I grew to crave those fleeting weekly glimpses of butts, their glutes flexing and contracting just below their skin. Often they shot it so you couldn't tell at first when it was a man's butt or a woman's butt, and I utterly did not care. Except for when they showed Dennis Franz's butt–which happened exactly once, in a shower scene–and Leonora made a face like a shriveled prune. But I loved Dennis Franz's lonely, blustering Sipowicz, and they made him stand there in front of a woman, and I could see that he was ashamed of how sad and droopy and bleach-white his butt was. But when that woman— her name escapes me now—came up behind him in the shower, and she gently, lovingly caressed his body and he could hardly speak for shock, I felt so tenderly toward Detective Sipowicz I had to fight back tears.

I did not know enough to want their bodies. All I knew was I wanted to see their bodies. It would take another few years for all the wiring in my head to fuse and connect the wanting to see to the wanting to touch, and when that happened…well, it never stopped happening.

For a long time, especially in college when I plowed through strange new bodies like a supervirus, I wondered whether, had Leonora done the responsible American grown-up thing and shut the TV off the instant that Amy Brennaman whipped off her shirt—had she conveyed the message to eight year-old me that gazing at these bronzed bodies coiling together was bad or wrong—I wouldn't have become what I was. But eventually I understood that without a counterfactual, it was a stupid question.

"All right," I said to Mr. Sweeney's great riven bowel, which lay there in two languid strips. "Speak."

I stepped back and gestured to the students. They approached gingerly, like a bomb-disposal squad. "What do you see?"

"Those red blotches—ulceration. Did he have colitis?"

"I would want to check the submucosal fat to make sure, but almost definitely. What else?"

"Those little bubbles like boils, are those diverticuli?"

"Yeah, and if they pop it's bad news," said India.

"Feel it," I said, handing them the sections. "There are two questions you ask at this stage. One, is it thickened in segments, almost ribbed, or is it the same thickness all the way?"

"It feels like all the way," Eva said, her face crinkling with revulsion as she slid the rubbery length between her gloved thumb and forefinger.

"Okay, so it's homogenous. Second question is, symmetrical or not. Is one side thicker than the other?"

"I think it's uniform," said Eva, passing it. The others nodded.

"All right, then. This helps us with differential diagnosis. Heterogenous and asymmetrical bowel walls tend to indicate malignancies, or serious conditions; homogenous and symmetrical means—"

"Hen xinku la shi," my father moaned.

A startled humane noise came from Wei Wei. A vulnerable *aww*. She was looking at him, her eyes brimming with sympathy, even pity.

I almost snapped at her in Chinese that my father didn't need her fucking pity, but I stopped myself. That would have been cruel, and it takes effort for me not to be cruel. My threshold for suffering is different from most people's: If your head is attached to your body and your heart is still beating, you are not my problem.

"That's true, Dad. Even if there is nothing malignant here, patients with colons like this experience straining and pain on the toilet."

"Did he suffer a lot?" my dad asked.

I replied calmly. "I don't know, Dad, but he isn't now." Empathy is a terrible drug sometimes. You hear about people so enslaved to their own empathy that they adopt twenty kids, or sell off all their belongings and leave their families to go midwife babies in war-torn Nicaragua, or move their kids to a leper colony. That's no longer empathy. That's mania.

But empathy is the vogue now in medicine. As if it were a brand new miracle drug just discovered by Science, like penicillin or chemotherapy. These students have been tested for it, trained in it, made to practice delivering bad news gently but clearly to moonlighting actors with the gift of tears. I have been told I need to be more empathetic. I disagree. There are plenty of empathetic people out there—social workers, television psychics, doctors without borders (I am a doctor with *firm* borders). The world needs people like me the way airplanes need gravity to fly.

When I did my death training, the actress was a middle-aged white woman. They had given me a slip of paper with the cause of death on it. All I could think was, was this her career? My parents were right.

This was what happened to people who went into the arts. They wound up having to spend a whole day with people in white coats telling them that their daughter was dead.

It wasn't that I didn't understand the point of the exercise. It was that I already knew it did not apply to me. By the time I would interface with a patient's family, their deadness would be settled fact. So I concentrated on her eyes as I spoke.

I had a friend in high school who could cry on command. Layla Cohen. She could go from neutral-faced to tears sliding down the edge of her nose in half a minute. It mesmerized me. I would ask her to do it over and over so I could watch. Her eyes would go suddenly vacant and little tremors would ripple across her face—a twitch of the neck muscles, a shiver under the eye, a subtle creasing at the corners of her mouth—and then all those little tremors would resolve themselves into a single glimmering tear, which would wobble in her eye for a moment before toppling out and streaking down toward her chin. And before the tear had even completed its run she would be all smiles again.

"How do you *do* that?" I finally asked.

"I imagine my mom dying," she said.

After that I was afraid of Layla. Her mom was a nice woman who worked for ABC News. Layla could slip into pure grief blithely, then pop back out again. Like it was a game.

By the time I was face to face with the middle-aged actress, I knew how her tears worked. I could name the muscles that were quivering across her face. Still, I watched her with fascination.

"Mrs. Otis," I said. "We did everything we could." This was the exact thing we were not supposed to say, but I wanted to draw this out a little, to give her more of a runway.

"I don't understand," the woman said. "Is she going to be okay? She's my only daughter." She was supposed to lay it on thick, punish us emotionally for any lack of clarity. Though I thought it was gauche for her to imply that having other backup children should somehow cushion this particular blow.

"I knew she was sick, but I thought she was going to get better," she said, her voice choked. "We're supposed to be going prom dress shopping today." And now her eyes began to shimmer.

"I'm so sorry," I said, earnestly. "I know this might be hard for you." I was supposed to say, "but she has died," but I was trying to focus on both her eyes at once—harder than it sounds at that distance. I said, "Maybe if you'd gotten here sooner…" I wanted to know if the lacrimal glands worked simultaneously or if her nervous system focused on one over the other. I'd noticed she was a lefty. Which eye would be first? It was the Great Tear Duct race.

She gasped in horror and clutched at her throat. "What…what are you saying?"

Somehow, she was getting to me. I was delivering the worst death pronouncement in the history of the Columbia School of Medicine, and she was making me pay for it. I had to admire her professionalism— it occurred to me that at some point she'd probably played a grieving mother or sister on *Law & Order* like every other New York actor. Maybe she had even been on *NYPD Blue* back when it was on. I wondered if I could IMDB her later.

I produced a tissue from my lab coat pocket and handed it to her. "I don't know how to tell you this, but"—and here I made a show of having to check my clipboard for the name—"Angela is in a better place."

Her eyes went huge. There! Water.

"I don't understand. Is she…"

"Oh! Yes. Dead. She's dead."

I'll be damned. It was a dead heat.

Like vomiting, crying is a reflex that can be triggered by seeing someone else do it. We don't exactly know why we cry, but the physiology is fascinating. The lacrimal gland can express three chemically distinct kinds of tears. The first are the basal tears, which continually bathe the cornea to keep it lubricated and clean. They're a very basic bodily fluid. Then you have reflex tears, the kind that gush out when you chop an onion or get pepper sprayed; under a microscope, these resemble tightly-packed snowflakes. Then there are the money tears—the psychic ones that spring forth in response to sadness, laughter, pain, pleasure. These are chemically similar to saliva (which has its own miraculous antiseptic power), but contain specific hormones, namely, leucine enkephalin, a neurotransmitter that acts as a natural painkiller—which may be why crying makes you feel better. Or so I'm told.

It was all I could do not to reach out and collect a teardrop from Mrs. Otis's cheek and taste it. Would it taste different from onion tears? Would it taste…simulated? Did it smell different? I *craved* this knowledge. But I just handed her the tissue, and watched her wipe those perfect, hard-won teardrops away. Her notes on me were scathing.

15.

The day of August's flight back to New York, he awoke, as he had every morning that month, to the sound of roosters crowing. He'd been working the pass all night in his dreams, and something expensive was burning on the range behind him, but he couldn't manage to turn around. In the darkness of his room, he fumbled for his watch and pressed the button to illuminate the display. 4:33am. All his life he'd accepted the wisdom that roosters crowed at dawn. Turned out they crowed whenever the fuck they felt like it.

He gazed out the little barred window. The moon was still out but the stars were fading, the sky a queer deep blue. The color of mold veins in a Roquefort, August judged. A cheese he had grown to love. He'd found there were very few cheeses he did not love. The French understood the value of stank.

August was a deep sleeper, but sometimes his eyes would flick open in the middle of the night and his mind would already be going at a hundred miles an hour. Back in Queens he'd get up and go to the 24-hour diner down on Steinway Avenue to smoke cigarettes over coffee and home fries and watch the sun come up. There was also a Lebanese bakery that would open for him if he knocked on the window, and he would buy a kanafeh and eat it right there on the sidewalk and lick the sweet white cheese off his fingers.

The hills above Buoux were quiet now. New York never got this quiet. It'd taken him a while to learn to sleep without the sound of garbage trucks and passing taxis. He lay there, looking at the moon. He wondered if he was homesick. He was not, he thought. Home was never such a big deal for August; he didn't own many things, and he'd never really missed anyone, per se. He didn't quite understand the mechanics of "missing" someone—was he supposed to just sit around wishing they were here? They weren't doing the same for him. But he did miss the city. It felt strange that he couldn't just walk down a few flights of stairs and have it all be there waiting for him, orange streetlamps and neon signs that burned all night, and gypsy cabs and steam grates. Here it was fields, and more fields, and dark cliffs washed in moonlight and silence, the daytime drone of cicadas finally stilled for the night. He'd barely seen a single traffic light in a month (they favored these demented traffic circles). And these people had never heard of a 24-hour diner. He once tried to explain it to Magnus and Albert, who acted like he was describing a hate crime. Who would even want to eat a T-bone steak at four in the morning?

Well, August for one.

The prehistoric springs of the bed winced as August heaved himself upright, and the vinyl mattress gasped. The tiled floor was cool on the pads of his feet. His scrotum was sweat-pasted gently to his inner thigh, and his penis was half-hard. He slept naked, always, so he pulled on a pair of boxers and eased open the door of his room, quietly so as not to wake his neighbors. He crept toward the bathroom, his penis still tenting his shorts, and while part of him warmed to the idea of the willowy, round-nosed Anouk seeing him thus, he still had Magnus and Albert to worry about.

The dorms were set into the hill above Le Roi Ubu, up a short but steep gravel path. There were four of them in the squat, stucco building, with a bathroom and a shower attached at the far end. The lack of air conditioning was fine at night, when a breeze (and mosquitoes) whispered through the open windows, but during the day, when they would haul themselves back to the rooms for *la sieste*, the heat was feral.

Then he would close the curtains and switch on the rickety table fan and lie stunned on his cot, stark naked, absorbing the heat, the cicadas unrelenting in the trees.

August lifted up the flimsy toilet seat and relieved himself. The noise in the bowl pierced the quiet.

Back in his room August pulled on a pair of sweatpants and an old Xavier football t-shirt and went for a walk.

He ambled down the path, the gravel crunching underfoot. Le Roi Ubu looked hooded in the darkness, all the lights out. He thought about testing the kitchen door. Maybe it was open, and he could make himself an omelette. He'd been watching Baratin carefully when he made omelettes—instead of loading it up with mushrooms and bacon and diced peppers like they did at the diner, Baratin used nothing but eggs and butter and a furious pan-shaking technique and about thirty seconds later the result was this exquisite golden pillow.

Instead, he walked around to the front of the restaurant, where the outdoor tables were. He sat in one of the wrought-iron chairs and fished his cigarettes out of his pocket. From here, in daylight, guests could look out over the lushness of the Luberon Valley, the lavender and wheat fields stretching out into the distance, guarded by white limestone cliffs. You could see little villages stud the hilltops, each with its proud little medieval steeple.

But now, all the moonlight revealed was the hooded mass of the hills set against the night sky. Here and there, in the offing, a few solitary lights. He'd imagined farmers would be up at this hour, but he didn't know how they could see anything in this darkness. Maybe they knew their fields so well they could tend them by feel, by smell. There were always farmers coming to Le Roi Ubu, bringing pallets of summer squash, eggplant, zucchini blossoms, and the most beautiful tomatoes he had ever seen. Dark red, yellow, velvety-purple. It was crazy. The way they bought produce here was a farmer drove up and say "I grew this at my house. You want it?" and handed you the most beautiful tomatoes you had ever seen and then right there and then you decided what the menu for that night would be.

He contemplated the produce section at the C-Town supermarket down the street from his apartment. Soft potatoes. Red Delicious apples waxed to iridescence. Iceberg lettuce. Shrink-wrapped cucumbers. Engorged strawberries that tasted acrylic. Optimistically, apricots.

It wasn't just that it was the most beautiful produce he had ever seen. It was how little Baratin seemed to do to it. At Timo's they'd had a whole shelf of spices, cumin and oregano and cayenne and meat tenderizer and paprika and sweet paprika and smoked paprika and curry powder, and August thought that this was where flavor came from. Especially after the foie gras incident he'd believed that his job as a cook was to take a cheap thing and make it taste expensive. He'd been good at that. But at Le Roi Ubu there were hardly any spices at all, not even in the sauces. There was salt, pepper, olive oil, and—with surprising parsimony—butter, and then some fresh herbs, and that was it.

Cupping his hands to his mouth, he lit his first cigarette. His eyes had adjusted to the darkness, and he looked around the patio. He had sat out here for the very first time the evening before, as the sun went down in waves of blue and purple all around the valley, and all the subtle machinery of the restaurant pulsed and swirled around him. He had showed up for dinner service, still groggy from bed, when Baratin intercepted him as he was stringing on a fresh apron.

No, he frowned. No, you cannot wear this. Go back and change.

August looked down—he was in his clogs and checks, same as ever. Was Baratin pranking him?

What is this face? *C'est la fin du stage.* It's tradition. Tonight you don't work. You eat. Go, you put on a shirt.

And so August dined, at last, on the work of his hands. Magnus had served him with perfect professional warmth, albeit with a smile playing over his Scandinavian mouth. Here, in the soupe au pistou, were the green beans August had sliced and blanched; here in the ceviche were the cilantro leaves he had painstakingly plucked from their stems and the sea breams he had gutted, filleted, and pulled the infernal pinbones from; here were the squash blossoms he had tenderly washed and piped with mousse. But most of all, here, in soft white rings, were the squid he had pulped and cleaned.

And God, they were good.

He knew these ingredients, remembered them in the bones of his fingers, but they seemed transformed—not just by the dark arts of Baratin and Julien, but by the very table they were placed on, and the smile of Magnus, and the ironed white cuffs on his sleeves as he laid them before him, and the simple ceramic plates made by Baratin's wife, and the setting sun coming through the trees and the floral scent of evening in the air, and the prickle of the breeze on his bare forearms, and the heft of the cutlery; it all swam together in his mouth and his head and his stomach and alchemized every bite into something close to edible gold.

This, he thought. If only Timo could see this.

He supposed he missed Timo. It was like having a dad. Of course August had a dad, but if he had gotten to *choose* his dad, it would have been someone much more like Timo. Baratin was kind, but he was more benignly tolerant of August than actively paternal. He had known at the beginning what August was only coming to understand now: a month was nothing.

He leaned back in his chair, the front iron legs coming off the floor. What had he learned, really? In the kitchen, he'd basically been a glorified food processor. He'd learned a few new skills—he had become a masterful filleter of fish—but he hadn't actually done much *cooking*. They'd barely suffered him to apply heat to anything. They'd let him use the deep fryer. Julien cracked that as an American, he would at least know how to use *that*. The only thing that had changed was when he arrived, he had assumed he couldn't make the ethereal green steak sauce from La Grenouille; now, he *knew* he couldn't.

He opened his lips to let the smoke float out of his mouth, and inhaled through his nose. This, at least, he had learned. Anouk had taught him. They would smoke together after *le perso*, the family meal, and once a week she would have him drive them in his cramped rented Citroën to the giant farmers' market in the nearby town of Apt. The restaurant was closed Monday and Tuesday, and on Tuesdays the whole town was taken over by stalls selling fruits vegetables honey wine meats cheeses soaps baskets linens; together, he and Anouk would walk through the winding medieval streets and she would teach him alimentary French by pointing at things.

L'ail, she would say, pointing to the most beautiful braid of purple garlic he had ever seen. She taught him how to select produce, how to ask the fromagière for a taste, to rap a knuckle against a melon to listen for ripeness, to sniff a tomato. And so August learned to speak a crude but effective French of nouns and elaborate hand gestures.

Le ris de veau, Anouk would say, pointing to the white lumpy gland of a calf, then at her own throat. It was an elegant throat, browned by the southern sun and taut-muscled whenever she concentrated intensely on piping a dessert. It pained August that he would have to leave this place without ever having pressed his lips to that throat.

But August knew he couldn't stay. His passport and ticket were right where he'd placed them last night, on his bedside table. It would be good to be back. He missed his apartment, where he could play John Lee Hooker albums as loud as he wanted and masturbate anytime he wanted. His flight was at 5:45 that evening. He'd checked the ticket over and over to make sure—he had to drive to Avignon to return the car, take the train to the Paris airport, then get on an airplane and fly home and Timo would pick him up at the airport and give him a big kiss on his forehead—which his own father had only ever done exactly once, when August was thirteen and he thought he was asleep, and he did it so softly and timidly that it felt to August like a butterfly wing swept once against his head.

The moon slid behind a cloud and the grey glow that had enveloped the valley dissolved. Timo needed him. Luna and Toussaint and Maria and the rest of the staff needed him. They were like family—they *were* his family. These people? They weren't. He couldn't even speak their language. He stood out in crowds like a parade float—children stared openly—and every time he walked into one of their ancient stone buildings he had to duck. This was no country for the August-sized. It would be a relief to be home, to be making money again—to be in *charge* again. He'd never worked so hard and achieved so little as he had in this place. Even when he was a kid at Jimmy Luisi's washing dishes, he'd had a real job to do. At Le Roi Ubu, even Habib the dishwasher was above him, because if Habib fucked up, the whole kitchen would slam to a halt; if August fucked up, and he did, with exhausting regularity, Baratin would just sigh, and take the job away from him, as if training him was more trouble than it was worth. August wanted his fuckups to *mean* something again.

In his kitchen at Timo's it was chaos, with cursing and joking and Spanish pop songs, but it was a chaos he controlled. Here he controlled nothing. Meanwhile Julien was only twenty-four, but seemed already to possess the ability to slow time down around him during service. In the full heat of the dinner rush, with steam billowing from the *four à vapeur* and the pots boiling on the range, calls for service from the maitre d', scallops and sausages sizzling in pans, Julien never seemed to panic, never moved faster than he had to. August saw himself in this, a little, and it gave him courage—he, too, had always found it easy to be zen in the midst of chaos. But it was Julien's movements that were the most spellbinding. Everything was elegant and precise. When he needed paper towels, he didn't just grab and rip from the spindle on the wall, he culled them around his hand gently, like a fork twirling pasta. His knifework was unhurried but decisive; nothing moved on him except the knife and his three knuckles. He seemed always to know how long each thing had been in each pan, without timers.

It seemed that Julien could cook by feel, but slowly August realized that that feel was the product of technique—a decade of it. After the day Baratin showed him how to fillet a fish, August understood the way it worked here. The process was so simple: master a menial and unfuckupable task, and then graduate to a marginally less menial task not by dint of creativity or intellect, but by the confidence of his superiors that he would not fuck that task up either. All that was required was to willingly do this over and over, squid after squid, tomato after tomato, for years, moving up the hierarchy until all of these tasks had insinuated themselves into his hands so completely they would not let him fuck them up if he tried, and then, finally, he would be a chef. And he *was* willing. Julien had what he wanted more than anything else in the world, and for the last few nights he had been waking up in the middle of the night, sweating in his little cot, paralyzed by the fear that he was already too late.

He stubbed out his cigarette and lit another. The smoke purled upward. He knew he was behind. At 14, when the Xavier Jesuits were trying to force-feed him algebra and American history, Julien had begun learning how to make demi-glace. When August was dissecting a fetal pig, Julien was being taught how to debone a duck. And if Julien, the best cook he had ever seen, was merely a sous-chef in this anonymous country restaurant without so much as a Michelin star, then what chance did August have at greatness? For that was the one thing he had learned. That he wanted to be great. No, wanted wasn't the word. He needed. Needed to be huge, adored.

He had no idea how a cook was supposed to get huge and adored. But he knew he couldn't do it from here. Maybe you had to get on TV. But all the cooks he knew in New York were like him, unshaven men in checks and clogs who put cornstarch down their pants to keep their balls dry in the heat. No one was going to put them on TV. The famous names on cookbooks weren't chefs, they were writers like Julia Child and Craig Claiborne. And August was not a writer. He was a talker. The moment he sat down to write something he got the commas confused with the apostrophes and the whole business felt like trying to knit a scarf with strings of melted cheese.

August was 22, he couldn't afford to dick around anymore.

Something rustled in the trees. Startled, August dropped his cigarette right into his lap. He slapped it away frantically and the fiery ember skittered across the concrete patio. There was a sound of crackling brush. August froze. A dark hooded figure emerged from the trees and lumbered across the lawn toward the patio.

The moon began to edge from behind its cloud. Was it a pig? It was huge, like a barrel with hooves. In the gloaming August could see his grey hair was matted and bristly, and two tusks shone dully at the corners of his snout.

It wasn't a pig. It was a wild boar.

August had never seen one before, not in real life. But there were pictures of it everywhere here. Anouk had taught him the French word for it: sanglier. And once he'd learned the word, he'd begun to see it everywhere; bars, restaurants, inns, and so on. The people of Provence seemed to treat it like a mascot. But he'd hadn't gotten to try one yet. And now he never would.

August sat mesmerized, rooted to his chair. Eight hours ago this patio had been full of women in colorful sundresses and men in collared shirts unbuttoned to the chest. Glasses of rosé frosted with condensation. And now it was just him and wildlife. He had never seen wildlife. He'd spent his entire life in New York where all they had were rats and squirrels who, far from being wild, were the shadow government of the entire city. Here, even domesticated animals like sheep and goats excited him, but there was nothing domestic about this boar. He looked prehistoric. As if he had been here, on this land, long before the women in sundresses and waiters in starched cuffs, and he would be here long after.

They didn't have this in America. He knew it because he knew the order forms for the Phylaktou brothers like some people knew song lyrics. They had every part of the pig you could ask for but no boar. Even Boar's Head, it dawned on him, didn't actually sell boar. It was as if the animal didn't exist in America. There was so much here that didn't exist at home. What good was home if it had none of the things he loved?

There was so much August did not know.

August watched the boar and the boar watched August. In the distance, the first filaments of indigo crept over the sky.

16.

"It's weird how this is what he made his whole career getting people to eat," said India, burrowed deep underneath the pulpy mass of August Sweeney's organs.

In order for India to get underneath the organ bloc to scalpel it free from the fascia, all five of us, including my father, were straining to hold him open. We stood on either side of him, aching fingers gripping the wet slippery five-inch-thick slabs of abdominal flesh to keep them from crashing down over India like the waters of the Red Sea.

"Not weird," grunted my father. "America is weird. Everyone in the world eat organs, only Americans waste." This was something he had drilled into me as a child: real Chinese people ate things like bao du, boiled cow stomach; if I flinched at any of it, he would taunt me. *You're not Chinese. Should I buy you some* laowai *food? Some...bologna?*

No! I'd yell, and take a huge bite of whatever was wobbling in front of my face. Bologna was the food of shame. Death before bologna.

"I feel like one of those people holding the giant American flag at football games," said Bushwick.

It takes time for a dead body to forget its habits. Like the way a poster needs time to forget being rolled up in a cardboard cylinder. And the deeper into a dead body you go, the more it comes to life.

Finally India emerged, panting. Her gloves were dripping pleural fluid. She nodded, and together the two of us reached under the organ bloc—the heart, lungs, liver, kidneys, stomach, and their supporting cast—and hoisted the whole thing out and laid it on the dissection table.

"So that's what's under the hood," India said, wiping her hands like a mechanic on a blue towel.

On the surface the dead have a convenient way of *looking* dead. Once you unzip the vinyl body bag the mind smooths the patient's body into banality, catalogue its stark bare parts with bureaucratic coldness. I do it to myself when I look in the mirror—I imagine what I will look like naked on a colleague's table. They'll see an Asian female in her mid-thirties. Five foot five. One hundred and twenty one pounds. Black hair of shoulder-length. Bangs. Degraded nail on right big toe. Pronounced appendicitis scar. Birthmark on left shin like a miniature storm cloud. Skin turned the color of a manila folder, except for the genitals, which are a deep saturated brown and spiky with hair, unlike the armpits, which are shaved. Breasts slack on the chest. Facial skin pulled tight and thin over angular cheekbones and sharp chin. Mouth prominent. Eyebrows severe. And that would be it. I'll resemble a wax replica of myself. I've always found this image comforting, somehow.

When I first interned at the Queens ME's office, it took fewer bodies than I expected for them to lose their power to shock. In fact, it took three—two women and one man. The bodies themselves were all radically different, but I realized they all had the same physical character: an arm lifted to check for rigor mortis would always thud the same way back to the table when I let it go. An eyelid, raised, would always stay where I put it. I found the predictability comforting: finally, a person I could not hurt.

But scrape away that coldly serene surface, and the dead body starts to wake up. To those of us who speak its language, it starts to talk. Sometimes it swings right into conversation, like an over-friendly waiter who wants you to know he's in a band, with giant rock-hard sarcomas or cirrhotic livers. Others would be quiet, cryptic, revealing their secrets only when the samples came back weeks later and I pressed my eye to the microscope. These were the ones who had hidden their diseases from all the doctors who came before me, whose signet-ring carcinomas crept undetected along the tissues of their bowels, or whose slivered brains revealed dozens of tiny buckshot-like emboli, meaning multi-infarct dementia, not the Alzheimer's the family feared they'd inherit. These were my favorites. These were the ones who whispered their secrets into my ear, and mine alone.

But there was nothing quiet about the viscera of August Sweeney. When the great blood-soaked contraption of the organ bloc was laid on the table and rinsed off, everywhere I looked, something was inflamed or calcified or oozing or caked in plaque.

The adrenal glands were the first to come out, and just in time: they were already starting to break down, like thick lobes of foie gras left out in the hot sun. The lungs resembled eggplants charred and withered over a direct flame. When I pierced the thin membrane of the gallbladder, black bile gushed, and three brown, perfectly cuboid stones clattered loudly onto the metal table.

My father picked it up to examine it. "What's this?"

I gestured to the students.

"Oh my God, are those gallstones?" said Wei Wei, rapping one against the steel table. "They're like dice."

"Or whiskey stones," said Bushwick, in the knowing voice of someone who owned a set of whiskey stones.

One kidney was white and palsied, the other was green, hard, and so riddled with holes it seemed to have been attacked with an olive pitter. He must have had kidney stones once a year. The liver looked like it came from a horse, if that horse had drunk a liter of whiskey every day of its life. It was humongous, with a hard pebbled exterior, and a nutmeg pattern throughout the interior like the marbling on wagyu beef, which is exquisite in beef, but in human liver means sluggish blood flow. Despite the engorged scrotum the testes were completely normal. All fluid. The heart, however, was a bowling ball. There were gasps when India finally cut it free of its moorings and lifted it, dripping and immense. I'd expected cardiomegaly, but I'd never seen a heart like this. There was so much thick muscle here it felt grafted from a human thigh. The ventricular walls were dense, even rubbery. Too much muscle is bad, for the heart—it means it's working too hard, straining to haul blood through constricted veins. And this heart had been working too hard for a long, long time. Maybe his whole life.

I was mystified. Not how this man died. How he made it this far at all.

By the time the individual organs were liberated from the aortic trunk and nested wetly in stainless steel colanders, it was past one. The students were trying to stifle yawns behind their masks, and were squatting and stretching to relieve the stiffness in their legs. Of course. The adrenaline of the morning had all worn off, and they were tired and probably starving.

My instinct was to keep pushing. We'd lost so much time already, and even a routine autopsy of a body this size could take all day; throw in the eyes and the bones, and we were in danger of going all night. These kids could take it. But my father had already gone all night, I realized—and he'd been going for days. Multiple times, as we worked, he'd tried to speak Chinese to the wrong person, like he didn't know which language was coming out of his mouth. Most of his sandwich, I suddenly remembered, had wound up on the floor. He needed to eat or he would collapse.

"Okay," I said, tossing my scalpel in the sharps box and removing my splash shield, "why don't we break for lunch?"

"Oh thank God," said Eva.

As they gratefully removed their masks and blood-soaked plastics, I took a minute to look them over. Bushwick carefully removed his foot protectors to reveal leather shoes that were clearly expensive, an insane thing to wear into my lab.

"You want us back in an hour?" asked Wei Wei.

I laughed. "You have thirty minutes."

As they lurched toward the door, my father clicked his tongue. I knew that noise, and stiffened. "Xiaotong, ni yinggai qing ke," he said.

"Shao guan, baba," I hissed angrily. Wei Wei had clearly understood him, but, no, I was absolutely not about to take them out for lunch. As hard as it might have been for him to understand, I was in charge here, not him. They would go to the canteen, and India and I would take him to the meh-but-quick Cantonese restaurant on 35th street.

"These are your students," he said loudly, in English, and they stopped in the doorway. "You are the professor."

"Oh, no, Ba, they don't...they don't want to do that." It was a ridiculous idea. Even if I wanted to take them to lunch—which I would, of course, have to cover—we didn't have time.

"Tshh. Of course they want to!" He turned to them, spread his arms wide. "You are medical students. You all work hard. Need a good meal! I take care of you!"

By the time I realized what he meant, he'd swept past them into the hall. The students stood there at the door, wavering awkwardly. He hadn't even given me a chance to argue with him. He wasn't just inviting them to a restaurant, he was inviting them to *our* restaurant. Now I couldn't refuse without humiliating him. He'd outflanked me completely.

"My family's restaurant is not far," I said, defeated. "My father would like to invite you to join us."

Expressions of surprise. Approbatory head-nodding. Med students would rat out their mothers for a free meal.

Dread wallowed around my guts as we pulled on winterwear over our scrubs and India locked up the lab. I loaned my father my coat, which cinched him tightly at the shoulders but otherwise fit him strangely well. He'd shrunk. I put on my hospital-branded fleece.

I checked my phone. There was the text I'd ignored from Mandragola earlier.

BTW I just got a call from his daughter. She seemed very confused.

That sounded like a problem for the guy with the window in his office.

I decided not to answer. I handled the dead people; he handled their families. That was why he made more than I did.

"Wait, Ba!"

He stopped, exasperated, just short of the elevator. "What?"

I pointed down at his feet, and the splotches of blood all over the hallway floor. He'd forgotten to take off his shoe covers.

Adrenaline is the most extraordinary substance. It changes, briefly, the very chemistry of our bodies. The brain burns as if with rocket fuel, the heart goes like a Gatling gun, sugar pours into the bloodstream, the pupils dilate, the lungs suck air—in many ways it simulates the feeling of being about to die. It's super-soldier serum: We can see better, clearer, farther. Everything slows down. Pain vanishes. Cold means nothing. We can run naked on a broken leg through a frozen forest and rip a branch off a tree. And right now, adrenaline was singing an aria in the veins of my father: he had barely eaten or slept, and still we had to trot to keep up with him as he sped west toward his favorite child, toward the restaurant I realized he hadn't been to since the stroke. The January air was nipple-invertingly cold. It had snowed three days ago, which in New York meant slush-moats lurked at each curb. Bushwick, in his Italian shoes, grand-jetéd into every crosswalk.

"Eeeeeeh!" cried my mother when she saw us troop in, kicking off the snow and stamping our feet on the red mat. "What are you doing here?"

"Wife!" my father said, striding up to her and taking her face in his hands. "I missed you so much!"

She went scarlet and twisted out of his grip like a hostile cat. She glared at me. "What's wrong with him?"

I shrugged. I could have said that when the brain heals, it leaves scar tissue. I could have said, to bypass old dead synapses and fried dendrites, the neurons jerry-rig new connections like someone stealing cable, and the person that emerges is never quite the same. I could have said, your husband is a different man now, but look on the bright side, you get all the novelty and excitement of a second husband with none of the inconvenience of divorce.

"He's hungry," I said.

We sat around a big round table in the back, and each time my father saw a familiar face he leapt from his seat and grabbed them in a big hug. When Big Pao came out carrying an exquisite tea-smoked duck, he seized and held him like a long-lost brother. Shocked, Big Pao glanced down at me for an explanation. Another shrug. But I was happy to see him. Big Pao was family, without all the complications. I was struck by how few people I recognized—how long since I'd been here?

Of course, complications are what *make* a family. Family is a pathology you spend a whole life trying to diagnose.

Steaming platters came and we dove in. The lazy Susan in the center of the table never stopped moving, as we loaded our plates with steamed fish pungent with garlic and ginger, silken tofu with sweet soy and scallions, braised pork domed over dried pickled vegetables, and anything else that my father called for. I should probably have been slowing him down—this was textbook post-fast binge eating. I could *see* what his stomach must have looked like, contracting over and over with nothing to calm it, its walls thick with pooled blood and sweating with its own digested fat, his intestines puffy and red. (The signals that convey hunger to the brain do not come from the stomach; the stomach is a relatively dumb organ, pounding away at whatever you put into it like a child with a big stick. Instead, it's up to the small intestine to let the brain know it's being starved of nutrients.) My dad was going to wind up bloated and moaning in a few hours and here I was, goading him on. When he forgot to order something, I'd call it out at the departing waiter. India and Eva were on either side of me and I was loading up their plates, urging them to eat more, try more. I heard things coming out of my mouth like "you *have* to taste this" and "wait no you need the sauce, here." There's nothing in the world like giving in to gluttony after spending a few hours with a dead person. Every bite becomes an act of gratitude that you are still here. This is why funerals have better food than weddings. Wedding food is catered, slung out of makeshift kitchens at scale, and designed to either sit in chafing dishes or be stable at room temperature. It's meant to look expensive but not *be* expensive, and it cannot be spicy. Wedding food is the corporate art of food.

Funeral food, however, is usually a glorious mess. Often a potluck, which under any other circumstances is a recipe for a dismal and incoherent evening—here, have a plate of chili, tabbouleh, cold stuffed mushrooms, and brownie bites from Trader Joe's—but somehow the act of cooking for the bereaved inspires home cooks to square up to the challenge. Funeral food is meant to console. It leans heavily on carbohydrates: macaroni and cheese, cinnamon rolls, thick noodles, buns, fried chicken. It's eaten gratefully, as a respite from awkward conversation, and guiltily, knowing that the person who has died will never taste another cinnamon bun again. Wedding food tastes like obligation. Funeral food? Defiance.

Eva had piled cold slippery gelatinous *liangpi* noodles on her plate and was prodding them with her chopstick, watching them jiggle.

"Eww," she breathed, excitedly. I was about to reproach her—it was one thing to express revulsion at a dead body who could not hear her, it was another thing entirely to do it in front of my dad—when she finagled a bunch of noodles into her mouth and closed her eyes, wincing at the *liangpi* coiling like a living thing around her tongue, insidious and cold. She struggled to swallow, but as she did, her lips curved into a weird, dazed smile. She wasn't struggling—she was savoring. Swiftly she collected more noodles and did it again, with the same reaction, all the while humming softly. It dawned on me that she was enjoying herself. And that she had been all day.

Whenever I'd asked her to reach into Sweeney's chest cavity she would emit these high pitched *eeee* noises, like a door creaking open on rusty hinges. It was annoying. She was clearly grossed out by autopsies, and was forcing herself to do this for the credit, the experience, the toughness, whatever. I didn't have time for it. But now I realized: she liked *feeling* grossed out. It had never occurred to me, because I never thought that one of them would understand: I knew this sensation—like ghostly fingers tickling the back of her neck. But for Eva there was a thrill in making these sounds, the thrill of vocalizing a physical sensation. The larynx is lush with nerve endings; it's a superb conductor of pleasure. (I reminded myself to save some of Sweeney's to study under the microscope.) What Eva was doing was physiologically no different from shrieking when whacking a tennis ball or moaning in pain or howling during sex.

I was fascinated. Not just in her—in all of them. Wei Wei had a look of childlike rapture on her face; I realized that my anger at her was gone, and I had an alarmingly maternal thought: when was the last time anyone had fed her real Chinese food? Even Bushwick seemed to have disembarked at last from the mental yacht he lived on, his aristocratically-white teeth tearing into scallion pancakes. Between bites India was looking at me accusingly.

"What," I finally said.

"Two years," she said.

"Yes?"

"Two years we been working together and I didn't even know this place was here. You been holding out on me."

"Yes," I smiled. "I have."

And that's when my fucking phone rang.

17.

Nine months later the kitchen phone rang.

It was the afternoon, around four, and August was breaking down a brace of rabbits. Ludovic, the host, poked his head into the kitchen and called, Eh, Big Ben! That was what they called August now, Big Ben; it had happened all the way back in his first month on the job, when he learned how to say Please teach me in French—montre moi s'il vous plaît—and thereafter used the phrase so constantly that the Roi Ubu brigade started calling him Le Montre, but then it was decided that since a watch was small and he was not, they should call him l'Horloge, but Julien, who with typical Gallic chauvinism saw no meaningful distinction between English and American culture, argued that August was no mere clock, he was Big Ben, and the nickname stuck.

Y'a une gonzesse qui te cherche, said Ludo, his beloved mustache smirking. There was simian hooting from Anouk in patisserie. It was known, for August had made it known, that for some time he had been shacked comfortably up with a woman named Martine who taught English at the local high school, and who was precisely twice his age. But it was not like Martine to call; it was Martine's way to simply arrive. Half of the kitchen knew her, having been her pupils once, and moreover, that was the way things seemed to happen here; if you wanted to see the person it was normal and fine to simply show up at their door and open it with a bright Coucou!, which was the kind of behavior that back in Queens would have resulted in assault, followed by acquittal. It was thanks to Martine (and, in the case of Magnus and Albert, Bruce Willis) that August had learned to communicate with the staff at all.

Apporte moi, said August, laying his knife flat on a rabbit's spine and cracking it with a burly fist. They had been delivered skinned and gutted but otherwise intact, their blue eyes lidless. He was carving the meat from the ribs and flanks and tying it with string into tidy little roulades. The bones would go the way of all bones, into the stockpot, the first step on the rainbow bridge to sauce.

Apporte-*le* moi, Ludovic corrected him. To carry you I need cows and a wagon. August grunted and nodded to his shoulder, indicating that Ludovic should wedge the cordless phone in there.

Oui, said August, his neck crooked awkwardly to hold the phone in place.

On ne dit pas *oui* au téléphone, on dit *allo*, called the departing Ludovic.

August? said a woman's voice.

August put down the knife.

Mom.

I'm sorry to bother you, I'm sure you're working.

I mean, I'm sorry I haven't called lately, it's just really expensive to call from here, said August, truthfully. It cost ludicrous amounts to call New York, and the 35 francs per hour they were paying him were barely enough to keep him fed on his off days. But then, even when he'd just been living a 25-cent pay phone call away, he didn't call much.

He added, But I'm fine.

That's good, Isabelle said. It's nice to hear your voice. I'm calling from the hospital.

The hospital? August dropped his voice to a whisper. What happened? Are you okay?

Your father had a heart attack.

Oh, fuck, said August.

The doctors say he's stable now, and he should be able to come home in a few days. And when he does—

Oh Christ, said August, oh fuck.

And when he *does*, Isabelle continued, I know he would like you to be there.

August barreled past his old little alcove, now occupied by Etienne, a whippet of a local boy who was the new stagiaire, and shoved open the back door of the kitchen. The day was windless and hot. Tiny white snails clung in bunches to the tall grass and August kicked them off as he listened to his mother.

Thomas had been at the club, Isabelle said. His weekly squash game. Collapsed in the middle of a point. She wasn't crying, but her voice sounded subdued. Gaunt, if a voice could be gaunt. The doctors said that he had enormous amounts of plaque on his arteries. More than he had any right to have. His cholesterol was much higher than it should have been—he was only fifty-five, and she had thought he was in good shape.

I can't just buy a plane ticket, said August. They're barely paying me enough for gas.

Don't be ridiculous, said Isabelle. We'll pay for the plane ticket.

Mom, he said, I can't just *leave*. The tourist season is about to start. They need me.

No, they don't. Your *father* needs you.

For how long?

I don't know, August, she sighed. I don't know anything right now. All I know is your father wants you here.

Is Jack coming back?

Jack's in school. He has finals.

And I can?

The silence on the other end was as clear as an ad in Times Square.

The day he had decided to stay, he had returned the car to the Europcar in Avignon and taken the bus back. For while, he walked everywhere. He didn't mind it. The villagers started to take an interest in this giant American they would see trundling along the side of the road. A man offered to sell him a mule, and August imagined himself riding into the market like Jesus into Jerusalem (his Jesuit education had not been entirely wasted), but chose not to, for the mule's sake. And he didn't know how long he would be staying. Until he had learned everything he needed to know, he supposed.

He spent the month of September badgering Baratin to put him on payroll, making sure he was the first into the kitchen in the morning and the last out. Finally Baratin agreed, and August bought a pummeled old Peugeot and fell instantly in love with it. He met Martine in the market one day in October—Anouk was the one who introduced them. When Le Roi Ubu closed for the winter, Baratin found him a stage in a bistro in Lyon, where they taught him butter sorcery and the mysteries of tripe. There he discovered why it had been that when he spitefully added kidney and brains to the menu at Timo's, customers inhaled them: kidney and brains were *good.* The way they fought him, the way they *felt* messy, was good in the way playing football was good, in the way it felt downright voluptuous to smash your body into another person's body and go crashing to the ground together and plough up the dirt and grass and spring to your feet unhurt and vibrating like a struck gong, ready to do it all over again on the next down. For months August ate and cooked every bitter, iron-rich, blood-thick inner organ he could. But still the week in March Le Roi Ubu reopened he drove south at 150 kilometers per hour and showed up at Martine's cottage door with a rosette Lyonnais and a bottle of champagne, or at least what was left over from his drive. They didn't even make it to the couch. August was cushion enough.

Mom, said August. This is my job.

And this is your *family.* It's time to come home.

August walked to the patio and looked out over the valley where all those months ago he and a boar had silently conferred. It was so *green* now. Soon, he knew, the lavender would bloom and it would be ablaze in purple, but for now, the green was almost primeval. It seemed to touch some part of him that had once swung from trees and gone around on its knuckles. He had never seen the boar again, but he had never—and as long as he lived, would never—forgotten how he had sat there, transfixed, even long after the boar had trotted off. He had sat there until dawn rose, until his ass went numb in the wrought-iron chair, until Magnus and Albert trundled down bleary-eyed to start setting up for service.

He wasn't so sure where home was anymore. And what did they even expect him to *do* at this point? He wasn't a doctor, wasn't a nurse. He knew nothing about taking care of people. And Dad was fine now, his mom had said so. She was just panicking—he knew that half an hour after he got home, he and his father would run out of things to talk about, and he'd just be in the way. He'd wind up back at Timo's slinging goulash and he'd never get out of Queens.

Mom, he said, finally. I can't.

It was nearly midnight, but Martine awoke; it was impossible not to whenever August Sweeney slunk into bed. But August was also making no effort to be subtle; the moment his head met pillow he groaned with a noise like an upright piano dragged over a hardwood floor.

Mm? said Martine, nuzzling up to him sleepily and running her fingers through his chest hair, then curving downward toward his groin. This was her typical evening greeting. It didn't always lead to sex; she just liked holding his balls. Some nights she would go back to sleep with her fingers laced tenderly into his pubic hair, and he would have to pry them off so that he could sleep too.

My mother called, he said.

Ah oui? Et elle voulait quoi?

She said I have to come home.

Ça m'étonne, she murmured, resting her head on his big shoulder. Her hair was a spray of brown curls that worked into his skin.

My fucking dad had a heart attack, August said.

Martine shot upright in bed, stark naked, and switched on the lamp.

So you are going?

Don't worry, I'm not leaving you, August said, reassuring her and reaching out to caress her left breast, his favorite.

She smacked his hand, and then his head.

Tu blagues? Your father has a heart attack and your mother asks you to come home et tu lui dis non?

Sure did.

In a fury she rose from the bed, swept the bedsheets around her, and strode out of the bedroom. Bewildered, August scrambled after her.

Wait! He's fine! She's just overreacting!

He found her in the living room, which was decorated with Japanese masks, all of which seemed to glower at him from the walls. Swathed in the bedsheet Martine resembled a Roman senator, and she spoke with imperiousness. Suddenly he felt naked. He *was* naked, but now he felt it acutely.

What kind of person are you? Your father almost dies and you feel *nothing*?

That's ridiculous!

Alors c'est très simple. You will get on the airplane.

It's not simple at all! They need me here. I need to be here. *You* need me to be here.

She dismissed him with a snort that held the full weight of French contempt at its core, like a roll of quarters clenched in a fist. All three hundred bare-assed pounds of him sank back on the couch as if she'd run him through with a sword. With Martine, he hadn't just fallen in love in his usual volcanic idiom—this time, the flames had kept right on burning, like a subterranean coal fire. This time he needed her like steak needed salt. And until this moment he'd assumed that she felt the same.

She picked up a packet of cigarettes from the dining table and lit one. Then she offered him one. He shook his head. This always happened to August when someone confronted him—suddenly it was like his throat dried up and his tongue shriveled. He'd never had a good comeback in his life. It was okay in a kitchen, where he could just work harder, do better, but with Martine he was helpless.

You don't understand, she said, her voice damp with smoke. How can I say. I cannot have children. You know this.

August did know. The first time she had told him this, August said, with perfect seriousness, Cool, so we don't have to use condoms, and Martine burst out laughing and kissed him on the mouth. But she wasn't laughing now.

So? he said sullenly. He couldn't believe she was attacking him for wanting to stay here—stay with her.

So I do not know about being a mother. I don't mind. There are lots of mothers in the world. But I do not have to be a mother to know when a child is full of shit.

I'm not a child, said August.

Yes, cheri. She knelt next to him and cupped his cheek in her palm. You are.

August lolled his head back on the couch and stared at the ceiling beams for a long time. Martine stroked his hair and waited. Finally, with his eyes still fixed on the ceiling, he said, I don't know what I'm supposed to do.

She folded her arms. Faux.

What?

You know what you have to do. You just don't want to.

But I'm not done here yet, he addressed the ceiling.

Why do you make this face. Le Roi Ubu, it is not the best restaurant in France, hein? T'es pas chez Bocuse quand même. I am not the only woman. And I am not more important than your mother.

She got up and picked up the telephone from its mount on the wall and handed it to him. Vas-y. Call her. Do the right thing.

Or?

Or, she said, picking up her cigarette from the ashtray and taking a meditative drag, you can get out of my house.

And so August took a deep breath and dialed. The housekeeper Magda picked up. His mother wasn't there. She was at the hospital because it was the middle of the afternoon and his father was still there so she was still there, so Magda gave him the number for the hospital and August called the hospital and asked the operator for Thomas Sweeney's room and almost hung up three times, apologizing to Martine for how expensive this call was, but she just laid her head on his great pillowy belly and cradled her fingers around his balls as if to say goodbye, and when his mother picked up the phone and August said Mom, I think I need a plane ticket, she burst into tears. Two days later the airplane's wheels floated off the tarmac and August realized he had made a terrible mistake.

August dropped his giant duffel bag on the blue foyer carpet with a violent thud and barreled past the startled Magda, who flattened herself against the wall to let him pass.

I'm HO-OME, he bellowed, stampeding into the family room. Everything in the Sweeney's Lexington Avenue apartment was as it had ever been. The wall-to-wall carpeting was still an unblemished cream color. Framed prints of impressionist landscapes, the lower third devoted to the details of their museum shows, projected a calm into the room. The scent of the place was instantly familiar to him, a sort of fragrantly chemical aroma, like some combination of his mother's perfume and Magda's cleaning supplies. The pillows of the green-and-gold upholstered couch had been fluffed invitingly, and August obliged them, toppling like a fallen tree into its cushions. His limbs were still stiff and cramped from being crammed into his middle seat for nine hours.

Hey! Hello? Where is everyone? he cried, prone.

Isabelle came trotting down the hallway, shushing him vehemently. August bounced off the couch and swept her up in a hug. He hadn't expected to be so happy to see her.

I missed you, ma! he said, even though he hadn't known it until that very moment.

You did? she said, her eyes widening in authentic surprise.

Of course! Where's the old man? said August.

Shh! she put a finger to her lips, around which August noticed wrinkles he'd never seen there before. Keep it down. He's asleep! Come into the kitchen.

Once in the kitchen, August started checking the cupboards, taking stock. There wasn't much. Beans, spaghetti, tuna. Table salt and a canister of ground pepper that had definitely been there before he went to France.

How was your flight? asked his mother, not knowing quite what else to say.

Long, he grunted. I'm starving. The food was a fuckin joke—shit, sorry, he said, remembering his parents' allergy to swearing as he opened the refrigerator, and his heart sank.

The boeuf Bourguignon on Air France had only added to his gloom, since it had never been anywhere near Burgundy, was only glancingly acquainted with beef, and had all been gone much too quickly—but on the flight over a notion had taken hold that he ought to cook something for his father, who he presumed had been eating nothing but hospital food for days; that stuff could cause you to give up on life entirely. And Martine had done such a number on him, guiltwise, that he'd wallowed in his own shame all the way up to Paris on the TGV, and then halfway across the ocean, which is where he realized that the only way he could make it up to his parents was to show them that he had not just been dicking around for the past ten months. He would cook his way out of the guilt.

It was summer in New York, so he imagined something light, like sole in lemon butter and a frisee aux lardons. But the moment he opened the fridge door those thoughts were banished.

A yellowish casserole leached oil in a baking dish. There was a ragged sphere of shrink-wrapped iceberg lettuce, a Ziploc bag of watery turkey breast in wax paper, and a few batting-practice tomatoes. In the door were some bottles of seltzer and a carton of Swanson low-sodium chicken broth. The butter drawer had become the I Can't Believe It's Not Butter drawer. A tub of Folger's moldered in the back beside a jar of—August recoiled—fat-free mayonnaise.

August had forgotten shit like this existed. Was this how *he'd* eaten?

Sixteen hours ago, he and Martine had shared a final breakfast: sliced velvety tomatoes from her garden laid on a toasted pain de campagne, glossed with olive oil, glinting with fleur de sel. They'd peeled open blood oranges—he could still feel the white pith under his fingernails. Then he'd gone down on her like a condemned man savoring his last meal.

Let me fix you a turkey sandwich, said his mother.

Baratin had always said, it's not quality of the ingredients that matters, it's the technique of the cook. With proper technique you can make anything work.

And butter, said August.

Obviously, snorted Baratin. You are not Jesus Christ.

Well, August thought now, Baratin had never gone up against the D'Agostino's on 88th and 3rd.

Before Provence, August had had no complaints about the American supermarket. But now he saw his parents' local grocery store for what it truly was: Hell's garde-manger. Crude, sinister lampoons of produce leapt out at him as he pushed his cart through the aisles, flinching at pinball-shiny apples and brussels sprouts you could have golfed with and engorged cabbages and thick-skinned green grapes, all of it engineered not for flavor, but for survival on the slow boat from Bolivia. Farmed tilapia and flounder fillets were caked in freezer burn. The meat section was a slight improvement; amid the hulking mounds of ground turkey in Styrofoam and hormone-swollen chickens, he found duck breast and prosciutto, and briefly rejoiced—that is, until he came to the bakery section. There was a basket of erect "French baguettes" sheathed in white paper sleeves. Eagerly he grasped one, and it wobbled like a pool noodle.

What kind of asshole did you have to be to even *make* this stuff, much less call it a baguette? This wasn't a baguette. This wasn't even bread. It was Nerf.

As August stood there, forlornly waving a loaf of bread back and forth, he saw the truth spelled out as huge and shimmering as pink neon balloon letters painted on the side of the 6 train: he had been cast out of heaven like Lucifer in the stories the Jesuits told him. He'd always thought Lucifer was a bad-ass. "Better to reign in hell than serve in heaven?" Indisputably bad-ass! Only now for the first time, did he understand what Lucifer's rebellion had cost him.

Of course this wasn't Hell, it was D'Agostino's. His punishment was not to burn, but to live as an enlightened man among the suffering. The only redemption lay in bringing them Truth. If ever he was to glimpse that haven of grace and warmth that he'd known at Martine's again, it would be because he built it for himself here, on this blasted earth, somewhere between the Lean Cuisines and the Hi-C.

Grimly he flipped the shambolic baguette into the cart, and trudged to the dairy aisle. If he was going to build himself a home here, a place he could minister to the fallen and benighted, he sure as fuck wouldn't be doing it with margarine.

Three hours later, August had pulled off something of a miracle, given what D'Agostino's had given him to work with—and that was before he confronted the equipment in his mother's kitchen. The flimsy pans were bowed in the middle from overheating, such that a knob of butter dropped onto the center fled at once to the outer rim of the pan. The pots were so thin he might as well have been placing the food directly on the electric coils. The one cast-iron pan had been scoured to gritty roughness; protein clung to it like Velcro. He'd taken one look at his mother's knife drawer and despaired. Years of being flung callously into the dishwasher had dulled the knives' sheen and edge to where they weren't even good for slicing cake. He missed the beat-up but indestructible pans at Le Roi Ubu, the fine-meshed *chinoises* that hung from the ceiling, and most of all the three beautiful copper pots that they used for sauces, which Habib the dishwasher cared for as if they were his own daughters. Thank God he still had his own knives in his duffel.

The duck breasts were hissing and smoking in the pan when his father appeared, padding unsteadily into the kitchen in his bathrobe and slippers. His hair was carefully combed, but he hadn't shaved in a few days. August had never seen him with facial hair. August had an apron knotted around his waist and his hair tied back and a tea towel over his shoulder. His first instinct was to wrap him up in his arms, but the man standing before him now appeared so fragile and gaunt that August—who had long ago learned to be careful of his strength—didn't know whether he should touch him. Besides, the Sweeneys were not a hugging family. It was not that they never hugged, it was more that when it was expected of them, on occasions like graduations, reunions, departures, they performed the action stiffly and gingerly, and broke apart with a stoic nod of the head that said, "well, *that's* taken care of." But now his father came over to him and held him, his arms more frail than August remembered. He felt a nervous tingle in his elbows—his father had always been solid. That was the word for him. Solid. No one would have called him the life of the party or a leader of men. Instead, Thomas Sweeney was the human version of a cast-iron pan. Slow to get heated, never flashy, and built to last a hundred years. At least, that's how August had remembered him.

The beard is dope, said August.

Your hair's too long, Thomas said into his son's shoulder.

An hour later the three of them were sitting around the table, while from the kitchen came the sounds of Magda cleaning up the colossal mess he'd made. August was deeply pleased with himself. With resourcefulness, ingenuity, and an entire tin of foie gras (this was the Upper East Side, after all; they weren't Visigoths), he had flung together a meal that even Julien would have been impressed by. Still, the conversation around the table was muted. It was as if now that he was finally here, no one quite knew what to do with him.

So honey, said his mother, how was France?

How was France? The question was insane. It was like asking him to describe the sensation of walking on the moon, or the taste of a 40 year-old Bordeaux. It was like asking him to capture a solar flare and stuff it into a Christmas stocking. The fuck was he supposed to say? Should he tell them about the cold bloody satisfaction of butchering ten rabbits? Should he describe the giddy exhilaration of sliding his Peugeot home through mountain roads at night, his brains smoked with wine and cognac and hashish? Should he speak of the sublime anxiety of finishing a sauce with butter, trembling as the sauce hovered on the knife-edge between life and death, a culinary version of autoerotic asphyxiation?

It changed my life, he said.

Well then, said Thomas.

That's wonderful, said Isabelle. This is all very impressive.

He *wanted* to tell them. But he knew that the moment he started to explain he'd feel like a cat who, having proudly brought its owner a gift, is mystified when the owner sweeps that gift up with a dustpan, retching audibly, and flings it, tasty mangled guts and all, into the trash. There was a reason he hadn't been here in over a year; even before he went to France, the Sweeneys had never exactly been the Sunday-dinner kind of family. After all, every time he did come, they grimaced as he regaled them with stories from Timo's. When he'd told them about Ivor hurling the suit out of the restaurant, he was laughing so hard tears were brimming in his eyes, until his mother pushed her chair back from the table and stamped off to the kitchen, where she began making a very pointed racket before returning, storm-faced, to bang the ham and broccoli casserole on the table.

Inevitably, at some point during these visits one of his parents would remind him that there was a job waiting for him at Grayson. They understood, they said, that he was having fun. But didn't he have ambitions? Where did he see himself in five years, they'd ask? And the truth was—or until now, had been—that August saw himself still at Timo's. Why would he want to change? You didn't get into this job to make money. That wasn't what it was about. He knew that there were chefs who had a lot of restaurants, but that just seemed like more time in the office, and less time on the line, where he was happy.

To Thomas and Isabelle this was just more evidence of his immaturity: a man did not do a job to be *happy*, he did it to be secure—not for himself, but for his family. Not that they expected August to have one of those anytime soon.

He had to change the subject. So August took a gulp of wine and said the first thing that came to his head.

Hey Dad, what's a heart attack feel like anyway?

Isabelle's fork clanked against her plate.

August, that is morbid, she said.

Thomas smiled wanly. It's okay, heart, he said, putting his hand on hers. I don't mind.

Like, it hurts, right? August asked.

Thomas pondered, looking vaguely past his right elbow. Not really, he said. I don't think it hurt. It was more like I was sliding downward, and it all felt very fast but also very slow. Circling a drain, maybe. Or like how a leaf falls from a tree.

He held out his hand, palm down, and made a swerving, declining movement. It was like I was swaying and falling all at the same time, he said.

Were you like, Oh shit, I'm having a heart attack? said August, taking a bite of duck. Not bad, he thought—basing the glaze on the cherry filling scooped out of a store-bought cherry pie had been a stroke of genius; it was tart and sweet and a little synthetic, but a good synthetic, like an airbrushed Playboy centerfold. He hoped the Folger's he used for the tiramisu would hold up too.

Thomas reflected. No. I don't think I did. I couldn't connect it to a specific idea like Heart Attack. I couldn't think. I couldn't move, either—or I couldn't stop myself from moving. I knew I was falling but there wasn't anything I could do to stop it. That was what really scared me.

It scared all of us, dear, but it's over now, said Isabelle with finality. I'm sure your father would prefer not to dwell on it.

It's all right, said Thomas. The boy wants to understand.

August knew that tone. It was the same tone his dad had deployed for endless fatherly lectures when he was a child. And just like that, his interest evaporated.

Too hard to die, right? Said August, raising his glass to his father. They clinked, and August swallowed his wine in one go. Thomas, however, merely moistened his lips on his glass before putting it down.

It was then that August noticed his father's plate. The mushrooms, long-simmered in fragrant *beurre noisette*, were congealing in a heap.

His gorgeous duck breast ballotine, lovingly inlaid with foie gras, had been pushed into the oozing gratin dauphinois like an innocent man being shoved in front of a subway train. The cherry glaze had hemorrhaged into the creamy potatoes.

What, you don't like it? said August.

It's very good, said Isabelle, who had at least eaten more than her husband.

Oh, very good, agreed Thomas, and hesitantly pried a single mushroom off the heap and put it in his mouth. I'm just not used... It's just very rich?

That's the point, said August. You look like Skeletor just got out of the shower. I bet the only thing they've been feeding you for days is chicken soup and saltines. How are you supposed to get better if you don't eat nothing?

Dear, said his mother, the doctors were very clear—

Yeah, yeah, August waved dismissively, but come on, one meal's not gonna kill you. You beat the reaper, man! You gotta celebrate!

He clapped his father on the back, shaking him effusively. He was just trying to liven up the situation—why was everyone acting like it was a funeral when no one died?

Meekly, Thomas raised a parsimonious, foie-gras-free forkful of duck breast to his mouth and chewed it slowly. The muscles around his lips tightened nervously.

I'm sorry, he said, I just don't seem to have much of an appetite right now.

August understood. It wasn't that his father didn't like the dinner. It was that he was afraid of it.

August had never been sick before—not properly, truly, immobilizingly sick. An ox-healthy child, he had never got the flu, never got stomach bugs. Consequently, he had always imagined sickness as basically a vacation where one lay on the couch and watched limitless daytime television, in much the same way as he imagined prison to be a place where you got ripped as hell from working out in the yard all day. To August, a heart attack was where you seized up and clutched your chest, and then they put the jumper cables on you and yelled CLEAR and then you were shook up but okay.

But his father didn't seem okay. Not even close.

In the weeks to come, August saw his dad turtle into himself. Having learned his lesson with the duck, August resolved to make simple foods his old man liked. But when he made him his favorite sandwich, he felt his heart break when he saw Thomas patiently remove the bacon, set it aside, and eat the lettuce, tomato, and mayo remains. If it had just been the food—he'd never really cared about food to begin with—it would have been all right, but the fear only spread. If a TV show got too stressful during its climax, Thomas would quietly take himself out of the room. He flinched at passing sirens. But what really killed August wasn't just his dad's sudden fearfulness—it was how he seemed to have given in to it without a fight. Fear was just a fact of his life now, like his bald spot, and like his bald spot, it would only grow. And worse, it wasn't the world that scared him. It was his own body. There was no escaping the fact that at any moment his heart could try to kill him again and there'd be nothing he could do.

August found himself walking on eggshells around his father-or at least trying to. More and more, the Sweeneys' apartment felt to August like the middle seat of an airplane—no matter which shape he twisted his body into he couldn't get comfortable, and the food was awful.

So he did the only thing one can do in a middle seat: hit the sauce. He started going out each night to clear his head, which for August meant walking to the bars on 2nd avenue and staying until the walls were moving to his satisfaction. When he got tired of drinking alone he called up Sidney Feinbaum, now a junior trader at Bear Stearns and self-described douchebag swimming in money and cocaine. Sidney introduced him to other douchebags who had more money and more cocaine, and who at first thought that having a six-foot-nine cook come out clubbing with them was a superb reason to deliberately pick fights with bouncers, bartenders, and boyfriends, which did not end well for the douchebags, who did not understand that August was not about to strike a fellow employee of the hospitality industry, at least not without cause. It was not that August disliked fighting. He liked fighting. He just didn't like being hid behind.

But the douchebags kept him around, because August was indisputably a good time. No one they'd ever met could eat more, drink more, talk shit more. Years in the kitchen meant August was more than fluent in the dick-centric demotic of the trading rooms of Wall Street. And August, for his part, was happy to tolerate the douchebags. He'd never eaten so well—or at least so opulently.

Every night they seemed to go to another throbbing, glitz-soaked restaurant, with leggy models arrayed at the bar drinking neon cocktails, wine lists where the bottles cost half a month's rent, and menus flush with things he didn't even know you could eat, like sea urchin and fried grasshopper. There were restaurants located underground like blue-lit nuclear bunkers and restaurants on the 107th floor of the World Trade Center. There were restaurants with giant glittering waterfalls and restaurants where the light fixtures were fashioned out of fedoras. Sidney and the douchebags used restaurant reservations like switchblades in a never-ending knife fight. August hadn't realized that people could get this competitive about where they ate. He didn't entirely understand why, since a lot of the food they were eating seemed pretty goofy to him, like little lobster morsels sitting in a passion fruit coulis.

This shit reads like Mad Libs, August said to Sidney one night, staring at options like Green Peppercorn Soufflé.

One of the douches scoffed. August, man, you gotta expand your culinary horizons. Turning to the waiter, he said confidently, I'll have the Eel Flottante.

But the cocaine was exquisite. He felt like Superman inhaling the energy of Earth's yellow sun. The next day, of course, he would awaken with a distinct sense of having been charred over a long slow flame, his mouth as dry as the inside of a crumpled bag of potato chips. It would be about 2pm, but so much the better—the later he woke up, the less he had to try to figure out what to do with the daylight hours. His goal was to ensure that each day, he would be in no state to do the thing he dreaded most of all: walk back into Timo's.

18.

Let me say up front that there is nothing erotic about dead bodies. I shouldn't have to say this but. Any pathologist will admit that when they are with live bodies it is hard not to think of them as dead. It's an occupational hazard. My variation is that after I am with dead bodies, I sometimes go out and look for live bodies that look like them. Not always. Inevitably many of my patients are geriatric, and while I have tried that—and it is fascinating (they are adoring and attentive, the women hiding their vulnerability with sarcasm and the men indefatigable with Cialis)—the proximity is too jarring. The line between alive and dead is too fine, so that I can begin to see what's coming for them, and I become uncomfortable. I always examine sexual partners clinically, but only the elderly know I'm doing it because they're doing it, too, each time they look in the mirror. It ruins the postcoital mood.

I'd known since the minute I unzipped his bag this morning that when I was finished with August Sweeney I was going to go in search of someone his size. By size I meant his enormity. The sheer *amount* of person he contained. People with bodies like his, with coils of muscle buried under fat, always feel like a thick memory foam topper on a very firm mattress. I wanted someone with that kind of endlessness, someone whose body would be a whole Hudson River School landscape, teeming with life. A man I could practically hike. And there was also the exciting thought that he could always throw me right out the window. I understand this is all perverse. But I've been reliably informed there is no ethical consumption under capitalism.

In my head I had been envisioning a football player, a bouncer, someone professionally immense, but in all cases it had been a man. That is, until the moment I entered Dr. Mandragola's office, abruptly summoned from lunch with my father by a phone call, and sitting there in his taupe Italian-leather armchair was a woman who could only have been August Sweeney's daughter.

As head of pathology, Mario Mandragola was entitled to a moderately palatial office, at least by the standards of a brutalist hospital building from the 1970s. There were wooden bookshelves behind his desk, and the wide windows faced the East River, but otherwise the walls were sheetrock and the radiator was thick with white paint. To compensate, he'd appointed it in his preferred style: conspicuously expensive. Hand-stitched leather. Blown-glass *objets*. Diplomas in mirrored-steel frames. The chair at his microscope desk he said he bought at Basel. And compared to the cool, assured elegance of the huge woman sitting before me, the office might as well have been a freshman dorm at a state college.

"Dr. Zhu, I'd like you to meet Astrid Sweeney," said Mandragola unctuously.

"Ms. Sweeney. I'm Dr. Zhu. I'm very sorry for your loss," I said. This is what I always say. I do not try to sell it; patients do not want me to actually be sorry. They just want the death to have been inevitable. It isn't always.

"So you're the one," she shook my hand, but did not stand from her chair. She wore a powder-blue suit. Not the usual uniform of the grieving daughter. Her hair was the hue of autumn leaves and had not been styled so much as laser-cut; her eyes were cold as chambered bullets. No red rimming around the orbitals. Her makeup was immaculate. This was not a woman in the throes of grief.

But there was her face, and there was the rest of her, and the rest of her left no doubt whose daughter she was: Her size was imperial, her proportions perfectly classical, from the tapering of her calves to the carved swerve of her jaw. She was the shape of Rembrandt's Bathsheba, of Gentileschi's Judith; I wanted to spy on her bathing, and I wanted her to cut my head off with a jeweled dagger.

I was so boggled at her presence that I almost missed what she said. What did she mean, you're the one. Words were having trouble assembling in my mouth. "I want you to know Ms. Sweeney that his—your father's—gift means, uh, a lot to this department, and to the students, and us…"

She folded her arms and glared at Mandragola. "Uh huh. Let me get this straight. Not only does he choose to do this without telling us, but he chooses this—no offense—girl to do it?"

"Dr. Zhu is a brilliant autopsist, Ms. Sweeney," said Mandragola, and I wished I had that in writing and notarized.

"But you're the department head. And you know who my father was?" The way she said *was* so easily intimidated me. Most families, children especially, struggle with the verb tense shift, from present to past. Not Astrid Sweeney. "So why aren't *you* doing this…" she waved her hand in revulsion "…thing. You're telling me my dad specifically requested her?"

My eyes went wide.

"He did. Or his lawyer did. As part of his bequest, he apparently stipulated—" he rifled through a few folders and handed over a document "—that his body be donated to science, and that Dr. Maya Zhu perform his autopsy, and then release the results to you and your mother."

I could feel numbness in my hands. How could he even know my name? Then I realized how it looked to her—to everyone. Young woman, famous man? The math was obvious. I struggled to keep composure. In front of a woman like her, this angry, we couldn't afford to look like the head didn't know what the hands were doing. But the hand had been deliberately left in the dark on this one. The hand was actually getting pretty angry at the head right now.

He could have warned me and he didn't. All he'd said when I picked up the phone—just as the tiger prawns with XO sauce hit the table—was, "Dr. Zhu, could you come to my office right away. Thank you." Then he hung up. That was it.

If Mandragola had thought about it for half a second he'd have realized he'd forced me to walk into this situation completely blind. I didn't imagine he cared about me—I certainly did not care about him— but he should have known better than to make me a liability here. An enraged family member was a pathologist's nightmare. Giving me a heads-up would have protected both of us. It was stupid of him, and I knew that Mandragola was not stupid (he was not exceptionally smart either, but that's an asset, for a department head). Maybe it was invigorating for men to be performatively stupid in front of a woman—God, what a woman—like Astrid Sweeney. That's what power really was: to not need to think things through, because other people would clean up your mess.

"That's absurd. My father didn't give a shit about science. He didn't give a shit about anything but cooking. Why would he even know what an autopsy was—and why would he pick some random…" She trailed off. Her eyes narrowed. Suddenly she stood and drew herself to her full magnificent height and glared down at me. "What kind of relationship *did* you have with my father?"

The way she leaned into the *did*, as if we'd all agreed I was sleeping with him and now the only question was the nature of the arrangement, unclogged something in my brain. The words came back and I chose them carefully. "I'm very sorry, I don't know what you're talking about. Your father and I didn't have any relationship."

Technically I was not lying. We didn't have a relationship. But I wasn't about to let her know what *had* happened.

I remembered the way he seemed to exert his own gravity, drawing me in. I remembered, because his fucking daughter was towering above me, all wrath and tits—her father's perfect feminine image—and she was doing the same number on me now.

She sized me up, scanning for lies. But panicked or not, I am nothing if not good at deceiving white people. I needed to defuse this situation.

"Ms. Sweeney, I'm sure there's been a misunderstanding. Your father and I were strangers." (Not a lie!) "And I'm sure his death must have come as a shock to you." (There is no earthly way it did.) "I'm wondering—did he never discuss his plans for anatomical bequest with you?" Using legal language with families tends to smooth their image of an autopsy into some kind of acceptable bureaucratic formality. It's one less decision for them to make at a difficult time.

"Anatomical bequest?" she snorted. "You mean carving him like a cow at the butcher's."

"That's not really what we—" Mandragola began in his most soothing teaching voice, but Astrid wasn't done.

"Of course he never talked about it with me." This woman could talk over men like they were television ads. I was speechless with longing. "We don't talk."

When August had started talking about her, I'd shut him down. Now I wanted to know everything. Usually I don't want people to tell me their secrets, but in the rare instances that I do, I know to shut my mouth until they get nervous and fill the silence. Activate Asian inscrutability. A trick I learned from my mother, whose method of balancing her general neglect was to mother me in punctuated high-intensity bursts, which meant interrogating me like a terror suspect. I folded my arms like she did, tilted my chin up slightly, and waited.

She looked out Mandragola's window at the Queensboro Bridge, an unlovely span of white trestlework I've always liked—it's the only bridge in New York that's all skeleton and no pretension. It's the bridge we always crossed in the minivan when we drove from Forest Hills to 47th St, where Xinghuacun was.

"I hadn't seen him in years. He was a shitty dad. He married my mom, cheated on her, and after the divorce treated us like we were a problem he could throw money at." I was impressed: usually even family members who loathed the deceased won't speak ill of them, at least not to others. Astrid didn't care. Her tone was unsentimental and practiced, the voice of a woman who was accustomed to ending conversations about her famous father quickly. But then she turned her piercing blue eyes on me. "But that doesn't mean I'm comfortable with any of this. Why do you even need an autopsy anyway? It's not like we don't know why he died. The man was an alcoholic who ate a pound of butter a day."

"All I can tell you, Ms. Sweeney, is what you've already seen. These were his wishes, as stipulated in his will and conveyed to us by his attorney." Mandragola was good in such situations. He'd risen up from the subterranean depths of the lab to this panorama thanks to his talent for quelling the misgivings that both doctors and donors tended to feel about pathologists. Even for the vast majority of us who haven't touched a cadaver since board certification, we have a PR problem: we make the rest of the medical world uncomfortable. Other doctors treat us the way cops treat Internal Affairs officers. Drug companies do not take us out for opulent dinners. The only perk of this job was that it blunted the fear of death. When I was in med school, the future pathologists were objects of pity and mistrust, who would soon be replaced by computers anyhow. "You'll just be a microscope jockey," I was told. We were bloodless walking textbooks who cared about sickness more than about patients and had no stomach for the real difficulties doctors faced. Unlike, I supposed, those poor dermatologists, who had three homes and saw patients once a week and spent the rest of their time sailing or exploring polyamory.

"You mean that walking sexual-harassment lawsuit Moe Eckstein?" Astrid said. "What exactly did he tell you?" I was wondering the same thing.

"He said that your father knew that there was a Dr. Zhu here, and that as part of his bequest, he wanted her to be the one who performed his autopsy. He also specified that his brain be given a full neurological screen, his genome mapped, and his skeleton donated to…" Mandragola made a show of checking his notes "…Xavier High School."

What did she do for a living? I was good at guessing what people did from their naked bodies—and I was fighting a losing battle with my brain to keep from imagining hers—but when they put clothes on I was hopeless. I didn't process clothes intelligently. One perk of my job was that I spent my life in scrubs I got out of a glorified vending machine. Her suit was well-made, her shoes sensible but elegant. She had the still-regenerating skin of a woman in her early 20s, but everything about her gave the impression of a woman comfortable with power. She had the directness and clipped delivery of a lawyer, but the sheer amount of color in the outfit, from the humid blue of her suit to the tint of violet in the eye shadow, seemed unconservative for a lawyer. Also, if she were a lawyer, she'd have said so already. If lawyers could carry their degree around in a holster they would.

Television, I thought. It has to be television. Family business.

"But I'm his next of kin. I'm his only child. You're telling me there's nothing I can do to stop this?"

Heat prickled on the back of my neck. She was trying to take him away from me. But since when was he mine? Since when did I feel possessive about bodies? I didn't like this. I didn't like any of this.

"Unfortunately," said Mandragola, "your father granted Mr. Eckstein power of attorney. So in this case, as his executor, it's up to him to give consent, which he did. But the good news is, Dr. Zhu is already nearly done with your father's autopsy. Isn't that right?"

I nodded with vigor, as if we hadn't broken for lunch with the man's entire organ trunk still intact on the dissection table like a great blood-soaked bunch of bananas, and his brain and eyes still firmly inside his skull. I hoped India had led them back to the lab quickly after lunch.

"So what, then, his skeleton goes to his high school?" she said. "And I get what. No body. No open casket."

"I understand you're grieving, Ms. Sweeney," I said. "But this was what your father wanted. I know it's hard to see right now, but he was doing this for you. Everything we find out, we'll share with you. His whole medical history, every genetic predisposition and neural pathology—it's all yours." I can do bedside manner when I have to.

"So that's all I get," she said. "A fucking medical file."

"Ms. Sweeney," said Mandragola.

"Nothing to bury. Fine. He wasn't there when I was a kid, why change a winning game now." Her voice cracked. *Please don't cry.* "He was Irish, for God's sake. You're supposed to have a fucking wake. You're supposed to look at the body and drink and do Rock the Boat. What am I supposed to do for a funeral, put a fucking manila folder in an open casket and light a candle?"

"We regularly offer support to families who make anatomical bequests," Mandragola said. "It's very common for families to hold memorial serv-"

"I want to see him."

"I'm afraid—"

"I haven't seen him in years. This is the last chance I'll have. He owes me this."

"That's not how it works, Ms. Sweeney," I said gently. "I need you to understand that your father's autopsy is quite far along."

"And I need you to understand," she said, drawing up to her full majestic height, "that I am not letting you—whoever you are—be the last person to see him before he's gone. I am his daughter. I'm entitled to see his body."

Not in the state of New York, she wasn't. I looked at Mandragola for backup. All he had to do was tell her it was impossible and it would be out of my hands. Strictly speaking, it *was* possible—no law prohibited me from bringing her in. But it was insane. Family members weren't allowed to view autopsies for the same reason they weren't allowed to view surgeries. They weren't prepared to handle it, and liability was infinite—I knew of pathologists who'd been sued for "mutilation" by families just for doing their jobs. But at the same time she did have the legal right to order me to stop. It didn't matter what the will said—as his closest relative, his body was technically her property now.

"I'm sorry, that's entirely at the discretion of Dr. Zhu, she's the attending pathologist. It's her call."

He looked at me simperingly, like he was doing me a favor, and in that instant I vowed I would take his job someday. I'd take this office and his keys and his fucking squash partner. I didn't know how to play squash. I'd learn. And I'd start it all right now. He thought he was the only one who could make power moves?

"Fine," I said.

She fixed me with a blazing stare and warmth rippled over me. I wanted this woman to see what I could do. I'd lost control of this entire day. That ended now.

"What do you mean, fine."

"I mean fine. Let's go see him. Now."

19.

What happened next was, August got famous.

August hadn't just wanted to get famous, he'd expected to. Not that he had any idea how it might happen. It just seemed like a natural outcome for him. Fame would suit him, what with its abundant privileges and minimal consequences. So he assumed someday it would find him, like a pig hunting for truffles. He was the truffle in this scenario. He just didn't think it would happen so fast.

But (and this matters for everything to come) he had never expected his fame to come from doing his job. It was the early 1990s. Chefs weren't famous—not really. There were luminaries in the industry, the appearance of whose names on a reservation sheet stiffened the backbones and focused the minds of back and front of house alike, but it was not as if they got recognized on the D train. They weren't rich. They did not glow. Real celebrities glowed. Once, exiting a nightclub, August saw David Bowie go in, and it was as though all the streetlamps on Delancey Street reverently swung their beams toward his lean, fluent frame, bathing him in light.

August never did go back to Timo's. In fact, he was surprised at how easy it was to abandon Timo. It wasn't the decision that was easy—that part was terrible. August was unaccustomed to feeling guilty, but during the long weeks he spent at his parents' home, each night as he crashed into bed, however drunk or high he was, it was the last thing he felt, biting at his bones like termites in the timbers of a house. Each night he swore that tomorrow, tomorrow would be the day he'd take the train out to Queens and present himself to his mentor. But each new day brought a new excuse, and months passed. The restaurants Sidney was taking him to beckoned (as did the women reliably assembled there; such women had never been seen in Timo's). Finally, accompanied by a boost from Sidney, who knew an investor, he signed on as chef de cuisine at a new industrial-chic Japanese-French restaurant in Soho, and when he went to bed that night, the termites were gone. Abolished forever. From this August learned an important lesson. It wasn't doing the thing that made you feel bad, it was how long it took to decide to do the thing. He would never overthink a decision again.

In the years to come August jobbed his way contentedly across New York City, the cocaine like wind in his sails as he tacked from the marble-bathroomed steakhouses of Midtown to the concrete-walled trendsetters of Meatpacking, from the bobo trattorias of Tribeca to the fusion factories of Soho. He liked month-to-month contracts, and disliked open kitchens. Every few months he would walk past La Grenouille, and gaze through the window at the tuxedoed waiters gliding along the carpeted floor. But coke cost money, and so did rent. Every time he started a new job, he had a clear, simple plan: get poached. There were three keys to this, he'd found. First, whatever the restaurant was doing, he had to learn it fast and do it brilliantly. He had to stay sharp, show up early, be flawless, and leave late. This was not hard for August, thanks to cocaine. Wherever he went he kept saying the magic words that had unlocked the wisdom of Baratin, *show me*, and soon he was conversant, though far from fluent, in a dozen culinary idioms. He learned to *ike-jime* a live fish by ramming a long metal skewer down its spinal cord. He learned the art of hand-pulling noodles, whirling and slapping them in white skeins. He learned he hated baking and never wanted anything to do with it. He learned that bad food held a strange mesmeric power over the rich fucks of

Midtown, for whom the act of deliberately overpaying—and being *seen* deliberately overpaying—for overcooked salmon caused a pleasure that dwarfed whatever a properly-cooked fish could ever offer.

All this learning, working, hustling—August took to it all like a lottery winner in a strip club. What made him feel like *he* was the one working the pole was the third thing: schmoozing. These guys (always it was guys) would invite him over to their table, and they'd all be wearing striped collared shirts and leather-holstered beepers on their belts. The hair gel would shine in the low lighting. They'd shake his hand, marvel at his size, invite him to wedge into the banquette with them, if he could fit, ha ha! The process made him feel like a racehorse on the block; they did everything but fondle his balls. He made himself be likeable, radiated confidence; his answer to every question was yes.

The problem was, the kind of guys who poached talent—especially talent like August who had a reputation for being poachable—weren't exactly the straightest arrows in the quiver. In time he learned to gauge their level of bullshit by volume, and how likely their restaurant was to last more than three months. Like if they mentioned their celebrity friend (who was, with startling frequency, John Travolta), who would bring other celebrity friends, and before long they'd be the Spago of Crown Heights, August knew to ask for a lot of cash up front. They'd always have the money. Then they'd burn through that money before the restaurant ever got its legs under it, and one morning August would show up to work and the place would be shuttered, all the lights off, and within two weeks the awning would be gone. It would be as if the restaurant never existed, wiped from the city's memory. For New York City has no memory, except when it comes to its grudges. As the self-appointed cultural capital of the planet, memory is a luxury New York has to sacrifice in order to be, as its very name ordains, new. Every great city has a role: Rome's is to be eternal; Paris to seduce; New York to forget, instantly, to rebuild and renovate and reinvent and replace, to be forever moving, like a great, city-sized shark that must keep swimming or die. New York is like the human liver, brilliant at absorbing toxins, forever sloughing off the dead cells of failure and re-growing thriving new tissue in its place. It is the skyline of Theseus.

As a child of the city, August found it equally easy to forget places he'd worked. People, though—people he would remember for decades. Nothing was harder for him than leaving a good crew. August always knew, within minutes, if a cook had a feel for it, the same way I can look at a person in line at Trader Joe's and know their heart is failing. It was something about how they would keep their shoulders back when standing at the cutting board, or how little they seemed to move when they were working, or how they knew where everyone else on the line was without looking. The secret to his success wasn't just his charisma or his palate—it was his eye for talent. Even after he got famous it was known that if August Sweeney thought you were the real deal he would twist arms ruthlessly to help you with your career.

It was in these years, around 1994, that one day, at a restaurant called Opus Five, a young Black kid showed up at the manager's desk and asked for a job. There was a SE BUSCAN COCINERO sign in the window because a prep cook had been deported back to El Salvador that week. August came out to meet him.

You got a resume? August asked.

No, said the kid, who looked like he was 18.

You worked in a restaurant before?

My uncle's got a bar. I worked there.

You like it?

Yeah. But we don't really serve food, except for frozen chicken tenders and fries and stuff. I want to cook.

There was something about how his voice went low and hard on the word *cook*. He meant it, and he meant it like August had meant it when he was that age.

He started him that day. It was training anyhow, so if the kid was a flop, he could just send him home. But all afternoon, he watched him carefully. At one point the other prep cook, Rigoberto, gave him a dozen heads of garlic to break down, and August saw the kid peel a clove, then pop one in his mouth and chew contentedly. A few minutes later he did it again.

Hey kid! August called from his station, where he was emulsifying a sauce. What was your name again?

Hal White, said the kid.

That's gotta make it hard to get girls, August said.

I don't date, said the kid very seriously. I'm too busy doin' me.

Over the next week, there grew a certainty in August's mind that this kid was something special. In the tumult of service, there was an assured calm about the way he worked, as if he were woven of some special fiber that hardened under pressure, and cooled under heat. He treated ingredients tenderly; he didn't slap or throw them around. Night after night he kept his station clean and his mind sharp. Sometimes August could hear him singing along to the radio in the kitchen, his voice soft but bulls-eyeing every note. He had a hell of a palate, too— once he'd tasted an ingredient he could pick it out consistently. After a few weeks, August asked him to man the grill station alongside him, and within an hour they were handing one another spices and pans before the other had even opened his mouth to ask, like they were telepathically connected. A baseball scout's job is to see a kid swing a bat a few times and know whether that kid has the tools to make it in the majors. Hal, transparently, belonged in the majors, and August wanted him on his team. For the next year, August poured his knowledge into Hal and took him out to party with his cook buddies. Hal, for his part, went from being a quiet, intense 18-year-old who didn't even have a fake ID to closing down bars with hard-drinking cooks who said things like, Always keep your dick clean, kid, you never know when you're gonna need it.

Once, at 3am, they were stumbling out of a bar on Sullivan called the Cub Room. It was a hot summer night and the rain had just stopped and the warm wet streets shone in the streetlights and the moon glowed hazily through the clouds and a plume of steam rose from a sewer grate. It was the kind of night where you could fall in love with New York City all over again, and August had $450 in a fat roll in his pocket.

Love folded itself into August's heart like egg whites into a soufflé and he put his arm around Hal's shoulders and said, As long as I got a job, my friend, you got a job.

He would keep his word. For the next two decades, whenever August switched jobs, he brought Hal with him. Night after night, year after year, they cooked side by side, moving together like twin butter pats sliding around a sizzling pan.

One night, about six months later, August and Hal had finally pulled themselves out of the weeds at Styng, which was the kind of place where they hired front-of-house staff based on their headshots. The restaurant-cum-lounge had been open for just three weeks, and they were slammed every night. Foodwise its motto was "There is no such thing as too much dry ice." August did his best to make sure that when the smoke cleared, his tunas tartare and chickens satay were still the shit.

It was just past 11pm. August ran a towel under the cold tap and mopped the sweat from his head and neck—lately he had noticed that he sweated constantly; all it took was five minutes of exertion and he'd be slick with it. Half the cornstarch in the kitchen went down the crotch of his green and gold Zubaz pants. Anyhow he slapped himself in the face with the wet towel, then emerged into the dark, pulsing dining room and headed for the bar.

In a few months, once New Yorkers got over the novelty of eating food served in the steaming bog from *The Land Before Time*, what Styng's dining room looked like would fade from August's memory, but always he would remember the bar, which was a long arc made of onyx, and lit from within so it glowed orange in the dark of the room. He walked over and Paulina the bartender—of whom August would remember only certain parts of her anatomy (small but thickly callused feet, areolae like silver dollar pancakes)—opened a beer for him.

Are you the chef, said a blonde sitting at the bar, alone. Her eyebrows were knifelike. She took a sip of a pomegranate-red cocktail.

Nah, I just stole his jacket, said August, pointing to the name embroidered in cursive on his chest: *August Sweeney, Executive Chef.*

Well, if you see him, tell him he's way too good for this place. She gestured to her faintly-smoldering plate. A brief streak of orange sauce testified that she'd fully enjoyed his seared scallops in romesco.

So what are *you* doing here, then? August lit up a cigarette, and Paulina rolled her pale, model eyes and slid a marble ashtray over to him.

She waved at the leather-walled, diet sex-dungeon décor. Waiting for the orgy to kick off, I think.

The woman wasn't dressed like the usual type you'd find sitting alone at Styng's bar. Her suit jacket was draped carefully over the stool next to her; she wore a conservative white short-sleeved blouse. Her heels were professional: clearly, she'd come from work. Or was working, thought August, with some alarm.

What are you, a critic? he said, warily. The thought of the cold light of critical evaluation shining on him suddenly made him feel like he was back in school, struggling his doomed way through a math test. But then again, didn't critics usually bring guests?

God, no, she said. You know how much those people have to exercise just to not die? I work in television.

August's eyes brightened, and nodded as if he recognized her.

You were on *Law & Order*, right? He'd learned that if you didn't recognize a New York actress, she'd been on *Law & Order* as like a bartender saying *Yeah he came in a few times, usually tipped pretty bad* as she wiped down the bar, and once you made an actress for whom that role was a big deal feel recognized, the rest was a glide path.

I said in television, not *on*. I'm a producer. Let me ask you: ever heard of the Television Food Network?

There's a food channel?

There is now.

What do you, like, just show people cooking?

Sometimes they even eat. It's very edgy.

What's the point? Who's gonna watch someone cook a burger?

Hey, our audience is growing every day, she said, gesturing to Paulina for another cocktail. Last night both of my parents watched. We got this new show we're trying, with this guy from New Orleans— it's called *How to Boil Water*. It's got hit written *all* over it.

August drank his beer and considered. And they pay you how much for this?

More than you're making here.

August laughed, coughed, and sat down.

He didn't actually learn her name until the next morning, when he left her apartment. It just never came up.

Her name was Jane Goodall. It really was. Being progressive, ethical parents, the Goodalls had named their daughter in a fit of admiration, hoping the name would inspire her on to punch through glass ceilings and travel the world. It never occurred to them that, while Jane was very proud of the name as a child—she even had a khaki uniform, and wore her hair in her namesake's sensible ponytail—they'd drawn a big, shiny target on her back. The day she started middle school the gorilla-mating jokes began, and had more or less never stopped since then (the "Me Tarzans" began around college). When pointing out that Goodall studied chimps, idiot, turned out to be an ineffective comeback, she learned the art of sarcasm. She was tempted to change her name, but that would mean betraying Jane Goodall, to whom she could not bear to be disloyal. This was a lifelong trait of Jane's: loyalty. So instead she crushed them academically, majored in anthro at Brown, and went (having added her middle initial, L, for Lily, to her resume) into television.

The beautiful thing about television, to Jane, was the simplicity of its mission: keep people watching. There was a limitless number of ways to *make* them keep watching, and a limitless number of ways to make them change the channel. She liked that every day when she went to work, she had a clear mission. Whether the show was about axe murders or puppets singing songs for children, her goal was to compel human attention. And she found, early on, that she got a warm downy soothing sensation in her brain when people were unable to look away from something she'd produced. She became driven, and then she became successful, or at least, as successful as a female assistant producer in her late 20s could be. It was a way to order her life, to understand the world; it was not that she craved attention herself, it was that she judged things—food, clothes, travel destinations—in terms of how likely they were to captivate. She led an uncluttered life in a sunlit loft on Mercer Street (this was SoHo in the early 90s; grimy, dangerous, with steam hissing from manholes and men sleeping in doorways. I don't acknowledge the new SoHo; I have no use for it), with not much furniture.

It was back to this apartment that she brought August that night, and he more or less never left. Her loft was much more conveniently located—more comfortable—than his studio in Crown Heights. (It would be a month before she saw his apartment, with Metallica posters on the wall and a mattress on the floor, but there were no dishes in the sink and the bed itself was neatly made; August had a thing about making the bed. He was oddly fastidious, for a slob.)

There was no quote-unquote courtship. Sex begot more sex, which begot intimacy, which begot a toothbrush in her bathroom, followed by her cleaning out a drawer for his clothes, and so on. August had no interest in the protocols of dating, and she was too busy trying to keep an infant basic cable network from dying in its sleep. Their fit was natural: Jane loved food, and August loved television. He'd park himself in front of her TV—she had cable, which he didn't—and would watch anything. Even the food shows. She showed him the pilot for the show with the guy from New Orleans—now titled *Emeril and Friends*, and the downy soothing comfort spread over her again as he watched, rapt.

This guy, he said, jutting his lower lip out, impressed, this guy talks like someone's got a hand up his ass, but he's got some game.

What's more, he could keep up with her. Neither one of them ever seemed to get tired; they saw sleep as a tedious necessity, the way miserable people saw food as fuel. They stayed out late and never ate in, not when there was a whole city out there curling its finger at them seductively. Her friends loved him and his friends hit on her shamelessly in front of him, and he would smile.

Around August, Jane could be the sarcastic, ballbusting dame that the world of basic cable required—certainly it turned him on— but she didn't have to be. She could be kind to him, and he kind to her, and kindness in their worlds was rare. To her friends, eventually, she would joke that her unexpected but alarmingly intense fondness for this immense man with a curiously delicate touch was "almost primatological," but it wasn't a joke; she meant it; he was the great ape she was destined for.

One morning, the sun was streaming through the tall factory windows of her loft. It was December. Jane woke to the sounds of August clattering around in the kitchen in nothing but a laughably small apron.

Eggs benedict, he said when she padded over and rubbed herself warmly into his bare back.

God, you're sexy, she yawned.

Is this what it feels like when you wear that fancy underwear? he said, thumbing the apron strings and swiveling his porcine hips. So free.

There's nothing liberating about lingerie, she said. Not when you actually have tits.

I got tits, August said, they're just hairy.

Jane laughed and leaned back on the counter and regarded him as he cracked an egg one-handed and strained out the yolk through his fingers.

See with hollandaise, he said as he began to whisk the eggs over an improvised double boiler, you gotta talk real quietly to it. It's emotional. If it gets too excited—he made a farting sound with his tongue—falls apart. So you gotta watch it like it's running a card trick till...there. See it balloon a little? He lifted the steaming bowl clear and tossed in some cayenne and salt; as he whisked, his arm held still as his wrist rotated rapidly. The winter morning sunlight was pale as the twin moons of his ass as he waltzed barefoot between the burner and the sink. He was so light on his feet. Almost unthinkingly he used the spatula to fling the discs of sizzling Canadian bacon into the air, intercept them mid-flip, then slap them flat down on the skillet again. It was like seeing Chico Marx play piano, except the piano was on fire. She could have watched him for hours.

Jane stood up straight. She *could* have watched him for hours.

I should put you on TV, she said into her coffee mug.

Fuckin' right you should, he said, bending low to rummage for a stainless-steel bowl in the cabinet.

I mean it, said Jane. I think you can host a show.

An explosive bang, a clatter of silverware, and a roared FUCK.

Jesus Christ, are you okay? said Jane.

August collapsed onto the floor clutching his head and laughing so hard there were tears in his eyes. He'd smashed the back of his skull into the top of the cabinet.

Do you have brain damage? said Jane. If you have brain damage the show's off.

Yeah, he groaned, his vision blurred either with tears or a concussion, but so what else is new?

She held his head and kissed him, and he kissed her, and they laughed into each other's teeth, and there with their naked skin pressed to the cool tile floor, the sun settling benevolently over them, there would have been a great deal more than kissing, had Jane not suddenly pricked her head up and said, Smoke, and August cried, The bacon!

As they ate their eggs, gently fragrant with char, a sudden wave of anxiety washed over August. Wait, he said, would we have to break up? Like, would it be bad for you if people found out we're…you know.

Jane pondered this. I don't think it'll be a problem, she grinned. What kind of producer would I be if I *didn't* fuck the talent?

They called the show The Feast with August Sweeney. It wasn't like they focus-grouped it or anything in those days; they didn't have the budget, so the producers just sat down in a conference room and tossed out names, most of which had to do with August's size—The Big Roast, Big Cuts with August, Large and In Charge, Beefy Meats, which, barf. Jane shot them all down. Sure, August's immensity was why people would watch at first, but she firmly believed that what would keep people watching was his lightness, his momentum when he got going.

August was perplexed that they wanted his name to be part of the title.

People are just gonna go, Who the fuck is that? he argued. No one knows who the hell I am.

Yeah, but now it's *their* problem, Jane smiled. It's like when you buy shoes and the salesman says it's made with like Illyria leather. You've never heard of Illyria leather, but since it's got a name, you assume it must be a particularly fancy leather. You assume other people with more money and taste than you shit themselves over Illyria leather, and maybe if you buy these shoes maybe they'll shit themselves over you. Same principle. Put some shmuck's name in the title of the show, suddenly people think they're *supposed* to know who that is, then they tell their friends, *Oh you've never heard of August Sweeney?* She made a moue of her lips. *You poor unfashionable thing.*

So I'm some shmuck, he said.

Oh baby, she said, you're gonna be the biggest shmuck on basic cable.

A week later, those words rang insolently in Jane's ears as she watched something very much like tragedy unfold in front of her eyes. Every cook she'd thrown in front of a camera, even Emeril, struggled at first. Some froze. They'd ceased trying French chefs completely when it turned out that their ability to speak English evaporated the moment the cameras came on. She'd been so sure August would be a natural. And in a sense, he was: once he began to talk he couldn't stop; he was boundlessly enthusiastic and fluent when he talked about ingredients and technique. The problem was, now that he was talking, he seemed to have forgotten how to cook. He looked to Jane as if he were being remote-controlled by a distracted child. A sideways gesture sent a bottle of olive oil flying. The cameras kept rolling. By order of management— specifically, the network president, Reese Schonfeld—they didn't do retakes. It all went into the can, and onto TV. There was, said Reese, a strategy.

August's eyes kept flicking back to Jane; he kept waiting for her to yell Cut and pinch her nose in the way she did when they were late for things, but she never did. He knew he was fucking up. He wasn't accustomed to talking about cooking, he just did it; you didn't ask a Major League pitcher to talk you through every step of his throwing motion as he was pitching, did you? When shit worked you didn't ask questions.

The TV Food Network studios (that was its name then) had recently moved from a sullen brick building south of the Lincoln Tunnel entrance to a majestic tower on 6th Avenue, a short dogleg around Radio City from the building where Thomas Sweeney had eventually returned, cautiously, to work as a minor executive at Grayson Medical Supply, never to rise higher. August had always imagined a TV network as being housed in something like NASA headquarters, with everything buffed and marbled and producers on headsets like they were at Mission Control.

Instead, the soundstage was three "kitchens" in various states of upheaval. Flats painted to look like wood leaned against lighting rigs; sinks had signs reading DO NOT USE; the whole thing seemed to be held together with staples and electrical tape.

Voilá, Jane had said, gesturing like a maître d'.

This is it? asked August.

Welcome to life on channel fifty, Jane said.

The set, if you could call it that, was a kitchen island on casters in front of a flimsy wall of cabinets. The oven in the fake wall was entirely ornamental, with a tiny orange bulb installed to simulate heat.

You're fucking kidding, said August, pointing to the range installed in the kitchen island. An electric stove? I'm leaving.

Jane shrugged. Take it up with the fire marshal.

Is this what porn studios look like? he asked.

They have nicer couches, said Jane.

He was on the verge of asking if they paid better but stopped himself. He knew they didn't. And he and Jane knew what this meant for him, financially. All his mercenary kitchen-hopping had only boosted his weekly take-home to about $600, and he was still working 80 hours, six-day weeks, but he felt pretty princely on that seventh day. Before moving in with Jane he would wake up around noon in his studio, which had a real bed now, and the bed had nice sheets, and he'd take a shit and wipe with extra soft toilet paper. You only got one asshole, he said, it was important to baby it a little.

August had lived comfortably, even blissfully, in this idiom until Jane had come into his life and he'd seen how someone with actual money lived. He wasn't stupid—he understood a junior producer at a tiny network no one watched wasn't exactly making fuck-you money, but it wasn't even the difference in incomes that jolted him, it was how much more she understood it. For August, money was like the tide, it came in and went out and hopefully you kept your head above water. But when Jane started talking about savings accounts and IRAs and even mutual funds it was like watching a weatherman on TV talk about air masses and pressure ridges. She'd asked him one night, gently, if he ever set aside a little for retirement, and August snorted and said Nah, I always figured when I get old I'll just knock over a bank. In truth, he was using the same checking account his father had opened for him in the 80s when he was working at Jimmy Luisi's.

Now August understood that he had to do better. She made him *want* to do better. On the rare occasions he saw his own apartment these days, August felt shame at how he lived; the shitty chipped enamel dishes, the frayed single toothbrush, the way the shower spat a bunch of times and whined when you turned it on. It wasn't enough anymore. He wanted to move out of the shitty apartment and shitty turn-and-burn world and into Jane's apartment and Jane's world. Jane was Queen Shit of Fuck Mountain, as far as August was concerned, and August wanted to be King Shit of Fuck Mountain right alongside her.

Reese had agreed on a trial run of 35 shows, for which they'd pay him $10,000—in seven days he'd make almost a third of what he made in a year. The plan was for each episode to do a starter, a main, and a dessert—they didn't really have time for gimmicks; the whole idea was just to get charismatic faces in front of a camera and have them make food and see if anyone watched. August had always wanted to flambé something. He remembered at La Grenouille all those years ago the whoops of shock when the waiter ignited a crêpes suzette. He was whisking his crepe batter, explaining the French concept of the *fontaine*, the well in the middle into which one cracks the eggs. Beside him, the cognac was slowly heating on the electric range.

The lights were in his eyes, and his upper lip was dewy with sweat as he whisked vigorously. He set the bowl aside and reached over the range to heat up his crêpe pan.

Then Jane saw it, almost invisible in the glare of the stage lights, over the pan of cognac: a faint blue flame.

The Food Network had a policy, in its early years, of never rerunning an episode, so this one would only air once, at 4:30pm on a Tuesday afternoon. There were no viral videos in 1995. No second life on the internet. Finished episodes sat on VHS tapes and the VHS tapes got tossed into boxes and when the Food Network outgrew its home on 6th avenue there was no point in labeling and shipping and re-filing all the thousands of slow-budget early episodes they'd filmed. To August's knowledge there was no extant footage of his sleeve bursting into flame. Nowhere on YouTube would anyone find a clip of him staring in amazement at the blaze on his arm, saying, Fire?, then looking helplessly at someone just to the left of the camera. But a quarter-century later, just before his brain shut down forever August would remember the sudden sparkling coolness that spread over him as the overhead sprinkler system switched on. He would remember the way, as the water arced in sheets, little rainbows coruscated at the edges of the lights.

An enraged bald man in a suit burst into the studio. *The fuck is going on*, he yelled.

Reese! said Jane. Minor fire problem! August wheeled around and lunged for the sink, his arm a pinwheeling blaze. He twisted the taps but no water came out.

Why doesn't this fucking sink work? Who makes a fucking fake fucking sink! August screamed, his voice soprano with panic.

It's just for show! Jane yelled back, unable to move. She hugged her chest protectively from Reese's fulminating glare, her blouse entirely soaked.

When the show aired, the thirty or so thousand viewers scattered around the Tri-state (the Network was so young then that they didn't get rated by Nielsen; the only way they knew how many people watched a show was from how many wrote in for recipes), would see a crew member barrel into frame with a fire extinguisher and blast August with white foam. They wouldn't see Reese roaring down the hall, skidding on the slicked floors, to throw open the door of the utility closet and finally wrench the shut-off valve on the emergency sprinkler system.

The system would remain off, the 31st floor entirely defenseless against fire, until one day in 1999 a fire inspector showed up and handed the network a $50,000 fine. By then it didn't matter. The Food Network was in over ten million homes, and so was August Sweeney.

About a year later he was at the Russian baths in Brighton Beach. Ivor the fugitive Serbian had introduced him to it years ago, and he tried to get there once a month on his day off. He had no idea what it was called, since all the signage was in Cyrillic, but he liked the psych-ward green tile, the dour lady of indeterminate age who handed out locker keys, and the nudity. He loved the nudity. The whole sweltering space full of naked middle-aged Slavs, steam curling from their massed shoulders and sweat glinting like dew on their thickets of chest and back hair (hair everywhere, indeed, except their heads). The necks of those who had necks were flabby and wattled. Their guts were ruddy and ballooned with vodka and carbohydrates, and below the guts, it was schlong city. He loved that you could see everyone's dick, at rest and at peace, and they could see his, for it reminded him that you never knew what somebody was packing. This was August's idea of a life lesson, and he would invoke it often when mentoring younger cooks. You just don't know, he would say sagely. The guy with the $2,000 suit and the perfect hair could have a stunted cock. But the guy who comes to clean the grease trap? Dick like Excalibur. No way to tell. That's why—he would pause for effect—you gotta treat everyone with respect.

He would feel like he was turning into his dad, when he talked like this. Or like a better version of his dad, because honestly, his dad never gave him lessons like that. Mostly his dad's lessons had been about stuff like "seeing things through to the end," which just didn't apply to people in the restaurant world, where most places failed in two years.

The whole place gave him a sense of being in a foreign country thirty years ago—it was both tourism and time travel, all for the price of a subway token and an hour on the Q. His masseur, a sturdy Georgian named Zurab, was a master of the *bushido* of the birch-broom. In particular, he appreciated that the Russians didn't make a fuss about the giant stooping to enter the steam room—they did not gawk or say things such as Whaddayou play for da Giants or sumtin; they just grunted in greeting as they shifted on their towels to make room for him. But then one day as he sat and glazed in a cloud of steam, enjoying the pleasant transit of a bead of sweat across his perineum, he became aware of two men across from him muttering to one another conspiratorially.

The men were long, pale, with gold necklaces and prominent ribs. One had dull, heavy-lidded eyes and a thin mustache; the other's nose looked like the tailfin on a vintage Cadillac. They had crude tattoos on their forearms and shoulders, and they kept glancing back at August as they conferred.

It took August a minute, but he understood: they were Russian mob. He knew they came here because Ivor had told him: You bump into someone, he said, you say sorry. Here it's mafia guys.

He shifted uncomfortably on the wet tiles. He didn't know why they were looking at him like this—they were almost smiling now, to the extent that either of these gaunt grim men could smile—but it made him nervous.

August racked his brain for how he could possibly have shown up on their radar. He hadn't borrowed any money recently—he hadn't needed to, given how his show had taken off. He'd been too busy to gamble. He hadn't switched drug dealers; he was loyal to a fault to Sidney Feinbaum's guy. It couldn't be a woman: he hadn't (it blew his mind) slept with any woman but Jane in two years. He really wished he weren't also stark naked, with his back still glowing red from where Zurab had gone to town on him.

Ah, shit, he thought. Muscle. They want muscle.

One nudged the other. August's throat went dry as he frantically tried to figure out a strategy for respectfully—very, very respectfully— declining.

I know you, said the one with the nose. No one had ever spoken to August in the steam room before. It just wasn't done. The steam room was the most intimate zone in the bathhouse, so it had unspoken rules: no prolonged eye contact, and no chitchat with strangers. This was Brighton Beach; if you broke these rules you could wind up in traction. They had bathhouses on Christopher Street where you could get away with that, but not here. But wasn't that the whole point of being mafia? You didn't just get to break the rules, you got to make people watch you break the rules. He remembered back when he was at Timo's, this group of wise guys would come in every week and one would bring his own bottle of Barolo, and nobody said a word. Timo would open it for them and most of the time they'd pour him a glass. They tipped magnificently.

Am I supposed to know you? August squinted. He figured these guys respected toughness.

You're August Sweeney? The man pronounced it Sveeney.

Who's asking? A tiny flame, like a pilot light, switched on at the base of his skull.

This is the guy! he said to the other man. I was just telling you about it! Was I just telling you?

He was just telling me, shrugged the one with the mustache.

His friend jabbed a bony finger in August's direction and said, Your show! Holodecks yes I can!

August blinked in confusion. Did this guy think he was on Star Trek?

No one had ever recognized him in public. Within a few years he would be so accustomed to people knowing who he was that it offended him when they didn't, and a few years after that, he stopped being offended and saw it more like a rare treat, a moment to be savored and lingered over like a fine Tokaji. But at this point, the Food Network was still just one step up from public access, and all their numbers showed that most viewers were middle-aged women. Before that first day of taping (once the fires were put out, he had settled down and found a rhythm), August had entertained fantasies of what he would do when people came up to on the street and said I love your show, can you sign my tits (of course he would be delighted to sign their tits) or how he would handle being shown to prime tables at restaurants and having half his meal comped (he would tip extravagantly). But these things did not happen. The money kept coming and he and Jane moved in formally and bought the biggest bed imaginable, an Alaska king that was more ice floe than mattress, but no one ever said, Hey you're that guy from that show, and so over time he just stopped expecting it, but now it was happening and instead of being asked to sign tits it was two Russian mafia guys with uncircumcised dicks.

Kholodets s yazikom, the man said again, enunciating each syllabus. You make it on your show.

Really? said the other one, then he narrowed his eyes. With the tongue?

Yes! *Kholodets* with tongue!

With *chrain*?

Of course with *chrain*! I told you, is crazy, this fucking guy is on American TV and he makes *kholodets*!

The beef tongue. They were talking about the beef tongue in jello. August burst out laughing. He'd made it almost as a joke months ago and he couldn't believe it aired. He'd seen it on the menu at Veselka late one night and out of morbid curiosity he'd tried it—it was, charitably, chewy. But he looked up how to make it (old cookbooks were, like, half aspic recipes, so it wasn't hard to figure out) and he did it on the show just for the hell of it. He was running out of ideas for episodes, since the Food Network wanted him only to make dishes people could actually do at home, which ruled out a lot of the stuff he'd learned in France. What he needed was a gimmick—like, this Batali guy was doing these crazy lectures about the chalkiness of the soil in Liguria or the rainfall in Piemonte, and somehow people were eating it up, but August couldn't do that; he wasn't an encyclopedia. He knew a shitload about meat and he was getting good at being on camera, but the food itself was boring him to death. So he'd started seeing what he could get away with—and thus, the Ukrainian jellied beef tongue.

You watch the show? he asked.

Thursdays 3pm Eastern! said the man (the Food network was not, in fact, on any televisions in the Central time zone, but they always gave the showtimes in both to project the illusion that they were). One day, I am flipping channels and I see there is big man holding the cow tongue. He is pretending it licks him, so I watch. And then—he suddenly grew emotional—then he is making *kholodets* and it looks like how my mother makes it.

With *chrain*? asked the other man again.

How many times I say? Of course with *chrain*!

Oh, the horseradish sauce, August said.

I tell everyone, there is a man on American TV who cooks like my mother. Most Americans, is all the time steak steak steak hamburger meatballs. Here nobody eat the other parts, like the how you say—he consulted his friend.

Liver, said the man, then volunteered, Or tripe.

August could only agree and shrug. He had learned to love tripe in Lyon, where *tablier de sapeur* was practically a municipal religion. If he'd had his way he would be doing entire shows about offal; he'd be grilling chicken hearts on skewers and wheeling out chrome-plated duck presses and extruding blood and making black pudding with it.

But you couldn't sell this stuff to Americans. He knew his parents had eaten it when they were kids, but never, not once, had they inflicted it on their children.

He meditated on this idea for the rest of the afternoon, into the evening, and throughout the night, even as meditation—and indeed cognition—became increasingly complicated by a cascade of cold vodka, whole bottles of sweet Sovietsky "champagne," colossal platters of oysters and deviled eggs and caviar and raw onions and of course, meats lavishly entombed in gelatin. His new friends took him on a rampage across Brighton Beach and they drank Georgian brandy out of a bottle shaped like an AK-47 and all three swore eternal comradeship and love, and when August said he loved someone he meant it. He loved these men who loved their mothers and beef tongue and New York City, and if this was what it was like to be famous he never, ever wanted it to end.

So what if you guys are Russian mafia! What's a little murder between friends? He cried at one point as they weaved down Brighton Avenue, arms linked across one another's shoulders.

They pulled up, and looked at each other, then at him. A few words in Russian darted back and forth. August, said the one with no chin. We are not Russian mafia. We are biznismen, okay? Import-export. Shipping.

I don't care if you guys are the fuckin' KGB, you know how to party.

They cheered, and went directly to a strip club. They bought August a lap dance and a pale girl in a pale wig rubbed her polyester panties along his thigh. Unsmilingly she took his hand and placed it on her tit. It had the tensile strength of a Goodyear tire. But August had been to many strip clubs and knew that you did not touch.

Here it's fine, said the one with the mustache, whose name August now knew was Vassily. You can touch.

August looked up at the woman whose tit he was handling. When dough felt like this it was time to stop kneading it, but this was not dough, it was a tit. She shrugged. You are friend of Vassily? she said.

Galechka, you know who this is? This is famous TV star chef August Sweeney.

I don't watch food shows. I watch the news. *60 Minutes*. You want blowjob?

Why, that was exactly what August wanted. He looked at Vassily, amazed. Vassily grinned crookedly, his half-lidded eyes cold in the dark golden light of the room.

$150 dollars, said the woman. Cash. So Vassily led him to the ATM, and he withdrew $150 and she led him to the VIP room and took the $150 and unbuckled his pants and blew him and August felt like a fucking god.

Vaguely he reflected that he shouldn't tell Jane, but why on earth would he. It was a transaction, like when she bought shoes. And he'd earned this. He'd been the picture of fidelity for two entire years. He was just blowing off steam.

You are really on TV? she asked, as she folded the money and put it into a clutch with gold Janus-facing G's. Maybe I will watch you.

He left the room, spread his arms exultantly to his new friends, and accidentally connected with a slight, bikini-clad waitress who flew with a little shriek into a velvet banquette; her tray of frosted shot glasses and a bottle of Grey Goose sailing high and crashing on the cement floor. August immediately felt terrible and ran to her, but the moment he knelt down to help her up he was headlocked by a bouncer, who shouted at him in Russian and raised his fist as if to punch his head.

August felt a calm come over him, as it often did in high-voltage situations. In kitchens, the deeper they were in the weeds, the more sure-footed he was, the more certain of what to do. He understood that as big as this man was, he could easily have stood up, lifted him off his feet, and tossed him over his shoulder. But that would not solve anything. Kneeling with the bouncer's muscular arm around his neck, he looked at the waitress. Are you okay? he asked.

Asshole, she spat.

The bouncer was still yelling and began to pull him towards the door. But then suddenly he went quiet and released him. Vassily and Yuval (that was the other one's name) had sidled up to them. They had their arms draped over the bouncer's shoulders, speaking in guttural Russian. Yuval held out his hand to the waitress and helped her to her feet, then handed her a thin folded sheaf of dollar bills. She took them and looked at the floor. A man in a suit with a diamond-studded tie clip ran up to them and shook Vassily and Yuval's hand warmly. He dismissed the bouncer with a click of his tongue. Vassily patted the man, clearly the manager, on the chest, then gestured to August, who heard his name pronounced with great ceremony as Vassily patted the bouncer on the chest. August made out words like *big star, TV, Holodeck.* The manager nodded as if he understood.

Sorry, sir, said the manager suavely. He is an ignorant man; he did not know who you are.

It's my bad, brother. He was just doing his job. I can pay for the bottle.

Not necessary. Our compliments. Please, go to table. I will send a girl over to you.

He retreated, and August stared at his new friends. He narrowed his eyes. I thought you guys said you weren't Russian mafia, he said.

A sly grin edged at the corner of Yuval's fleshy lips, the grin of a man who has appraised another man's bare genitals and now there can be no more secrets between them.

I said, he smiled, we were not *Russian* mafia.

We are from Ukraine, said Vassily. Whole different country.

In this way August Sweeney learned: fame made you invincible.

Invincible, except for this: As Galina drew his rigid penis into her mouth, a sudden swarm of virions had erupted from a small sore on her gums, carried upward on a gush of saliva. They bound themselves to the glans of August's penis and went furiously to work, soaking in through the epidermis and into the craze of nerve cells just under the surface. Each virion glommed on to a neuron, sliced it open, and fired its viral payload—the capsid—into the cell. Once inside, the capsid shot toward the defenseless cell nucleus and penetrated it like a spermatozoa piercing an egg. It fused permanently with the coils of DNA that formed August's chromosomes, becoming as much a part of him as his sense of smell. This was herpes simplex virus-2, and not a soul in the world would know until I got my hands on his brain.

20.

Not a word passed between me and Astrid the whole way down to the lab. Standing mutely in the elevator and walking through the subterranean tunnels, it was like we were each waiting for the other to call the bluff. I wanted her to bail, to jab the L button on the elevator and flee when the doors opened, and I wanted to see how this would play out. As the elevator filled with people I stepped closer to her. She smelled amazing. She smelled like the moment you step out of an airport after a long, long flight and inhale the air of a whole new country. If ever there was a woman worth making bad choices for.

Not until we reached the door of the autopsy lab did I speak. And what I said was: "Your father is dead in that room and there is an enormous amount of blood."

"And?" she said, coolly.

"Those look expensive." I pointed at her shoes.

"They are."

I handed her a set of protective garments from the cabinet and she shrugged off her suit jacket and hung it up. She crossed her foot stork-like over her knee, bent to tug the booties over her heels, and then slipped on the gown. I knotted my own gown, and came around behind Astrid to help tie off hers. Her sleeveless top exposed her upper shoulder blades—which were at my eye level—and as she reached up to arrange her surgical cap I could see her trapezius twitch under her skin. I let myself watch the muscle fibers shiver for a moment, spellbound.

Her spine was flawless, free from the kind of kyphosis I often saw on women with large breasts.

"Ready?" I said, then opened the door.

Normally, the orientation of the dissection table meant that when one walked into the room, one was confronted with the body's genitals. But I had called India on the walk to the elevator, because I do not have the luxury of playing power games with my staff; I wasn't about to spring this on her as he'd done to me. I told her who was coming and made sure Astrid could hear me say, "please cover the body and the organ bloc—and oh…close his eyelids?"

They'd all made it back just in time, and I was relieved to see that Sweeney now lay under his original body bag, with only his head visible. All Astrid could see were her father's bare Hulk-sized feet at the base of a craggy white mylar dome. Small mercies.

Having retreated to a respectful distance, India, my father—who I was strangely glad to see had come back for more—and the students gazed at Astrid in wonderment. The resemblance between her and August was haunting.

When she saw her father's face, the wrinkled eyelids gently closed, Astrid raised her hand to her lips, then withdrew it sharply at the touch of the latex glove.

No one spoke. We waited. Alongside her father she seemed almost small, and getting smaller the longer she gazed down at him. As if all word and thought had gone out of her. She breathed shallowly, not wanting to let too much of the room's smell into her nose at once. Her eyes had none of the moisture of imminent tears. She just seemed to be unable to move.

"Why can't I stop staring at him?" she whispered.

"Have you ever seen someone deceased?"

"No. Not even at a funeral."

"How often do you get to see a thing you've never seen before?"

When I worked for the Queens Medical Examiner I watched her

bring family members in to identify bodies. Almost no one ran. In fact it was hard to get them out of the room.

"He just looks tired. I don't ever remember him looking tired."

"You know, you're lucky," I said softly. "You're getting to see him one last time. Most people never get to see how normal death is. Up close like this, it's not so bad, is it?"

"It's not," she said.

"But we never see it anymore. It's easy to be scared of what we never see."

Astrid said nothing. Finally, I couldn't take the silence.

"It's good you're here," I said. "It's just...it's rare that people take the time to *be* with the dead. Most people just want to wash their hands of it, which means they never get closure, they never even see the body, and then the guilt makes them buy six-thousand-dollar coffins. It's like buying an indulgence. It's outsourcing grief. It just—"

She said, "Could you *please* stop talking."

Behind us I heard them gasp. My ears went hot with shame.

"Can't get away now, can you," she snarled, then added, as if driving a nail into a board, "August." The word came out of her mouth like it was a foreign language. Like she'd almost forgotten how to pronounce it. But now I saw her eyes begin to redden. Her jaw clenched and her beautiful neck went taut in resistance but those muscles have no control over the tear ducts. She inhaled sharply through her nose; it was no use. The tinier the body part, the less authority the mind has over it.

"It's oka—" I began to say.

Astrid seized the body bag and wrenched it aside.

And things had been going so well.

There was his spine, craggy and white. She lurched for, of all things, the linen bin. "That's not a—" I began to say, but she flung open its lid as everything she'd eaten all day forced its way up and out of her. The balled-up discarded gowns muffled the sound of splashing.

Stomach contents I saw every day, but on the table, with the jets running, green-tinted water sluicing around fragments of final meals. Actual regurgitation was rare.

Astrid emerged from the bin pale, her eyes red-rimmed and full of rage. She pointed a trembling finger at her father, whom India had hastily covered back up.

"Did you...did you think this was some kind of *joke*? Did you think this would be funny?" she shouted at me—really shouted, like no one had raised their voice to me in my whole life. Even when my father would get mad at me his voice would go low and dark. I was dumbstruck. This woman had a foot and fifty pounds on me and she looked like she wanted to do to me what I'd done to her father.

"It's *disgusting*. What kind of sick—what kind of—" she was looking wildly at all of us, at India, at my dad, at the students. "How can you do that to a human being? You cut him open like an animal!"

I was trying to mentally locate all the scalpels in the room and make sure I was between her and them. "Ms. Sweeney, please—"

"I thought I asked *you* to stop talking," she said.

"Ms. Sweeney, I did warn you."

"Oh please. Oh please. That's a real fucked up power play, you know that? 'Oh yeah, come down, let me show you the corpse of your father I just mutilated.'"

That word. That word was a knife in the back of everything I believed in. "We don't," I said dangerously, in the voice my father used to use on me, "use that word." I lowered my mask so she could see my face. Blood pulsed in my cheeks.

I sensed behind me the students edging toward the door.

"Stay where you are," I barked. "You're here to learn. What we have here is a distraught relative who is struggling to process what—"

"I am standing *right* here. I'm not some dead body you can just rip open and talk shit about. You're *all* responsible."

"Ms. Sweeney," I said, my voice tremulous, "your father not only consented to this autopsy, he eagerly sought it. He made an anatomical gift, and we take those wishes very seriously. I understand that you've had a shock, but this is what the process looks like. We've been doing it since the 16th century. We honor our patients, we certainly don't mutilate them."

"Oh, I'm sorry, what would you call it when you strip someone naked and gut him like a fish and pull out his organs?"

"My job."

"Your job is vile."

"My job saves lives. What do you do?"

Her eyes went wide. I don't think she'd expected me to fight back. I certainly hadn't. I realized this was not a productive avenue of persuasion or de-escalation but I had not been in a fight since I socked Feifei on the public bus in Shanghai and now my vision was blurring around the edges and my fingers were tingling and I didn't know what I was supposed to do.

"I'm a lawyer," she growled, "and I sue people. I'm *real* good at it."

Family members had screamed at me before, but they had never threatened. I was not accustomed to this feeling of wanting to fight and throw up and run away all at the same time; indeed, I had scrupulously lived my life in order to make sure that I never felt this way.

"And don't think malpractice insurance will cover this. See this?" she pointed to her blotchy, seething face. "This is a few million in emotional damage right here."

To get good at fighting you have to have been in a lot of fights. That's the only way you learn to *use* your adrenaline instead of letting it overwhelm you—like it was doing to me now. I've never wanted to learn, because the human body can't actually get used to violence or aggression. These aren't things you build up a resistance to, they're things that invade the body and rewire it forever. Severe stress eats holes in the stomach. It rips up the gut. It corrodes the dendritic pathways of the brain until it responds to every problem the same way: *attack*. Eventually it can rupture a heart.

I'd seen more than enough inflammation in August Sweeney's intestines to know that when I took his brain out the years of stress would be carved on it like Roman soldiers' graffiti chiseled into Egyptian temple walls. Poisoned by daily surges of cortisol and adrenaline, the hippocampus and amygdala would be stunted, which would have bleared his memory and warped his emotions. Maybe that had something to do with why his daughter was screaming at me.

"Hey!" It was my father's voice. "You cannot talk to her that way!" He barreled forward, jabbing an irate finger up at her though she was a head taller than he was. "She is a doctor! This her office. You should be respectful! I know your father and I know—"

"*Ba! Bi zui!*"

For an instant I thought he was about to have another stroke. I had never in my life told him to shut up. But then again, he never would have complied before.

When they take out my father's brain—which he often reminds me he forbids—they will no doubt find the same corrosion, probably near to the ischemic parts where the stroke happened. I would like to do it myself but I do not think I will be allowed. Still, I think often— especially when we fight—of what it would be like to hold his brain in my hands, to slice it finely and explore the damage: the years of hacking into frozen ground on a collective farm in Heilongjiang when he should have been in high school; leaving his country and people and daughter to plunge into New York, and New York in the crack-epidemic 80s, no less; spending decades holding a business together with his fingernails while laboring over a blazing wok. But who but me would ever really see him? What in the world could be more filial than to study every burn, every scar, every ache that my father suffered while building a life for me?

I realized my urge to run away or throw up was gone. I put my hand on my dad's shoulders and turned to the students.

"Why don't you all take five while Ms. Sweeney and I talk," I said.

"India, there are some slides in my office that just came back, lungs from the ARDS case last week. Can you take them through it a little?"

India bit her lip. It looked like she didn't want to leave me alone. *I'll be fine*, I gestured.

When they were gone Astrid narrowed her eyes at me. "Why did that man say he knew my father?"

I regarded her for a long time. Confronted her gaze, you might say. Held it. The more I looked, the more I saw the hurt in her eyes. Or just inflammation. Same thing. Soon it stopped feeling confrontational and started to feel like right before you kiss someone.

"That old man is my dad," I said quietly.

She snorted. "You're joking. What the hell is he doing here? What did you do, call him when you saw my dad? Is this what you do when you get to chop up a famous person? Show him off? Like, 'this guy was on the TV! Everyone come on down!'"

"That's not what happened," I said. "He recognized him because they were colleagues—they used to be. I didn't invite him. He showed up. He's sick."

"And you brought him here? Some doctor."

"I'm an excellent doctor."

"I don't get it. How can you possibly do this for a living?"

I reflected on this for a minute. She was asking, she really was. I thought about saying, *because someone has to*. I thought about explaining the incomparable value of autopsy to medicine. I thought about telling her how every surgery or checkup she's ever had, every antibiotic she's ever taken, happened because of the doctors who risked public outrage—and worse—to study human anatomy. I thought about telling her how in 1788 medical students studying anatomy at Columbia were attacked by a mob and twenty people died.

I thought—fleetingly—about admitting to necrophilia, just to throw her off-balance.

"Because I love it," I said.

She snorted. "You love it. You couldn't even close his mouth. It's ghoulish."

"You understand that he wanted this so badly he donated a lot of money to this hospital, and left specific instructions for how to handle this body."

"Why? Who would want…that?" She pointed at his organs piled on the dissection table.

"I do," I said, and then more quietly, "everyone should."

She closed her eyes. She looked exhausted. Her own adrenaline was wearing off too, and instead of a magnificent pillar of rage she now looked bulldozed. The fact of his deadness was setting in and hardening, a psychic rigor mortis. I wanted to cut to the chase.

"Ms. Sweeney, why did you come here? What do you want?"

"I want *him*!" she cried. "I came here to get *him*! To collect his body. To bury it properly. That's what you're supposed to do when someone dies."

I sighed. "I'm sorry. I really am. I can't tell you how many people make postmortem plans for themselves, but never get around to telling their families about them. But he was clear that the full report, when it's done in a few weeks, is to be given to you. When that happens, I will take you through every part of it and answer any questions you have. Don't you realize? The gift he was making—it was for you."

"So I don't even get to bury him?" she said, choking up. "I just get, what, a printout?"

"Technically…" I hesitated. Why was I about to tell her this? Something to do with wanting her to *choose* my way, rather than force it on her. I wanted her to understand me, see *me*. "I assume your parents are divorced?"

"Obviously."

"Then you're the legal next of kin. You technically have the right to collect his body right now. A person can't consent to his own autopsy. His lawyer could because he has power of attorney, but strictly speaking, his body…it belongs to you. He isn't a person anymore. He's property now. Your property. You could collect him now. If you say so, I'll call my team back in"—God, what mortifying stories was he telling them about me—"and we will restore his organs, sew him up, call whichever funeral home you want, and they'll bring the van around and you can do whatever you want with him after that."

It took her a minute to absorb this.

"What's the point?" she sniffed. "That is not my father. Not anymore. You pulled it all out of him."

I had the sudden sense that I had the advantage now, and pressed it.

"I have news for you." I pulled the sheet back from his face. "That *is* your dad." I went to the organs articulated and glistening on the dissection table. "*This* is your dad." I picked up a small plastic cassette and waved it under her nose; she flinched. "*This* is your father. And in a few days, the lab will send a micron-thin sliver of it back to me, sliced so finely I'll be able to look at every molecule under the microscope. And, when I do, I will know more about who he was than anyone alive. If you really want to see him, then let me do my job."

All the wind seemed to go out of her. She sat down on a stool, her back to August's body. In the silence I could feel the borborygmic rumble of a subway pass under us. The ventilation ducts thrummed. In the walls water rushed in pipes. We were in the bowel of the building, the last stage of the digestive process of human healthcare. Born on the third floor, dead on the first floor, excreted out the basement.

"Nope," she said, and swiveled around to face him, his eyes still staring at the ceiling. "Somehow it's even worse when you can't see him."

"Because you know he's there. I'll tell you a secret: even I don't like turning my back on them when I'm alone in here."

She snorted. "Funny. Knowing he's there. It's…not something I'm used to."

And then, unexpectedly, the dam broke, and Astrid Sweeney began to talk.

What is it about my face that makes white people want to open up to me? Is it the bangs? Words came out of her like blood from a severed artery. She said, Do you know what it's like to have everyone know your dad except you? Do you know what it's like to have people tell you the man who walked out on you and your mom is their personal hero?

Once she'd started she couldn't stop. Right now, she said, the entire restaurant industry of New York City, of the whole country, was going into mourning. There would be obituaries, memorials, dedications. Grown men would weep openly, on camera. Searching, heartfelt essays on what August Sweeney meant to us all would be published. His shows would stream forever on one service or another. It was easy before, she said, to just tell people when they brought it up, because of course they always brought it up, the egomaniac had given her a name that was practically the same as his, and just look at me, she said, and I was at pains not to say I haven't stopped looking at you since the first moment I saw you. But at least when he was alive, she said, it was easy to just say, calmly, we're estranged. That word was sharp. It sounded like syringe. It punctured things. It implied at least that he must have done something wrong. But now, what was she supposed to say? We *were* estranged? And what, have people pity her, this poor child who never got the chance to reconcile with him? She knew what they would think: if August Sweeney had been *their* dad, they would have found a way to make things whole again. *They'd* have done it right. And maybe if it had been them, they wouldn't have let him die like that. Alone. Unforgiven.

She let out a sigh like a new couch outgassing. It was almost worse now than when he left her the first time, she said. Jesus. Because now he wasn't just a celebrity, he was a legend. An inspiration. Her face wrinkled as she said it and I could tell she was tasting bile.

And you know what the worst part is? she said. It's not that you couldn't speak ill. She'd done that. It's that ever since she was seven there'd been this hole in her life, like a shadow where he was supposed to be. She choked up. This huge looming shitting fucking shadow, following her around. But at least it was there, and that was the closest thing she had to him. She learned to orient by it. Like the shadow on a sundial that tells you the time. She was used to it. Her father had come to represent the dark corners of herself, and she'd learned to avoid it like an elephant graveyard. And now even that's—she pressed her fingertips to her lips and blew them away—*pfff.* Now what did she have?

"Money?" I offered.

Startled, she laughed, and brushed away tears.

"You know he did try that, once he got rich," she said. "His way of trying to be a dad. He paid my tuition, covered law school, would have Moe send me money on like, birthdays. I'll say this for him, he wasn't cheap. It wasn't just me. He threw money at people. Like it was nothing. To me he was the most selfish man in the world, but to everyone else? I'd hear stories—a waiter's car loan paid off. Gambling debts covered. He'd hire an immigration lawyer for a dishwasher's, like, cousin. Which is almost worse. How could a man who took such good care of his employees be the same guy who couldn't—" she grimaced, trying not to cry again.

When it was clear she wasn't going to continue, I said, "Can I ask you something?"

She pressed a hand to her forehead, then waved it vaguely.

"When you pulled away the sheet. What did you want to see?"

"God. Who knows. People go crazy sometimes."

"I've seen hundreds of family members identify bodies." I spoke softly but firmly—those psych rotations hadn't been a waste after all. "No one has ever gone crazy like that. You knew what you were doing."

She stared at the cabinets arrayed with buckets. Each held an organ suspended in formalin.

"The day I graduated from college, he—Dad—just…showed up. Out of nowhere. Said we were all going out to dinner, on him. Like it wasn't even a question, it was a fact. I hadn't seen him in forever but I saw how happy it made my mom. So I said yes. And you know what?" She rubbed her mouth ruefully. "It *ruled*. He took us on this spectacular night out—my mother, my boyfriend, my friends, me. He took us to this underground Japanese restaurant where they didn't even have a menu. They just brought you stuff, insanely good stuff. Life-alteringly good. Then we went to a Ukrainian dive bar in St. Marks where they were selling top-shelf shit for four dollars, somehow? We played air hockey. Then a Spanish place that stayed open late for him, with wine, wine, wine. Everywhere he went they knew him, brought us drinks and food we didn't ask for. I watched the sun come up from a diner in the West Village. It was the best night of my life. He told everyone I was his daughter, told them I'd graduated from NYU that day. He was *proud*. And then...he was gone."

She looked at the floor, the linoleum sheened pink with blood and pleural fluid. She seemed diminished, as if the mere memory itself had turned her back into the child version of herself.

"Poof. No calls, no dinners, nothing. Do you have any idea what that's like? To know he was capable of that kind of love? One incredible night and then seven years go by and you never quite get over the hope that one day he'll come back, that it'll be like a movie and maybe he bails you out of jail or you bail him out of jail and then you finally get to sit down and make up and then it could be like that again, that he could love you like that again, and then you get a call from a lawyer, and he's dead. This is the first time I've seen him since that night."

She raised her gaze to meet mine. Her irises were the same brown-gold as his. "I just wanted to *see* him."

Grief does strange cruel things to people who have no experience with it. Grieving is an art, the hardest one to master. It takes practice. That is why what I do matters. The value of an autopsy, for the family, is to explain clearly why someone is dead. To present the whole story of their death in the cold firm language of science. It helps deadness become settled fact, as opposed to some invisible commute of the body from hospital to morgue to funeral home to coffin to earth. The autopsy gives the family a toehold on the towering wall of grief. What she wanted, I could give her. I could help her.

A psychopomp is a "soul guide" whose duty it is to escort the soul to the afterlife. Every culture has one—Hermes, Anubis, the Valkyries, Xolotl, ancestral spirits, Saint Peter, on and on. Sometimes they look like us, sometimes they're animals, sometimes they are the aurora borealis. They speak to the elemental human fear that when we die our soul will find itself in a new place, and not know where to go. We've always done a good job of giving the dead what they need. It's the living we've failed. In China, there is a funeral tradition we call *shou ling*—or my grandparents did, until the Communists came—but it has many names. The Jews call it *shemira*. In the American South, it is called sitting up with the dead, and it was standard practice until Americans began to outsource to the funeral home. Family members took turns sitting all night with the dead at home, guarding them, until they could be lowered into the ground the next morning. Like so many great traditions its origins were more practical than poetic: bodies had to be protected from flies and rats. It is rare now, but I know some morticians are trying to resurrect the practice by helping people host funerals at home, and encouraging people to bathe and dress their loved ones themselves, then keep them on ice for a few days. To be able to sit there and keep loving the person you're grieving, to have them right there next to you, is like fast-forwarding to the acceptance stage of the process.

When my father and mother die, I will do this, I will do it alone, and some piece of me will go into the ground with them and never come back.

At this rate I have no one who will do the same for me. I think about this sometimes. I don't mind, I think. I am going to science when I die, like Sweeney. I want to float around in formalin, have pieces of me slivered off and slid under a microscope, the whorls of my cells held pink and blue in paraffin. Sweeney wanted that, too. He wanted to be *seen*. Who wouldn't?

I put my hands on her shoulders. "So look," I said, and gently wheeled her past the prone form of her father over to the dissection table, to the massed pile of organs.

I laid his gargantuan liver on a white cutting board. Blood pooled below it. "Feel this," I said, and took her gloved hand and laid it on the organ. A healthy liver is a pleasure to touch—velvety, almost silky on the surface, its color an attractive burgundy. Sweeney's liver was not healthy. It was bulging and caked in fatty tissue.

She stiffened, but she didn't bolt. "This is so fucking weird," she breathed.

"The liver," I said, "is made out of cells called hepatocytes. When you drink, those are the cells processing the alcohol, but they also process pretty much everything else you put into your body. But you feel that pebbling? Like stucco? Or a carapace? But, like, greasy? See those little yellow flecks? Cholesterolosis. That's what happens when everything you eat has half a stick of butter in it, or you drink a bottle of wine a day. The hepatocytes basically suffocate and die, and turn into collagen fibers. Once that happens, drinking is like pouring alcohol into a brick."

"Is this what cirrhosis looks like?"

"Not yet. In another year or two, yes. At that point the cells get replaced with scar tissue, and the damage is forever. This liver, though…this you can fix. The liver wants to heal itself—you basically regenerate an entire new one every seven years—and if your dad had made lifestyle changes—"

"Ha!"

"Right." His doctors, of course, had told him. They'd surely said those words, lifestyle changes. I had told him too. I'd told him he was going to die.

I took out a white plastic cutting board and laid the liver on it, and sliced it in half. I held up the halves to her like loaves of fresh bread. She didn't recoil this time.

"There. The white marbling all over it. We call it a nutmeg pattern."

"What does that mean?"

"This pattern is caused by backpressure—sluggish blood. It means his heart was failing. It was working so hard trying to pull blood back through his circulatory system that when he stood up too fast he would have gotten lightheaded from blood struggling to make its way back up. Like salmon swimming upstream. Look at this heart now. See how muscular it is, how craggy and thick? Bad sign. And here's why. This up here is the aorta. Put your finger in there—go on. Feel it. That's what we do here, we actually put our hands on disease. Feel how studded and lumpy and hard it is. That is atherosclerotic plaque, probably caused by cholesterol—I don't know yet. But I do know that it meant that it was starving the heart of blood. Every pump would have felt like trying to suck a smoothie through a tiny little cocktail straw—wait, I have to ask. Is there a history of heart trouble in your family?"

"On my dad's side? I think. I mean, I never really met my grandfather but I know he died of a heart attack. He was pretty young."

I nodded. "I'm not surprised. But given his lifestyle his whole system would have been fighting itself for survival. These little cubes? Hold them. They came out of his gallbladder. He'd have felt it, like a sudden stabbing pain right under the ribs. The kind of pain that drops you to your knees. He probably didn't know what it was but it would hit him at random moments. His kidneys, on the other hand—look at these. They're tiny. Like shrunken heads. The renal arteries are as full of plaque as the rest of him, so the kidneys get starved. He'd have seen it in his urine—the color would have been alarming, either dark yellow or brown. Every few years I'm assuming a kidney stone would break off and travel down to his bladder and it would be like someone had shot him in the back."

Like magma, her anger had cooled and resolved itself into solid ground, a new territory to explore. She wasn't waiting for me to hand her organs anymore. She was lifting them herself, learning their weight. She picked up a dark green sac, almost black.

"Careful with that. You're holding the spleen. Squeeze too hard and it'll burst. Here. Watch."

I placed the spleen on the board and opened it with a flick of the scalpel. Black bile gushed from it. I was showing off. I didn't care. She was absorbed.

"All of this?" I said, sweeping my hand over the organs. "It doesn't just affect who you are. It *is* who you are. I don't just mean he had trouble breathing, or numbness in his lower legs, or when he'd start sweating it would soak through his clothes."

"He had a sweating problem," Astrid nodded.

"I know," I said, reflexively, then caught myself. "The heat gets trapped under all the adipose and the body can't cool itself fast enough."

"My mom told me at the beginning of every service he would grab a fistful of cornstarch and throw it into his underwear. She still gets like wistful when she uses cornstarch."

Did my father do that? I didn't know. When he died—and it would be so much sooner than I'd ever imagined; people with his pathology don't usually keep hanging around for decades—how little I would know about him. I knew him as a father and a business owner, and these are not intimate ways to know a person, not when he practically ran my childhood as if it were a business. It was the anthropologist's dilemma: how could I ever know what he was like when he wasn't playing the role of stern father? I'd never know the man he was before I came along—I'd never know him as a *person*. He would always just be the wiry, glowing filament of authority who cast his particular stark cold light over my world. All the other parts that made up who he was were hidden from me. It was like trying to do an autopsy on just the left side of a body. What dirty jokes did he tell when he got drunk with his friends? Had he ever tried drugs? Why did my mother love him? How did they have sex? It wasn't like I wanted to know these things, and never in a million years would I ask. Yet I knew as surely as I knew my own social security number that when he was dead I would regret not knowing for the rest of my life.

"All these little things," I said, "these flimsy bits of plumbing and electric wiring, that's who we are. It's how long we can sit in a chair and work without our mind wandering. It's how fully we can taste something, how hungry we are—your dad would have been hungry always. The work that a body this size has to do just to perform basic metabolic functions—to breathe, to move blood, build cells, survive— burns tons of calories, and so it has to be fed constantly. It's like the heart. The harder it has to work to pump blood the more blood it needs to do so. For him, at this size? Doing a physical job, with a stomach like this?" I prodded his bloated stomach sac, which wobbled ominously, as if so much as looking at it wrong could make it blow. "At 2am he'd eat a leftover sandwich cold from the fridge. But the size is only a part of it. Your dad was sick everywhere. You could have seen the signs. Every time he stood up he grunted as if his knees had rusted over. He spoke in short, clipped bursts because if he went on for too long he'd get wheezy at the end of the sentence. He'd rub his hands together constantly, like a cartoon villain, only he was doing it to bring feeling back into them. He thought it was that his cooks' fingers got desensitized to heat, but really it was cholesterol and edema. Coronary artery disease."

I was almost in a trance now, a haruspex hovering my hands mystically over his organs. They were all talking at once. The lungs hard and dark with fibrosis. The thick shaggy lace of the omental "cake" covering his menacing stomach. The colon dimpled with diverticula. And then there were the still-buried treasures of his spinal cord and testicles and brain and genome. Even without them August Sweeney was speaking to me now as if he had sat up on the table, swung his legs around to touch the floor, and struck up a conversation. This was what I was put on earth to do: to see the life left in the dead.

"He knew he was in trouble but then there'd be days when he'd wake up and he wouldn't feel like there were knives in his kneecaps and all he wanted to eat were soft-boiled eggs with a little flecked salt on them, and they'd be glossy and warm and sublime, and he knew that you couldn't feel this good if you were sick. People don't like accepting that something is wrong with them. The sicker we are, the more likely we are to try to convince everyone around us—and ourselves—that it's not really that bad. It's why half the country was so ready to believe Covid was just the flu. So he went to work. He went out drinking. He stayed out late, woke up early, drove himself even harder. Because as long as he could do it he couldn't possibly be dy—"

"*Fuck* you," Astrid breathed, backing away from the table. "You did know him."

I looked at her for a long, long time. I didn't know how she'd react. I could have lied and just said I was a big fan of his shows, but I couldn't have named even one. Arguably, I'd concealed a relationship, which might be enough for her to try to take him away from me, and Mario was so spineless he'd let her. Would she do that? What did I know about her? She was a lawyer, so, litigious. She was estranged from her father, and therefore emotional. She was genetically destined for a heart attack before she hit fifty. But beyond that, who was she? What would she do?

Then it was obvious. She was a daughter who wished it had all been different, who until today—until she held her father's dead heart in her hands—had carried in her core the belief that someday it would be. She was just a kid who learned long ago how to be alone. I knew something about that.

I peeled off my gloves and dropped them in the trash. I untied my mask and took off the splash shield and the surgical cap, letting my hair fall to my shoulders. I let her take a good long look.

"It's not what you think."

21.

One night in 1996, at around 2am, August burst from the bedsheets like a giant whale breaching the surface of the ocean, in pain so instantaneous and total he couldn't draw breath to scream; he just thrashed as little wheezes of agony escaped his lips. Jerked awake from a deep sleep, Jane's first thought was that somehow August was being electrocuted.

Help, he gasped. Help.

What is it? What's wrong?

I don't know. I think something exploded. Ice? Get ice? Oh shit, oh shit Jesus.

She ran to get an icepack and came back and he pointed to his right lower back. August's eyes were shut so tight he could see little starbursts, like it was *Fantasia* and they were trying to animate his pain with little dancing flares of color and music and the ice wasn't even remotely helping, somehow the pain was getting even worse. The pain was deep in the middle of his body, where ice wouldn't reach. He didn't know you could feel this much pain, he'd figured that at some point there was just a maximum pain you could feel but this just. Kept. Going. Wasn't he supposed to go into shock? He *was* in shock. The pain was searing and grinding but his breathing was shallow and his hands had gone numb—he opened his eyes to look at his fingers, which felt fried with static electricity. Could he even still move them? With effort he curled his fingers into a weak fist, and then saw Jane hovering over him, her face white with fear, asking him what to do.

Call 911, whispered August, curling into a fetal ball. Now.

Jane sprinted to the phone.

Through his haze of pain, August could see Jane whirling into action while they waited for the ambulance. She was packing a bag, throwing in wallets and IDs and clothes and food and a few magazines, anything that looked like it might be remotely useful. God, she was good in a crisis. Where's your insurance card?

What insurance card?

Oh my God. Don't tell me. You don't have insurance?

No! Who the fuck can afford it?

You can! The network has an HMO!

Can we talk about this, he grunted, after I have pants on?

Jesus, she said, startled. You're naked. She grabbed a pair of boxers and sweatpants and somehow muscled him into them with the force of a mother lifting a car off her baby. He'd never seen her so scared, but then again, he'd never been so scared either. He couldn't begin to imagine what could possibly cause this kind of pain, but it had to be serious. Like, an internal organ had burst, an important one; for all he knew toxic shit was leaking into his body. Through the fog of pain he tried to remember what part of a human body was back and on the right. He could summon up in his mind the carcass of a pig— and then, the fetal pig that decades before he had dissected—but he couldn't begin to think of what was inside *him*.

The EMTs were there within five minutes. A man and a woman.

Buddy, said the woman, what you got there is a kidney stone.

I've had 'em, said the other. I tell you I'd rather have a tooth pulled out. No novocaine or nothin'. Least it's over fast.

In the corner of the bedroom, Jane hugged herself and chewed a hangnail.

Can you sit up, said the woman as she put a blood pressure cuff on him.

August tried, and immediately the room spun. But he held on, and finally, they got him into a big metal wheelchair, which bumped over the ridge of the doorjamb and it was like someone had ripped out a dozen stitches from August's back.

Sorry, big guy, said the woman, can't lift you.

You happy you don't live in that fourth-floor walkup anymore? said Jane in the elevator, smiling wanly.

The woman snorted. Ha! We would of had to get you out with a crane, buddy.

I love you, baby, said August, shutting his eyes to try to keep the elevator from revolving, but also surprising himself by how ardently he meant it. They had been saying I love you for some time now—and it wasn't like he hadn't meant it—but not until now did he understand just how much he meant it. What would he do without her? Collapse? Be flown out a window trussed to a crane? The intensity of his love almost began competing with the intensity of his pain and the two crashed into one another like vast atmospheric pressure systems and whipped up a hurricane inside his heart and he did not know what to do and his vision went bubbly and bleary and he realized these were tears.

Jane held his hand in the ambulance. He seemed so small and tender to her then, like a bear cub. If the Alien from *Aliens* busts out of my stomach you gotta promise to kill it, okay? he grunted to the woman EMT as she took his vitals. It's gonna lay its eggs all over this ship.

He was trying to force jokes through the pain and she saw he wasn't doing it for the EMTs' benefit but for hers—he did not want her to be scared. This was what love was, Jane thought. When you're suffering, but all you care about is making sure the *other* person is okay. She felt at that moment that he would have jumped in front of a subway train for her, and maybe she would have done the same for him.

They took him here, to NYU. I've read the file. He lay on the stretcher, which barely accommodated him, and hissed through the pain as the stone scraped its way down his ureter with all the delicacy of claws on a blackboard. Jane gave the duty nurse his information. No, he didn't have insurance. Yes to the drinking question. Yes to the smoking question. Yes, he used substances. Marijuana, cocaine. Not *that* frequently. Around them was the sullen chaos of a New York City ER at 3am.

I remember those nights. The central bullpen of the ER was like the most dismal casino in the world, with no windows and machines everywhere blinking and pinging. Gurneys parked haphazardly in the hallways with moaning derelicts and drunks the cops had brought here. Most of them we could all tell had grave underlying conditions but all we could do was treat whatever they came in with (mostly using naloxone), monitor vitals until the garbage cleared their systems, then offer to connect them to a clinic and you just knew they were never going to go and there wasn't a goddamn thing you could do about it. It was expected that at least once, we would break down crying at the futility of it all, the utter failure of the city or the system or society to treat these people like human beings. It was all considered to be an important lesson in humility. But I was not interested in humility. When an incoming trauma case would puncture the monotony I would feel something close to elation. I could sure-handedly pull a bullet from seared tissue. I knew I was bound for the autopsy lab, so I relished learning what these trauma cases had to offer: they were the near-misses.

Jane was in full producer mode: wrathful, commanding, magnificent. She would not permit them to just leave him in triage; a room *would* be found and a doctor would be summoned. The nurses seemed to marvel at her authority. An exam room was opened for August. He was still writhing as they wheeled him in. The RN walked into the room and froze. She smiled delightedly.

It IS you! She clapped her hands. I *love* your show. Oxtail! I didn't know white people even heard of oxtail!

August had absolutely no idea where her home was—her accent

was Caribbean or African, he didn't know the difference—but if she knew who he was maybe she would get him the good drugs. He very much wanted drugs now.

She made him describe his pain all over again, which now he could do with some fluency, even through gritted teeth. Anything to expedite this. His mind homed in on the drugs as a singular goal. He knew enough about scoring painkillers to know that asking for painkillers specifically, by name, was the best way to make sure you did not get any painkillers. So he told her the pain was an eleven out of ten and held Jane's hand tightly and pathetically and in short order she came back with a doctor who ordered him an entire bag of morphine, all for him, and by 4am August was purring in the warm embrace of the woman he loved. He said he was hungry and she produced from her tote bag a sleeve of Ritz crackers with cheese and a Tupperware of pasta salad. What a hero she was. What a *woman*. He was just a shitty cook who'd abandoned people who loved him all his life—oh, he knew it, don't think he didn't know it—and here floating over him, cradling his head and stroking his thinning hair, was a god damned angel. In the middle of the night, while he was being a whimpering baby, she'd pulled herself together, gotten the paramedics there, packed a bag, bullied the whole damn hospital into doing what she wanted, and all of this while wearing a pink hoodie over his oversized Pantera T-shirt.

August was almost grateful to his kidney stone now, for it had shown him true love. He knew what he wanted now with a clarity he'd never felt before. But the kidney stone was stuck fast in the ureter, and so they took him away to a room where they aimed a giant machine like a humongous overhead projector at his stomach and bombarded him with ultrasound for an hour to break up the stone into crystals.

A day later, smoked on Percocet, he keened in pain on the toilet as the crystals carved their way out of his urethra and she knelt next to him and held his hand and he looked up at her, his eyes welling with tears, and asked her in a small trembling voice if she would marry him.

Tell me this isn't about health insurance, she said, but there were tears in her eyes.

They held the wedding at Jing Feng Dim Sum restaurant on Chrystie Street. Emeril was there, and so was Batali; so were Vassily and Yuval and Galina, which was Vassily's idea of a joke. Julia Child sent her regrets as well as a three-foot *croquembouche*, a tower of choux pastry spiderwebbed with spun sugar and pyrotechnic with flaming sparklers.

A year later, like her father before her, Astrid Sweeney massacred her mother's vulva on her way into the world. It wasn't anyone's fault; Jane had been tended lovingly to by a midwife who had done their best to adhere to the birth plan she'd typed up and printed out on a dot-matrix printer. She'd wanted an epidural and got one, and it worked sublimely. The baby's heart rate was strong, even forceful. But the baby was in frank breech position—like a diver in pike, with its feet up around its ears. Jane was adamant: she did not want a C-section. She had a mortal horror of being cut open—it had haunted her nightmares all her life. *Not unless I'm about to die*, she'd told August in her first trimester. Her eyes bored into his. *Promise me.*

The midwives and nurses at Mount Sinai were saints in scrubs (a week later August would show up with an entire catered feast for the nurses' station in tow, as a gesture of gratitude). They spent hours trying to rotate her, first pressing on her belly, then plunging their gloves inside her dilated vagina to try to scoop her head around. But finally, the baby was coming, and there was nothing to do but let it come. Jane pushed for three hours. They performed an episiotomy and she screamed. August had to leave the room because he was going to faint. When he finally collected himself he reentered the room and saw Jane, sobbing, leaning against the edge of the hospital bed, legs splayed and trembling, with two tiny feet dangling out of her. They had freed the baby's feet first and let them hang so gravity could do its part. Don't push, said the midwife. *Just breathe.* He held her tight and met her wild gaze but Jane was somewhere he would never, as long as he lived, be able to go. The only sound in the room was the beep of the heart rate monitor as they all held still, the nurses and midwife watching the legs. And then the baby's legs began to slide downward, followed by its hips and belly. Gently, as if defusing a bomb, the midwife reached inside Jane and freed the baby's shoulders, and Jane threw her head back, howled, and they were parents.

Jane was back at work after eight weeks, even though she would continue to wear mesh diapers for months after that. The more damaged she'd been by the delivery, the more she refused to let it control her. She pumped almost constantly in her office and kept the bottles in a minifridge. The only concession was that she ceased to wear heels. The doctors forbid them to have sex for at least six months.

August, however, was back to work within days. He didn't have a choice. He was now the executive chef and minority partner of a massive, overpriced Nu-American restaurant in Herald Square, and he couldn't very well quit because it had his goddamn name— AUGUST—on the door. But mostly, Hal was running the show because August's shooting schedule was punishing. His show was live now, with a studio audience, and he'd have mid-tier New York celebrities like Mike Piazza or Marla Maples join him; he'd teach them to eat things like knuckle and duck tongue. It was called *Nose to Tail.* The idea had first taken root after meeting Yuval and Vassily but he'd pitched it to Jane after the kidney stone incident. He found that every time he cooked something he thought was too kooky—at least, too kooky for the white female viewers with disposable income who were pretty much the only audience his advertisers acknowledged—his shows got these very intense, almost emotional letters from viewers. He became convinced there was an audience for a program about eating the weird cheap parts of the animal, and no one else was doing it. Jane's stroke of genius was to rope in the celebrity element, because even people who wouldn't in a million years eat, say, glands, *would* gladly tune in to watch contemptibly famous people do it. He wasn't the biggest ratings-getter at the Food Network, but his audience was devoted, and the easiest for advertisers to profile and target.

Two months after Astrid was born a limo picked August up at their apartment, drove him right onto the tarmac at Teterboro Airport, and he boarded a private jet along with half a dozen other Food Network stars, bound for Miami for the network's first Food and Wine festival. Any guilt he felt at leaving her was dispelled by the shining wood paneling and cream-leather seats of the jet, and by Batali handing him a flute of champagne and kissing him messily on the cheek.

I want you to think, muttered Mario, tugging him close as the jet accelerated down the runway, of every motherfucker who didn't believe in you. I want you to think of how sick to their fucking stomachs they'd be if they saw you right now. Think of them biting their own goddamn tongues off. This is the best revenge. Never forget that.

August thought of his parents, which he realized was unfair, since right now, his mother was spending most of her days helping take care of Astrid. But he did wish they could have seen this. They'd been to his restaurant—though true to form they had ordered the chicken—and made approving noises. Spiting *them* really wasn't satisfying.

I need some enemies, August said to Mario. You got any enemies I could borrow?

Oh, don't worry, my friend. They'll find you.

Until that week in Miami, August had still thought of his show as a slightly more upmarket version of his catastrophic first episode. In New York, much of the early studio audience had been coaxed into the building, told to whistle and clap on cue, and then when they were being fed afterward, August realized that they had literally been hauled in off the street with the promise of a meal. His fame had not come overnight;

it had grown slowly, in fertile soil, like a giant blue agave fruit. But now, four years on, it was like he was Axl Rose. All the shows in Miami were filmed live and outside, in front of an audience of a thousand people. The chefs all had a blast crashing one another's shows, walking on stage to gale-force—and unprompted—cheering from the crowd. The noise was stunning—it had physical mass. It hit him in the face and crashed over him like an ocean wave and flooded every last nerve ending in his body with pleasure. It felt like fucking someone with his whole body.

August snuck up the stairs to Mario's show (not that August could actually sneak anywhere; the whole crowd saw him coming and began to cheer) and relieved a camerawoman he recognized of her equipment. This was a common gimmick he did on his show: when he got really excited, he'd run offstage and grab the cameraman, hoist the camera to his shoulder, and aim it directly at whatever he was cooking, zooming in and out like it was a dramatic scene in a kung fu movie. Now he slowly crept up behind Mario, who couldn't understand why the audience had started laughing until he turned around and saw August pointing a camera at him.

Man, said August, you sure look a lot prettier through this thing than you do in real life!

The crowd's laughter was like serotonin applied to his brain with a turkey baster.

When he came back offstage he handed the camera back to the woman, a brunette who had her hair tied back in a sleek ponytail. She was wearing loose-fitting jeans, boots, and a tight black t-shirt that accentuated her broad shoulders. When he came near her he felt something crackle in the air.

Alexis, right? August said. She looked surprised that he knew her name. There's a beach party tonight. You wanna come?

She smirked. You sure?

By midnight they were both ripshit and she was on top of him in his suite, and August could not get enough of the muscles on her arms, how they swelled and plunged like dolphins cresting the water; these were the images that came to him when he was drunk and inside a strange woman.

I want you to punch me, he said, as she bobbed up and down.

Where?

He thought about this. Not the face; he had to protect the face. Stomach, he said. Right here.

She squared up and drove a right cross directly into his diaphragm.

Thus it began. August did feel pangs of shame at first, but he had always had a tremendous faculty for excusing his own behavior. If anything, when you thought about it, he was doing Jane a favor. They couldn't have sex at all. But this put August in a bind. She knew how perpetually horny he was—he just *wanted*, that's who August was—and six months without sex would drive August insane. He would be cranky, distracted, and useless to anyone. She'd notice, and feel bad about herself, and the last thing August wanted was for Jane to feel bad. She just needed time to heal. He didn't want her to feel like she was depriving him, so really, a single meaningless hump like this? All he was doing was tiding himself over until his wife, whom he loved very much, was restored. It would, he reassured himself, be good for their marriage.

Then it happened again a few months later. And then again. It didn't happen *all* the time, but it felt inhospitable to say no to the women who openly tried to seduce him at his own restaurant. And in a sense, this too was Jane's doing. For as the millennium drew near she orchestrated an extraordinary PR campaign on August's behalf. He wasn't a household name by any means; he had clout in New York about equivalent to whoever happened to be playing third base for the Mets that year. But the food world was only just waking up to the idea of celebrity, and Jane was way out ahead of anyone else. She wasn't just booking August on daytime shows where he'd teach Matt Lauer or Oprah how to make a terrine of chicken livers and apricots, she was piping him and other Food Network cooks directly into the tabloid air supply. She had him courtside at Knicks games hanging out with Matt Dillon or Billy Joel, or doing cameos during sweeps on *Mad About You*.

Four years passed like this and they became rich and they were happy and Astrid basked in their love, and one morning Jane opened up the Post to see a grainy black-and-white picture of her husband apparently trying to vacuum another woman's soul out through her mouth and the litigation she hit him with could have registered on the Richter scale.

22.

The second I confessed, something extraordinary happened inside my body. It was as if suddenly all the deadbolts and latches and clasps inside me, all this heavy metallurgy I didn't even know I was carrying, cracked open at once and there was a physical rush of blood to the head, a marvelous fizzing in my lungs. I'd never told anyone I was in love with them but it was likely that it resembled this sensation. No wonder Catholics did this every chance they got. Confession had a whole physiological component I never knew about? Had anyone studied this? Couldn't the cops put people inside MRI machines as they admitted to embezzlement? Who cared about civil liberties—this was about science.

"That's it?" she said. "*That's* what all this was about?"

I had almost forgotten she was there.

"I swear," I said quickly, my face crimsoning like my mother's when she drinks. Aldehyde dehydrogenase deficiency. Controllable with Pepto-Bismol, oddly. But what had I been *thinking*? "That's the whole story—or I thought it was. It was years ago. I never told him my name! I didn't give him my number, my workplace, anything. I promise you, I'm as confused as you are."

She sighed. "So all this. All this mess. It was just another guilt-inducing impulse decision for him."

"I'm sorry."

She turned to her face her father—I had almost forgotten *he* was there—and pressed her thumb to her forehead and rubbed it like she was trying to flatten it out. "God, that's just so on brand for you."

"I really didn't know this was happening. I didn't even recognize him at first. But I can't get over how much you—" I stopped.

"Look just like him? Yeah. I've heard."

"Sorry."

She just looked at him. It was as if she wanted to speak to him but knew there was no point. He was past remorse, past guilt. It is so hard not to envy the dead when you spend so much time with them. Diogenes the Cynic ordered his disciples to throw his body over the city walls when he died, so that he could be ripped to pieces by wild animals. His disciples protested. He said, Fine, then put my staff next to me so that I can fend them off. They said, But you will be dead, you will not know they are there. *Ahaa*, said Diogenes, sounding like an elderly Chinese man. *Ahaa*.

"It's funny," she said quietly. "Everything you told me, everything on the table over there. You still haven't told me why he died."

"That's because I'm not done," I said. I touched his hair. Had it thinned since our meeting? Stress. "I have to get inside here. His brain has to come out."

She winced but nodded bravely. Unconvincingly.

"I need more hands for this. I need to bring my tech and my students back in. Is that all right with you?" I said, like a police officer asking to examine a small child's bruises.

She nodded stoically.

"I need to tell you," I said. "The next part is rough. You don't need to be here."

"It's fine." A vein twitched at the side of her throat. Her head gave a microscopic shake, as if fighting off a tiny insect. Clearly it was not fine.

"Ms. Sweeney, I'm serious. To get it out we have to...do things to his face."

"What do you mean, things. You mean, worse than this?"

"Frankly, yes. You really don't have to put yourself through this. There is absolutely no need. I'll write all of this up for you. I'll call you with the results, I'll walk you through everything. You can stay if you want."

I was giving her a way out. The truth was, I didn't want her to see what came next. I had wanted her to understand that she was wrong, that was all—and she had. She was exhausted. She needed to go and grieve however she grieved. It would take her a long time to learn how.

"I don't..." she hugged herself and looked up at the ceiling. "I don't think I want to be here anymore."

I touched her shoulder. "Why don't I leave you alone for a minute to say goodbye. When you're done, just throw all the PPE in that bin. We'll be outside."

I left her there and went to the office. "Jesus," said India, "we were about to call the cops!"

Immediately my father began lobbing questions about her in Chinese at me. I could not answer them all.

I waited until I heard the lab door open and shut, and came out to see her. The color had returned to her face; her blue suit shone like armor.

"I assume you have my contact," she said, looking down at me.

"Yes."

"Then I will look forward to hearing from you with the full report." She nodded curtly, and was gone.

We reentered the lab to find a scalpel sunk to the hilt in August Sweeney's left thigh.

The way you remove a brain is, you prop the head on a block. You press the scalpel firmly as you slice from the back of one ear, up over the hair whorl, and back down to the other ear. It's a deep cut that goes to the bone. Then, remember how in elementary school there was that one kid who could flip out his eyelid? Or how August inverted hundreds of squid tails? Imagine this, but with the entire face; you pull the skin of the crown and forehead down to meet the bottom lip. The exact opposite of how Carole Burnett described the pain of childbirth. You invert the face.

When India and I did it, Eva clutched Wei Wei's hand and made a noise like air being let very slowly out of a balloon. My dad held it together until India revved up the Stryker saw and touched it to the base of his skull. It sounded and smelled like a dentist's drill on steroids and with a screech he spun away, flapping his arms histrionically. I burst out laughing.

Almost to herself, in a voice so quiet only I could hear her over the noise, India murmured "Damn. You *do* laugh."

I let go of his scalp and stared at her. She switched off the saw. Even under her surgical mask I saw her smile evaporate. She had crossed a line.

"Sorry—" she began, but I shook my head and looked at my dad pacing back and forth, ranting to himself. He was hilarious. But more than that he seemed…happy. From the minute I first saw him, filthy and stinking, he had been all smiles. Unnerved, I had chalked it up to delirium and brain damage. But he had slept now, and showered, and eaten, and still he radiated excitement—his fascination with Sweeney's body, that was real. His wanting to stay with me was real. No brain was normal, in the end. What if the stroke had just freed something that all the years of struggle and stress had kept shackled? What if this was who he had wanted to be all along and he'd just crushed that part of himself because he knew the world was cold and harsh, and so he learned to be cold and harsh to protect us?

And was I any different? All my obsessive control, my certainty that if I relaxed my grip the ceiling would cave in. But every rule had been thrown down and stomped on today and the ceiling had stayed where it was. I had handled it, hadn't I? We had handled it. Maybe it wasn't Sweeney's brain that needed examining, it was mine. But that would have to wait.

"First time for everything," I said, and took the saw from her. Bone shrieked as I drove it into his skull.

India held a wet towel above the saw to absorb the spray of bone dust. It only took about thirty seconds to cut around the perimeter of the skull cap. I offered the steel wedge to the students.

"Who wants to pop him?" I said.

Eva raised her hand timidly. She came around to the end of the table. I patted her lightly on the back. "Just jam it in there and twist. Easier than opening a bottle of wine."

"And whatever you do, don't open your eyes," warned India, in a surprisingly good Harrison Ford growl.

Eva took a deep breath. Then another. Then another.

"Aiya, just do it!" I heard my father cry.

She winced, shoved, and twisted, and with a crackling sound the skull cap came free. Carefully, India reached inside with the scalpel and cut away the dense cushioning of the dura.

"Now, Eva," I said, and she lifted the skull cap like the lid of a casserole. There, blood-smeared and wrinkly, was his brain.

Carefully India cut the optic nerves, cranial nerves, and carotid arteries, and hoisted the brain and handed it to me as if it were a newborn baby. I transferred it to the colander and washed it gently, then held it to the light. When I saw it, my breath caught in my throat. There, under the temporal lobe, plain as day. That resident who pronounced him dead last night had no idea. No one did—it was nowhere in his history. Not Astrid, not his friends. He'd probably hidden it well. If he'd wobbled or slurred, or seemed confused, they'd just assume he'd been drinking because he probably had. If he was hypomanic, who would have been able to tell the difference? A doctor would have chalked it up to a bad heart and hypertension.

"What do you see?" I asked them.

"It's the right temporal lobe," said Bushwick. "Those dark grey lesions. Like mold. Is that hemorrhagic necrosis?"

"It sure is. What else?"

"It's swollen in the frontal cortex next to it. It looks like edema," said Wei Wei.

"Good gross examination," I said. "I see I've managed to scare you all out of rushing to diagnosis. But go ahead. You should know what this is."

"Encephalitis?" said Bushwick.

"Good. And I'll spot you something: he hadn't travelled abroad in over six months. So best guess at what caused it. No tricks this time. This is 101. Classic. If you go to Edinburgh you can see brains that have been floating for two hundred years with exactly this pathology."

They thought hard for a moment.

"Oh my god," said Eva. "Herpes! Herpes!"

"Herpes!" they cried, jubilant.

"What? What is it?" asked my father.

"Herpes, Ba. It's a sexually transmitted disease. I don't know the word—"

"Paozhen," said Wei Wei. I stared at her. How the hell did she know that? "I worked in a clinic in Chinatown."

"Paozhen?" He clicked his tongue at his friend on the table. "Aiya, August. So irresponsible! You should have been more careful. Xiaotong, is this why he died?"

I put Sweeney's brain on the dissection table. I ran my fingers over its bunched smooth gyri, traced the interhemispheric fissure. It was clean, healthy. There is nothing like getting your hands on a brain: it is tantalizing and frustrating. To see a brain and imagine that you have any idea what is going on inside is like looking up at the stars in the night sky and thinking you have a grip on the universe. Of all the organs it is the least impressive to look at, a clump of drab tissue the color of boiled noodles. No wonder that early anatomists declared that human consciousness lay in the heart or liver (and even today, despite knowing better, we rely on an entirely cardiological language of love). The heart is more majestic, the liver more miraculous in its regenerative abilities. Whoever would have thought, looking at a human brain, that this was the organ with a galaxy hidden inside. It is why we had to invent the concept of a soul; what kind of maniac could ever look at this gelatinous loaf of tissue and think, *Yes*, here *is where everything we are or think or want or know comes from.*

The brain is there to humble you. I touched the necrotic part of the temporal lobe: pebbled, friable. Inside my father's skull, part of his brain looked like this. But he was still here, maybe more than he had ever been—or maybe it was just a mirage, a halo effect, and soon the hammer would fall again and all of him would be gone.

They were looking at me for answers. All day long I had been the very picture of authority. I had been the barbed, brilliant, bloodless doctor I had always thought that, as a woman in medicine, I had to be; I answered every question like I was snipping a flower from its stem. And I was bone-tired. We'd been at this twelve hours now—usually an autopsy takes, like, five—but it wasn't the work. The work I could do forever. It was the talking. Words had been coming out of my mouth all day. Measured words, careful words, prudent words.

Did you know, one of my favorite things about autopsies is the silence? I missed the silence.

Why did August Sweeney die? That was the question, wasn't it? Why, after all the punishment his body had been through, after surviving decades of a lifestyle that would have killed a lesser man years ago, did it pick last night to suddenly give up? Was it his heart? His brain? His liver? I thought about explaining the complex interplay between ischemic tissue and the endothelium, where blood clots form. I thought about saying something about needing to disambiguate underlying causes from concomitant ones. These were the answers I was supposed to give when the real answer was that I just didn't know. I was not supposed to say, "I don't know." I was *supposed* to know.

I did the most wonderful thing.

I shrugged.

"Come back tomorrow. We'll figure it out."

Half an hour later, the students were gone. They had helped us bag Sweeney's organs and store them in his chest cavity. India and I then used twine to sew him up loosely. I lowered his brain and heart into buckets of formalin. India boxed up the cartridges of organ samples to be sent to the lab, where they would be fixed in wax, slivered to micron-thinness, then placed on a microscope slide and stained with blue hematoxylin and pink eosin, so the molecules would appear as marvelous pointillist whorls.

Tomorrow, they would come back. An ophthalmic pathologist would come down from the 5th floor to teach them to remove eyes. We'd go more thoroughly through everything they didn't get to see when Astrid showed up and I threw them out of the room—I hadn't even gotten to log half of what I'd seen during the gross examination, and the students never got to probe the coronary arteries, barely got to check the ravaged lungs for emboli, never got to examine his prostate. Eva deserved to know what was in the feces sample she bravely collected. I wanted them to get their hands on his testicles. I wanted them to know—and I wanted them to help. And in a week when the slides were delivered, they'd come back and I'd walk them through how to read the fine print of human tissue.

I'd offered to take India out to dinner, but she had a long train ride home. So now it was just me and my father. It was almost 8:30. He was slumped on a stool by the cabinets, resting his head on a pile of clean blue towels.

"Come on, Ba. Let me take you home."

He shot upright. "Eh? Buyao hui jia."

"Are you kidding? You're exhausted."

"I'm hungry. You haven't eaten either. Let's go eat."

I agreed to walk him over to Xinghuacun, where Big Pao could feed him, then my mom could drive him home and hopefully put him to bed for a week. I was too tired to be hungry, but at least there I could make an easy exit. I wanted to go to bed.

But when we stepped through the sliding glass doors into the night of 2nd avenue the January wind was stinging. We walked north bunched together for warmth—I'd given him my coat, which he had lost so much weight he could fit into, and I was wearing three sweatshirts I'd scavenged from my closet. My father asked if we could walk toward 3rd, to put distance between us and the river.

The bars of Turtle Bay were full. Everyone unmasked, hugging, leaning in close to shout in one anothers' ears over the thumping music. Even now, with Pfizer's synthetic mRNA woven like chain mail into my cells, it jars me to see it. I wonder if I'll ever get used to it. I remember when the only full rooms in New York were the ICUs and the morgues. People have forgotten—that's what New York does. But we who were there remember.

On 47th and 3rd he stopped in front of a restaurant called Sanglier.

"We eat here," he said.

"What? Why? We're three blocks away."

"Come on," he said.

"What is this, French? You don't even like French."

"You have to eat here tonight," he said. "It's your duty. You can't know who he really was if you don't eat his food." And now I saw it, framed in the front window: a picture of August Sweeney. Below it: 1970-2022.

"Dad, no. This is morbid," I said in English. I didn't know the word for morbid. "We can come back tomorrow."

"No. Tonight." I recognized the tone like struck flint in his voice. It meant *I will fight you to the death on this.* The old iron was still in him.

"We smell like dead people," I argued.

"It's New York. Everyone smells bad."

I understood. He wasn't ready to end this day yet. He was worried that if it ended the spell would break somehow. Maybe I wasn't ready either. But the place was absolutely packed—there were people waiting inside by the window, staring at their phones. Of course. An icon had died. People had come from all over to bask in the energy of his death. To draw power from it, to feel the heft and mass of their continued existence.

In other words no way were we getting a table.

"Cabron!" I heard from down the block. "Oh shit! Oh shit, it's James T.!" It was a stocky man with absolutely no hair on his face or head.

My dad turned, then smiled warmly. "Chucho! My friend!"

The man flicked his cigarette into the street and bearhugged my father, lifting him clear off the ground. "I missed you, son."

"I miss you too. I am so sorry about August. Chucho, this is my daughter. She is a doctor."

Chucho held out his arm, fist crooked toward him, to bump wrists with me. "Your dad makes the best Chinese food in Manhattan, girl. Chef's favorite place to go after service. But you look like shit, James T. You workin' too hard. Come on in, we fix you up."

"But there is a line," said my father.

"Not for you, hermano," said Chucho, tugging him inside by his elbow. "Ay Shanice," he asked the hostess, "you get this man a table, aight?"

The hostess's eyes went wide and she gestured at her screen, then at the line, then at the screen, in desperation.

Chucho laughed. "Chef would have got you, I got you. Come on." And he led us into the sweating heart of the restaurant. Oh, well, I thought. I was all right with morbid.

A few feet from the kitchen door, my dad seized my elbow and looked me in the eye, gravely serious.

"Xiaotong," he hissed in Chinese. "Don't tell *anyone* he had herpes!"

23.

Hal White was sitting in a banquette at Osmazôme, reviewing punch lists and eating an experiment. It was a longshot—octopus lavished with smoked tomato foam—and it wasn't there yet. If he was being honest the octopus was a vehicle for the foam. A few years back August had sent him on an eating tour of France for a few months, and he'd snuck off to eat his way across Catalonia, and he'd come home obsessed with Ferran Adrià and Juan Mari Arzak. Now they finally had the budget for things like PacoJets and an ultrasonic bath, and he kept trying to replicate what he'd seen and tasted, but it never came out as good as what he'd tasted there—or what he and August came up with together. This dish was no different. It was fine. You'd eat it. But you wouldn't remember it.

When he and August tested dishes together they stood at the pass, as August liked. But when Hal did it alone, as he had been doing more and more, he preferred to do it in the dining room. He wanted the food to fit the space. Hal believed in harmony at every level, from the lighting to the silverware to the way the shaved truffles fell over a poached quail's egg. It was less science, to him, than alchemy; it was about bringing the elements into balance. The octopus was almost there, briny and coddled in a smoky foam that made you feel like you were on an island off the coast of Scotland. He'd read that some guy in Denmark was blowtorching moss he pulled out of the North Sea and serving it to people for three hundred per person. Hal wondered if he could get his hands on some peat to burn. The octopus needed something, but Hal couldn't quite taste it in his mind. He needed August to bring it home. But August was late.

The late afternoon sun coming through the front window spread mellow and bronze across the oiled Douglas fir floors. It was autumn of 2005. The dining room was empty; soon it would fill with staff for family meal. At the bar, Rhoni and Heather were deep in conclave over a new infusion involving wormwood. The bar was a spectacle all on its own, a sleek crescent of wood carved from a single tree. The velvet barstools were so comfortable that no one wanted to get up, and so wide that, massive as it was, they could only seat ten covers at a time. If they switched it up with normal, narrow stools, they could easily fit fourteen in there—40% more money in the door. Hal knew they were leaving money on the table all over the place, or burning it in places where it made no sense, or comping shit that should never have been comped. The money element of a restaurant came naturally to Hal, but the money wasn't his department. Running the kitchen was.

The door swished, a thudding footfall: August, in sunglasses and a huge dun-colored duster, carrying a plastic bag of takeout.

You're late, said Hal.

Cool thing about owning your own place, he said, easing himself into the banquette, you're never late. What is that?

Smoked tomato foam. Trying it on the octopus. Hal slid the plate over to him. It's not there, he said.

August forked a slice of tentacle into his mouth and nodded. It's close. Come on.

Slapping the beautiful $2,000 inlaid-wood table that would, after another year of being washed twice a day, bulge and warp and have to be replaced, August headed for the kitchen.

How many VIPs on the books for tonight? August asked as they set up, back to back.

Not that many. Andy Garcia's bringing a bunch of people. Don't know who.

Huh, said August, buttoning up his custom-tailored white jacket. Some days you get Godfather one, other days you get Godfather three. Oh, by the way. I'm gone again tomorrow.

You *just* got back.

Some kind of food festival. I think Switzerland? I'll bring you back some chocolate.

Fuck chocolate, bring me a watch. Open a bank account for me.

They schedule me for these things and then they're like, Oh hey, can you be on a plane next week, we scheduled you for this, do you want to go? And no one tells me. I need a new assistant.

I thought you liked Josie.

I did like Josie. She quit a month ago. This one's named Aurora. She's gonna get me into trouble, man.

What you need is a middle-aged dude with a Blackberry and no life, Hal said quietly. Won't have no trouble then.

August laughed. He pulled the octopus out of the salamander and poked it with his finger. And you know what it is, right? I got so many fuckin' agents and managers now that it's like my life is a giant block of cheese and they keep carving out pieces so each one could get their 10%. I'm not gonna put up with this shit anymore. I'm laying down the law. From now on, first week of every month, I'm here. In the restaurant. Cooking.

You know what happened, man? said Hal. You fucked up. You're not just famous anymore. You're a whole damn celebrity.

What's the difference? August said.

Famous means you make money just by being you. Celebrity, though— it's like you're a publicly traded company. That means other people make money off you being you. You're a whole economic ecosystem, man.

What if I just want to be a cook, August asked.

Fake your own death, Hal advised.

August laughed. Wait, he said. Try this. He took a takeout container out of the bag he'd been holding. It was Korean takeout, some bulgogi over rice. He picked out a clump of kimchi, julienned a few pieces, and scattered them on top of the lightly-charred octopus.

Oh shit, said Hal when he tried it. Oh, shit. With the smoked tomato like prickly air on his tongue, the kimchi funk gave a sharp crisp tang to the sweetness of the octopus. Hal slumped against the counter, dejected. I'd never have thought of that, man, he said.

You'd have gotten there, said August, and Hal knew he believed that. He also knew it wasn't true. Understand that in 2005, people weren't smacking kimchi on everything like they are now; there were no Youtube channels with two million subscribers teaching home fermentation; there weren't half a dozen companies selling $15 jars of doubanjiang. So no, Hal wouldn't have finished a dish whose foam alone took nine steps, one of which involved a centrifuge, with a clump of fermented cabbage from a takeout container. August would never say it—he'd never even think it—but Hal understood: this was why August was August, and he wasn't and never would be.

And where was August, at this point in his life? In heaven. He had opened Osmazôme in early 2005. He owned 50%, and Sidney Feinbaum, now off the coke and heavily into collateralized debt obligations, put up the other half; Hal was installed as chef de cuisine, and ran the day-to-day. August was determined to make the place a pleasure palace. He finally had the budget to cook like he'd wanted to at Timo's all those years ago, because he wasn't in Queens anymore; now he was in Tribeca, and everyone around him seemed to have fuck-you money. If he wanted abalone he went to Masa Takayama's fish guy; if he served pork it had been raised on acorns and weekly handjobs. Truffles flew like dollar bills at the Hustler Club. He got the duck press he'd always dreamed of. The toilet paper was so soft it practically sang a lullaby into your anus. No one got out for less than $200 per person. Finance guys came to order $4000 wines and play credit card Russian roulette. Critics bitched about the price point ($114 for a porterhouse!) but they couldn't deny that there was magic in August's touch.

Getting here hadn't been easy. Jane's lawyer was a flaming sword of vengeance named Debra who'd persuaded the judge that not only was August's success due entirely to Jane's hard work, but his manifest use of Schedule 1 substances made him an unfit parent, meaning maximum alimony and minimal visitation. She wasn't wrong, either. Before the divorce, Jane had built August: The Restaurant into a celebrity zoo where the waitstaff learned during *training* how to robustly supplement their incomes by calling in items to New York's gossip columnists. It was a new millennium in New York City, and August's had become a magnificent little ecosystem: the columnists got their stories on a gilt-edged plate, publicists knew they could plant those stories, the semi- or hemi- or demi-famous got to act like divas, the restaurant was booked weeks in advance, August's celebrity stock rose like the sun, and everyone (except, of course, the back of house) prospered. The only wrinkles were that A) having a restaurant named after you turned out to suck, in that any time he talked about it it sounded was like he was talking about himself in the third person, and B) as a *restaurant*, August's was appalling—the food, which took forever to arrive, was like the product of a collaboration between a coked-up branding guru and a second-grader, with offal-themed dishes like bone marrow-stuffed chicken tenders ($26) and deep-fried calf thymus rolled in crushed Cheez-its (they called it *Cheez de veau*, $31). This bothered no one but the critics, but who needed critics when you had Keanu Reeves cuddling Winona Ryder in the corner, and so August: The Restaurant hummed profitably along until the planes flew into the towers.

That night August: The Restaurant was no different from Xinghuacun. They were thronged. August was like a man possessed on the line. He physically shoved cooks who were in the weeds out of the way and took over their station. He caromed around the kitchen, sweat soaking through his shirt and monogrammed chef's jacket, like everything he saw was burning and he alone could put the fires out. He had friends who worked at Windows on the World and Wild Blue, the restaurants on the 107th floor, but he hadn't been able to reach them all day—cell phone networks were overwhelmed—and the images in his mind wouldn't stop coming, no matter how hard he worked.

The next morning one of the bartenders called Michael Musto of the *Village Voice* to dutifully report that Cyndi Lauper had gotten drunk and wept at the bar and Michael stopped her and said sadly, Sorry, kid, I don't think anyone's gonna give a shit for a while. New York sank into recession, and a year and a half later August: The Restaurant was a Sephora.

The two years after it closed were the longest August ever went without cooking in a restaurant. At first, he had thought it would be liberating—no one depending on him, no payroll or purveyors to worry about. He did worry that his celebrity friends wouldn't take his calls anymore, now that he wasn't pouring Moët down their throats as cameras flashed. But when he texted Johnny Knoxville—who shared with him a deep love for the smut-scented wines from the Jura—Johnny called back immediately sounding thrilled to hear from him. Ethan Hawke welcomed him into his townhouse; he ran into GZA at a party at the Hayden Planetarium, and the two snuck off together to smoke Cubans on the balcony and reminisce about how New York used to be. He had begun to reach that echelon of fame where it was *more* comfortable to be around other people of the same fame-tier than around ordinary people. It was easier to let his guard down when didn't have to worry about whether or not they wanted to get something out of him.

It didn't hurt that after 9/11, when the entire world seemed to go crazy, suddenly the Food Network became an oasis of comfort for millions upon millions of Americans. At first, it was amazing—August was one of their biggest names, and he was so busy he didn't have time to miss the restaurant, which if he was being honest, he didn't. But slowly, he started to notice that little things on his set were changing. They brought in new appliances, saying it was a partnership deal, but instead of the sturdy stainless-steel stuff he'd been working with before, everything was brightly colored and curvy and edgeless and…cute. The sweet leather apron he'd always worn on camera was swapped out for a loud blue one.

It made him angry. He *liked* his set. He'd fuck with it—that was his signature, rather than having a catchphrase (he never did come up with a catchphrase that stuck). He'd run off set to pull a cameraman over, break things by accident, even grab a light and hoist it up to shine a 400W flashlight on something when he got really excited. This was a huge part of his appeal, that he could trash the illusion for viewers and thereby become even more authentic and real. I mean, it was basic cable. Who cared? Then it turned out audiences looked forward to it, the way they'd look forward to Julia Child dropping an omelet, or an actor on SNL breaking.

One day he walked into the studio to find a new set, with pastel-yellow walls bedecked with sheaves of garlic and corn, and a fake kitchen window looking out on a fake yard with fake trees.

What the fuck is this, August yelled at his producer, who was not Jane, Jane having ditched the Food Network shortly after the divorce and moved to an upstart network called Bravo, which seemed mostly to rerun episodes of *Cheers*. Why's there a yard out there? I've never had a yard in my whole fuckin life!

The producer, who was accustomed to being yelled at by men with large egos, shrugged apologetically. People want calm. We're just giving people what they want, and right now they want to feel like they're in someone's nice but not too nice country house and they want to see comfort food.

The fuck? I don't do comfort food, Nancy. That's my entire shtick. I do the freak-you-out food, that's why they watch me.

Everyone's freaked out enough, she said. No one wants to be even *more* sick to their stomach. *I* don't even like watching the show these days.

So what, I gotta go back to showing them how to make meatloaf and tuna melts? Roast chicken?

See, I told them you'd understand, said Nancy. I mean, you can still put the August Sweeney experience on the side. But yes, roast chicken would be perfect. Or tell you what. How about a goose? Goose is fancy.

He began to say yes to any offer that involved travel. Not wanting to alienate him entirely, the Food Network sent him on an offal tour of France and Italy. He would have rather gone to China or Argentina, but they said no one would watch. This guy from Les Halles named Tony Bourdain had tried it that year, and the ratings were eh. The word was the guy kept talking about Godard and Wong Kar-Wai, like he was making food cinema, not food TV.

At the end of the trip he brought a camera crew to Buoux and Le Roi Ubu, where everything was absolutely unaltered since 1992, except that Julien was gone, and Martine had married the man who ran the local video store. He tried it anyway, but she just laughed and removed his hand, and said, So, you are still a child.

August liked the travel show—he flew first class, local fixers set everything up, the food was free—but bit by bit he started to find fault with things. The champagne in first class was the cheap stuff. They were constantly filming entrances and exits to places, making him go out and come back in again. They made him shoot his first greeting with Baratin four different times; by the end his jaw hurt from forcing a smile. At meals, he had to wait for the camera guys to get the shot of the food, and by the time he actually got to eat it, it'd cooled. The falseness weighed on him. By the end the only thing that gave him any joy was the part where he got to cook alongside new people. Then the cameras would hang back and let things happen, to the point that he could forget they were there. August always knew how to find a rhythm with these people. He would cease to be the authority, and become their sous-chef, which he hadn't been in years, and it felt good to just let other people coach him again, as Baratin and Ivor and even Jimmy Luisi had coached him. There was nothing like having a dictatorial French grandmother field-marshal him around the kitchen with a wooden spoon.

Thank God, said Nancy, when she gave him the good news that network brass had greenlit the new show he'd pitched (with her help). I was *not* looking forward to telling you you were canceled.

You were going to cancel *Nose to Tail?*

Oh yeah, she snorted. You were a dead man walking around here. What? Did you think you were going to be making, like, fried earlobe on TV forever? You gotta *evolve*, August. Evolve or die.

The new show was called *American Cook* and the concept was elegantly simple. It was more a reality show than a food program: August would spend a week working his way up through the stations at a restaurant. He'd start with the prep cooks, and by the last day, he'd take over the kitchen for a service, and it would end either in triumph or disaster (usually a combination of both, and if it looked like August was cruising the producers were not above sabotaging him by surreptitiously turning off burners or hiding ingredients). They filmed thirteen episodes, which took thirteen weeks. The restaurants were all across the country. He did Cajun in New Orleans, Chinese in San Francisco, German in Milwaukee, Mexican in San Antonio. It was punishing work—he was in his mid-thirties, but with the heart, back, and knees of a man twice his age—and August *loved* it. The show was a hit, not just because it was exciting, but because August seemed so unutterably happy the whole time. I've gone back and watched some episodes now, and I can see it: even when he is frantic, stuck deep in the weeds, trying to rush out a plate of enchiladas to a table that has been waiting half an hour, he cannot stop smiling.

With the new show came more money, and with it he built Osmazôme, and the opulence of his nights was transformed. Now, instead of neon clubs and Polish models, he was ushered into the after-hours luxury of New York's culinary plutocracy. They would lock themselves into one anothers' restaurants and break out the '85 Margaux and carry out deranged experiments with animal flesh, such as, what would happen if you whipped uni with xanthan gum, rolled it in tempura batter, and deep-fried it, or could you cook an entire dry-aged steak with just a blowtorch. There were ortolan dinners where diners covered their heads in silk napkins and popped an entire endangered bird, bones and all, into their mouths. Sometimes celebrities would join, actors who made black and white films with no music, or Brooklyn rappers whose lyrics were as rococo as their beats were spare. It was like August had the keys to a vast secret city that came alive only at night, after all the little people were tucked safely in their beds.

From time to time his sorrow over losing his daughter swallowed him whole for days. It would come on suddenly, the way ten thousand cicadas will all start chirring at once, and it would blot out everything else. August would binge guilt the way he consumed everything: in massive, blackout volume. He would shut himself in his apartment and drink and call Jane, who had no interest in letting her daughter hear her father like this; if he wanted to talk to her, she said, he was welcome to try calling when he wasn't inside a bottle of bourbon. He would apologize to her over and over, and Jane would tell him that she did not hate him, which happened to be true. She had cut him surgically out of her and Astrid's life, but she would never lose her interest in him, less as a husband than as a phenomenon she discovered. You wouldn't ask Howard Carter to stop caring about Tutenkhamen, or Isaac Newton to turn his back on gravity.

He always swore he would get himself together and come see her, and then when the feeling passed he'd feel so humiliated by his behavior that he'd be too embarrassed to call.

So now we are back to Osmazôme. The same night. In the middle of service August burst into the kitchen, ruddy-faced.

Hal, get out here! They want to meet you.

Hal looked apologetically at Lucia, his sous. Can you pick up thirteen?

He's not even a real Italian, she groused.

Andy Garcia was at a six-top in the corner in an elegant turtleneck sweater, with a group of cheerful, well-scrubbed friends he did not recognize.

This is the guy! August crowed, putting his arm around Hal's shoulder and steering him toward the table. You gotta understand, I'm just the pretty face around here. This man, Hal White. This man is my brother. He's the man who made everything. August beamed at him like a proud father.

The suckling pig terrine? said Andy Garcia, his voice dark and resonant, Beau. Ti. Ful.

Glad you enjoyed it, said Hal, smiling and shaking the actor's hand. It all comes from Chef's brain, though.

Even after a few years of this, it always threw him to see faces he'd seen in movies turn up in person. He'd served Julia Roberts, Tobey Maguire, Halle Berry, and each time it happened he'd be struck by how they seemed to *deserve* to be the kind of people who froze you solid when you looked at them.

C'mere, said August. I want you to hear what this lady right here said. She called—what was the word? I never heard it before.

Tenebrous, said the woman warmly. She was middle-aged, with pale brown hair and a prominent nose. Her scarf was purple and green.

Tenebrous! said August, his arm still around his shoulder. I don't even know what it means but I love it. This lady is a writer. Andy says she's brilliant.

She waved it away. Oh, please. I dabble.

Dabbled your way into the Orange Prize, Andy Garcia said.

Go on, tell him what it means, August said.

She looked at Hal and suddenly hesitated, and in her hesitation Hal, who knew perfectly well what tenebrous meant, and who also knew that he was one of only two black people in the entire room because this math was as automatic for him as breathing, saw clearly what she was trying *not* to say—

It means…like the night. It feels like a warm summer night, she said.

Nifty save, Hal thought. He was about to thank her politely and retreat to the kitchen when August gave a delighted gasp.

Uma fuckin' Thurman! And just like that he was gone, beelining joyfully to a luminous woman who had just walked in, leaving Hal to stand awkwardly with his guests, who Hal knew perfectly well hadn't wanted to meet him. August had wanted them to, because this was maybe August's best quality: he did relentless PR for his people, and Hal loved him for this. But talking to famous people was stressful and uncomfortable if you weren't one of them. What were you supposed to say that wouldn't make you sound stupid and ordinary?

He tried to remember that they were his guests. August took hospitality seriously, which meant Hal took it seriously. In these situations August usually would pull up a chair and sit down and jaw with the guests—and not just with VIPs or women who might slip their numbers into his jacket pocket. When he was in the restaurant he tried to talk to everyone, because he knew so many of them had come to see him. What August could never understand was that his magnetism was non-transferable, and that the famous and powerful were comfortable with August because he was one of them. Hal was not, and never particularly wanted to be. Or at least, he never wanted to be famous. Powerful, on the other hand—he fucked with powerful.

Hal thought about sitting down and hanging out with Andy Garcia and this woman and whoever else these people were, turning on the charm, and letting them go home to tell their influential friends about the talented black chef they'd met, and wasn't it great that someone like him had succeeded, and who knew what would happen next.

But he had a restaurant to run. Dupes were piling up in the printer, and the kitchen was shorthanded. August was doing his job; for now, Hal needed to do his. His time would come, and when it did he would be ready.

Two years later, Lehman Brothers collapsed and took half of the deliberately overpriced restaurants in New York City with it. Sidney Feinbaum barricaded himself in his FiDi penthouse and resumed cocaine in earnest, certain the FBI was about to break down his door. Osmazôme never stood a chance. For all its absurd prices, the restaurant had never broken even. It was too expensive for the average tourist or Food Network fan to visit—that was the point, to lend the network a veneer of gastronomic hauteur even as it was taken over, lock stock and barrel, by the Sandra Lees and Paula Deens of the world. But whatever hauteur it had was badly stunted when the Michelin guide gave it no stars in its first New York City guide, for the Tire God took a dim view of celebrity chefs not named Bocuse. The foodies all went to the Spotted Pig, and the finance bros, the ones who had not been truly rich, but rather consumption smoothing, certain that they could Norman Vincent Peale themselves from acting rich to *being* rich, never returned.

Hal had been right about the difference between fame and celebrity, though. A lot of people now held stock in August Sweeney. He had become an AIG or Wells Fargo unto himself: too big to fail. (A quality not shared with his heart, which in the spring of 2009, during a late-night binge with Batali at Babbo, sent out its first distress signal. August was smoking a cigar and chowing down on a plate of confit gizzards when his sinoatrial node, the little button that keeps the metronomic rhythm of the ventricles, briefly ceased conducting electricity to the muscle. He experienced an intense sensation of being suspended in mid-air, like when he'd fall from a great height in a dream, just before bouncing awake in bed. His head bulged from the sudden lack of oxygen. Then his heart shifted straight to fifth gear and stomped the accelerator. Oh shit, said August, in a small frightened voice. He placed the cigar in the ashtray with shaking hands.)

These arrhythmias would happen regularly over the next few years, to the point where August grew used to them, but he rarely saw doctors. He simply didn't have time. He had a career to resurrect. He and Hal opened a new place in the Time Warner Center with powerful corporate backing, militantly-regulated food cost, HR infrastructure, and menus designed by McKinsey. They named it Astra, not out of any interstellar enthusiasm, but because the name sounded expensive all over the world. (August for his part, saw it as a gift to Astrid, who was now in middle school, and who secretly watched her father's shows when Jane wasn't around.) It was a colossal hit. As the years sped by— we are accelerating now, the nails sink one by one into the coffin— August's power grew until he was sovereign over a small empire. A constellation of Astras developed in Vegas, Dubai, London, Shanghai. That each Astra practically printed money was sweet, but what August really loved was opening a new one. Hal would fly out for a few months to set up and train the kitchen, then a week before opening, August would descend in a hurricane of energy and media attention (and Food Network TV crews, for this, too, he had fashioned into a show) to hone the staff to dagger-sharpness. He and Hal would stay for a month, crushing service together and roving the city afterward with local chefs, plunging into the bacchanalia of a whole new country, and waking up late the next morning in luxury hotel rooms, rarely alone, ready to do it all again. They were making fuck-you money and living fuck-you lives.

It must be said, however rich he got, August never grew lazy; perhaps if he had, he might still be alive. He loved to break in a new kitchen brigade, to forge it into a bayonet of efficiency to be thrust at every service. I suppose August would have been excellent in the military. He didn't even despise authority, so long as it was an authority he trusted. And now, as the authority himself, he had the gentle power of men who were born big, and have always been big, and therefore feel no need to make themselves big. He had the elephantine calm one finds in creatures too large to have any natural predators. When he was in the kitchen, he was rarely a screamer. He was quick with his judgments—when cooks needed to re-plate or cook something longer or be faster, he would say so firmly but unhysterically. In this way he developed a fanatically loyal crew who stayed with him for years.

Late in 2017, while he was filming his third season of *No Guts, No Glory*, his publicist called him out of the blue.

I need to know, she said, if anyone's ever sued you for sexual harassment.

Sued? I don't think I ever got sued. I had some people that couldn't handle the vibe too good, but that's it. Why?

Oh, Jesus, she said.

Wait, he said, am I *being* sued?

You better hope not. Can you tell me something? How many of your restaurants have women running the kitchen?

August thought. His mind vaulted across the globe. None, he said.

Great. Fan-tastic.

Mia, what's going on?

Just tell me if there are stories out there that I have to know about. Like are there women who work for you who are going to say you touched them inappropriately. Like touched their thighs or tried to kiss them or sent them pictures of your dick.

What? I don't know.

His face was very hot all of a sudden. He thought back to the cold slimy feeling that had spread over him when he was thirteen as he watched Victor's hand snake down that girl's jeans. What was her name? He couldn't remember. Lately he had been having more trouble remembering things.

No, he said, that's crazy. I don't remember doing that. I'm not that kind of guy.

She sighed, and in the sound in his ear was the grating hiss of the undertow, drawn back over pebbles, before the wave crashes down.

August, you've tried to kiss *me*.

The next six weeks seemed to happen in slow motion. It was as if a seam opened in the earth under August's feet, and then just kept widening and widening as the walls shuddered around him. Every day seemed to bring a new Eater article or tweet thread or Medium post in which a woman who'd worked for him described how he'd run his hand up her leg, or screenshot texts he'd sent while stratospherically high, or ask loudly in the kitchen if her pussy was shaved. These were women he thought *liked* him. Hadn't they laughed? Didn't they respond to his texts with "lol we'll see about that" or crying laughing emoji—they were posting them right there on Twitter, couldn't people *see*? When he *had* had sex with them, hadn't they been enthusiastic participants?

For almost a decade, when August went forth into the streets of New York, he had been welcomed everywhere he went as if he were an old beloved friend. At a bar, at a barber—hell, at the DMV—the moment August walked in the door people were happy to see him. New York is a city purpose-built to teach human beings anonymity, dispensability, and unimportance, but for August every day felt like being the main character in a Hallmark Christmas movie, who returns to her small town where there is neither poverty nor meth addiction, where everyone recognizes her and offers her a cup of cocoa and a sweater. This is why there is no more magnificent place to be famous than New York: people mostly leave you alone until you want something, in which case they will gladly donate their own organs to you, anesthetic optional.

Now, though, a frost began to settle over August's city. It wasn't overt. People still served him drinks and asked for selfies. No one was crossing the street to get away from him. New York doesn't work that way. It was just that the warmth began to wane. The smiles were professional. Interactions were businesslike—or worse, apologetic. Where with women, he at least vaguely understood the mistrust that now colored every exchange, when men stopped him on the street to say, Hey, buddy, I'm with you, it's all bullshit, a veil of shame would settle over him, because slowly he was coming to understand that it was not bullshit.

When John Besh was forced out of his restaurant group, Batali called him in a panic. He wasn't even worried about himself, he said. I've got money. I can go live on the farm in Michigan and fish and be fine. But a thousand people work for me.

You're gonna be fine, August said soothingly. Besh was a dick. People love you. But in his head, he remembered the night at the Spotted Pig when Mario slid his hands under a waitress's shirt and squeezed her tits like he was trying to juice them. Unbidden, the thought came into August's mind: *and how many of those thousand people did you touch like that?*

For August had made a terrible error: he had gone on Twitter. He had Hal set up a dummy account, and late into the night he would sit up in bed staring at his phone, his face illumined in the darkness. He had never seen so many people be so angry. At first, he would forward Hal and Mia the most unhinged tweets, like the one calling for his dick to be hacked off and braised and fed to him, which wasn't even how you cooked penis; you had to grill it yakitori-style or it would just melt.

Have I taught them nothing? August texted. It was 3:15am.

He thought it would eventually blow over. After all, what he did was no different than what any chef he knew did. The dirty jokes, the occasional playful grope, the pickup lines—that was how people in kitchens expressed love! Everyone knew that. That was what the industry was about. If they wanted strict HR policies and stuffed shirts who watched every word they said there were plenty of offices they could go work in. Night after night, August would scroll, certain somehow that if he could just make it to the bottom he would find good news. But Twitter had no bottom. It was all abyss.

The anger was so total, so far-reaching, so pure. It seemed to stretch a ghostly hand out from his phone screen and wrap its fingers around his throat. The suspicion that he had done something terrible, something that could not be undone, became harder and harder to ignore.

I hate this part of the story. I need to say this. I've known men like August. Who hasn't? They were the grad students who ran my labs in college, for whom fucking undergrads was like a video game. They were the middle-aged detectives who'd visit the Queens Medical Examiner's office and slip me, the extremely underage-looking intern, their numbers. They're the celebrity pathologists (yes, we have those, they're the ones who families call when their sons die in police custody and the coroner calls it a suicide) you see at the hotel bar after conferences, buying drink after drink for cute young residents, and I have to figure out how to peel them away and get them back safely to their rooms.

From what I can tell, no one ever accused August of the really vile shit. He did not punish or cold-shoulder women who didn't play along. There are no reports of him demanding naked massages or pressing women up against walls or offering better shifts in exchange for fellatio. None of that. He was, as they go, garden-variety.

But fuck that garden; prune it. August didn't have to threaten women to make them feel threatened. Because with every caress or text or leer he was still telling those women the same thing that I've always been told by the men who run my departments: that I have to play by their rules. That my access to their world is conditional, and can be revoked. I have no patience for it. I have no sympathy. August Sweeney was a pillar of a system that by any measure of justice should be reduced to rubble. It won't, but that's no reason not to try.

My anger here is not salient (but still, it thrives). My job is not to judge the man's heart, it is to cut it open. I am telling you the story of why he died. And this? This is part of the story.

The weeks passed in a fog, confusion giving way to anger, then to numbness.

I hate to do this, said Nancy. We know what you've done for the network.

It's time to lie low for a while, said his agent. Let's talk in a few months, okay? Get some rest, recharge your batteries. I know this resort in Tulúm, I'm telling you.

It's only temporary, said Hal, whose time had come at last. It's just a leave of absence, man. The company thinks it's best. I'm just gonna be running things til you come back.

He could have fought. Maybe he should have. Pitched fits, bellowed about how he built this network, or how he found Hal when he was nothing. But the truth was August was tired. His bones scraped. He was fifty years old, but felt ninety. He'd been on his feet for thirty-five years. He either couldn't shit for days on end, or he couldn't stop shitting, and there was blood on the Charmin either way.

The killing blow came from Padma Lakshmi. He had nursed a crush the size of the Chrysler building for her for decades, ever since his first of many guest judge appearances on *Top Chef*. They'd been friends. But when the stories about his behavior hit the internet, her anger at him was instant and white-hot. She barred him from ever appearing on *Top Chef* again, retweeted accounts of the women who accused him, and publicly called on him to step down from his show and, quote, try to rectify the harm he'd done. He'd called and barked, What the hell does that even mean?

It means you need to make things right, August, she said. I'm really angry with you. I thought you were better than this.

Fine! Tell me how. What am I supposed to do?

Oh, so it's my job to tell you? she said sharply, Figure it out. I have shit to do, August. Shit that isn't teaching boys who never grew up how to act like men. Maybe try reading a book.

Wait, what book?

Goodbye, August. She hung up.

Winter came to New York. One night he went to a new restaurant a former cook of his had opened—this kid from Little Rock who'd clawed his way up—and a woman stood up, aimed her phone at him, and yelled and yelled. Everything stopped. Bartenders making cocktails froze mid-shake. The servers—many of whom August knew—did nothing. Other people took their phones out. August stared at the lovely scallops in front of him and for the first time in maybe his entire life felt his appetite vanish.

He had to get out. New York, that great, ever-regenerating liver, had decided that he was a toxin and had to be purged.

Batali had gone to Michigan. God knew what he was doing there but August saw the appeal. Just to go into the wilderness and vanish. But at the same time, New York was his home. He'd never even bought a second house. Where was he supposed to go? He was rich now, at least; he could go somewhere where he'd be among his kind, where the whole point was that there were never any consequences for anything as long as you kept a fat chunk of cash in the bank. But as soon as he thought about it, he felt depressed. He loved being rich, but he couldn't stand rich people. Their hands were soft. He liked cooks. He was always at home with them. Maybe Mario could be happy outside a kitchen, but August knew he never could. What stung most about being exiled from his restaurants and test kitchens was that standing at the pass, commanding his brigade—that was the one place he had always been happy.

A month later he knocked on the kitchen door of Le Roi Ubu. Baratin opened it.

Come in, he said. You look hungry.

24.

Every student discovers something jarring after their very first gross anatomy class: how hungry it makes them. It consistently freaks them out, but it shouldn't: it's just the adrenaline rush of encountering the dead giving way to a primal urge to fill one's stomach and feel alive. It's also that under the skin, human muscle just flat out looks like brisket.

After hundreds of autopsies, it still happens to me, but never more so than it did right then as I gazed lustfully at the food people were shoveling into their mouths all around us. Chucho had lugged a table from the back room and set us up in an alcove near the kitchen door. The dining room was small but spacious—it had the feel of a place designed by an enormous man who longed for space to stretch out—but the lighting was dim and ochre-toned. The speakers were playing some old-school blues, with an emphysemic guitar crying for a woman dead and gone.

"Jesus," I said, holding the table's candle up to the menu so I could read it. It was surprisingly brief—only a handful of options. Their food cost must have been tiny. And what was equally surprising was what wasn't there: no chicken, no steak. The menu was entirely uncompromising. "They weren't kidding. Pork knuckle, duck's blood, heart. I didn't know waiguoren ate any of this."

"I am going to eat an entire animal all by myself," said my dad. "I don't even care which one."

"Have you ever been here?" I asked him. He shook his head. He and my mom didn't eat out. It wasn't (just) that they were cheap, it's that they felt uncomfortable in non-Chinese restaurants.

The server was young and tattooed and intensely attractive. But I was too tired and hungry to get horny tonight. I shelved my plans to find a former linebacker.

"Thanks for being with us tonight," they said, and their gratitude seemed real. I did not trust this attitude. "I'm happy to answer any questions you have."

"You order," said my father absently; he was staring in unabashed amazement at the server. I braced for something offensive to come out of his mouth. But then he shrugged as if to say, *I've seen weirder things today.* The server noticed and shrugged back at him, a small smile on their lips.

I looked at the menu. Fried sweetbreads with lemon aioli. Spit-roasted Uyghur lamb's head rubbed with cumin and za'atar. Tablier de sapeur. Honest-to-God Rocky Mountain oysters—where had they even gotten them? I wanted all of it. And a drink. I wanted a god damned drink.

I held up the menu, drew a circle with my finger around the entire thing, and said simply, "Yes."

The server laughed. There was a tiny gap between their front incisors.

"Good choice."

The food when it came caused us to make animal noises. Plate on plate of unfussy earthy pleasure, cooked exactly as much as it needed to be, and no more. No chemical legerdemain was allowed; this was food that cupped your face in its hands and kissed you slowly, and then licked your face. Everything my father had taught me about yielding to strange textures had been worth it. But it was also patently the work of August Sweeney. The server brought forth a wild boar shoulder braised slowly in milk, with fried sage leaves that crinkled fragrantly on the tongue. The milk in the braise had separated into white curds, which had been heaped on top of the unutterably tender meat. On Instagram it would have impressed no one, and when I tasted it I just about dissolved with pleasure. August's taste—the thing that made him a legend—had survived him.

I watched my father as he ate slowly, pensively. Was he as seduced as I was? Was it even possible? How many times must August have come to his restaurant—our restaurant—and Dad had never once come here? The cruelty (well, a cruelty) of the restaurant business is that most cooks can't afford to experience the food that makes headlines and realigns the industry. My parents were never going to go to Le Bernardin, and if I ever took them, they would spend the whole meal rictal with anxiety over the price and the service. I don't think my father would even enjoy the food, either. He would have admired the craft, maybe, as one admires intricate blown glass or a highly photorealistic painting. But would it have *meant* something to him? No. For him, such a meal would have been like going to the ballet and thinking only about the ballerina's bloody, aching toes.

It's easy to be romantic about food. An absolutely colossal industry exists to *make* us feel romantic about it: TV shows where illustrious chefs talk about their childhoods and sauté things in gorgeous slow motion, as if cooking were tai chi set to Vivaldi; media-friendly cooks who invoke "love" as an ingredient in their food, but do not specify measurements; lyrical essays devoted to the mystic emotional power of a single tea egg or taco; memoirs where the writer has substituted extra-virgin olive oil for a personality; constant reminders to eat locally and ethically and thoughtfully and responsibly and organically and sustainably; and all of this is before you even set food in an actual *restaurant*.

No one seems to want to admit the truth: food is *work*, and then you shit it out. Which is why those vanishingly rare moments when eating really does feel as sublime as we hope it will must be guarded, kept safe. Even trying to write it now, putting it down in black and white, I feel like I am letting the magic out of the balloon.

I had never seen my father eat so slowly. Instead of shoveling food into his mouth as if it might be taken away from him, he chewed each piece gently, like he didn't want to damage it. His eyes were closed; he looked like he could hear music. From time to time he nodded faintly to himself.

Neither of us said a word about the food; we did not have to. We both knew. For the first time all day, maybe in years, he and I were at peace. We had nowhere to be except right here. No one was waiting for us. He was something I had rarely seen him be since that night all those years ago when I stood on a chair in Queens and sang out a poem: he was happy.

And that's when my father spoke, so quietly that I could barely hear him over the music.

"Why did he have those strange rocks in his gallbladder?"

I blinked. "The gallstones?" I wasn't sure how to explain this in Chinese. Maybe Wei Wei would have known the words. I had to use English. "Cholesterol buildup. The gallbladder secretes bile, but if it doesn't flow smoothly, debris starts to harden. It can be painful if it blocks something."

"Like a kidney stone," my father nodded.

"More or less," I said.

"He used to drink so much beer at Xinghuacun," he reflected. "I did not know his liver was so bad. How could he drink at all?"

"Because the liver is *amazing*, Ba. It will keep working even if 80 percent of it is dead. And if he'd stopped drinking it might have even healed—you saw it, it was a wreck!" I might have been a little drunk, but I become very excited when I discuss the liver.

He looked down at his food—in fact, a perfectly-seared calf's liver. "You are a good teacher, Tongtong. I did not know."

I almost fell off my chair. Was he having another stroke?

"I'm a terrible teacher, Ba. I didn't even want those students there."

"You are a good teacher," he said firmly, not looking up from his food. "You taught them the truth." His tone was final.

I didn't know what to say. I looked around the dining room, which was becalmed since we had walked in. I saw Chucho leaning by the kitchen door, arms folded, scanning the tables. A cook came out of the kitchen, a tall, powerfully-built Black man. Chucho put his arm around his shoulders and the bigger man inclined his head to rest it tenderly against Chucho's. They stood like that a while, their bald heads touching.

Chucho saw me and pointed us out to the other man, who smiled warmly when he saw my father. Chucho gave a questioning thumbs-up. I managed a smile and pressed my hands together prayerfully and touched them to my forehead, as a wave of gratitude crested over me. I looked at my dad, who was collecting sauce on the tip of his fork, then placing it carefully on his tongue to figure out what was in it.

"Xiexie, Baba." I said. "That means a lot."

We finished our meal in a silence too perfect to puncture.

Around 9:30 my mother pulled up outside in the Plymouth.

"Aiya, Jianguo!" she cried, hurtling out of the car to wrap him up in a gigantic down coat. "It's freezing! What are you wearing?" She looked at me. "You too, get in. I'll drive you home."

"I'm completely out of your way, Mom. I'll take a cab. Just take him straight home and put him to bed. Tie him to it if you have to. He needs rest."

"I'm not a child," my father groused.

"No," cackled my mother, "you're an old man. Get in the car."

As he opened the passenger side door I touched his shoulder. It was so frail. "I'll see you Sunday, okay?"

He looked at me, surprised. He smiled and reached down to grip my hand. "Good, good," he squeezed. "We'll make dumplings."

Dumplings. It had been a long time since we'd made dumplings together.

"Good, Baba. See you Sunday." I was tempted to kiss him on the head but it might have given my *mother* a stroke. "Drive slowly, Mama."

When they were gone, I walked toward 2nd avenue, but when I got there I closed the taxi app and kept walking, breathing on my hands to warm them as I walked. The doors at the hospital slid open; it was warm inside. I rode the elevator down to the basement and touched my keycard to the lock on the lab door. I walked down the hall, my sneakers squeaky on the floor where Yenni, the janitor, had already mopped up the blood my father had tracked out of the lab. I walked past the lab to the cold room at the end of the hall, punched the code, and tugged open the door.

There, half-zipped into the white mylar bag he had arrived in, was your father.

25.

On the night the pig head rotted, August Sweeney hung around the kitchen at Sanglier until everyone else went home. Then he went to his office, drank half a bottle of Lagavulin, and thought about everything he'd survived. He felt like writing his memoirs, then he remembered that two people had already done that for him. He hadn't bothered to read either book. Why would he? He already knew the damn story.

He leaned back in his chair. He felt a warm coppery glow at the thought that he was still here. Diminished, perhaps. Slower. His knees hurt all the time. When he got out of a chair he made bovine noises. And increasingly, he'd felt furry in the head. He'd forget things, space out. But tonight, even without the pig head, service had been beautiful. He'd been through exile, lawsuits, cardiac events, a pandemic, and he was still here. Alive. He wondered what that girl at Shanghai Village who'd told him he was going to die would say now.

August sat and thought and drank and thought and listened over and over to Louis Armstrong sing "St. James Infirmary." Then he called Moe Eckstein.

Jesus, August, it's one in the morning.

What are you, asleep, Moe?

Maybe yes, maybe no. Maybe none of your business.

Moe, you're like a lousy cartoon of a lawyer. Get a pen. I want to change my will.

You want to what?

Change my will. I, August Sweeney, being of sound mind and healthy body—

Yeah, you're both of those things.

Lucky for you. You wouldn't be my lawyer if I was. Did you get the fuckin' pen? Write this down. I want an autopsy. When I die.

There was a brief pause. Okay, Moe said.

I mean a big one. Full. Everything. Look inside my brain and eyeballs and marinate me in formaldehyde.

Okay. And I'm telling them they're doing this why?

Why the fuck else? I want them to find out what the fuck's wrong with me.

Okay. So you're saying you think it's something *other* than you've eaten a stick of butter every day for twenty five years. Got it. Writing it down. With my pen.

A lawyer, a doctor, *and* a comedian! You must be your Jewish mother's dream. Meanwhile I'm fifty-one years old and I'm going to die.

I'm sorry to hear that.

Don't say sorry, Moe, it's not your fuckin' fault. It's mine. There's something wrong with me. There's always been something wrong with me, inside. This—making food—is the only thing I've ever been good at. Everything else has blown up in my face. My wife didn't love me because I gave her a shitty time, my kid doesn't love me because I give her a shitty time.

Another pause. Okay.

Okay, he says. I pour out my guts and he says Okay. That's why I love you, Moe. You're a shitty lawyer but you know how to eat. But I'm not fuckin' around here, you understand? I don't know what's wrong with me. But I want them to find out. I don't care how much it costs, you hear me? I want a full like slideshow of everything that's fucked up inside me. I want them to separate the lobes of my brain like it's an avocado and look around inside, and then I want them to write it all down and give it to Astrid. She oughta know why her dad was so fucked up.

…Like…an…avocado. Got it. Anything else, before you die?

August lifted the bottle to his lips and took a long sip. The fragrance of peat smoke made him think of the crematory.

Yeah. There's a girl I want to do it. I don't know her name. Chinese girl. Does autopsies. Don't know where she works. But she told me her dad runs that place Shanghai Village in Midtown. Find out who she is and where she works. You send me to her. I'll make a donation or something but it's gotta be her. And once she's done, I want her to donate whatever's left to a medical school. And not to some fancy medical school that can get all the dead bodies they want. Give it somewhere they'll appreciate it. Sew me back up and let those kids dissect me. Let them learn some fuckin' *knife skills*. I want them to see the cuts on my hands and the skin grafts on my legs and how my nose is fucked from the coke. Let them see how I lived. And then when they're done with me, when they've poked around every part of me from my ears to my asshole, I want—are you writing this down?—I want them to toss the organs and strip off the muscle and take my skeleton and hang me in a high school classroom so they can put like a hat on my skull and a fucking tie on my neck and give me a name like fuckin' Wilbur. I'm gonna be Wilbur the skeleton forever.

Moe waited until it was clear August had finished. And am I stipulating in the will that you be called Wilbur?

Fuck you, Moe. You're gonna die someday too. But listen to me. They gotta use every part of me, nose to tail. Nothing wasted. Because—listen to me—listen to my voice and write this down: just because I'm dead doesn't mean I'm done.

A minute later he called Moe back.

Jesus fucking—

One more thing, said August. Chucho Rivera gets the knives.

The idea for Sanglier had come from Jane, of all people. He'd spent two years in France, vanishing from the public eye almost entirely (as well as from Astrid's life; she'd graduated college in spring 2017). He declined nearly all media requests, fell in love a few times, and cooked his way from Provence to Gascony, mostly in out-of-the-way country restaurants. He never publicized his *stages*, he didn't want to draw attention. In this way he was able to be with his people and do his work. Eventually someone would recognize him, and he'd move on to the next place.

Then one day in April another call came. It was Jack. They hadn't spoken in forever. Their mother was in the hospital. She'd caught the virus.

There were no flights, so August took a private jet. But when he got to the hospital he couldn't even get near the door.

I don't need to describe the scene that met him, do I? These were the nights when the sirens never stopped. We weren't doing autopsies in those first months—we didn't know how the virus spread yet, and the fear of catching it from a body shot through the pathology community. Our discipline does not attract the cowboys, like the pulmonary surgeons who dove down the windpipes of coughing, gasping patients. And even if we wanted to get inside the victims' bodies, we couldn't—for weeks, OSHA barred us from performing autopsies. The assumption was that given how dangerous it was to be in a room with a coughing patient, actually cutting open their lungs would be lethal. Meanwhile upstairs, the hospital staff who didn't get sick were being ground into paste, working endless shifts soaked in sweat, death, and terror.

One night in April, after a twenty-hour shift, I left the hospital through the back entrance. Two huge refrigerated trucks were parked out there. That was where we were putting the bodies now that my little morgue had overflowed. In the pre-dawn light I pried off my face mask, which had merged with my skin, and sucked fresh air into my lungs. But all I got was the stink of diesel. I'd felt guilty all day for my ICU patients who'd had the bad luck to draw me as a doctor; there were hundreds of other doctors and orderlies who could have treated them better than I could. I *should* have been tending to the people in these trucks instead. *They* were my patients, mine alone. No one else but me knew how to care for them; no one but me could tell their families the full story of their deaths. Out of every doctor in that hospital I was the only one who could have made those deaths anything more than a haunting statistic, and there was nothing I could do except stand there in the shadow of the trucks and cry.

It was months before the first autopsy reports were published, and one thing they showed was that often, when those pulmonologists were forcing breathing tubes down patients' throats like fatted geese, their lungs were already so choked with debris and inflammation that there was nowhere for the supplemental oxygen to go. The ventilators administrators and governors had been knifing one another in the back for—and that the federal government had inexplicably been stealing from them—weren't nearly as useful as we thought. But in April, we didn't know. No one knew anything; the entire global medical establishment was flying through a hurricane and all anyone could do was try to keep the plane level. So Isabelle Sweeney died at 79, like so many others—more than any human mind has the strength to imagine—alone and in a medically induced coma.

Months later, they held a small memorial for her out on Long Island. In black masks, August and Jack scattered her ashes on the pond she loved sailing on. A few people came. Jack had a family now. Jane came also. She had been, since their divorce, closer to Isabelle than August had, largely because she and Thomas had continued to care for and visit their granddaughter. After Thomas died (his heart finally gave out in 2010, and August understood that Sweeney men were not meant for long lifespans) she and Astrid had grown closer. They would drink gin together and Isabelle would coldly reduce every man who had wronged Astrid to smithereens. But that weekend, Astrid was pent up and heartbroken in a Radisson Suites in Milwaukee, a young associate in the middle of a very expensive trial she couldn't take so much as a day off from.

Afterward, August and Jane took a walk along the water. Funerals have a way of reconnecting us. People find themselves in this strange emotional bubble where all they want to do is say the things they've left unsaid until now. Eulogies are cruel things: for some reason humans refuse to say the kindest, most loving things we have to say about a person until they're dead. The person in the coffin can't hear the compliments any more than Diogenes could feel the fangs. If I were president I would require that eulogies should be read to the person *before* they die; this might even have the added salutary effect of making people lead better, more compassionate lives: who wants to hear on their deathbed the eulogy equivalent of a student recommendation by a professor who doesn't really know them?

I'm off-topic. The closer I come to the end the more I find myself reluctant to let go. But August and Jane are taking a walk. This is important.

So you're an orphan now, Jane observed.

August stared out at the water, his eyes red-rimmed. He had been crying a lot, which surprised no one more than him. He had been stoic when Thomas died. In a sense Thomas had died for August many years ago, when he stopped *living*. At least that was what August told himself.

Fuck, he gasped, suddenly short of breath. You know this really hurts. It *hurts*. I don't even know why. *You* saw her more than me.

Cause you're alone now. You're the worst person I've ever met at being alone.

She stood next to him impassive, wearing his enormous blazer. He'd given it to her when the wind kicked up.

You've been gone how long?

Two years. Thanks for noticing.

You always thought that if you ever truly fucked up, if the whole world demanded your head on a plate, she was the one person in the world you could come to and not be alone. And now that option is gone. It's just you, babydoll.

How the hell do you know that.

Cause I'm a mom whose daughter is an adult now. That's the only thing I'm good for now that she makes money. I'm like insurance.

August stuck a cigarette in his mouth and lit it with shaky hands. You want one? he asked, the smoke racing into the alveoli of his lungs, swiftly filling the precious few spaces that were left.

You still smoke? I didn't think anyone still smoked.

It's about all I do these days, he muttered.

Oh, no. No. I did not spend two hours on the Grand Central Parkway to stand here and let you, of all people, feel sorry for yourself. I will jump off this dock into the water and drown.

How am I supposed to feel? I got no restaurant, I got no show, I can barely even get arrested these days. I'm trying to handle it. I know things went bad, and yeah, it's my fault, but you gotta see…Here words failed him. Whenever he tried to paste words onto his inner turmoil, it turned out like a four-year-old's macaroni self-portrait, all globs of glue and clumps of uncooked pasta that made no sense to anyone but himself.

So? Lots of cooks have no show. In fact, lots of cooks now have no restaurant. You have talent, you have name recognition, and you have money. Stop feeling sorry for yourself. Go make something so fucking great it gives the whole industry a light in the darkness.

I don't even know what you're talking about.

Yes you do. Hospitality is going through an apocalypse. You want to make things right? You want to make amends? Come back and help rebuild it. Here's some free PR advice: if you want to have a career again, you need to give people a really good reason to come back to you. Help make the industry better than it was before. Get a little place somewhere and run it well. Take care of people. Pay them. Feed them. Hire a lot of women. Don't fucking smell their hair.

That wasn't me. That was Mario. Who sniffs hair?

Listen to me. They say half of the independent restaurants in America are going to die. The only places that are going to survive are going to be the, like, Houlihans and so on. The whole system is fucked. But it was always fucked, right? Nothing about the economics of restaurants has ever made sense. The industry is going to need a new model. Equitable. Something that actually takes care of its people instead of treating them like cannon fodder. But it's going to take money, and no one with the guts to do it right actually has any money right now.

A girl in a kayak knifed silently across the pond. She was wearing a pink life vest. Sunlight rippled in her wake.

I got money, said August, quietly, hope moving across his chest like the kid in the kayak.

I know, she said. I still have access to your bank statements.

You wanna help? He said, hopefully. We could team up again. We were a hell of a team.

She faced him, and even with her mask on he saw a faint smile crinkling at the corners of her eyes. Not in a million years. And don't think it's because I'm not over you. Believe me, I got over us years ago. Didn't even need therapy.

So why—

She shook her head and reached out to stroke his arm sadly. Because you fucked up my daughter's life, August. You hurt her in a way she'll carry all her life. And I'm never gonna forgive you for that.

In January 2022—here we are, and somehow it feels too soon—the kitchen at Sanglier was slammed. Dupes flew out of the printer and August barked them as they came in at the pass, euphoric. I use this word medically: he was in a state of elation disproportionate to its cause, because the cause was that Angelo had just raced in from the back to announce that the dishwasher was down.

Down? cried August, mopping his forehead with a towel and following Angelo back to the stainless-steel behemoth that cost as much to lease as a Lexus. Fuck you mean, down? It's brand new!

Chef, you don't smell that?

August sniffed. He did smell it. It was a very bad smell. Not electrical smoke, at least. Something spoiled, fleshy, squelched inside the machine.

All the dishes come out smelling like that, Chef, said Angelo, wincing at the stench. I gotta get in there. But right now, no clean dishes.

Dishwashers are the kidneys of a kitchen; if even a tiny blockage happens, the whole system is on its knees. August knew the proper thing to do was to slow down the whole line: you couldn't make food if there was nothing to put it on. The bar couldn't pour drinks right into peoples' mouths—or at least they couldn't charge for it. But something in him, some shimmering lucidity like winter sun through a skylight, said, *It's okay, you got this.* That something was euphoria, a burst of chemicals swerving around the parts of his brain caved in by encephalitis. But August didn't know that.

August was all action. He hauled Claire and Santos off the line, instructed them to wash dishes by hand, and took their place, manning garde-manger, fryer, and grill all at once, while Chucho rode shotgun on fish and the binchotan. He dispatched a runner to tell Priya, the manager, to spread the word among the front-of-house staff. He was a general and this was a battlefield, and he wanted his hands on his artillery. He was going to make it work. He'd taken Jane's advice and gone all-in on Sanglier. He'd financed it entirely on his own, which nearly cleaned him out, but established it as a worker-owned restaurant where all employees made a living wage and, in lieu of tips, pocketed 12 percent of shift sales. This not only appealed to the critics, it cured the tension that had always existed between front and back of house, whereby the servers knew that the more they sold, the more they made, while the cooks knew they would make exactly the same (shitty) wage regardless of how busy the place was. Now, when one person made money, everyone made money—and people were making a lot of money. Or they had been. But now the dishwasher was broken and everyone in the building could see their take-home vanishing like sand in an hourglass. August wasn't going to let that happen.

Sanglier was in many ways an experiment, and every part of it had been crafted with deliberate intent. He wasn't comfortable throwing around the big words Jane had, like equity. He phrased it as, a place where we all take care of each other. He was done with TV, done with empire-building. This was all he wanted. This was supposed to be the restaurant he'd run until he died. He hadn't poured his heart into this restaurant. It *was* his heart, chambered and beating and blood-bathed and electric. Sanglier was his legacy. He wanted it to mean something.

The printer spun and meat sizzled and steadily the towers of plates arrayed above the range shrunk down. Claire and Santos tried to keep up with the dishware while August and Chucho split the dupes between them. They whirled in sync, their movements smooth and elegant. August felt music in his muscles, a thriving drumming beat. Five years ago Chucho had just been a skinny kid from Guadalajara whose brother was a prep cook at the first Astra, and now here he was right alongside him, all grown up and riding the wave. Who the hell needed Hal?

Jane had turned out to be dead right. As the pandemic raged on (and on and on) almost all of the Astras had died, impaled on their own astronomical rents and consultant fees. Only Dubai and Shanghai survived. At some point in 2021, Hal, who had entirely usurped August's empire, reached out to him. He said he wanted to explain. August had ignored him. Sanglier was on the verge of opening; there would be time to consider forgiveness later. Right now, he was getting too much mileage out of spite.

He checked the clock. 8:14pm. At least an hour left of rush to go. Claire galloped by with a rack of fresh glassware for the bar. The speakers were playing Wu-Tang Clan. August felt as if everything around him were moving in water, slow and floating. He could smell when meat was cooked, prod it with a finger, and sling it onto a plate with one hand while he reached for the sauce with the other. Plated in seconds. Whatever had broken the dishwasher hadn't broken him. Nothing could break him.

At 8:36 a dupe came out that read across the top *****VIP*****

Oh, shit, said Chucho.

The fuck? We didn't have any VIPs on the books for tonight.

Maybe she's a walk-in?

These fuckin people. Just make a fuckin reservation! August snorted and set aside one of the few remaining plates.

Moments later Priya burst in.

Table 9. It's Padma. Padma Lakshmi. She's a walk-in.

August's blood seemed momentarily to reverse course and drain toward his feet. (This sounds figurative; it is not; he was already experiencing backpressure as his blood strained to make it back to the heart, which began to beat even harder.)

You're fucking kidding. Padma's here?

Table 9. She's with her kid.

Her daughter. If she was here with her daughter...suddenly August's head felt cloudy (this had been happening more and more) and he struggled to grasp what was happening, but it felt like trying to use chopsticks to pick up three peanuts at once. James T. at Shanghai Village had showed him that trick once. He took a deep breath. She wouldn't have just come in at random. This was on purpose. She wanted to be seen here. There would be pictures online.

Silently, she was giving him her blessing.

Priya. Tell her not to worry about the menu. I got her covered. And her money's no good here. This is on me.

You understand I love her, Priya said.

I got it, said August.

I would die for her, she said.

Go! Out!

His chest felt thick, sluggish. Chucho was looking at him funny.

You okay, Chef? You look even more gringo than usual.

He didn't answer. His brain was churning like the frog who kicked the cream into butter. He knelt in front of the lowboy fridge, his hands finding ingredients. Spicy. She liked spicy. He found the habanero oil. He found a sauce, he couldn't even remember what it was, but he tasted it and it was exquisite, sweet pungent acidic joy caroming around his mouth. Scallions—he would halve and char them. He couldn't quite see what he was doing but it felt right—no, better than right, it felt *good*. He felt soft at the edges and sharp at the hands. She'd get it—she'd taste what he was about and know that he *had* listened, he *had* grown—

Chucho, can you get me one of the snakeheads from the walk-in?

A snakehead. Yes. She'd get it. A predator, an invasive species. Like him, once. He would show what he'd learned. An apology in fish. He didn't even want the fillet—he just wanted the cheeks. He knew and she knew, the cheeks were the best part. His tongue felt dry. Why did his tongue feel dry?

He stood up from the lowboy and all his blood stayed in his ankles and August had to grip the hood to keep from toppling over. Santos rounded the corner at a trot carrying a stack of barely-dry plates and almost ran into Chucho carrying the snakehead.

Last one, chef! he said, as he and Santos did a little dance around each other to avoid colliding. At which point Angelo ran up and cried, Yo chef! I found where the smell in the dishwasher was coming from! And raised high for all to see: a giant smashed dead rat.

A tinny shriek, and the plates smashed to the floor. Chucho jumped about a mile in the air and a wet fish shot out of his hands and landed headfirst, with a burst of steam and sizzle, in the deep fryer.

They watched in horror as bubbles streamed from the fish's open, serrated jaws in the yellow oil. The head began to crackle and brown. August seemed to be unable to move. He knew he should move, save the fish, but his body was not having it. His body was good where it was. Then that old feeling came over him, the sudden clutch and flutter in his chest. Not now, he begged. The edges of his vision began to darken. Pain began to ripple over his core, pain like he had never felt before, pain so total he could see through space and time.

He knew what he needed to do. He saw it clearly. The answer shone in front of him, radiant as the sun and roaring in his ears. With a mighty effort August lurched forward one step. He could fix this. He could fix everything.

I have a great idea, said August.

And fell.

Astrid.

I imagine this—all this—isn't the autopsy report you expected. But it's the one you deserve. It's the one your father would have wanted. His death was the last thing that would ever belong to him, and he wanted you to have it.

I don't want you to think I did this because I was in love with him. I did it because I am in love with him. Which, I get it. Lousy timing.

Love gets way too much media attention, though. Whenever I take a heart out of a bucket of formalin there is a Victor Hugo line I always think of: "the heart saturates itself in love, which like a divine salt, preserves it." But I think you and I both know Victor Hugo didn't get it quite right. We know the heart can embalm itself in plenty of things: solitude, self-reliance, spite. It is a tough organ that holds up well in a variety of solutions. The heart fights to survive harder than any other organ in the body.

But let's talk about decay, Astrid.

The human body has only two settings: Grow and Decay. From the first very moment of fertilization the main business of an organism is to grow, because a living thing that does not grow is decaying. On a purely technical level "death" occurs at the moment—not always easy to define (Magic Max in *The Princess Bride* was more right about death than he gets credit for)—when the switch flips irrevocably from the former to the latter. But this suggests that the two settings are equal: they are not.

Growth is eager, but decay waits. Growth is rapid, decay is total; decay is absolute. All things fray unbidden. As light drives out dark, growth holds back decay. Cells divide, are reborn, shore up old membranes, restore exhausted organs. But like darkness, decay is still the default setting. Life, like light, requires *energy*, and life is insatiable. To pump blood, to maintain its cell membranes, to sustain the powerstroke of actin and myosin—the piston of muscle—it must feed constantly on oxygen and amino acids and blood. The slightest interruption in this biochemical banquet, and decay storms the castle. Starved of energy, that muscular piston freezes in place. Cell walls collapse and flood the body with water. And yet, decomposition is an active process—itself a kind of life. Anaerobic bacteria swarm out of the gut to feast on withered proteins. As they do, they excrete gases and compounds, namely putrescine and cadaverine, the sources of the mephitic stench that moves us to bury our dead—the stench of the pig that slugged your father in the nose. But if handled right, if managed, decay is also one of the great sources of flavor in the world: another word for it is fermentation.

You wanted his body, I know. But by now his eyes have been donated—imagine that, for a second! Someone out there is seeing with his eyes! His brain floats in a tub, dermestid beetles have eaten away his remaining organic tissue, and his skeleton now hangs in a science lab on the third floor of his old high school. So this is the best I can do: a book of his body.

I have done my research, Astrid. I have been forensic. And where forensics have failed I have filled in the blanks. I have taken my time. I have talked to his friends and lawyers and cooks, I've read the literature, watched his shows. I'm sure I've made mistakes, too; there were many times when all I could do was guess, and sometimes those guesses have been complicated, but I think I got it right in the main. I know your father better than anyone alive—and the sad thing is I know no one alive better than I know your father. I am working on that. India and I go to lunch together sometimes now. It is a start.

Knowing your parent, finally, not as a parent but as a human being complete and entire, is every child's nightmare and every parent's deepest yearning. It sure as hell is what he wanted for you. And so I have written it all down here for you, and now that I have written it, I am never doing this again as long as I live.

You want to know why he died? It was exactly what the exhausted resident thought it was: a heart attack. A tiny thrombus, a clot, about four millimeters wide lodged in the coronary artery. The whole heart caved in around it. But anyone could have told you that. My job is to tell you how that tiny clot came to be there. That tiny clot was just the single apricot kernel that housed a whole tree.

By the way, the genetic screens have come back. I was right. You have probably inherited familial heterozygous cholesterolemia from your father, as he inherited it from his. Consult your GP, but you should start Lipitor now, and follow dieticians' advice carefully. The good news is that you could not have contracted herpes from him; it can only be passed on by the mother. This does not mean you do not have herpes. A quarter of all Americans do.

Your father's body was cold, finally; the last of his heat had dissipated. The other body from the morning had been picked up by the funeral home, gone into the maw of the grieving process. It had been a swift autopsy, the diagnosis obvious: pulmonary embolism secondary to lung cancer. No surprises. But who had she been, outside of those lungs? I hadn't thought about it. I remembered that she was delivered to me as patients sometimes are, with their last effects in a clear plastic bag. She'd had a pair of black slippers and a copy of *The Economist.*

I unzipped the bag and looked at August. Then I dragged a stool over from the corner and perched on it beside him. My 289th body of the year.

Outside in America the public grieving had already begun. Elegiac tributes had begun to appear online, long twitter threads. Montages, oral histories, remembrances. Essays striving to unpack what he meant to America. The people he had mentored would tell their stories, and the people he had wronged would bite their tongues, mostly. There would be a memorial service of some kind, I hadn't asked. I did not want to know about it. I didn't need it. They were trying to bring August Sweeney back in words and video but even now he was passing into history, no longer a man but a memory. Except in this room. For me he was still here, cold and lonely. Still my patient. Still mine.

I hate that we heave bodies into the ground. I hate that we cremate them. I hate that we hide from them when they die. But most of all I hate that so few of them will ever be seen by the precious few of us who actually know how to look. The human body is a house, no more, no less, a magnificent house with plumbing and wiring and ventilation and sewage, all of it built to last the better part of a hundred years, and all of us, every one of us, gets just one. When we die, it's like the power goes out, the gas disappears, the water permanently shuts off. And yet, for a while, the house stands. It still has stories to tell.

A human being can go into the ground and be dug up a million years later and we can tell from their bones what kind of food they ate or how they walked. A man can fall into peat for two thousand years and we know his last meal was porridge. There is always life left in the body. The trick is knowing how to look for it.

His arms were slack by his side. The last thing you dissect in a gross anatomy course is the hands. This is for emotional reasons. You might imagine that the hardest thing to dissect would be the face, but somehow the embalmed face so swiftly distorts and warps under the scalpel that its power to shock evaporates. The hands are far more intimate. The fingers curl inward with rigor mortis, as sleeping babies' do. The hands speak even when the voice is silent.

These craggy mottled hands were responsible for the best meal of my life.

I took his hand in mine, the hand I'd touched all those years ago, and this time I held it. It was cold and hard, the fingers slightly bloated. I moved my fingertips over the calluses and scars, felt the ridges of his nails. I felt a hangnail on his thumb. My breath was visible in the refrigerated room.

I do not know how long I sat beside him, my little hand in his great cold fist. I was listening. This was my job. The thing I was put here to do and I would sit here as long as it took. I am the haruspex, I am the *shomeret*, I am the shou ling, I am Hermes, I am the Archangel Gabriel, I am the one who speaks for the dead, who sits with them, who guides them home. I listened as I held his hand until enough warmth had gone from my hand into his that I could not tell where my body ended and his began. My limbs stiffened in the cold and my breath clouded the air. I did not move. I sat there listening. I was ready to begin.

ACKNOWLEDGMENTS

Every book that is written, much less published, issues debt it can never repay. Here is this book's ledger, however incomplete.

Monica Prince, Andrew Gifford, and Adam "Do You Really Need This Many *Law & Order* References?" al-Sirgany at Santa Fe Writing Project saw 97,000 words on cadavers and fine dining and thought, "that sounds like us." Justin Brouckaert at Aevitas Creative swooped in at just the right time and said the words every writer wants to hear: "I want to work on whatever you want to work on." The first time this book ever truly felt real for me was the moment I saw Benjamin Shaykin's cover art.

One does not simply walk into an autopsy lab. Nor into a Michelin-starred kitchen. This book would simply not exist were I not lucky enough to know Dr. Nicholas Barasch and Dr. Christine Anne Garcia, who put me up in their home, read early drafts, and answered a tidal wave of technical questions. Dr. Jeffrey Nine might be the only pathologist in America who would let a writer into his autopsy lab for two weeks. Evetta Katz told me I had to put her in the book, and I did. Hardly even changed her name. Dr. Kay Negishi was the first to bring me into the house of the dead.

On the food side, I couldn't have done this without Alexandra and Kirk Kelewae. Albert Riera, Damien and Yves Mourey, Frederic Cordier, Joelle Danneyrolles, and the entire Poirson family, who made my research in France possible. Reine Sammut and the staff of Auberge La Feniere suffered me to clean squid and their walk-in freezer. Thank you also to Annys Shin, Anna Maltby Patil, and Matt Buchanan for allowing me to test-run much of this project in print.

I've been taught by a hell of a lot of people. Anthony Piccolo taught me to open my head and sing. Tom LaFarge changed my life, may his memory be a blessing. I'm indebted to the faculty at George Mason's MFA program: Mary Kay Zuravleff, Susan Shreve, Tania James, Steve Goodwin, Courtney Brkic, Tim Denevi, and Kyoko Mori. Matt Davis and the Cheuse International Writers' Center sent me to France, which is the best thing you can do for someone. Lisa Page at GW gave me a job, which is a close second. The DC Council for the Arts and Humanities provided years of much-needed support.

I tell my students that it's not your story or your vision that keeps you going in this business, it's your friends. I consider that my career began the night I met Helena Fitzgerald and Evan Simko-Bednarski, and almost 15 years later, I'm grateful for the false starts that brought us together that night. Nathan Morgante, Dan Chinoy, Zach Powers, Lily Diamond, Robbie Maakestad, Rajpreet Heir, Marisa Siegel, Lyz Lenz, Sarah Wheeler, Darcy Gagnon, Hannah Grieco, Greg Larson, Karissa Chen, John Cusick, Lauren Kirchner, Shrayana Bhattacharya, and the entire MPA/ID family provided aid and comfort. Particular thanks go to The Meandering Jews, Ruthie Birger (who gave Bushwick his name), Rebecca Shaykin, and Michael Pareles, and to This Is Fine, Arathi Rao, Michael Eddy, and Arjun Vasan. Dahlia Wilson was the best reader and copy editor anyone could ask for, 12 years old or not.

Not only did Rion Amilcar Scott award me my first cash prize for writing, not only did he help me get my first short story published, but he introduced me to *Barrelhouse* magazine, and in so doing gave me something every writer needs but never expects: a home. Thank you to Dave Housley, Joe Killiany, Becky Barnard, Chris Gonzalez, Christina Beasley, Tara Campbell, Matt Perez, Dan Brady, Mike Ingram, Siân Griffiths, Aaron Burch, and Tom McAllister.

Basma Muhammad, Fatima Golou, and the staff at Preparatory day care in DC took care of my children at their most feral *and* helped potty train them, which is actually better than sending someone to France. Henry Hoyle, Laura Shen, Jenny Sarma, and Chris Sarma have all but co-parented with us.

My grandfather Ed Kander set aside his own dreams to raise and protect a family of artists. My great-uncle John Kander taught me that there is no greater joy than making art with your friends. Jason and Diana Kander trusted me with their own stories, and opened up a world I never thought I'd be a part of. And this book would not exist without the generosity of Qi Guiping, who gave Maya Zhu her Chinese name, and routinely drops everything to help take wonderful care of her grandchildren, and—vitally—pack our freezer with homemade dumplings.

I was always warned that my brother, Jacob Ashworth, would grow up to be taller than me; I didn't realize that meant that before I knew it *he* would be the one I looked up to. My parents, Susan Kander and Warren Ashworth, taught me that you can and should make a life in art, that you should do it with pleasure, and that above all it is a privilege to entertain. All the restaurant designs in this book were my father's first.

To my sons: Gabriel, you were named for the angel who wakes the dead. Isaac, you were named for someone who laughed. When you read this book someday, know that it was written in spite of your best efforts.

And most of all, to Shannon: there is not room here to express how grateful I am. There would not be room in the entire Library of Congress. Every good idea in this book was yours. Everything I am, you made me.

ABOUT THE AUTHOR

PHOTO: Evan Simko-Bednarski

Samuel Ashworth has been a bartender, a dancer, and a reporter. He has gutted seafood in the back of Michelin-starred restaurants and assisted with autopsies in a Pittsburgh hospital. His fiction and nonfiction appear in the *The Atlantic, The Washington Post, Longreads, Eater, Hazlitt, Gawker, The Rumpus*, and so on. He is a professor of creative writing at George Washington University, and assistant fiction editor at Barrelhouse Magazine. A native New Yorker, he now lives with his wife and two sons in Washington, DC. He is on Twitter and Bluesky at @samuelashworth.

Also from Santa Fe Writers Project

The Book of Losman *by K.E. Semmel*

Introducing K.E. Semmel's *The Book of Losman*, about a literary translator in Copenhagen with Tourette syndrome who becomes involved in a dubious and experimental drug study to retrieve his childhood memories in a tragicomic effort to find a cure.

"Semmel has written a fine and funny novel. Are we merely the sum of our experiences — or is there something deeper, something ineffable?."

— Owen King, the author of The Curator

Mona at Sea *by Elizabeth Gonzalez James*

This sharp, witty debut introduces us to Mona Mireles — observant to a fault, unflinching in her opinions, and uncompromisingly confident in her professional abilities. Mona is a Millennial perfectionist who fails upwards in the midst of the 2008 economic crisis.

"Mona at Sea is sharply written Millennial malaise that dares to be hopeful."

— Georgia Clark, San Francisco Chronicle

K: A Novel *by Ted O'Connell*

Professor Francis Kauffman has unwittingly landed himself in prison where he's faced with an insurmountable task: execute a fellow inmate. Charged with igniting a political insurrection amongst his students at a university in Beijing, Kauffman is sent to the notorious Kun Chong Prison, where his existence grows stranger by the hour...

"A startling, beautiful book. Its nightmares will haunt readers, and its dreams will make them fly."

— Erin McGraw, author of Joy and 52 Other Very Short Stories

About Santa Fe Writers Project

SFWP is an independent press founded in 1998 that embraces a mission of artistic preservation, recognizing exciting new authors, and bringing out of print work back to the shelves.

  @santafewritersproject |  @SFWP | sfwp.com

Made in the USA
Middletown, DE
11 April 2025

74142224R00189